FORBIDDEN INSTINCT

The Summer Park Psychics
WANDERING SOUL
WHISPERING HEARTS
LINGERING TOUCH
THE SUMMER PARK PSYCHICS OMNIBUS

Other Works
CRAFTING A WRITER'S LIFE: Building a Foundation

Coming Soon

The Blades of Janus
PERIHELION

The Department of Homeworld Security Omnibus 1

Gray Card (second edition)
Resident Alien
Business or Pleasure
Tied up in Customs
Entry Visa
Duration of Stay

Cassandra Chandler

Copyright Page

This book is pure fiction. All characters, places, names, and events are products of the author's imagination or used solely in a fictitious manner. Any resemblance to any people, places, things, or events that have ever existed or will ever exist is entirely coincidental.

The Department of Homeworld Security Omnibus 1
Copyright © 2020 by Cassandra Chandler
Print ISBN: 978-1-945702-31-0
Digital ISBN: 978-1-945702-30-3

Gray Card
The Department of Homeworld Security, Book One
Copyright © 2015, 2019 by Cassandra Chandler
First eBook edition: October 2015
Second eBook edition: August 2019
First Print edition: December 2019
Second Print edition: August 2019

Resident Alien
The Department of Homeworld Security, Book Two
Copyright © 2016 by Cassandra Chandler
First eBook edition: April 2016

Dedication

For everyone who has yearned for a place to belong.
You are not alone.

Don't miss out on any of the alien action.
Subscribe to Cassandra Chandler's newsletter at
cassandra-chandler.com!

Greetings, Reader!

When I sat down to write *Gray Card*, I knew I wanted to create a story about a nerdy girl who falls in love with an alien. I didn't know that it was going to be the first of many stories set in Evelyn's world, or that—fourteen titles later—*The Department of Homeworld Security* would be one of my most popular series!

These novellas are designed to be quick, fun, and easy to read. I want to give you all a break from your routines and provide some pure escapism for you to recharge and return to your lives hopefully feeling a little lighter.

Some of you have asked for more—not just in terms of new novellas, but new content about the characters you've come to love. With that in mind, this compilation of the first six *Department of Homeworld Security* novellas includes bonus content at the end of the book!

In the bonus content, you'll find short stories about how the main characters of *Gray Card* and *Resident Alien* initially met. I couldn't decide which perspective to share with you, so I wrote both!

I wanted you to see not just how Evelyn was smitten with Adam when they first meet in "Close Encounter", but why he approached her in the first place—and couldn't walk away afterward. And it was just as important in "Listen" to share why Brendan was seeking out extra-terrestrial intelligence as the daring reason that Kira broke protocol and answered his transmissions. There's also a short bonus epilogue for *Business or Pleasure*.

This omnibus includes stories featuring Lyrians and Scorpiians—better known on Earth as "Grays"—and Cygnian-Sadirian hybrids. It was so much fun to come up with these new aliens and explore parts of their cultures and physiology (and some of the Earthling characters definitely explored their physiology).

I think I can safely say that this universe is just getting started. I'm so glad you've decided to take the journey with me. There are many more stories to come in *The Department of Homeworld Security*, so stay tuned.

Thanks for reading!

Cassandra Chandler

CASSANDRA CHANDLER

GRAY CARD

THE DEPARTMENT OF HOMEWORLD SECURITY

Gray Card

The Department of Homeworld
Security
Book One
(second edition)

Cassandra Chandler

Dedication

For A.E. Ash—nerdgirl extraordinaire.

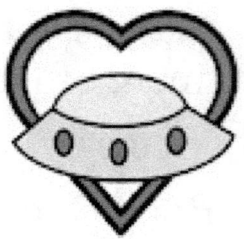

Don't miss out on any of the alien action.
Subscribe to Cassandra Chandler's newsletter at
cassandra-chandler.com!

Chapter One

Two things were working at ruining Evelyn's day. First, she was wearing a dress to try to get Adam—the love of her life—to see her as something other than a friend. Second, Adam was having an argument with some jackass.

With irritating sweat trickling down her spine from the relentless summer heat and Adam so obviously upset, she wondered if now was the best time to try to make the leap. She watched him as she debated the wisdom of her decision.

Evelyn had never seen Adam's dark eyebrows furrowed over his perfectly straight nose. She'd never seen his gorgeous eyes—one the blue of the waters off Oahu and the other as green as the immaculate grass in the park behind him—narrowed in anger.

The skin over his jaw held its usual light coat of stubble. She could still clearly see the taut masseter muscle flexing within his cheek. Even his face was toned.

What was she thinking? Blonde-from-a-bottle, too small up top, too big at the hips, her narrow face accented by huge horn-rimmed glasses...

Wait—superheroes sometimes wore big glasses to put

people off-guard and conceal their strength. She wore them to remind herself that she was strong too.

Evelyn wasn't going to let herself be cowed by her measurements or society's standards. She was going to go for it. Eventually. As soon as she could get herself to move.

The man Adam had been talking to sauntered off, hands in the pockets of his dark suit. He would probably have a heat stroke any minute, but looked as though he hadn't a care in the world. Unlike Adam.

Adam had his hands on his hips, feet braced far apart as he stared at the sky. His muscular legs couldn't be hidden by the khaki cargo shorts he always wore and his jade green T-shirt seemed barely able to keep itself together over the joy of embracing his broad chest.

Reining in her libido, Evelyn wiped her damp palms on her dress to dry them off, then slid her glasses farther up her nose. This wasn't the time to push the envelope. She could tell him how she felt later. From the looks of it, right now Adam needed a friend. She would be that friend.

She only wished she was in her normal clothes. Jeans and one of the T-shirts she'd made for her gaming group during her undergrad studies would be much more comfortable. She'd been wearing something similar when she first met Adam, plus a sign around her neck that said, "Help! I'm an alien stranded on this primitive planet!" It was her standard costume when she went to comic book conventions.

Adam had actually been concerned when he approached her, and not because he thought she was nuts —like most people. It didn't take long for her to figure out he wasn't local, with all the weird idiosyncrasies in his use of English. Until today, she actually had never seen him speak with anyone else aside from ordering food at a restaurant.

Time to find out how she could help.

The sidewalk baked her feet through her sandals as she approached him. "I'd ask if everything is all right, but it obviously isn't."

Adam closed his eyes and took one last deep breath. "I've had better days."

"You don't look like you're up for a bunch of personal questions, so I just have one. Do you want to talk about it?"

"Not really." He finally looked at her, apparently not registering her dress at all. "I thought we were meeting at your place."

"I know you spend your mornings here. And a lot of afternoons and evenings. I thought I would surprise you. Surprise!"

Evelyn waved her hands in the air briefly. The faintest hint of a smile fluttered across Adam's lips. She decided to build on that.

"Do you want me to go kick that guy's ass? Because I

will. I mean he's tall and all, but he's kind of skinny. I think I can take him. Especially if I hide somewhere and pop out at him."

"I have to go." Adam's light voice was barely audible.

"Go where?"

"Home."

"What, like...*home* home?" Evelyn's stomach clenched around the freezer waffles she'd had for breakfast.

Adam had never mentioned having to go back to whatever country he was from. He always said he wanted to focus on the moment and enjoy the time he had. She couldn't believe that time was up.

"When?"

"Three days."

"Three days!" She raised her hands, then slowly lowered them while she let out a deep breath. Bringing her voice to a more conversational volume, she said, "Wow. That's...soon."

"I requested an extension, but it was denied."

"Is that what that guy was telling you?"

"Yes."

"I guess this means the *Planet of the Apes* marathon is off. I can't see you wanting to spend ten of your remaining hours locked up in my apartment watching movies."

"That actually sounds wonderful."

Adam looked so sad. She probably mirrored his expression.

"Maybe we can go for a walk together first?" he asked.

A walk in the summer heat sounded awful, but being with him, helping him through this and spending every possible second with him overrode any complaints. She tried to smile, but only managed a nod.

"Sure."

They fell in step beside each other, walking close enough that their arms brushed. Adam caught her hand in his and entwined their fingers.

That was weird. He had always been stand-offish physically, only touching her to catch her if she stumbled on a trail or something.

What if this whole time he'd felt the same way about her as she did about him? What if she'd wasted moments they could have spent in each other's arms instead of watching sci-fi movies and eating popcorn on the couch?

If she looked at him she might start to cry, but she was dying to see his expression. She held her gaze steady on the ground. She wouldn't risk letting him see her cry. This was obviously hard enough on him as it was.

Evelyn tried to focus on his closeness. His hand dwarfed hers, his skin surprisingly smooth, given all his rock climbing and other adventurous pastimes. He had somehow persuaded her to come along on a few of them. She was in the best shape of her life thanks to their walks in this park, and they'd only explored a fraction of it. They wouldn't map every inch of it after all.

Her brain practically whirred as she tried to think of some way—any way—that they could have more time together. She wasn't ready for their relationship to be over. She wasn't ready for him to leave.

"You could always put in for another visit, right?" she said.

"No. Where I'm from, they're very strict about where citizens can go. I was amazed they let me come here at all."

"Sounds like a pretty crappy place." Evelyn thought she murmured her sentiment quietly enough that he'd miss it, but his hearing was keener than that.

"I've never thought so before."

Before now, she finished for him. Not out loud, though.

"There are reasons behind the laws." Adam sounded more like he was trying to convince himself than her. "I understand why the limitations are in effect."

"Let me guess. You'd rather not explain them to me." She tried to smirk, to let him know she was joking, but her mouth wouldn't cooperate. It just kept pouring out smart-alecky comments—as usual.

"I'd rather enjoy the time I have left as much as possible. And I'd like to spend it with you."

Evelyn could set her own schedule since the professor supervising her PhD work was gone for the summer. The research journals she was supposed to be going through were piling up from the time she'd been spending with

Adam, but she couldn't bring herself to care at the moment. Besides, she'd have plenty of time to catch up on them. As soon as Adam left.

This time, she managed to look up at him and conjure up a full—if fake—smile. "Whatever you want."

Chapter Two

Three days left in paradise. Adam could hardly believe his request for an extension had been denied after his latest successful campaign. Tau Ceti-6 would think twice before launching an attack on neighboring systems again.

Peace was mandatory in the Coalition. Adam's ship was in the vanguard of the fleet that guaranteed it for the septillions of sentients in the Milky Way.

The translation session that prepared him with the knowledge and language he needed to blend in where he would be staying on Earth made his mind provide a direct translation of many idioms. He suppressed a laugh at the quaint naming convention this particularly Earth culture had adopted for the galaxy. They had named it after spilled milk.

He could imagine Evelyn's jokes at his thoughts if she could hear them. *"Better than crying over it. Get it? Spilled milk?"*

Soon, imagining her jokes would be all that was left to him. The thought sent a sharp spike of pain through his chest, surprising him with its intensity. Moons, did he really only have three more days with her?

Holding her hand wasn't enough. He needed her closer. She didn't protest as he pulled her arm around his back. When he clasped her waist, she rested her hand on his hip. The years of training for command were barely enough to help him control his body's reaction. Her touch was like fire—as he'd suspected it would be. Her small frame tucked in next to his perfectly. He couldn't help but wonder how well they would fit together in other ways.

Stopping by a small manmade pond near the entrance to the park, he luxuriated in her warmth next to him, the softness of her skin and the firmness of her grip on his side, as if she was trying to keep him with her. The longing that swelled up in him made his chest feel tight, like his heart was filling with a lifetime of memories they could never make together.

A pair of swans paddled lazily across the still water. The white of their feathers struck a stark contrast to the brilliant green grass on the bank behind them.

Adam had seen birds from all over the galaxy on his homeworld, Sadr-4. Always in captivity. Even the Proteus —a bird that shed small fireworks of energy and glowed like a star—couldn't compare to the simple beauty of these swans.

Earth was unspoiled, untouched by the genetic engineers who peddled their wares at all the ports he had visited. Every person he had met in the Coalition was the product of those geneticists. He was one himself—not that they were eager to claim a faulty model as their work, no matter how successful his military career.

"Are you okay?" Evelyn asked.

This wasn't the time for darkness. Evelyn was at his side, her warmth pushing away his memories of cold space. Holding her close, her velvet voice at his ear, he felt a shiver pass through him.

He was far from okay. But he smiled and nodded, looking out over the water.

"It's beautiful here," he said. "I'm going to miss it."

"Don't they have parks where you're from?"

"Not like this." Adam felt her gaze on him and shrugged. "To say they've gone a little crazy urbanizing everything would be more than an understatement."

"Blech. Overdevelopment. It's almost as bad as underdevelopment. I still don't get how you spend so much time camping and stuff."

"You seem to be taking to it well. We've spent much time together in the wilds."

"You know my rule. I have to be able to reach a modern bathroom within ten minutes. That's hardly what I'd call *the wilds*."

Adam laughed and the tightness in his chest loosened a bit. "I suppose you have a point."

"You didn't have to spend so much time with me." Her voice was low and tight—strain showing through. "You could have been outdoors even more. That is why you came here, right? For the nature?"

"I wouldn't change a thing." He pulled her closer against his side. "You look lovely, by the way."

"Oh, please."

He let his gaze roam over her, drinking everything in. Her hair was walnut brown, but she colored it a pale gold. It was gathered up on the back of her head as usual and held in place with a clip. The rich brown of her eyes reminded him of fertile soil. They were keen and expressive, even behind her glasses.

She was blushing. The paleness of her skin couldn't hide the pink tinge coloring her cheeks and rising up from the low-cut bodice of her pale yellow sun-dress. Her shoulders were bare except for the thinnest of straps holding the garment up.

Much of her back was open to the air. Adam wondered how she had managed to put sunscreen on, knowing how quickly she burned. A surge of jealousy coursed through him as he imagined someone else—anyone else—touching her skin.

"Let's move to the shade."

"Okay."

He led her to a bench near the main path that wound deeper into the park. Ancient oaks stretched their limbs above, sheltering them in cool shadow. He sat next to her —as close as he could.

Moons, he really was losing control.

Visiting Earth had been his reward for thoroughly defeating the Tau Ceti. The High Council hadn't been pleased with Adam's unorthodox request to visit a planet designated as a preservation site, but with it being time for Adam to decide whether to re-enlist, they'd been inclined to comply. Anything to keep Adam at the head of the fleet.

Sitting next to Evelyn with a warm breeze flowing over them, Adam realized they never should have granted his request.

Sadr-4—his entire civilization—had intellectualized their existence to the point that bodies were seen as little more than vessels for their minds. Vessels that were to be modified and crafted to fit the needs of society or the whims of the parents, if they had enough resources.

The society itself was full of distractions——technology keeping everyone's attention occupied, and Coalition regulated cocktails balancing their emotional states. No one seemed to notice that there was anything beyond supplements, technology and genetically crafted skills.

Adam's parents had ordered the political package. They expected him to become a leader, sitting safely in Sadr-4's capital and ordering people around from a desk while they watched on in admiration and enjoyed the status his position would bring them.

"See that man? He's from our DNA."

Well, at least the ability to command had come through.

Everything else had gone wrong. Instead of the color

his parents had settled on, he had one green eye, like his mother, and one blue eye, like his father. That was the first sign that the geneticists had lost control.

Adam was much taller than his parents wanted. He towered over most citizens, intimidating rather than inspiring. He lacked the graceful limbs and angular features as well, and his sheer size... There were some ships where he could barely fit through the mechanical tunnels.

He hated to use the word, but he was a glitch.

His parents received a full refund and Adam was transferred from the civilian pod where he had been born to one that specialized in preparing Sadirians for the Coalition's military. From what he'd seen of other citizens, he was better off with the firm but comparatively kind people who trained him—most of whom had similar origins.

Coalition citizens didn't know just how often the reproduction process glitched. The military was primarily composed of unwanted results—people who couldn't quite fit in with societal expectations.

But Adam fit in on Earth. He loved it here.

He wanted to keep breathing air that was processed by trees instead of re-circulators. He longed for the deep laughter brought on by embracing the ridiculous dichotomies of life, and for this—holding someone dear to him close at his side. He had three more days to get his fill, and then he would never be able to return.

"We should get married," Evelyn said.

"What?"

"We should get married."

"That's not something to joke about."

"I'm not joking." She turned to face him, eyes bright and wide. She sat up straighter and leaned toward him with a broad grin on her face. "If we get married, you can stay here as long as you want."

He had a vague understanding of the various laws on her planet about people from different countries marrying, but she couldn't possibly fathom what she would be getting herself into. "I appreciate the offer, but—"

"You're not interested. I get it. My mistake."

She sat back—eyes shuttering, smile gone—and started to turn away. Adam couldn't stop himself from reaching out and gently caressing her cheek, bringing her gaze back to him. The thought of marrying her, of living with her on Earth for the rest of his days... It was tempting.

There were cases where citizens of the Coalition had been assimilated into another culture, but they were extremely rare. Aside from the intense amount of bureaucracy he would have to navigate, it would mean giving up all of his resources, his rank, even his citizenship.

With his military background, the High Council would probably insist on implanting him with a tracker and a device that would fry anything more sophisticated than a standard computer if he came too close. The Coalition didn't want anyone getting homesick for their technology —or doing worse.

A planet with Earth's technology level could easily be exploited. Adam could pass off rudimentary Coalition tech as his own and make a fortune, then use his knowledge to turn that into political power.

No one would believe he was staying on Earth for love, even *if* that was what Evelyn was offering.

"We can't get married just to fool them into letting me stay," he said.

"Who said it would just be for them?" She tilted up her chin, gaze boring into him. "I have been crazy about you pretty much since we met. I will pass any test they throw at me about why I'm marrying you."

"Evelyn…"

He didn't know what to say. Did she mean she loved him? He hadn't dared to hope, to even consider that possibility. Maybe attraction, perhaps lust, certainly friendship, but love? The way his heart was beating, it was difficult to convince himself that he didn't love her too.

If he stayed, he would have to give up everything…

"Marry me," she said, her voice dropping almost to a whisper.

Adam leaned toward her, not pausing until their lips touched.

Stars above... So soft. So warm.

His tongue slid into her mouth, dormant parts of him awakening with a suddenness that shocked him. Without hesitating for a moment, Evelyn matched his passion. She wrapped her slender arms around his neck, opening her mouth to him and seeking out his tongue with her own. The first touch sent fire flooding through his veins.

She pushed him back on the bench, shifting her dress to straddle him. A throbbing ache built in his groin—his dick went ramrod straight, wanting relief from her so badly he could hardly stand it.

He ran his hands down her back, clenching her hips and rocking her against him. She moaned into his mouth, burrowing her fingers through his hair and crushing her lips to his.

"Excuse me!" A shrill voice cut through his euphoria. "Kids sometimes come to this park, you know!"

Evelyn was first to stop the kiss, sliding back onto the bench next to him. Her eyes widened when she noticed his erection. Then she grinned and draped her skirt over his lap to help cover him.

"Thank you for the reminder," she said. The woman who had broken into their perfect moment glared at them, then turned and stalked down the path. Evelyn called after her, "Have a nice day!"

She broke into laughter, the joyful sound mingling with the wind rustling in the leaves overhead like the most beautiful music. She stood and offered Adam her hand.

"That lady is probably going to call the cops. We should go. That is, if you're *up* for it. See what I did there?"

Normally he would have groaned or sighed at the terrible pun. This time he just laughed along with her, letting her pretend to pull him up. He wrapped his arms around her waist and lifted her from her feet, kissing her again.

He hadn't intended to rekindle the passionate moment they had shared, but the softness of her lips and her inviting mouth overwhelmed his control. By the time he set her back on her feet, they were both panting.

"My place," she said. "Now."

Adam nodded, grabbed her hand and sprinted for the exit from the park.

Chapter Three

Evelyn barely had time to shut the door to her apartment before Adam was all over her again. He lifted her with his hands on her ass, pressing her back against the door and grinding his hips against hers. The stupid skirt of her dress was too long and she couldn't quite manage to get both legs over his waist.

Realizing her difficulty, he reached under her skirt and slid it up to her ribs. He ran his hand along the back of her thigh as he used it to lift her higher. She finally wrapped her legs around him, loving his groan of pleasure as his erection pressed against the thin fabric of her panties.

Dresses suddenly didn't seem that bad.

His kisses were relentless, stealing her breath away. The room was spinning when she caved and tapped his shoulder to signify her need for a break. He reached up and started tapping her shoulder too.

She couldn't keep from giggling. It was a weird moment for his sense of humor to manifest, but that was sort of the way he worked. He leaned back, a dazed expression on his face that thrilled her to her toes.

"I had to come up for air," she said.

"Are you all right?" Adam smoothed her hair away from her face.

"I'm fine. We just might want to slow down a tiny bit."

He used his grip on her leg to pull it away from his waist and gently set her back on her feet. "Of course. I shouldn't have—"

Evelyn slapped her hand over his mouth before he could continue. She'd already figured out that he was the *takes too much responsibility for everything* type, and she wasn't about to let him second-guess taking their relationship to the next level.

"None of this *shouldn't have* crap. I just needed a breather. I have now had it and am ready to resume." She smiled and took his hands in hers, then turned them around and started walking backward toward her bedroom, leading him along. "That shoulder pat thing was pretty funny by the way."

"Right. Funny." He looked a little uncomfortable. Worse—he paused at the threshold to her room. "I don't know if this is a good idea."

"Oh no, no, no. You are not getting out of this."

"Evelyn…"

She squeezed his hands and said, "Why shouldn't we do this? I mean if we really do have limited time… I don't want any regrets."

"Neither do I. I just—" He let out a sigh. "I don't want to disappoint you."

"Why would you think that's even… Oh."

The idea that someone as gorgeous and masculine as Adam could have performance problems was beyond ironic, but it was the only thing that came to mind when trying to think of how he might disappoint her.

She wrapped her arms around his shoulders and pulled herself up on her tip-toes to nibble his earlobe. He groaned and put his hands on her waist. That was progress. Now if she could just get him into her bedroom.

"You don't have to worry about that with me," she said. "Besides if things don't go exactly as we hope, there are lots of other things we can do."

"What kinds of things?"

"Are you looking for dirty talk? I'm not sure how good I am at that, but I'll give it a try if you want."

"No, I…" He lowered his head to her shoulder. "I think I should go."

"What?"

Her stomach started to churn. She gripped his shoulders and pushed him far enough away that she could see his expression and try to figure out what was going on.

His lips were slightly parted, eyes still unfocused, and he seemed a little unsteady on his feet. Maybe he wasn't feeling that stable himself. He lifted a hand as if to touch her cheek, then winced and curled his fingers into a fist before lowering his arm back to his side. Resolve was seeping into his expression and Evelyn had a feeling she was not going to be pleased with his decision.

"Do you want to go?" She did her best to hide her own desire, her desperate longing for him to stay, whether they had sex or not.

Adam stared at her for what felt like a long time. "This is more complicated than you think."

She was tempted to say something about their body parts and inserting tab A into slot B to break the tension, but she resisted.

"Help me understand," she said.

"We have different customs where I'm from. We do things...differently."

How different could it be? Evelyn shrugged. "I'm open to trying new things."

"We aren't. I mean, *I* am. But where I'm from... We keep things simple. This is already much more than what I've experienced before."

The ground seemed to shift beneath her. All they'd done so far was kiss. Sure, they were the best kisses she'd ever had and that bit against the door was fabulous, but they hadn't even passed second base.

"Wait, you're not telling me you're a virgin, are you?" she asked.

"No, of course not. I've just never experienced anything this intense."

She tried to make sense of what he was saying. He'd had sex before, but hadn't done anything as intense as their make-out session.

Well, that took all the pressure off. If Adam wound up leaving, she'd make sure he had some amazing memories to take with him. Hell, maybe she could convince him to marry her just for the sex.

"So, you've had sex, but it's always been boring?"

He let out a laugh and his shoulders lowered a bit. "That is a good way of putting it."

"Oh, I will show you a good way to put it." She cringed. "That sounded better in my head. I did say I'm not good at dirty talk."

"I'm not going to be able to tell. I thought you patting my shoulder was some kind of move."

Laughing, she said, "Then why don't you let me show you some real moves? Just promise to tell me if you object to anything."

"I don't see that happening, but I promise."

"Boring sex, huh?" She wrapped her arms around his neck. "You are *so* going to marry me."

Before he could say anything else, she kissed him. He let her lead this time and she kept it light and slow. For the moment. She walked backward into her room, keeping her grip on his neck and her lips on his. She didn't want him having any more second thoughts.

She guided him carefully to her bed, avoiding the model planets, stars, and spaceships she had painted and hung from her ceiling that were low enough to hit his head. She'd have to do something about that later. He was taller than she'd thought, and she hoped this wouldn't be the first and last time he was in her bedroom.

When they reached the bed, she let her hands drop to his stomach, tracing the muscles she'd suspected were there. She pulled up his shirt, dragging it over his head and throwing it on the floor.

"Holy crap!" Evelyn couldn't stop her outburst.

She gaped at his perfect pectorals coated in fine dark hair, the lines of sinew and muscle cording his shoulders and arms, the rows of abdominal muscles standing at attention in orderly rows down his stomach, the two graceful divots marking the iliac crest of his pelvis...

A brief moment of self-doubt sparked within her. Adam could have any woman he wanted.

Evelyn brought out her mental fire extinguisher. He wanted *her*.

He was brilliant. She knew that because he was one of the few people she'd met who could keep up with the vagaries of her mind. He had to be most enamored with her intellect and personality, based on the vast discrepancy between their physiques. Which made it all the worse that he was leaving.

Sadness was just as unwelcome as self-doubt. And she had promised Adam—and herself—a good time.

"Is something wrong?" he asked.

"No. Absolutely not." She grinned at the terrible joke.

Always falling back on humor. "Get it? *Abs*olutely?"

Adam raised an eyebrow.

"Sorry. I can't help myself. And this—" she gestured at his chest "—is so magnificent. It's a little intimidating, with me and my three-bags of chips a week habit and Internet addiction."

"I think you're beautiful."

"I bet you say that to all the women who promise you the best sex of your life."

"I've only ever said it to you."

Evelyn's brain just stopped. Jokes, thoughts, plans— they all evaporated. He ran a finger over her ear, pushing a stray lock of hair away from her face. He stared at every feature, as if he was trying to memorize her. She actually…believed him.

Her body kicked in as her brain bowed out. *Want. Need.* She would show him that he belonged with her, letting her body lead the way.

Chapter Four

Thinking about his home world cooled his ardor somewhat until Evelyn kissed him again. Adam let himself sink into the sensation of her lips against his, her cool fingers on his chest—exploring, teasing. Her hands were bold, hungry, unlike anything he'd ever experienced before. There was so much need behind her touch.

Feather-light, she dusted the backs of her fingers against his navel, trailing them over the smooth skin of his stomach to the fastener of his shorts. She worked the button deftly, opening them just enough to reach in and stroke him through the soft cotton of his underwear.

He drew in a breath like he was surfacing from an ocean. Without using *Coupling*, the drug the Coalition provided citizens to meet their sexual needs or facilitate sex with a partner, even that touch made lightning arcs of pleasure streak through him. He was used to stimulation coming from chemicals flooding his body, not from his actual senses.

He could feel her smile against his lips.

Turning her lips to his ear, she gently raked her teeth over his jaw. "Tell me your lovers at least touched you here."

"Not like this." He was surprised he could get out the words. His chest felt tight, his entire body filled to the brim with feelings that threatened to shatter him at any moment.

She sank to her knees before him, then quickly untied the laces of his boots, helping him out of them. His socks joined the pile of discarded clothing, along with his shorts. She slowed as she pulled his boxer-briefs down his legs, her breath hitching as she stared at his erection.

When he was completely naked, she looked up at him with a wicked smile.

"Did they touch you like this?" she said.

He wasn't sure what she meant. Before he could ask, she licked the crown of his dick.

His entire body jerked in response to the intense pleasure that reverberated out from his groin. She kept her gaze locked on his, that smile curving her lush mouth as she took another long lick from the base of his shaft to the crown.

"Cygnus X! What are you doing?"

"Making you have nerdy outbursts, apparently." She ran her cheek down the length of him, practically purring.

"What?"Adam forgot for a moment what they were talking about. All he knew was that he wanted more.

"Cygnus X?" she said.

Moons, how could he have made such an error? His

translation session changed almost all of his vocabulary to match that of Earth, even in their naming of things, but exclamations of that sort seemed outside of the mental programming. Evelyn had taught him quite a few slang terms and epithets, but he didn't realize his own had been translated into her language. At least he could explain it away with relative ease.

"I must have read it somewhere," he said.

This was too dangerous. He had to stop. He reached toward her to pull her away, but when his fingers touched her silken hair, he found himself instead taking out the clip and casting it away. All that honey-gold spilled around him, framing her face as she smiled up at him. Then she parted her lips and took him into her mouth.

"Evelyn!"

She circled her hands around him again, her eyes finally lowering to his dick. "Wow, you are huge. I'm going to need quite a warm-up to accommodate you."

A warm-up after this? Adam's skin was on fire, his muscles writhing with need—to hold her, to push himself into her over and over until oblivion claimed them both.

But she had been seeing to his pleasure. Moons, how she'd been doing so. He wasn't sure how to reciprocate. What she was doing to him was primal.

"Tell me what to do," he rasped.

"I do like a man who can take orders."

If only she knew. Adam commanded starships. He was

used to being the one who gave orders, and he was used to being obeyed. But in her hands, in her mouth, he found he would do anything to please her, anything to stay with her.

The thought was natural, the decision effortless. He was only surprised it had taken him so long to realize how strong his feelings for her had become. Beyond the amazing things she was doing to his body—her humor, her wit, her spirit, were all things he couldn't live without.

Exist, yes. Live? No.

"Have a seat," she said. She leaned back from him and stood, then bent to take off her sandals.

Adam sat on the bed. He couldn't keep from staring at her, wondering what was next. He was always wondering that with her. He never knew what she would say or do. It was what made their time together so magical, part of why he loved her.

How could he have not realized that? He *loved* her. Absolutely. And that was why giving up everything to be with her wouldn't be a sacrifice at all. It was a necessity.

The realization snapped what was left of his self control. He gripped her waist, pulling her onto his lap. He crushed his mouth to hers, his tongue delving, exploring.

She moaned against his lips, pressing herself against his erection. He slid his hands up her back, finding the zipper for her dress and making quick work of it. The warmth of her skin called to him, but he wanted more.

Flipping her over onto the bed, he pulled her dress

down her body and cast it away. He slid her panties down her legs, letting his fingers delight in the warmth of her skin, the fullness of her thighs. Her body was decadently feminine.

"This seems like the point where I should tell you I have a birth control implant," Evelyn said. "I'm not that active and have been tested recently for…unpleasantness. I'm all good. You?"

Cygnus X, how could he have not thought of something so important?

He swallowed hard, his dick pulsing as he stared at her. Nothing had ever affected him as Evelyn did.

"I was rigorously tested before coming here to be sure I wasn't carrying anything harmful," he said.

"Awesome. Well, now that we have that out of the way…" She reached for him, drawing him down to lay beside her.

So much warmth. He pressed his chest to hers as he kissed her again, marveling at the softness of her skin.

She had mentioned concern about them coupling. Her body needed to be prepared for him naturally. Perhaps it would be best to start smaller.

He cupped her sex, then slowly slid his finger into her core, amazed at the different textures, the sensation of her body inviting him in. He had never touched a woman this intimately with his hands.

"More. Adam, more."

She couldn't be ready for him yet. He slid another finger into her, never pausing in his movements.

"Oh God, yes!"

His dick was so hard. It throbbed with need, longing to fill her. But he wanted her to enjoy their coupling as much as he was certain to. A third finger joined the others, her body clenching them tight.

"Wait, wait! Stop!"

Adam quickly pulled back, wondering if he'd hurt her or offended her somehow. She was panting, one hand on her forehead.

"That's enough. I'm ready."

Those were the most beautiful words he'd ever heard. He didn't trust himself to speak, to think, to do anything except press her back into the bed, his shaft finding its perfect place immediately.

Soft. Hot. Wet.

He wanted to go slowly, but once he touched himself to her, it was over. He buried himself deep, crying out from the intense sensations scattering through him. His body was a live conduit, sparking from the overload to his senses.

He wanted to be deeper, he wanted to feel more, to give her more. Gripping her thighs, he pulled her legs up to rest on the bed, holding them in place against his arms. The angle gave him more—just a little more—but he would take whatever he could get, whatever she would give him.

She gripped his neck, holding on as he rocked her against the bed. Her eyes were clenched shut, mouth open as she gasped for breath.

Her back arched, head thrashing as her hips bucked against his. He kept going, pumping into her, barely controlling himself as he felt her body coil around his, the rhythmic contractions pulling on him, urging him to give in to his own climax.

It lit like a fuse from where they were joined. The flame traveled up his body, through his chest, down his legs and arms, consuming his mind, his memory of anything before her, before *this*. He screamed with the pureness of it, as all that he had been before was burned away. Still thrumming, chest heaving for breath, he collapsed on top of her on the bed.

She was his. She would always be his. His body still wanted to move within her, on top of her, but he was too relaxed—more than he had ever been.

He didn't know how much time passed before she said, "Um, getting a little difficult to breathe down here."

"My apologies."

She laughed as he rolled over onto his back, which reassured him that she was all right. Evelyn propped herself up on her elbows and grinned at him, her full lips pulled in a devastating smile. Her face was still flushed, eyes bright, hair a glorious halo of gold around her soft features.

"You are so beautiful," he said.

"Eh, you probably say that to all the women who let you fuck them senseless."

He laughed again, deeper and longer than he ever had. His chest felt spacious, like shackles that he hadn't known he wore had been cast off.

He felt infinite.

This couldn't end. Ever. He stood and helped her to sit up, then knelt in front of her again.

Adam took one of her hands in both of his. He couldn't stop smiling. "I'm not going to marry you because I want to stay here. I'm not going to marry you because of what just happened, even though it was truly the most amazing experience of my life."

One corner of her lips pulled into a knowing smirk. "But you *are* going to marry me."

"Yes. Because I love you."

Chapter Five

Had she just heard him correctly? Love?

Evelyn's heart was too small to hold all the emotions she was feeling. It seemed to split in two. One half pounded frantically in her chest and the other lodged itself soundly in her throat.

"Marry me," he said.

Adam's smile was gentle, even though what they had just done really kind of wasn't. She'd suspected he would be passionate in bed if she could convince him to let go of some of that self-control, but...

Wait, what did he just say?

"Evelyn. Marry me."

Her brain didn't seem to be working, but luckily her mouth was doing fine. "Okay."

His smile brightened and he rose up on his knees to kiss her again, hands cradling her face. The kiss was gentle and slow, as if they had all the time in the world. Maybe now they actually did.

"I have to go."

She shook her head to clear it. That didn't seem right. "Great. Because that's what every woman wants to hear after a declaration of love, mind blowing sex and a proposal."

"I only have two and a half days left. If I don't get everything in order, I'll have to leave no matter what."

"Well then, why are you kneeling naked in my bedroom? Go!"

She waved her hands at him to shoo him on his way, but he caught her by her wrists, then pulled her against his chest and wrapped her arms around his neck. She laughed as she fell into him, still exhilarated from everything that had happened.

He kissed her again, one of those mind-numbing, earth-shattering kisses. She could feel his erection poking her thigh and wondered if she might be able to convince him to stay a little bit longer.

"Are you sure you don't have another fifteen minutes? I can teach you about this thing we call a *quickie*."

Adam chuckled deep in his chest. He nuzzled her neck and said, "You make it sound tempting, but I really do need to go. There's much to do to make sure everything is in order."

He stepped away from her and started to gather up his clothes.

"Far be it from me to disagree with my fiancé." She still couldn't believe it. Fiancé? Was she really engaged?

"I hope you do keep disagreeing with me. And making me laugh and surprising me at every turn."

"I'll do my best, but it might be *hard* to keep that *up*." She giggled. "Get it?"

"I'll *pun*ish you for that later."

She couldn't believe he'd made such a terrible joke. Sure, she usually earned a laugh when she made them, but the fact that he'd loosened up enough to make bad jokes of his own...

Evelyn threw herself back on her bed, covering her face with her hands. "Oh my God, you're perfect."

"The student becomes the master. You did teach me all about puns."

She laughed, then rolled off her bed and headed for her dresser. Adam had already managed to get dressed and was tying his boots.

"What are you doing?"

"Getting dressed." She pulled on a pair of jeans and grabbed her favorite T-shirt—a 50s style flying saucer hovering over the words, *I believe*. With the shirt halfway over her head, she said, "I don't know if you picked up on this over the last couple of months, but I don't usually sit around my apartment naked."

"I'll have to fix that." He grinned at her, tugging her shirt down the rest of the way.

"Oh, I look forward to that. But in the meantime, since you're going to be gone for a while and we'll probably be pretty busy when you get back," she waggled her eyebrows, "I'm going to see what I can get done at the

University. Meet you here tonight?"

"I'll be back as soon as I can, but I don't know how long it will be."

She slid her hands up his chest. She would never get tired of feeling him, touching him, being close to him. She wrapped her arms around his neck and pulled herself up so that their noses were touching.

"Then give me a little sugar to tide me over," she said.

"You are ridiculous."

"You are not kissing me."

"I'll have to fix that too."

"They better let you stay," she said. "You have a lot to do."

He kissed her then—soundly, deeply. The model planets above their heads seemed to spin as his lips caressed hers, his tongue stoking the fire in her belly yet again. Evelyn used what willpower she had left to push him away.

"If you don't leave now, I'm going to tie you to the bed and keep you here until I'm well and truly done with you," she said.

"Done with me?"

"That was a poor choice of words. I don't think I'll ever be done with you."

"Good. Because I know I'll never be done with you."

She walked him to the door, holding hands the whole way. She felt giddy, so excited at the new prospects before her that she hardly knew what to think.

At the door, Adam said, "That thing you mentioned about tying me to the bed... Do people really do that?"

Evelyn grinned. "Later."

He kissed her once more before he left. A lingering kiss, his gaze promising more. She could hardly wait until tonight. But in the meantime, there were some research journals that she could bury herself in that might help her pass the time.

Chapter Six

"I'm staying."

Adam burst through the door to the planetary liaison's office, a little gratified that his entrance made Todd jump behind the heavy wooden desk that dominated the large room. Adam planted his feet on the ground, daring Todd to object.

Something was wrong. Instead of being cowed, Todd leaned back in his chair and smirked. He draped one of his arms across the surface of his desk and kept the other out of sight beneath it. From the angle of his elbow, his hand wasn't resting in his lap.

Amateur. Todd was broadcasting the weapon he had strapped to the underside of the desk. Why he had a weapon pointed at his door was the mystery. Without seeing it, Adam couldn't tell the range or dispersal pattern he was facing.

"I've told you the High Council's decision," Todd said. "You'll have to take it up with them. In person."

Adam stalked to a low table along the left wall of the room, hopefully out of the path of whatever Todd was hiding beneath his desk. Turning, Adam leaned against the table, crossing his arms.

"Actually, *you'll* be taking it up with them," Adam said. "I'm done with the Coalition."

"You can't just quit the Coalition."

"My latest tour is complete. My obligations are fulfilled. I'm officially releasing my citizenship so that I can stay on Earth."

Todd stood and smoothed the jacket of his suit—dark fabric made of native materials of extremely high quality. He walked around the desk and leaned against it, mirroring Adam's posture.

"I know it's nice here, but you can't just stay. It was enough of a stretch that you were allowed to come here in the first place. This is precisely why Earth is a preserved planet. There are too many temptations here for someone like you."

"What, you mean a glitch?"

Todd's lips flickered into a sneer for the briefest of moments, but Adam caught the expression. Todd recovered himself quickly.

"A conqueror," Todd said.

Adam couldn't argue that point. "Not anymore."

"Really? You can guarantee to the High Council that you won't snatch up some choice technology when you get bored with all your nature hikes, cobble it together into something that actually works, and bring these primitive people to their knees?"

An image of Evelyn before Adam on her knees sprang to mind. He had to clamp down on his body's reaction with all his willpower to keep himself from getting hard just from the thought. When he looked back at Todd, the bastard had a smug smirk on his face.

"I see. You've tasted even more of the forbidden fruits of this planet than I thought. The women here do have their charms. I have yet to find one immune to my own."

Adam couldn't believe that the planetary liaison had taken such liberties with the people he was supposed to be protecting. Adam kept his expression as impassive as he could, seething inside.

Todd shook his head and walked back to his chair, but didn't sit. "My advice is to find a few Earth women to teach you their tricks and then hire someone on one of the stations to service your new appetites when you get back."

Adam had made a dangerous assumption about Todd—and was paying for it. Being assigned to Earth was an important role for a planetary liaison. They were supposed to be carefully screened. They were also supposed to protect the populace of the planet they were overseeing, not offer them up as entertainment.

"I'm only interested in one woman," Adam said. "And she's on Earth, so that's where I'm staying. Draw up whatever forms you need. Citizen revocation, contracts of conduct, relinquishing my assets."

A spark lit in Todd's eyes at the last. Adam was hardly

surprised. Apparently, Todd had been on Earth long enough to be corrupted by the vast resources of the planet. He masked his expression, most likely realizing that he wasn't being as discreet as he needed to be.

"You can't just buy yourself a spot on this planet." Todd sat again, leaning back and steepling his fingers, elbows on the arms of his chair. "If people could, the place would be overrun. Half the planets with preservation status would be."

"I'm not some tourist looking for a permanent vacation. I don't make these choices lightly."

Todd was silent for a while. The unwholesome gleam in his eyes caused Adam's stomach to clench.

Now that Adam was listening to his body more, he received the message clearly. Battle was coming.

"You love this Earthling?" Todd asked.

Adam hated to admit it when his senses were warning him of danger, but he had to. "Yes."

"Then I'd like to meet her."

"I don't see why that would be necessary."

"It is necessary," Todd said. "I have to decide if this is some sort of ruse to allow you to stay. The High Council won't just take your word that you fell in love with an Earthling during your leave."

They should. Adam's teeth started to hurt from grinding together. Adam had done so much for the Coalition, he'd worked directly with the High Council for years. If they didn't trust him, they didn't trust anyone.

The thought didn't sit well with him on many levels. If they didn't understand trust, he might be better served to put his faith elsewhere, like in himself. And in Evelyn.

"I'll arrange a meeting," Adam said.

The first volley had been fired, but Todd didn't understand who he was dealing with. Adam would set up the meeting in a safe location that he scouted in advance. But before he brought Evelyn anywhere near Todd, Adam needed to arm himself with information.

A weapon would have been preferable, but if he was caught planet-side with one, the High Council would certainly refuse his request to stay. Adam needed to call his crew and get them working on this. He needed to know exactly how deep of water Todd was treading.

Chapter Seven

Getting engaged was not good for concentration. Neither was incredible sex. Evelyn stared blankly at the pages of the journals she was supposed to be indexing for about an hour. Her body tingled from the memory of Adam's touch as her mind replayed vivid scenes from their morning together.

Nope, she wasn't getting anything done today.

Maybe a walk in the park would be nice. She decided to go back to where it had all begun, to the very bench where she and Adam shared their first kiss.

The day wasn't getting any cooler, but the bench was still shaded from the afternoon sun. She sat and closed her eyes, smiling as she thought about their morning.

"I don't suppose you'd like some company?"

Evelyn jumped at the unexpected voice—the unexpectedly close voice.

A tall man stood before her. He was wearing a charcoal gray suit that fit his lithe frame perfectly, accenting his narrow waist and broad shoulders. His nose was straight and thin, like his lips, and his cheekbones were high and sharp. His dark hair was combed back from his face and full of enough product to be formed into a perfect helmet.

If it wasn't for the aura of douchery he was giving off, he might have been handsome in an avant-garde supermodel sort of way. As it was, Evelyn could only think one thing as she looked at him.

"How are you not dying?" she said.

He blinked, a momentary lowering of his eyebrows and curling of his lip making her more than a little uncomfortable. He covered the expression quickly with a smile as fake as a mannequin's. That plus the hair-helmet and she actually let out a little laugh.

He didn't look like a real person. It was more like he'd been stamped out from a plastic mold.

"I'm afraid I don't follow you," he said.

"You're in a dark three-piece suit in hundred degree weather and you're not even sweating. That's weird." She shook her head and said, "I don't mean to be rude. I'm just having a really awesome day and my verbal filters are even lower than usual."

This time, he let his sneer stay a bit longer. When he pasted a smile on his face again, he accompanied it with lowered eyelids. He sat next to her, sliding his arm behind her on the bench.

"A good mood is nothing to apologize for," he said. "And good days should be celebrated."

Evelyn scooted forward on the bench and turned to face him more fully, trying to figure out what the hell was going on. Heavy eyes, half-smirk on the mouth, lips a little pouty, body angled forward...

"Oh my God. You're hitting on me," she said.

The extremely strange stranger sat back quickly, scowling again. This guy was not good at hiding his emotions. His smile was a little more genuine when it returned, but there was a reptilian vibe to it that made the hair on the back of her neck prick up in warning.

"Maybe I am," he said. "Would that be such a bad thing?"

"I guess it's true what they say about getting more attention after you're engaged. Which, I am. As of today. Hence, the super-awesome day."

"Even more reason to celebrate." He leaned forward a bit, and Evelyn scooted back further.

She held up her hands and said, "Ho there, cowboy. Ease up on the spurs."

Now he looked genuinely confused. "What?"

"I'm not sure where that came from. But I do know where I'm going. Which is away. From you. Right now. You have crazy-eyes. Seriously—you're creeping me out."

She managed to get a few steps from the bench before Mr. Mannequin called out to her.

"Is that really such a good idea, Evelyn? Making a good impression on Adam's liaison will go a long way toward helping his paperwork through."

Thoughts raced through her head. Liaison? Was this the

lanky guy Adam had been arguing with earlier?

She turned back around to gape at the man. Tall, thin, dark hair. Yeah, he could be the same guy. Same expensive suit, anyway.

"Wait," she said. "You're not telling me I have to have sex with you for you to put Adam's paperwork through, right? Because if you are, I will find whatever authorities I need to report you to and—"

"Please." The liaison stood up, contempt practically rolling off him. Shaking out his jacket, he smoothed his hands down his lapel and then straightened his tie. "I have my pick of women. Why would I want you?"

Evelyn felt his words ping off her ego like pebbles thrown by a wayward child. The little girl with braces and acne she had once been was now dating the quarterback of the football team—and the head of science club—all in one delicious package.

"Is this some kind of test to see if I'm actually in love with Adam?" she asked. "Because it's a pretty shitty test. I'm just saying."

"Your feelings are insignificant. Just like the wayward glitch whose been leading you on."

Despite herself, a small ember of doubt lit in her mind. Adam wasn't leading her on. He loved her. She was sure of that.

"First of all, Adam is not a glitch. He is awesome. Second, I'm pretty sure I can find a lawyer who will be happy to turn this festival of bad manners into a case for letting Adam stay here no matter what a petty bureaucrat with delusions of grandeur has to say."

"You really have no idea who you've been fucking, do you?"

"Language! There are kids in this park sometimes." Evelyn was growing increasingly uncomfortable with this guy.

It was broad daylight, and they were near the entrance to the park. She could see a few people on the other side of the pond. They were out of earshot for a regular conversation, but if she started to scream, she wouldn't be in this alone.

"What does he see in you?" the liaison said. "I suppose it's impossible to understand the reasoning of a madman."

"I certainly am not following." She made little gestures with her hands as she explained her joke. "See what I did there? I'm actually implying that *you're* the madman."

The liaison slid his chin to the side, as if he was chewing on something. Evelyn had the weirdest idea that he was going to unhinge his jaw and swallow her whole. She took a step back, and he smiled.

"That's right, little monkey. Be afraid of me. But the person you should really be afraid of is Adam."

He slid his hands into his pockets, suddenly smug— which made her even more nervous. He could have anything in there. Mace. Bear mace. A teeny tiny gun. She should probably be more cautious, but he was seriously pushing her buttons.

"You're not making any sense," she said.

"Let me use smaller words for your primitive mind. Adam is lying to you."

Evelyn didn't buy it. She crossed her arms and jutted her chin at the liaison. "About what?"

"Who he is. Where he's from."

"Aha! He hasn't told me where he's from, so how is that a lie?"

"And you say you're going to marry him? Do you even know his full name?"

"Adam Smith." She'd have to ask Adam his middle name the next time she saw him.

A tiny sliver of misgiving crossed her mind. Saying Adam's name aloud… It sounded kind of fake.

"'Adam Smith' is a cover identity I made for him when he decided he had to see this backwater during his shore leave. Didn't know that, either, did you? Your love is military. A General responsible for the deaths of billions."

"Okay, wackadoodle. Now I know you're crazy. I think that would have made the news, given that there are only seven billion people on the entire planet."

"On *this* planet."

"Just so you know, this is the part of the conversation where I run away screaming for help."

The liaison pulled a small silver disk from his pocket

and squeezed it with his thumb. Evelyn told her body to turn and run, but she couldn't move. She felt suspended, as if not even gravity was pulling her down. Some other force —something she didn't have a name for—was holding her in place. Her stomach lurched at the bizarre weightlessness that her brain couldn't manage to process.

"Now you're going to be quiet and listen to me, *monkey*," the man said. "And then you can tell me if you think your precious glitch is worth all this trouble."

Chapter Eight

"Open a secure channel with K-35-b7." Adam paced within the small space of his skimmer, an uncomfortable energy coursing through him that he was unfamiliar with. His skin was crawling with the need for action.

This was a new battlefield for him.

The viewscreen that took up most of the main wall of the craft flickered to life, his second-in-command filling it. Around the edges of Khel's blond hair, Adam could see weapons hanging on the wall. A familiar plasma rifle and a wickedly curved blade.

My command room.

"General Serath," Khel said.

Adam felt a chill at hearing his true name after so long. He pushed through the discomfort.

"Khel." Adam nodded toward the screen.

Khel was a glitch, like Adam, but even taller and thick with muscle. Adam had reviewed Khel's file thoroughly, and still shuddered at the thought of all the tests they had put the man through to understand what had gone wrong with his genetic engineering.

"Activate a full link with the *Arbiter's* computer and

that of my skimmer using maximum security protocols," Adam commanded.

"Yes, sir." Khel's arms moved outside of the area Adam could see. After a few moments, Khel leaned back and said, "It's done."

Adam crossed to the viewscreen and began entering commands at the control panel at its side. A smaller, transparent screen appeared within his communications window with Khel, providing data on the *Arbiter's* status and location.

"You're three days out from the Sol system," Adam said.

They would arrive exactly when Adam's shore leave ended. Khel was nothing if not efficient.

"At standard speed." Khel's blue eyes glimmered with something akin to hope. "Do you need us to expedite your retrieval?"

"Tired of command already?"

Khel didn't pick up on Adam's joke. It wasn't surprising, since Adam had never made one before visiting Earth.

"The *Arbiter* is not as effective without you at command," Khel said. "The crew is eager for your return."

The crew had no idea Adam was thinking about leaving the fleet. Khel…would not take that well. Adam needed to keep his focus on the matter at hand.

"That must wait," Adam said. "I need a full report on

Earth's planetary liaison."

Khel's mouth opened and closed a few times. "Sir?"

"Something is very, very wrong here," Adam said. "And Todd Simms is at the center of it."

"T-14-b5." Khel again shifted as his hands slid over the controls back on the *Arbiter*, feeding data to Adam's skimmer through the secure link.

Adam almost wished he was back on board. Though he could investigate the matter remotely, it would be much easier to mete out punishment if he had the resources of the *Arbiter* at hand—and he was certain there would be a severe penalty for what Todd was doing.

An abrasive buzz brought Adam's attention back to the viewscreen. Khel's pale eyebrows were furrowed.

"Report," Adam said.

Khel shook his head. "This makes no sense. His file is locked. My security codes can't grant me access."

"That's not possible." Adam stopped reviewing the scrolling data Khel was feeding him and entered his own security code.

Nothing happened.

Adam's heart felt as though it had turned to lead. He was the highest ranking military officer in the fleet. The only people in the entire Coalition of Planets who could restrict his access to information on other citizens was the High Council itself. But they wouldn't concern themselves with such a small planet...

Something else had to be going on. Todd must have connections that Adam didn't suspect. Which meant he was even more dangerous than Adam feared.

Evelyn…

"General?" Khel prompted.

"The soldier assigned to Earth's listening station has been sending regular reports, correct?" Adam said.

Khel tapped on his control panel a few times. The furrow between his eyebrows deepened.

"Records indicate there is no soldier assigned to Earth's listening station," he said. "All reports have come directly from the planetary liaison."

"That's against protocol," Adam nearly shouted.

He couldn't believe what he was hearing. No matter who Todd Simms was connected to, the High Council would not stand for this.

"We'll have to gather data through other channels," Adam said. "Put Ari and Vay on this. With his investigative expertise and her cultural knowledge, they should be able to find something useful. Just be sure they know to proceed with the utmost discretion. They are to report to you and I and no other, understood?"

Khel nodded briskly. "Understood. Should we increase our speed?"

"Yes. I want to see how deep his connections are," Adam said. "Let's see if he learns of your expedited schedule. I'll be in contact with you soon."

Adam tapped the command to end the transmission, his dread growing.

He had to check on Evelyn. After confronting Todd earlier, Adam didn't know what the man was capable of. He ran from the ship, only pausing for long enough to make sure that the cloaking field was in place before tearing through the forest toward Evelyn's apartment building.

She didn't live far from the park. Adam reached her dwelling in less than half an hour, sweating and out of breath. He unlocked Evelyn's apartment with the key she'd given him.

Her purse was on the side table just inside her apartment. Adam locked the door behind him, then set his key and wallet next to her belongings. He took a moment to look at them jumbled together. This simple domesticity was supposed to be his future, and now, he was fearful for her life.

Normally, she would be sitting at the computer desk in the area adjacent to her kitchen, but she wasn't there or on the couch. The kitchen was quiet—which left the bedroom.

He walked briskly down the hallway, eager to see her again.

"Evelyn, I…"

He paused in the doorway to her room. Evelyn was sitting at the foot of her bed, hands clasped in her lap. Her glasses were low on her nose and she hadn't bothered to push them back into place. She was staring blankly at the floor in front of her.

Adam's throat seemed to close. Something was very wrong. He practically leapt into the room, then knelt at her feet.

"Evelyn, what's happened?"

Her eyes were glazed when she turned to him, not the bright, sharp gaze he was used to. She almost looked as if she'd had a mind-wipe.

Cygnus X, it couldn't be.

"I met your liaison today," she said.

Rage surged through him. What had Todd done to her? And how could Adam not have thought to protect her sooner?

"What did he do?" Adam asked.

She must have read the guilt on his face. Her eyes focused and the brightness seeped back into them, fueled by anger. Adam felt hope flutter in his chest. He knew this Evelyn. And—thank the stars—she knew him.

"It's my turn to ask the questions. Here's the first one." Her brows drew down on her forehead, her lips pulled into a frown, and she pushed her glasses up the bridge of her nose forcefully. "Are you an alien?"

Adam felt as if the ground had given way beneath him and he was free-falling. Not since his first zero-g maneuvers had he been this disoriented.

His stomach was ricocheting against his ribs, his heart frantically looking for escape. His mind whirled pointlessly, offering nothing helpful, except the one word that escaped his lips.

"Yes."

She shoved him, hard. He was surprised by her strength and already off-balance enough that he toppled over. She leapt up, towering over him, hands clenched into fists at her sides. For a moment, he wondered if she was going to kick him where he lay.

"You jerk," she yelled. "I can't believe I actually fell for your scheme. You used me!"

"What are you talking about?"

"You want to stay on Earth so bad you'll do anything, even marry me." Her voice hitched on the words, but rage quickly pushed aside any sorrow on her features.

"You've got it backwards."

"Right, because I'm just a stupid, un-evolved, hairless monkey from a backwater planet that's as rich in resources as it is lacking in technology."

The sentiment was all too familiar. Damn him, Todd must have told her so much. Things that were forbidden for an Earthling to know.

This was Todd's plan. He was setting them up, trying to make the High Council mandate a mind-wipe. They might even decide to take *all* of her memories of Adam.

But he and Evelyn could fight this, as long as they

fought together. Adam needed her by his side.

"That's not true." He tried to get through to her with the humor she had taught him. "Besides, don't Earthlings think they evolved from primates rather than monkeys?"

"I swear, I will kick you in your teeth."

Her voice was deadly calm, but she was talking to him, at least. He could get through to her. He had to.

She started pacing back and forth, pulling strands of hair loose from her ponytail. "Earthlings! God, I'm just an Earthling to you!"

"You're not *just* anything to me. You're the woman I plan to marry. The woman I love."

"Drop it! I know you're just trying to get your Gray card."

"Gray card?"

She stopped pacing and lifted one shoulder in a half-shrug, a crack in her defenses opening that Adam desperately needed to navigate. Her voice lost a bit of its edge. She was falling back on humor, as always.

"Like a green card, but for aliens."

He remembered the tiny gray creatures in so many of the TV shows and movies she had shown him. Grays.

Adam couldn't help himself—he started to laugh. He laughed so hard that tears streamed down his face.

"It wasn't that funny," she said.

Pulling himself together, he managed to stand, wiping at his eyes. "How can you say something like that and still doubt why I want to marry you?"

She lifted her chin, eyes blazing. "What, that I'm not funny?"

Adam took a deep breath, then let it out slowly. He was going to set this right.

"You are hilarious," he said. "You are ridiculous. Absurd."

"Such flattery. How could I possibly resist you?"

He dared to reach out and gently cup her elbows. She didn't pull away, but she did look like she might head-butt him. She had even more fire than he knew.

"You are completely unpredictable," he said. "You make me look at the universe with new eyes. You make me laugh at myself, at everything. You taught me how to enjoy life rather than just existing. You think I want to marry you to stay on Earth? I don't give a damn where we are. I just want to be with you."

Her lips softened ever so slightly. He might not have noticed at all, except he was having trouble not staring at them. She let out a sigh and her arms relaxed a bit in his grip.

"Were you ever going to tell me? Maybe after the first kid came out green?"

"Wouldn't she be gray?"

That earned him the faintest glimmer of a smile.

The time for dissembling was over. If Todd had stepped on the mine of telling Evelyn they were aliens, there wasn't any more damage Adam could do. And there was plenty he could fix.

She pushed her glasses up her nose and crossed her arms again. He was expecting more questions about his origins, so was surprised when Evelyn said, "She?"

What a thing for her to focus on. It made his heart pound, his stomach fill with butterflies. His life with her would be full of laughter and wonder, love and family. He was certain of it.

"Or he. As long as it's a surprise, I don't care."

"It usually is with us monkeys. You'll just be lucky if you get out of the delivery room without me throwing poop at you."

"Gross. And again—inaccurate. You aren't a monkey, or did Todd neglect to mention your origins?"

"He had plenty to say on other topics."

Adam didn't doubt it. "Humans did evolve from something resembling a primate, but not on this planet."

Her eyes widened and her lips parted. That caught her attention. "Where did we evolve, then?"

"Sadr-4. We're from the same planet. Millennia ago, a colony ship went off course and crashed here."

"That's not in any of our history books."

"Their ship was destroyed and they had no means of manufacturing anything. Survival, dealing with an alien world, vying for resources with the already-evolving Earth hominids—that closely resembled our own ancestors... I think they had plenty to handle. Their origins just got lost along the way."

"Hence lost colony?"

"Exactly."

"So you and I are the same species?"

"Fundamentally. Our DNA has just been a bit... altered."

"Altered how?" She stared at his chest and leaned a little closer, unclasping her arms so she could gently tug on his shirt. "I didn't notice anything out of place earlier."

"You wouldn't. Everything is in order and carefully controlled. Geneticists take care of all the details of childbirth in the Coalition of Planets."

"*All* the details?"

"Yes. Women don't want to deal with the pain and discomfort of carrying children in their bodies when they and their partner can just place an order for exactly what they want." In most cases.

"Your parents must have been thrilled with you," she said.

"Actually..." He swallowed hard, struggling to speak the words. But she needed to know. "I'm considered defective. The command abilities my parents requested came through, so I'm of great use in the military, but physically... I don't exactly fit in at most Coalition social events. That's one of the reasons I prefer life on a ship. My parents received a full refund."

Her eyes snapped to his, anger sparking in their loamy depths. Adam hadn't previously felt the pain of his parents' rejection the way he did in that moment—one of the downsides of becoming more aware of his feelings. Looking into Evelyn's soulful eyes—connecting with the empathy he saw there—made it worth it.

"That's awful," she said.

"It's just the way things are. My society isn't as emotional as yours. Or as physical."

"Not as physical, huh?" She smiled briefly. The distance he felt between them was narrowing, but he hadn't quite closed the gap yet.

"As you discovered. We still have sexual urges, but there are many other things vying for attention. And the biological drive to reproduce has been rendered obsolete. The Coalition has developed various chemical solutions that meet most of the emotional and physical needs of our citizens."

"You mean people take drugs instead of having sex?"

"Quite often. But if the drugs don't satisfy the person's drives, they find like-minded individuals and have sex with the assistance of *Coupling*."

"Coupling?"

"The chemical mix that facilitates sex. It takes the body through the entire process within a few minutes, from arousal through orgasm." Adam couldn't believe how easy it was to talk to her about this. He hadn't even spoken so frankly with the women he'd used *Coupling* with. "People most often use it alone, but if taken with a partner, the drug does all the work for us. We have to act quickly to keep pace with it, in fact."

"How romantic," she said. "And you've only ever had sex while taking it?"

"It would be unheard of to attempt sex without it. I was already seen as unusual for preferring sex with a partner. I suppose I'm something of a throwback in more ways than one."

She slid her arms around his neck and leaned forward until their chests were touching. "You have to love the classics."

"Do you?" Adam had clearly stated his feelings and intentions, but she had yet to say those words back to him. He knew he wouldn't truly rest until he heard them. Until he knew for sure.

"Love you?" Her face relaxed and the warmth flowed back into her smile. He felt as if his heart had stopped.

"I do," she said. "I love you, Adam Smith. Whatever your name really is."

Chapter Nine

If Evelyn doubted Adam's feelings before, all of that was wiped away by the expression on his face when she told him she loved him. His eyes softened, his lips parted, and he looked at her as if he couldn't believe what she was saying.

They really had it bad for each other.

He lifted his hands to her face, tracing his thumbs over her cheekbones, then leaned forward and gently pressed his lips to hers. It wasn't long before his mouth became more insistent. His hand slid around her waist, pulling her closer.

Evelyn tightened her grip on Adam's neck, reveling in every feeling. She didn't wait for an invitation, but trailed her tongue along his lips until he opened his mouth to her. His tongue met hers, thrust for hungry thrust.

He gripped her ass, rocking her against his erection. He parted from her for a moment—just long enough to lift her shirt and pull it over her head, then fling it away. Thankfully, she had put on her best bra before going to the University. He ran his fingertips over the lacy fabric.

"How do I get this off of you?"

"There's a clasp in the back."

"Turn around."

"Is that an order, General?" She had meant it as a playful tease, but a shadow crossed his expression.

"What else did Todd tell you about me?"

"Nothing that we need to discuss right now." She brought her hands to Adam's face, running the backs of her fingers along his cheek. "I know you're a good man, whatever planet you're from or rank you hold."

"I'm not proud of everything that I've done, but most of my missions were about keeping the peace. It's important to me that you know that. And most of those missions, the people that I stopped…"

She moved her hands to the back of his head. "We have time. I want to know everything about you. But right now, I need this."

She dragged his lips back to hers, kissing him deeply. Grabbing his shoulders, she turned him around so he was standing at the foot of her bed, then gave him a shove. He went along with it, sitting down on the bed hard and falling back on his elbows.

"Now, can we please stop talking?" she asked. "I have much more interesting things in mind for us to do."

She reached behind her back and unfastened the clasp of her bra, then smirked as she pulled the lacy garment off and threw it aside. His gaze locked on her breasts and he nodded.

"Very good," she said. "I hope you're as good at taking orders as giving them."

Adam grinned, then leaned forward and wrapped his arms around her waist. "I'm yours to command."

"Oh, I really like the sound of that."

She ran her fingers through his dark hair. It was so soft. That was probably part of his DNA. She tried not to think too much about that—all the implications associated with his origins.

Evelyn wasn't close with her parents, mostly because they didn't understand a word she said. But they loved each other. The idea of being grown in a petri dish, and then returned to sender…was just too terrible.

"I can't say that I like your expression right now," Adam said.

"I'm not obeying my own orders. Now is not the time for thinking."

"What is it the time for?" He gave her a gentle smile, his hands slowly roving over her back.

"Kissing would be good."

"Where shall I kiss you?" He started to work the front of her jeans, undoing the button and slowly pulling down the zipper.

"Like I said, you have really good instincts."

"In that case, there's something I've wanted to do."

He leaned forward and clasped one nipple in his mouth, flicking his tongue over the surface until it tightened.

Evelyn gasped, burying her hands more deeply in his hair and hugging his head to her chest. She kicked off her shoes as he slowly worked her jeans down over her hips, taking her panties with them.

He moved to her other breast, teasing, kneading, caressing. Her body ached for more. She wanted him all over her, inside her.

As if he sensed her need, he slid his hand between her legs, two fingers gliding effortlessly into her while his thumb traced lazy circles around her clitoris. She grabbed his shoulders to keep her balance.

"I'm going to fall over if you keep doing that."

"I'll catch you."

Her smile transformed to a gasp as he hit a particularly sensitive spot. "Oh God, that feels so good."

"Then let me keep doing it."

Warmth coursed through her body where his hands were working. At some point, she wasn't even sure when, he put his other arm behind her, helping to hold her up.

"I want more," she said. "All of you. Now."

Her body ached as he pulled his hands from her and stood. He unfastened his pants and pulled out his dick, barely pausing as he picked her up and spun them around.

Her knees hit the edge of her bed and she let herself fall back. Adam followed, covering her body with his. He reached between them to guide himself to her core, then buried himself to the hilt with a groan of pleasure.

Or maybe it was hers. It was hard to tell, and she didn't really care to sort it out.

He immediately started thrusting deep. No preludes, no hesitation. Evelyn wanted to give him more. New sensations, new pleasures.

She wrapped her thighs around his waist so he had even better access, and raked her fingernails down his back. She felt his shiver with every part of her, everywhere they touched.

The valley of his spine seemed particularly sensitive. She trailed her fingers down the length of it, splaying her hands over his ass and squeezing the muscles that were rhythmically contracting—pushing him deep within her, pulling out to the protest of her body.

Her body was lighting up everywhere. She must be glowing. No one could feel this good—this energized, this ready to explode—without glowing.

"Moons, Evelyn," he grunted out. "That feels…too good."

He kissed her before she could respond, so she dug her nails into him, playing with the threshold between pleasure and pain. He rewarded her by pushing himself up on his hands and angling his hips to grind against her clitoris with every thrust.

The fireworks began, small explosions at first, that quickly built into a cascade of color and energy, making every cell in her body feel alive.

"Adam!"

His own cry mingled with hers as his thrusts became more desperate, uncontrolled, the force of them rocking the bed. Her body clenched tightly around him, joining the pulsing of his shaft.

He buried himself deep and stayed there, head back, eyes tightly shut, a look of such rapture on his face she knew she'd never be able to forget it. The thudding of her heart in her ears slowly subsided, tension she hadn't noticed melting away into the mattress beneath her.

Adam lowered himself to his elbows, careful not to put too much of his weight on her as he had the first time. He nuzzled her ear, nibbling on her earlobe and kissing her neck.

"We need to keep doing that forever." It took several breaths to get out her sentence, but she managed it.

"Absolutely."

He rocked against her again, kissing her deeply. She could feel him softening inside of her, her body no longer stretching as much to hold onto him. He didn't seem willing to end their union, which was fine with her. The relaxed connection was wonderful in its own way.

They were going to get married. The thought sprang up unexpected, but no longer accompanied by surprise.

This felt right. The two of them together. It was how the universe was meant to be. She was sure of it—could feel it in her bones.

They just had to convince the insane liaison to let Adam stay.

Chapter Ten

"I want to see your ship."

When Evelyn made the request, Adam was hardly in a state to refuse her anything. A shiver flowed over his skin as he thought of the warmth of her body. There was nothing like the incredible feeling of belonging and connection when he was inside of her, their arms around each other, holding each other as close as they possibly could.

He felt like he was melting into her sometimes, a union beyond anything he'd experienced. Remembering that and enjoying the forest around him, he could almost forget about the challenges they faced.

In the full bloom of summer, the trees overhead were thick with rich green foliage. Insects that couldn't bite off his head chirred pleasantly around them and birds called out to each other. The entirely wholesome sound of dirt and rocks crunching beneath their boots blended in with the woodland melody. The only thing that would have improved the hike was if they could hold hands, but the trail was too narrow for that.

"Earth to Adam." She laughed. "I guess I should say,

'Sadr-4 to Adam.'"

"I have no idea what you're talking about." He smiled anyway, delighting in learning a new game. She was the most playful being he had ever encountered.

"It's an expression we Earth-humans use for when the person we're with seems to be zoning out. I guess that idiom was overlooked when you learned English."

"A few were. I am a bit distracted. Bringing you to my ship is a big deal."

"Why do it, then?"

"Because you asked."

That and because he needed to check on Khel's progress investigating Todd Simms. Adam's ship held all of his weapons as well. He would feel safer once Evelyn was on board. Perhaps she should even remain there with him until everything was sorted out.

"So..." Evelyn said. "If I asked you to throw me down on the ground and have sex with me right here and now, you'd do that too?"

Adam stopped so suddenly that she ran into his back. Making love to her in the forest? Could they really do that? His body grew hard at the thought of Evelyn in a green field, the wind playing over their naked bodies as...

"Do not get your hopes up!" she said. "I shouldn't have used that as an example." She slipped past him, hands held up as if to fend him off, but she was smiling. "It is amazing enough that you've been getting me out in the wilderness so much that this hike isn't making me wheeze. I am not ready to throw down with you in a field full of bugs and dirt."

"Not ready *yet*." Adam grinned at her as she gave him a fake look of disapproval over her shoulder.

His body slowly got the message that now was the time to walk, as disappointing as that was. She wasn't too far ahead as he resumed his trek toward the ship.

"It is awesome to know the actual location of another inhabited planet," she said. "And so close."

"The Milky Way is much more populated than you think. There are protocols in place to keep Earth from figuring that out."

"What kind of protocols?"

"There are teams assigned to all the planets with preservation status. They do what's necessary to allow any sentient inhabitants—even ones that originated from a lost colony—to develop along their own natural progression without gaining too much knowledge too quickly. Earth also has a listening station in orbit. Cloaked from detection, of course."

He was concerned that there wasn't a Coalition soldier assigned to Earth's listening station yet. It was most likely an intentional oversight by the planetary liaison—to protect his operations on Earth. Adam would be certain that his crew downloaded the memory banks of the listening station before departing, though he was certain

Todd had altered the data to reflect what he wished for it to say.

"Wait, so you guys are stopping us from realizing that aliens are real?" Evelyn said.

"We're stopping you from getting hard evidence. Can you imagine the panic that would ensue if everyone suddenly discovered that not only were they not alone in the universe, but they're right next to a galactic highway?"

She stopped to stare at him, wide-eyed. "Are we?"

"It's close."

"I'm glad you guys decided to go around the planet instead of through it when you set that up."

She grinned in the particular way that let him know she was referencing a sci-fi story that he hadn't experienced yet. They had a lifetime for her to share everything with him. He couldn't wait to get started.

Evelyn turned around and resumed picking her way along the barely discernible trail that led to his skimmer. When she started to get off course, he corrected her with a gentle touch.

"It's still pretty shitty of you guys to decide that for us," she said. "Somebody should give the powers that be a talking-to. Maybe you could do that when this is all settled."

Adam was glad she wasn't looking at him in that moment. He didn't say anything, not wanting to lie and not wanting to let her know the truth. If the High Council let him relinquish his citizenship—to become an Earthling himself—he would never be allowed to leave the planet again.

He didn't care. Space was cold and uninviting. Evelyn was everything he had wanted his entire life. Warmth, connection, love.

And her homeworld was so full of life, just like her. He would gladly live out his time on Earth, perhaps have some children with her—naturally, having no idea what they would be like.

The thought made his breath catch in his chest. Children. Natural children—not designed in a lab or ordered from a catalog. Moons, he wanted that. Desperately. Immediately.

"You're falling behind." She turned to look at him, a slight crease between her eyebrows. "Are you okay?"

"Children. I want children."

She smiled and put her hands on her hips. "What, like now? Because I told you, I'm not having sex in a forest. We can talk about me going off birth control after we're married. We have other concerns at the moment."

"You do want them though, right?"

"Eventually, sure. I'd love a few rugrats underfoot. But you need to keep your head in the game until we've dealt with the liaison."

She turned back to the trail, taking a few steps before he caught her up by her waist and lifted her into the air.

Her laughter rang through the trees, startling some nearby birds.

"No sex in the forest!" she yelled.

"I know." He set her on her feet. He wanted to kiss her, but if he did, he wasn't sure he'd be able to stop. "What about sex on my ship?"

Evelyn glanced over her shoulder at him, eyes widening and lips parting as if she was about to speak. Instead, she pushed his arms away from her waist and bolted up the trail. Adam followed, laughing all the way.

Chapter Eleven

In the center of a clearing filled with green grass, the most beautiful vehicle that Evelyn had ever seen perched like a resting bird of prey. The exterior was black, polished to a high sheen. Two wings stretched from the ship's underbelly, curving down toward the earth in graceful arcs. Four legs held it up from the ground.

Adam said it was a skimmer, but it didn't have a name past that. She wanted to name it right then, but could only come up with ridiculous things like, *Starshadow*.

She waited at the edge of the clearing as Adam approached the vessel. His gait changed as he grew nearer to it, shoulders more squared, spine stiff, hands curling into fists. His demeanor put off an energy of command that she found both incredibly sexy and a little intimidating.

He lifted a hand to his ship, and as soon as he touched it a line appeared in the smooth skin of the hull. The line was joined by two others forming part of a rectangle. When it started lowering, she realized it was a ramp.

Adam gestured to the opening. "Well? You wanted to see my ship."

"Right."

He reached out to her, his smile softening. "Come on."

She smiled back, then ran across the clearing. She was about to go on board an actual spaceship. An *alien* spaceship. She'd dreamt of this moment her whole life.

Still, she wasn't sure which was causing her heart to thump in her chest—the ship, or the man whose warm hand clasped hers.

"Is this why we never hiked in this section of the park?" she asked.

"If I came too close, the cloak would turn off automatically. Besides, there were plenty of other places to explore."

"I'm only interested in exploring this at the moment."

"By all means." He led her up the ramp and onto the ship.

The interior was small. He had told her it was a one-person ship and pared down to the barest essentials. The Coalition didn't want their technology accidentally falling into the wrong hands, after all. Skimmers had just enough to get people to their destination and back.

The walls were white, the floor was gray, and everything was made of metal. Evelyn had a momentary bout of claustrophobia. Adam's love of the outdoors made more sense after seeing his ship. If he spent all of his time in places like this, an open horizon would be a welcome change.

The walls had what looked at first like designs

engraved on them, but eventually she realized they were controls. Indentations that might be hand-holds seemed to accompany a few stations she could make out.

"There are no chairs," she said.

"We need to stay alert while we're on duty, so there aren't any."

"Are we just going to do it on the floor, then?"

His grin was huge. Her body began to tingle thinking of other huge parts of him.

"There's a sleeping chamber up that ladder," he said.

She turned to look where he was pointing and sure enough there were hand and footholds recessed into the wall leading up to a hatch in the ceiling.

"How do you work the controls if you need to use your hands to hold on?"

"We have artificial gravity. For safety, we also hook up to harnesses during shifts to keep us in place in the event of power loss."

"That is so cool."

Evelyn didn't dare ask to take the ship for a spin. She wasn't even sure if Adam was supposed to fly it during his vacation when he was by himself, let alone showing off technology for Earthlings. She asked one of her many other questions instead.

"Are you going to get in trouble for bringing me here?" It was at the top of her mind.

"The liaison is the one on the disintegration pad. I still

can't believe that he told you about us. That is a serious crime."

"Are you going to report him?"

One of Adam's shoulders lifted slightly. "I'm looking into it."

"What aren't you telling me? I know when you're keeping me in the dark."

"The liaison—Todd—is dangerous. Telling you about us and showing you some of our technology might be the least of his crimes. I have my crew looking into it, but until the situation is resolved, I don't want you to be alone."

"If Todd wants to get to me, I doubt a crowd will stop him."

"I was thinking I'd stay with you."

She finished her circuit of the ship, then walked to Adam and wrapped her arms around his neck. "My own personal bodyguard. I like the sound of that."

"Guarding your body is only one of the things I have planned."

He slid his hands around her waist and pulled her close, pressing his lips to hers. He smelled so good—like fresh cut grass and peppermint. His hands roved to her ass, lifting her slightly and pressing her against him.

She pushed away from him, then started backing toward the ladder that led to the sleeping chamber. "Why don't you show me the rest of your ship?"

He didn't answer and didn't follow her. In fact, he didn't move at all.

"Adam?"

He was standing completely still, his face a mask of fear. When she reached out to him, a sharp pain tore through her fingers. She shook her hand, tingling jolts of energy shooting up her arm.

"I wouldn't try that again. Unless you're okay with losing the use of that hand."

Her heart sank at the voice behind her. Todd.

When she turned, she wasn't surprised to see him holding the same shiny disk that he'd used on her in the park. His other hand held an ordinary gun.

"I just don't see the allure." Todd shook his head, his gaze traveling over her body. "Unless you have certain skills that add to your worth. After I deal with the General, maybe I'll do a few experiments of my own."

Evelyn glanced at Adam, took in the anguish and rage on his features, and knew she was on her own. She looked around the ship, but there were no weapons lying around. The only escape was the open ramp, which led to the expanse of forest beyond. Help was miles away.

"Yes, monkey. You are trapped. Let the panic seep in." Todd kept his gun pointed at her, but turned to address Adam. "Did you really think I would believe you were giving up everything for *her*? You arrogant glitch. I wish I could let you live to regret sticking your nose into my operations."

"You can't kill him!" Evelyn stepped forward, but stopped when Todd raised his weapon higher, sighting her down the barrel. She held up her hands and said, "How will you explain his death to your superiors?"

"When I deliver his corpse to the High Council, they're going to give me a medal for protecting Earth from his conquest."

"You're delusional." She was baiting him on purpose, keeping him talking, gathering information, trying to find anything that might help get her and Adam out of this.

"You're the only one who's delusional here. You really think that he's doing this for you?" Todd's lip curled in a sneer and he tilted his head away, as if he could barely stand to look at her. At least he lowered his gun a bit. "A General decides to suddenly leave his prosperous career, give up his citizenship, and relinquish the vast resources he's accumulated over decades of successful campaigns to live on a primitive world where he'll have no access to real technology and can never leave the planet again? He's not after you. He wants Earth. But I got here first."

"You can't leave?" Evelyn turned to Adam, not believing Todd's words. "If you stayed with me, you were going to give all that up?"

Adam's brow furrowed slightly and his eyes narrowed.

It was true. And he wasn't going to tell her. He was planning to give up everything to be with her and he wasn't even going to let her know what he was sacrificing.

"With the riches this planet possesses, it would be more than a fair trade," Todd said.

Evelyn closed her eyes, visualizing the situation, trying to find a way out. On board, there was nothing to help her. But outside the ship there were plenty of thick, heavy branches perfect for thumping an insane alien over the head with. She only had to manage to get outside and sneak back in without Todd realizing it.

Right. Only that.

The first step was getting out without getting killed. Playing along with Todd's story seemed her best bet. She only hoped that Adam would realize she was acting.

"I can't believe you would do this to me!" Evelyn bit her fist for effect. She doubted Todd had watched any 50s sci-fi movies where the women were constantly doing ridiculous things like that. "After everything we did… And it was all a lie!"

"Stop yelling!" Todd lifted his gun again, pointing it right at her face.

"I'm sorry, I just… I'm so emotional right now." As she'd hoped, Todd's sneer deepened. He looked a little green. "I don't want anything to do with this! Do whatever you want to him. I just want to go home. I promise, I won't tell anyone that aliens are real."

Todd stared at her for a moment, then his thin lips pulled into a smile. "No, you should tell them. Waste your life trying to convince people that aliens are real. That will be so much more amusing than just killing you. Go on."

He shooed her with his gun. Evelyn wasn't sure if he was baiting her, trying to get her to turn around so he could shoot her in the back—but it was the best chance she had. She turned and bolted, heart pounding in her chest.

She could hardly believe it when she reached the trees. Pausing, she looked back at the ship, but didn't see Todd watching her. Adrenaline flooded her system, making her lightheaded.

She didn't have time for that. Focusing with all her will, she started looking for a branch that she could use as a weapon. It didn't take long to find one solid enough to do damage, but small enough to wield.

She wanted to run back to the ship as fast as she could, but surprise was crucial. She only prayed that Todd would do more grandstanding before killing Adam.

Tears burned her eyes, but she blinked them away. Adam needed her. There was still hope.

She picked her way through the trees as quietly as she could, approaching the ship from a direction that wasn't easily visible from within. Reaching the ship wouldn't be hard. Getting up the ramp without Todd seeing her—that was the challenge.

She paused under the ramp and listened. Todd was still talking, taunting Adam. She let out a shaky breath. That meant Adam was still alive.

The ship was small and low to the ground. Evelyn could shimmy up onto the ramp at its midpoint, minimizing how long she'd be visible from inside. Branch in hand, she practically crawled on her belly till she could see into the ship.

Todd was focused on Adam. Even better, with her gone, Todd had moved so that he was standing near the ramp with his back to her. Evelyn had a clear shot.

She took a deep breath and held it, rising to her feet and noiselessly crossing the short distance between them. All the while, internally she chanted, *Please, please, please...*

When she brought the branch down on the back of Todd's head, hard enough that the wood made a loud cracking sound, she could barely believe it had worked. But Todd fell to the floor, the gun skittering out of his hand.

Evelyn kicked the silver disk out of Todd's other hand, then ran to get the gun. She shifted her club to her non-dominant hand, and wheeled around with the gun in the other.

"Take that, you... Oh," she said.

Adam was standing with the small silver disk held out toward Todd, who was still face-down on the floor. From the looks of things, Todd wasn't going anywhere any time soon.

The look on Adam's face was priceless. His eyes were wide, his mouth hanging open. He just kept staring at her.

Evelyn couldn't believe her plan had worked. She was still shaking with adrenaline and felt like she might burst into tears or maniacal laughter at any moment. Or maybe throw up.

Instead, she pointed her branch at Todd and said, "Take that, asshat! Nobody messes with my planet or my man!"

A broad smile spread across Adam's face, though the wonder remained. "I will make sure everyone gets the message."

Chapter Twelve

Securing the liaison more permanently was a simple matter once Adam made a few adjustments to the suspension disk they commandeered. Figuring out what to do with him after was more troublesome.

Adam was just glad Todd couldn't talk while in stasis. Evelyn would probably hit him with her branch again. She'd kept it close by and was even talking about turning it into some sort of memento.

Thanks to her, the biggest problem Adam faced at the moment was dealing with her proximity and not being able to do anything about it. Once she had learned that his crew was on the way to take Todd into custody, she insisted that they not take their eyes off their prisoner, referencing half a dozen movies where the villain managed to slip away when the protagonists let down their guard.

Kissing Evelyn in front of Todd would just be awkward for everyone. Not that Adam really gave a damn what Todd thought.

Adam was saved when his second-in-command walked up the ramp.

"Khel," Adam said. "You arrived sooner than I

anticipated."

They aligned their forearms and clasped each other's elbows in the customary greeting among the military ranks.

"The *Arbiter* is the fastest ship in the fleet," Khel said.

Two other crew members entered the skimmer and saluted Adam. He acknowledged the gesture with a nod.

Before coming to Earth, he would have dismissed them from his thoughts, trusting them to follow standard procedures without further interaction. Now, his attention lingered on the woman.

She was part of his crew, but they had never communicated through anything other than reports. Reports that he primarily ignored.

"Vay?" he said.

Her blue eyes widened and she tucked a lock of her short blonde hair behind her ear. It was a bit too long to meet regulations, but he let that pass.

"Yes, sir," she said.

He glanced at her companion, a hulk of a man who towered over her, his head and face devoid of hair. Ari— one of the highest ranked security officers from the *Arbiter*.

"Why did you bring the *Arbiter's* cultural programmer along on a security mission?" Adam said.

"I..." Vay clasped her hands in front of her, her cheeks turning pink as she held Adam's gaze. "I've been assisting with the research on Earth's...special situation." She glanced at Evelyn briefly before continuing. "And we didn't want to bring in too many people before you have a chance to review our report."

"General." Ari stood straighter, staring over Adam's shoulder. "Vay is fully trained in security protocols. By assigning her to this low-risk mission, she has an opportunity to observe a new planet while also assisting with the retrieval of the prisoner."

"I approved it," Khel said. "Vay makes an excellent point about the sensitivity of this matter. It seemed an efficient use of our resources."

"Very well." Adam handed the suspension disk to V-21-b3. Vay. "But your cultural observations will be extremely limited."

A bright smile spread across her face. "Even seeing Earth's ecosystem will give me invaluable insight into—"

Ari cleared his throat. Vay stopped speaking abruptly, resuming the placid expression she'd entered the ship with.

"Understood, sir," she said.

She put the suspension disk in a portable artificial gravity control unit and adjusted the settings till Todd's stasis field switched to anti-gravity. Todd floated into the air, enabling them to easily transport him to their ship.

"When you put him in the brig, make sure to turn off communications," Adam said.

He trusted his crew, but he didn't want Todd to even try to turn any of them. Besides, Todd was a jackass. Adam wanted to spare the guards from having to listen to him.

After Vay and Ari had left with the prisoner, Evelyn finally spoke up.

"That was way too gentle for my tastes. Couldn't they have knocked him down the ramp or something?"

"I'm just glad to be rid of him," Adam said.

Khel cleared his throat, then said, "You might not be rid of him, yet."

"Explain."

"You were right about this liaison. Not only was he smuggling contraband off of this planet, he was selling to some very important people. People with vast resources."

"Credits can't protect criminals from Coalition law. Contraband is illegal for a reason. Take this, for example." Adam handed Khel the gun they had taken from Todd.

"A projectile weapon?" Khel asked.

"That fires balls of metal using an explosive powder."

"That's barbaric." Khel shook his head as he examined the weapon. "The damage this would do to someone's flesh..."

"Exactly," Adam said.

"I suppose you guys use ray guns and just instantly disintegrate people in a civilized fashion." Evelyn flashed a brief, small smile.

Her shoulders were hunched and she was huddled

against one of the walls as if she was trying to disappear into the paneling. The idea of her disappearing from his life terrified Adam more than the thought of the High Council itself seeking revenge on him after this.

He had watched enough of her sci-fi movies to understand what she was referencing with *ray guns*.

"As a matter fact, we do." Adam turned to Khel and said, "Forgive me, I haven't introduced you to the woman who saved me."

One eyebrow hitched up Khel's forehead. "That is a story I would like to hear."

Evelyn held up her branch. "Not much to tell. I just snuck up behind Todd and cracked this over the back of his head."

"A stick?" Khel said.

"A heavy stick." She wielded the branch with both hands as if it was a sword, swinging it through the air a few times. "I'm pretty good with wood."

She looked at Adam, a huge grin on her face. She didn't have to explain the joke for him to get it. He let out a loud laugh.

Adam didn't miss how Khel jumped at the sound. He had never heard Adam laugh before. Adam wasn't sure anyone outside of Earth had.

Evelyn grinned back at Adam. "So is it over? Can we finally get on with our lives?"

"I'll still need to put in the official request, but maybe

Khel can help with that now."

"What request is that?" Khel asked.

"I'm staying. You will begin the procedure for me to relinquish my Coalition citizenship immediately."

Khel looked as if Adam had struck him. Rather than explain with words, Adam walked over to Evelyn's side and put his arm around her shoulders. Khel had the decency and good sense not to say anything, even though he gaped at them for a while.

"With all due respect," Khel said, "I don't think I've communicated how serious the situation is. Dozens of arrests have been made, but we don't yet know how high Todd Simms' connections reach. What we do know is that they all blame you for their current circumstances."

Adam had never given much thought to making enemies. He'd never had anything to lose—nothing that really mattered to him, anyway. Now, the thought of Evelyn in danger turned his blood to ice in his veins.

Khel's voice softened as he said, "You aren't safe here."

"If I leave, it won't fix anything." Adam was desperate for any reason, any excuse to justify staying. "Eventually, word will get out and they'll know that they can use her against me."

"Not if both your memories are wiped," Khel said. "She's not Coalition. She shouldn't know about any of this anyway."

Evelyn held up her hands, including the one holding the

stick. "Hold on a minute. First of all, stop talking about me as if I'm not here and don't understand what you're talking about. Second of all, please explain exactly what you're talking about. I mean, I get the whole, *I'm in danger, he's in danger*, thing. But how much danger?"

Reality came crashing down on Adam. If he stayed on Earth as they had planned, he wouldn't have access to any technology. He wouldn't be able to protect either of them. At least if he returned to his command, he would be able to keep a ship in orbit. He could assign people he trusted to watch over her.

Quietly, he said, "Evelyn, if I stay here with you, we'll be dead inside of a month."

Her eyebrows lifted, but to her credit she didn't look afraid. "Okay, that's a lot of danger. How are we going to deal with it? And don't you dare talk about memory wipes. I don't like the sound of that at all."

Adam didn't either. Bad enough that Evelyn should forget him, but to forget her? The man he had become since he arrived on Earth would vanish. He didn't want to go back to who he was before. Still, he couldn't think of any other way.

"Khel, head back to the ship. One way or another, I'll send word soon."

Khel nodded before retreating down the ramp. Adam waited to speak until he was sure he and Evelyn were alone.

"I can't stand the thought of anything bad happening to you," he said.

"Can you stand the thought of anything bad happening to you? Because I'm about to hit you on the head with this stick. And I'm pretty good at it. Just ask Todd."

She wasn't laughing. A bad sign.

"There's no way that I can protect you," Adam said. "When they come for us—and they will—they'll kill us both. Or worse. You saw what Todd was able to do with a simple suspension disk. That's our equivalent of a zip tie. These people are corrupt. They will not respect the law. They'll come armed."

"So, have your buddies leave us some weapons. At least we'll have a fighting chance."

"I won't break the laws I've spent my life defending. Evelyn, I can't protect you. Not if I stay with you."

"Then take me with you."

Adam's blood started rushing through his ears. His mind filled with visions of a possible future with her.

Evelyn by his side on his ship. Evelyn safe behind the protection his rank and resources could afford them. Evelyn warming his bed every night and his heart every day. Evelyn far from her family, torn from her homeworld…

"You don't know what you'd be getting yourself into."

"I imagine it would involve whisking me away to a far off planet and traveling through space as a regular pastime." When Adam didn't deny it, she went on. "Do you even remember what my bedroom looks like?"

"My people are not what you're used to. You'd be giving up so much to be with me."

"You were willing to give up even more to be with me. Besides, that's one of the benefits of not being genetically programmed for a specific role. I'm adaptable."

She had certainly proven that. Still, it seemed too good to be true.

"What about your family?" he said.

"We mostly talk through the Internet. I'm sure you can rig up a video call from Sadr-4. I'll make sure there isn't a view of space behind me. And if we do get a chance to visit around the holidays, you can get your fix of the great outdoors."

Could this actually work? Hope started to seep into his mind.

"They'll especially want us to visit when we start having children," he said, stepping closer to her.

Evelyn tilted her head back and laughed. "Oh, your doctors are going to love that. We might have the first one on Earth so someone from your crew can observe and learn."

"They'll probably faint."

"I would think your crew is made of sterner stuff."

His mind raced to meet this new challenge. There would be paperwork involved—there always was.

Procedures to follow and protocol to fulfill. But having an Earthling join the Coalition was a much simpler process than what he would have faced to relinquish his own citizenship.

Having Evelyn at his side aboard the *Arbiter*, being able to keep her safe, to truly *be* with her… It was more than he could dream.

"I promise, we will make this work," he said.

"Well, there's one other promise you need to keep first. An implied promise, anyway."

He sifted through his memory, but couldn't figure out what she meant. Then she kissed him, and memories, thoughts, plans, all vaporized in the heat of just feeling her. When she pulled back, her smile was wicked. One eyebrow was raised expectantly.

Swallowing hard, Adam asked, "What promise is that?"

"Sex on a spaceship."

With a broad grin, he lifted her into the air. She wrapped her legs around his waist and laughed again.

"I am a man of my word."

Epilogue

K-58-b7 sat in her favorite window of listening station T5-Alpha, watching the changing patterns in the clouds covering Earth. The heavy feeling in her chest would not go away.

She shifted her gaze to the ship that was also orbiting Earth—that she could only see with the help of the nanites populating her brain. A faint shimmer along the edges of the massive ship's hull let her know its cloak was fully engaged.

The *Arbiter*, flagship of the Coalition of Planets. Commanded by General Serath himself, highest ranked military officer in the fleet.

"Why haven't they contacted me yet?" she murmured.

"Please restate inquiry." T5-Alpha's measured voice sounded over the station's intercom.

"Nothing." K-58-b7 shook her head. "Cancel inquiry."

She'd been alone too long. Talking to herself would only confuse the station's computer.

But talking to Brendan…

The tightness in her chest intensified. Any moment now, the *Arbiter* would contact her. She would most likely be reassigned, since she'd already been alone on the station four times longer than she should have been. She would have to leave Earth. And him.

I wish I could at least say goodbye.

The base of her skull tingled, a silent inquiry from her nanites that switched her despair to panic.

"No, don't try to contact him."

If the nanites tried to initiate a connection with Brendan, the *Arbiter* would certainly detect it. He would likely be taken aboard and receive a mind-wipe, clearing all memory of their conversations.

She could bear the thought of never talking to him again much better than the thought of their relationship vanishing from his mind, as if it had never existed.

And if they looked more closely at her—and her nanites —at how she managed to contact him while bypassing T5-Alpha's controls and accessing the station's systems directly…

She shivered.

No, she wouldn't try to contact Brendan, even to say goodbye. She would wait for the *Arbiter* to contact her, and—

Her thoughts cut off as the engines of the enormous vessel brightened. The aft thrusters fired, and before she knew it, the ship was just an afterimage on her retinas. It was gone.

Gone, and she was still there.

She should contact the ship, let them know that she'd been forgotten. But she had everything she needed to survive on the station. If she was reassigned again, she would be alone—just her and the malfunctioning robot friends in her mind.

At least stationed on Earth's listening station, she had *him*. She had Brendan.

Her heart pounded as she thought about the consequences of continuing their forbidden communication—and knew she would do it anyway. For as long as she could, as long as they had.

She shifted her gaze back to Earth, eager for his next transmission.

—

I hope you enjoyed *Gray Card!* The fun is just beginning with *The Department of Homeworld Security.* Read on for K-58-b7's story. I'm sure she'd be fine with you calling her Kira.

USA TODAY BESTSELLING AUTHOR
CASSANDRA CHANDLER

RESIDENT ALIEN

THE DEPARTMENT OF HOMEWORLD SECURITY

Resident Alien

The Department of Homeworld
Security
Book Two

Cassandra Chandler

Dedication

For Allie S.—a great listener.

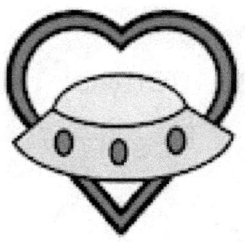

Don't miss out on any of the alien action.
Subscribe to Cassandra Chandler's newsletter at
cassandra-chandler.com!

Chapter One

"Greetings, my fellow interstellar travelers. This is Brendan Sloan, speaking to you from the little blue marble third from Sol. Without context, that doesn't give you much of a clue as to where I am, but if you're advanced enough to pick up this signal, I'm betting you can trace the source."

Brendan picked up the toy rocket that he kept on his desk and fidgeted with the stabilizers on its base. His stomach was full of butterflies—not the good kind—from his conversation with his sister, Paige.

She had been scheduled for a flight out of Louisiana earlier that day, but ran late at a cleanup site her environmental restoration team was working on. The plane had crashed. No survivors.

He felt terrible for the people who had been on board and for their families. And at the same time, he was grateful beyond measure that his baby sister had been spared. He was still having trouble wrapping his head—and his heart—around the situation.

"I'm keeping it short today, as I have something of a date." He hoped that Kira was listening. He needed to talk to her immediately—to hear her voice and know that she was okay as well. He spoke his mind, eager to finish the transmission.

"Humans have a need to bond. We bond with a partner, with our friends and family. With comrades-in-arms and comrades-in-ideas. It's part of what makes us strong as a species and something I hope our cultures will share. And if not, perhaps we can teach each other and grow through our own interactions."

He set the rocket down in front of a picture of him and Paige. He had his arms around her shoulders and was hugging her tight. Her expression was equal parts amused and annoyed.

They had the same blue eyes and red hair, same smile and scientific curiosity, but what they each added to the world was so different. She fought for the planet, hands on —often from the inside of a hazmat suit. Trying to get people to stop damaging their homeworld.

He worked with the government to create technology that was decades ahead of anything on Earth—tech that was supposed to be used to improve everyone's lives, but was usually turned into weapons to use against others. Hence his hiatus from his most recent project.

He ran his hands over his face, careful not to knock his headset out of place, then let out a sigh and leaned back in his chair.

"I look up at night and my eyes show me a sky filled

with thousands of stars. My instruments let me know there are so many more out there, galaxies full of them in an infinite universe. And my reason tells me this—we cannot be alone. This is my official request to parlay. Please come in peace."

It was a silly dream and a waste of time—sending transmissions into deep space in the hopes that he might get lucky and reach an alien civilization, maybe hitch a ride and find a more peaceful home. But it kept him distracted from the problems on Earth and how very little he had been able to change anything. Yet.

Time and distance would help him come back to the communications project he was working on refreshed and with new perspective. Maybe he'd even figure out how to use their results to benefit all of humanity instead of only the people he worked for.

And thanks to taking time off, he had met Kira.

Officially, Brendan had been told that Eric was his *liaison*. Eric checked in with Brendan once a month. Their conversations were superficial, but Brendan was sure Eric was under pressure from his superiors to get Brendan back on the project. Eric knew Brendan needed a break and more time to unwind. Brendan was pretty sure that was why they had assigned Kira to be a sort of handler for him. She talked to Brendan every day—pretending to be an alien.

His government sure was going the extra mile to help

him recharge and get back on the job. He didn't want to admit how well it was working. If he knew he'd be working with Kira—that they might meet face-to-face—he'd ditch his lakeside cabin and head back to civilization in a heartbeat.

He wasn't sure when it had happened or how, but their talks had become the highlight of his day. He thought about her all the time. He even dreamed about her. Maybe today was the day he would tell her how he felt. After Paige's brush with death, he didn't want to risk never telling Kira the truth. Even if it made him feel like an idiot.

Falling for his handler was bad enough, but somehow he'd convinced himself that she felt the same way about him. He was probably going to make a royal fool of himself.

He flipped off his transmission, watching the power draw levels drop. Waiting—but never for long. He adjusted his headset and leaned forward.

"Brendan Sloan." Kira's voice flowed into his ears, rich and deep and sexy as hell.

He closed his eyes and smiled before responding. "Kira I'm-too-mysterious-for-a-last-name."

A hint of laughter laced her words when she spoke again. "I thought today's broadcast was going to be about your theories on the best spots in the Sol system for setting up extra-terrestrial bases."

"I changed my mind."

"That's a shame. I'm looking to build a summer home."

He let out a laugh. Talking to Kira always made him feel...less alone in the universe.

"For you, only the best," he said. "Earth all the way."

"No bias there?"

"Come on. Try to stop and smell the roses on Jupiter, and you get a chest-full of ammonia crystals."

He was encouraged when she let out a little snort, so he continued.

"Then there's Mars," he said, "with its barely-there atmosphere and all those satellites taking pictures. How's anyone supposed to have any privacy? And robots running around on the surface, poking and prodding everything. I wouldn't want to live there."

"Right. Because once robots move in, there goes the neighborhood."

"They're up all hours whirring and running around. They pretend they're collecting samples, but you know they're just partying."

She laughed and it about did him in. He wanted to see the face that belonged to that steel-and-brandy voice. He could imagine her sitting across from him on the couch, leaning her elbow on the back of the cushions as they talked long into the night.

"Besides, you don't need to build a summer house in the Sol system—you're welcome in my cabin any time. There's no guest room, but it has a big bed."

He cringed the moment the words left his lips. *Smooth.*

Still, his mind leapt at the chance to add him to the scenario in a very carnal way. He shifted in his seat.

"And a very comfortable couch," he said. "Which is where I would be...in that event."

"It's a tempting offer, but I'm kind of stuck here."

"Right."

Wherever *here* happened to be. Probably a bunker outside of Bethesda.

He imagined her working in a sort of call center for handlers—everyone with headphones on, sitting in their cubicles and listening to their assigned assets while they shot rubber-bands at homemade dartboards.

"You sounded a little tense," she said.

"Picked up on that, did you?" Of course she did. Nothing seemed to slip past her notice.

"Do you want to talk about it?"

He shook his head, even though he knew she couldn't see him. "Just had a close call. Too close for comfort. It's made me think about not taking things for granted. Or letting opportunities pass."

She was silent, so he went on.

"Look, I know you're my handler."

"I have said no such thing."

"Right. I forgot. You're an alien." Because *that* was more likely.

"I've never confirmed that, either."

"Yeah, and you haven't denied it. When you first responded to my transmission, you wouldn't tell me how you picked it up and the only people capable of doing that are the ones in the group I work with."

"Or the advanced alien civilization you're trying to reach."

"There you go teasing me again."

"Sorry."

He could practically hear the smile in her words. It was contagious.

"I may just be a nerd to you—"

"You're not *just* anything to me," she said.

There was heat to her words. That was much worse than teasing him about being an alien. If she didn't care, why would she get so worked up? Why would she say something like that? He expected her to backpedal, but her tone was still serious when she went on.

"I wasn't supposed to talk to you," she said. "I'm just here to listen. But I couldn't...*not* respond. I had to talk to you, to get to know you. And I don't regret it. No matter what happens next, I'll never regret getting to know you."

His heart picked up. It sounded like she was saying goodbye.

"What's going on?"

"There have been some changes here," she said. "Big changes. I don't know when it will happen, but it's only a matter of time before I'm removed." Her voice cracked and she coughed as if she was clearing her throat.

His stomach felt like it had suddenly turned to lead. No daily talks with Kira to look forward to? No one to bounce ridiculous ideas off of and philosophize about society's ills and strengths?

The loneliness that had plagued him throughout his life started pushing back into his heart. He knew she had been lonely too, before they started talking. He could hear it in her voice. It was part of what bound them together. In all the world—in all the universe—they had found each other. He didn't want to lose her.

"I'm shocked they haven't already shut me down," she said.

His dread increased.

If she was anything like Eric, she'd been trained as a spy—received the full package. Brendan never let himself consider the baggage associated with being a handler. Sure, he considered that she might be using techniques to win his heart and seduce him into a course of action that might not be his own choice, like going back to work early. But hearing her talk about being *shut down* brought other aspects of her role to light. Ugly possibilities.

"Are you safe?"

"Yeah, just in deep trouble. But I don't care." Her voice was strong—almost harsh. But it softened as she went on. "Talking to you, getting to know you...has been the greatest experience of my life. I wouldn't trade it for anything."

"If your job was to convince me to come back, it worked. Tell them it worked. Tell them whatever they need to—"

"Hang on a second."

There was a pause when all he heard was the blood rushing through his ears.

"Something's wrong," she said. "I have to go."

"Kira, wait," he said. "I love you."

The signal died.

Chapter Two

"I love you."

Kira was already shutting down their com-link as Brendan said the words. She sat stunned, staring at Earth through the main planetary viewport of listening station T5-Alpha.

He loved her?

When he'd started talking about pair-bonding in his transmission, she couldn't resist the urge to imagine herself in that role with him. But it was a dream. There was no way they could be together—not after she'd broken Coalition protocol by making unauthorized contact. Her future was an eight-by-eight cell—if she was lucky.

A normal soldier would get a mind-wipe and return to duty. Kira was not normal. She couldn't let anyone find out how very not-normal she was.

Her performance levels were low enough that the genetic engineers who created her considered her a glitch. Thankfully, they decided she was salvageable as long as she was augmented with a nanNet. She couldn't be wiped unless they removed the network of nanites from her brain first, and if they tried…

Her stomach cramped. If they found out how very wrong she had turned out, they would want to figure out where they made their mistakes. By any means necessary. She had a feeling a cell would be paradise in comparison.

Thinking about it was too much. She needed to focus.

She activated the control-band built into the forearm of her uniform. Her biodata displayed, showing everything within normal parameters. An image of her face rotated in the upper-right corner.

The geneticists had selected brown hair, brown eyes, and skin that looked tanned even though she hadn't been in direct sunlight…ever. It was really too bad that her levels were so low. At least she *looked* like the Sadirian ambassador they had hoped she would become.

Shaking her head, she dismissed the screen and pointed the station's scanners at the patch of clouds that held her attention. The vid-screen in the band gave her a magnified view.

There it was again—light reflecting off something metal. Something rising out of the planet's atmosphere.

General Serath had departed on the *Arbiter*—the lead vessel in the Coalition's fleet—only hours ago. There were no Coalition-approved spaceships on the planet. The vessel approaching—and she was sure it was approaching —wasn't following protocol.

Not that anything about this assignment had followed

protocol.

The *Arbiter* hadn't even checked in with her while it was in orbit. If it hadn't been for the monthly contact with the planetary liaison, she would think she had been forgotten. Observers normally were only assigned a planet for six months. She'd been listening to Earth for two years.

After finding Brendan, she wasn't eager to be reassigned. That was why she had waited for the *Arbiter* to contact her. When the *Arbiter* left orbit, she was confused but relieved. At least she would have a chance to tell Brendan goodbye. Glancing back at the approaching sliver of light, she wondered if that "goodbye" would be more permanent than she originally anticipated.

"T5-Alpha, I need an ID on the vessel currently approaching the station."

After a brief delay, the station's interface sounded through the communications output of her control-band, level and emotionless.

"No vessels are on approach."

"What?" Kira looked back out the viewport that followed the curve of the small, disc-shaped station. The ship would reach them in minutes. It wasn't even cloaked.

Wait, the station *was* cloaked. How did they even know where she was?

For a moment, she considered that it was a coincidence. An unknown ship was departing from Earth and just happened to be on a direct collision course for the invisible station.

Unlikely.

"I have visual contact. Scan again."

The delay was a bit longer, but the interface came back with, "No vessels detected."

Something had to be wrong with the scanners, but she didn't have time to run a full diagnostic check. If the station wasn't detecting a threat, it wouldn't defend itself —or her. Not without her help.

The approaching ship was close enough that she could make out its shape—a small equilateral triangle getting bigger by the moment. Adrenaline spiked through her system.

"It's the Tau Ceti!" Kira jumped to her feet and ran toward command, hunching over to stay clear of the low ceilings while shouting orders to the interface. "Raise shields. Send a distress call to the *Arbiter*."

"Shields inactive. Communications are offline." The station made the statements casually, as if it wasn't reciting their death sentences.

"By whose order?"

"Access code 471-PLT-113894—planetary liaison. Earth designation Todd Simms."

Kira's fingers were slick with perspiration as she climbed the ladder that led to the upper deck. Coincidence was no longer a possibility.

The *Arbiter's* communications with the Coalition had

been logged with the station while it was in orbit. She knew that the planetary liaison had been taken into custody. What she didn't know was why his codes hadn't been stripped or who was using them.

The command deck was the most open and spacious part of the station, with a lowered circular area surrounded by monitors facing its center. One person standing in the middle of the circle could see everything, commanding the station as necessary. Kira ran to the center of the space. A chill swept through her as she looked around.

One by one, the monitors flickered out. The station lights dimmed and she heard systems shutting down all around her.

She was too late.

Her heart pounded as she walked to the viewport that made up one wall of command. The Tau Ceti ship approached at a steady pace, as if they knew her dilemma. They had probably caused it.

Listening stations weren't built to withstand attacks. Nobody cared about the data she gathered and analyzed except anthropologists and bureaucrats. Her reports probably never made it past the planetary liaison's desk.

The liaison...who had been taken onto the *Arbiter* right before it sped out of the Sol system. The man who had secured her assignment, convinced her that there wasn't an oversight when the months turned into years. The one who insisted that her reports go through him instead of directly to the Coalition.

He had come onboard the listening station three times since she'd arrived, to "check in and make sure she was holding up okay". The last time, he had insisted on doing a systems check.

She ran to the nearest console and keyed in every command she could think of, trying to get a response. Nothing. He must have put in a failsafe—programmed a code that would give the Tau Ceti control even if his standard codes were stripped.

She closed her eyes and took a deep breath through her nose, then blew it out.

Any moment, the Tau Ceti would open fire and destroy the station. They might not even know she was onboard. Except if they were working with the liaison, he would have told them. Wouldn't he?

With the access they obviously had, if they wanted her dead, they could vent the station or open the airlocks. Her uniform would keep her alive for a few hours, if they didn't vaporize her.

Life support was still on but the lights were dimmed. Dim lighting would help the Tau Ceti, protecting their sensitive eyes. They must be planning to board the station. What could they want, though? All she had was data, and the liaison could easily have shared all of her reports with them.

Except for the most recent one. They must be looking

for something.

Whatever they wanted, she had to stop them from getting it. If she could get to the sun-facing side of the station before they docked, she had a better chance of... What? Taking out as many of them as she could? Hiding for a few extra minutes before they found her?

If it came to that, she would end her own life. The first thing the Tau Ceti did after hatching was cannibalize the rest of their broodmates. They called it their own twist on genetic engineering. "Only the strongest survive."

They applied the same principle throughout their lives —not just at birth. The strong survived by eating the weak, even if the meal consisted of sentients. The thought turned her stomach.

She wasn't bloodthirsty by nature, but she had been trained as a soldier. Strategies formed in her mind as the ship loomed closer. She was running out of time.

Countdown. She smiled as the idea popped into her head. She might even survive.

She wasn't just a soldier. She was augmented.

She wasn't just a glitch. She was an aberration.

The liaison knew about the nanites in her brain that enhanced her memory and provided her with a direct link to download her interpretations of what she observed. The nanites made her singularly qualified to be assigned to a listening station. He had probably shared that information with the Tau Ceti. Which meant they knew that she had a constant backup of the station's data in her head— including the data they were after.

But she was a glitch. Glitches started their lives surprising the geneticists who tried to control their DNA. The engineers who had augmented her would be shocked to know the nanites were more than just an upgrade to her brain. They were her constant companions. Her friends.

The station might not defend her, but her nanites would.

She took a deep breath and held it. This was going to hurt.

Her awareness of them started as a tingling at the base of her skull. It rapidly moved through her brain till it concentrated on her forehead. The station's systems were locked out to her, but the nanites had a way with machines that she didn't. She willed them to make the connection.

Searing pain tore through her mind as the nanites powered up and sent their broadcast. Her brain felt hot, her skull practically cooking the skin under her hair. She groaned as she fell forward, hands planted on the console before her. The monitor flickered.

Her command was simple—self-destruct.

In ten minutes, the station would explode in a fiery burst of energy. The cloak generator was in the most protected part of the station so that it would be the last to go. Even if someone happened to be looking in her direction, by the time light could escape the field, the Earthlings would only see a bright flare that quickly winked out. Coalition destruct sequences didn't leave anything behind except an energy signature.

Because her nanites could convince the station that they were part of its systems, there wouldn't be any notifications or broadcasts. All she had to do to survive was drag herself to the escape capsules and hope that the chaos of the explosion covered her departure—or that all the Tau Ceti were on board when it happened.

She gave the nanites a few moments to reorganize themselves within her brain, then sent a shut-down command to let them rest. They weren't intended for that kind of use, and she imagined it taxed them about as much as it did her.

Swallowing was hard. Her mouth was bone-dry. Walking was worse. But she focused on putting one foot in front of the other, wincing as the pain in her head retreated to a dull throbbing ache.

She reached the escape capsule just as she heard the docking clamps engage. The airlocks were a level above. She was in the underbelly of the station.

Heavy footsteps sounded above her, the quiet station suddenly filled with echoing shouts and guttural yells. She waited as long as she dared, hoping to give more of the Tau Ceti time to board the station. She wanted as many to be caught in the explosion as possible. If she was really lucky, their ship would be disabled as well.

The voices were getting closer. She slid into the capsule

and programmed the first coordinates that came to her bruised mind. As the capsule detached from the station, she let out a deep sigh and closed her eyes.

Chapter Three

Brendan sat at his table in front of a plate of cold bean burritos. He only vaguely remembered preparing them. Going through the motions of making lunch calmed him down enough to know that he wasn't going to have an appetite for a while.

His first thought had been to call Eric, but he wasn't sure that was the best idea. If this was a ruse to get Brendan back on the project, that would be playing right into their hands. If it wasn't...

Two ideas presented themselves. Either Kira really wasn't supposed to talk to him, and letting Eric know about it would possibly get her into serious trouble, or she was in such serious trouble that Brendan might already be too late to help her.

He pushed away from the table and started to pace. The cabin was too small. Stifling him. He couldn't think.

He walked outside and slammed the door behind him. A walk along the lake's shore would help clear his head.

Two courses of action. Call Eric or don't call Eric. Maybe he could make the call, but sort of hedge around the issue. Maybe he could ask Eric to talk off the record.

Of all the people Brendan had worked with, Eric was the only one Brendan trusted. It was still a lot to ask.

His chest ached. He rubbed it absently, staring out over the water. He wanted to hear Kira's voice again.

Summer had settled over the mountains, but the air kept a hint of the crisp snap of snow nearby. Sunlight glinted off the lake, reflecting the peaks in the distance and the pines that lined the shore. A cool breeze made the trees sway and reminded him that he probably should be wearing a jacket over his long-sleeved shirt.

It was peaceful—until something rocketed past him so fast that its slipstream nearly pulled him off his feet.

He stumbled forward, arms flailing as he regained his balance. The projectile was about the size of a car, only shaped like a bullet. It was hard to make out details, since the whole thing was chrome, gleaming in the sun.

His mind tried to make sense of what he was seeing. Some kind of low-flying plane? A missile?

That last possibility made his stomach clench. Maybe Kira wasn't the only one in line to be shut down.

If it was a missile aimed for him, though, they had missed. The thing was speeding away.

Halfway across the lake, it slowed to a stop and... hovered above the water.

Brendan rubbed his eyes and looked again. It was far away, but he could swear it was at least four feet above the surface, ripples spreading beneath it. It turned back in his direction and approached slowly.

"What the hell?"

His instinct told him to run and his curiosity told him to move forward. He settled on staying put.

The object stopped when it was only a few feet away, definitely hovering above the water. Its exterior looked like chrome, but it was shaped more like a quartz crystal than a bullet.

Six planes made up its body, the sides about ten feet in length with four-foot wide and three-foot tall pyramids formed on both ends. It swiveled around him, keeping the apex of one pyramid pointed at his chest. Then it drifted down to rest on the water.

After a few moments, the top panel of the object popped up, revealing a compartment within. The panel slid to the side, folding seamlessly into what he could now tell was some sort of aircraft.

Or spacecraft.

Brendan shook his head. No way. It couldn't be. He took a step closer and stood on his tiptoes, trying to peer inside.

Something moved and he jumped back. A figure rose from the opening, clad in shining silver fabric that clung to her form like a second skin.

At least, he thought it was a *her*. He couldn't be sure, because she was wearing a helmet that looked like it was made from the same opaque gleaming metal as the capsule.

Whoever—or whatever—was inside the suit had a gorgeous figure. Long legs, curvy hips, narrow waist, and a chest graced with two—and only two—breasts.

Brendan held up his left hand in the Vulcan salute and said, *"Klaatu barada nikto."*

The figure stood motionless for a few more moments, then lifted a hand to her helmet. She tapped the side and parallel lines appeared in the smooth chrome as it broke into one-inch segments. The segments folded back on each other until the woman's head was uncovered.

Well, uncovered by metal.

The breeze lifted her long strands of chestnut hair, obscuring his view at first. She shook her head to get her hair out of her face, and time seemed to slow like in a swimsuit commercial.

Dark eyebrows curved gracefully over her large brown eyes. Even as far away as he was, Brendan could see how thick and long her lashes were. Her nose was straight and narrow, her cheekbones defined, her chin strong, and her lips full and sensual.

"Brendan Sloan." Her voice was steel and brandy. The same voice he'd heard every day for months.

His stomach was in his throat, his chest tight enough he could barely breathe. He was so lightheaded he thought he might pass out.

What a first impression that would make. He managed

to get hold of himself, forcing air into his lungs so he could breathe her name.

"Kira…"

She brushed the last unruly strands of hair behind one ear and smiled. The way her cheeks pulled up, the crinkles around her eyes, the dimples…

Kira was here. She was safe.

And standing in a spaceship.

He had made so many jokes about her being an alien. He thought she was playing along when she danced around the issue rather than calling him out on it. But now ─

That sexy as hell voice of hers pulled him back to the moment as she said, "I come in peace."

Chapter Four

Kira couldn't believe that Brendan stood right in front of her. He was even more beautiful than she'd imagined.

He stared at her with blue eyes—wide and expressive. The sunlight shimmered on his pale skin. His red hair was short, sticking up in disheveled spikes on top of his head, then settling down to frame his face in a neatly formed beard that covered his jaw and chin. The beard drew her attention to his full lips.

She had only seen beards on people in the data she screened from Earth's broadcasts. The genetic engineers seemed to do their best to minimize body and facial hair on Sadirians—except for eyebrows and eyelashes. Well, and the pubis. They generally stayed away from that area.

She loved Brendan's beard. She wanted to run her fingers along his jaw and feel its texture.

The thought shocked her. Why would she want to do something like that?

Shaking herself, she focused on her immediate problem —the danger they were both in. If the Coalition found her talking to an Earthling, Brendan would get a mind-wipe and she'd end up in prison. If any Tau Ceti survived and managed to track her down, she and Brendan were just plain dead.

When she had put in Brendan's coordinates, she hadn't been thinking clearly. She was still putting her brain back together after the minor miracle she'd pulled off with the station.

Looking at him now, being so close to him, she couldn't honestly say that she wouldn't have come anyway.

She'd wanted to meet him.

Now she needed to keep him safe. The only way to do that was to keep the Coalition and the Tau Ceti from finding them. She needed to be off their scans, which meant no tech. Her nanites were already powered down and she planned to keep them that way for now.

She unlatched the bands at her forearms that held her uniform's controls, then did the same to the collar that held the segments of her helmet. With that out of the way, she grabbed her uniform's seal and slid it open down the length of her torso.

"Whoa," Brendan said. "Um, Kira?"

She glanced at him, noting that his eyebrows had hiked way up his forehead. A quick look at their surroundings didn't reveal any threats. The escape capsule should notify her of predators as well. For the next few minutes, anyway.

"What is it?"

He stammered for a few moments, then asked, "What are you doing?"

"Stripping." She wiggled out of her uniform till it was around her ankles, then unlatched her boots and stepped out of them.

"I can see that. I can really, really see that." He shifted his weight and clasped his hands in front of his body. "But why are you doing it?"

"Coalition tech shows up like a nova on scans. My uniform and the escape capsule are filled with it."

She grabbed the capsule's med-kit and tossed it to Brendan. He scrambled to catch the small metal case.

"The med-kit is shielded from scans, plus its tech is inactive."

She keyed in the destruct sequence—manually, thank the stars—then programmed new coordinates that would take the capsule deep into the lake before it exploded. She sat on the edge of the capsule and swung her legs over the edge before sliding into the shallow water.

"Wait!" Brendan dropped the med-kit and rushed forward, water splashing up his jeans.

Gravity was faster.

As the water closed around her legs and waist, the cold hit her like a blow. Her knees gave out and she sank deeper before Brendan grabbed her and lifted her from the lake. One arm was under her knees and the other around her back. Her arms settled around his neck without needing her command.

After a few gasping breaths, she managed to say, "Much...colder...than...expected."

"This lake is fed from runoff from the mountains." Brendan gestured with his head across the water to snow-capped peaks.

That explained why her skin was covered in bumps and her heart was trying to beat its way out of her ribcage both as punishment and to escape from the stinging cold. Kira had been through a lot in her training, but liquid water wasn't all that common. And cold water was very different from the freezing atmospheres her teachers had exposed her to—in her uniform.

The option of taking it off while stranded on an alien planet hadn't been covered. It was generally believed that if things were bad enough to take out their uniform, the soldier wearing it would be dead anyway.

But she was alive. And she intended to stay that way.

The orientation session that prepared her for her assignment in Earth's listening station gave her rudimentary knowledge of the environment and things she might encounter if she had to go planetside. It was a rarity, and she certainly had never heard of it happening under the circumstances she was facing.

She pulled on her training anyway, trying to calm her heartbeat. Deep slow breaths, focus on the objective. But all she could seem to think about was Brendan's warm chest pressed against her side.

The escape capsule silently drifted away from them, then sank under the water when it was several meters away.

"Where's that going?" Brendan asked.

"Under the water so the explosion won't be visible."

"*Explosion?*"

"The water should protect us from the blast."

"That's not particularly reassuring." Brendan was already headed for the shore. It didn't take long for them to clear the water.

He bent so she could grab the med-kit. As he stood again, he said, "How far away do we need to—"

A dull boom-whoosh sounded behind them. Brendan flinched, tucking Kira closer against his body, wrapping more of his around her.

He was protecting her.

The thought made the bumps on her skin intensify. Held in his arms, she had the same internal sensations as she did in zero gravity.

He looked over his shoulder at the spout of water that was already starting to fall back to the lake. "Okay. I guess that was that."

"I would have told you if we were in danger."

"Right. Because showing up in an escape capsule that you then promptly destroy is a sign that everything's peachy keen."

"Peachy what?"

"It's an idiom."

He stared into her eyes for long enough that she grew uncomfortable. Her stomach was fluttering and her skin still tingled from the cold. Strangely, she felt hot at the same time. Especially where they touched. The feeling spread to…places she was not used to paying attention to.

The form-fitting undergarments she wore under her uniform were wet from the lake water. She was cold and her body was trying to find equilibrium. That was all it was.

She knew the thought was a lie.

"You're shivering."

His voice was gravely and lower than usual. His pupils were dilated too, as if he was excited.

It was probably from the shock of her arrival—not from her proximity. She wondered what her nanites could tell her about what else was going on in his body.

"Clothing would be useful given the cool temperature in the region," she said.

Slowly, he let her go, as if he didn't want to. The ground shifted beneath her feet. Sand. It squished up between her toes, abrading her skin.

She was about to say something when Brendan pulled his shirt up and over his head. Sunlight gleamed along his shoulders and highlighted the smooth skin of his pectoral muscles, abdomen, navel…

Something deep inside her destructed as her gaze seemed locked at the fastener for his jeans. Heat pooled in her belly, tingling spread between her legs. She felt almost like she'd taken a hit of *Coupling*, only the effects were much more intense.

"Here."

He handed her the shirt. It was still warm from his body.

"Won't you be cold now?"

"My cabin isn't far. I'll live."

She handed him the med-kit, then slipped into his shirt. The soft fabric whispered across her skin. A rich, sweet scent surrounded her. Brendan's scent.

He took her hand and started to lead her toward the grass. Earthlings referred to *blades* of grass. But he wouldn't lead her into something dangerous. She trusted him.

She stepped onto the green foliage.

The plants poked at her skin, tickling the sides of her feet. She took another step. Both feet were on the life-forms. The leaves were cool. Some of the sand stuck to her was wiped away. More of it seemed to be grinding deeper.

Cygnus X, she was a soldier. She had been trained to withstand torture. But she had never been planetside before. Not in an undeveloped, pristine environment, teeming with life.

She paused and said, "Wait."

"What's wrong?" Brendan turned to face her, creases appearing between his eyebrows.

Focusing on him made her feel better. She gripped his hand more tightly.

"There's too much… Too many…" She shook her head and closed her eyes. Even that wasn't enough to shut out all of the stimulae.

Birds were singing nearby. The hush of processed air whispering through the station's vents had been replaced with leaves rustling in the trees. The swells and ebbs of the wind were nothing like the steady drone she was used to. They left her breathless, made her wonder what would happen next.

She opened her eyes and looked up at the sky—a clear and crystalline blue with a few fluffy white clouds breaking up the monochromatic backdrop. Very different from the speckled black canvas visible from the station's viewports—from every viewport she had ever used.

The wind picked up and the trees bent, branches turning over and leaves waving like thousands of tiny hands. It was beautiful and terrifying.

"I don't think I can walk," she said.

"Are you hurt?" He stepped closer, but not close enough. She wanted to wrap her arms around him and hold on forever. Or at least until they could get inside.

"I'm not hurt. I'm just…overwhelmed. I've never been outside of… Well, I've never been outside before."

"You can't be serious. Don't you have...planets where you're from?"

"We do, but they're mostly dome-worlds or otherwise covered in tech. I was raised on space stations and ships. I've only been planetside for training." Training that seemed absolutely inadequate at the moment. "And there was no grass. And I had shoes."

Planets like Earth were rare. They were valuable. That was why the Coalition had assigned Earth preservation status. Most soldiers were unlikely to ever encounter a planet so rich in life. Her training hadn't covered anything like the springy green plant-matter beneath her feet.

"Are you agoraphobic?" he asked.

"No, there's just...so much here. Clouds and birds and —" She swatted at a small flying insect that buzzed past her face.

"I get it." He smiled. "Earth's a happening place. I tried to tell you it's the only place to be in the Sol system."

She surprised herself by being able to smile back at him. "I came for the company, not the scenery."

That...was not what she meant to say. It was the truth, though. She cleared her throat and looked away, but not before she caught how the furrows between his brows eased.

"Come on." He let go of her hand and turned around, then crouched in front of her.

"What are you doing?"

"I'm going to give you a piggyback ride."

"A what?"

"Lean forward and wrap your arms around my neck. Just don't choke me."

He shifted so that his back was brushing her stomach. Was this some sort of Earth mating ritual? She shook the thought away.

He patted his shoulder, as if encouraging her. She leaned into him, holding onto his neck carefully.

"I'll need you to carry this." He handed her the med-kit, then said, "We're playing hot potato with this thing."

"Hot potato?"

"Forget it." He laughed, then reached back and gripped her thighs. She let out a gasp as he lifted her into the air, with most of her weight spread over his back.

"Relax." His voice was gentle. "I've got you."

The fluttering in her stomach intensified as he started walking, carrying her along with him. She felt like she'd been given too much *Balance*—the chemical mixture most Coalition citizens used to maintain their contented state of mind.

She hadn't used it herself for years, though the Coalition made sure she always had some on hand. Even the med-kit had several vials. But she hadn't bothered with *Balance* since she'd been sent on her first assignment.

Balance always gave her a weird buzz that she didn't like. Maybe it was because she was a glitch. She was more likely to use *Coupling*. The physical release it generated was enough to keep her content. Too bad *Coupling* wasn't part of a standard med-kit. She could introduce Brendan to Coalition mating rituals.

Moons, where had *that* thought come from? She glanced at Brendan, but looked away quickly. Her face was probably as red as a skeelbat's belly.

At his age, Brendan was statistically likely to have had multiple sexual encounters—none of them involving a drug that would take care of everything for him. Earthlings did things manually.

Kira was suddenly very aware of his hands on the bare skin of her legs, on her chest and pelvis pressed against his back. His hands were large and strong. And warm. All of him was warm. She wondered what it would be like to snuggle up with him under a blanket and explore their anatomical compatibilities.

"You okay?" he asked.

She had never lied to him and wasn't about to start. "I'm not sure. This is weird."

"*You* think this is weird? I'm the one giving a piggyback ride to an alien."

She laughed and started to feel a bit lighter. She had made it this far. The Coalition would send someone to investigate what had happened to the listening station. She would be presumed dead, if they even knew she had been there in the first place. They would discover the Tau Ceti involvement when they scanned the energy field of the explosion and take action. She wouldn't have to do anything.

And she could live out the rest of her days happily on Earth. Once she acclimated.

"You not wanting to be found…" Brendan said. "Does it have anything to do with you talking to me? You said you weren't supposed to make contact."

"That's part of it. My superiors wouldn't be happy to find out we've been communicating. But they aren't the ones I'm worried about."

"Okay, now *I'm* a little worried."

"Don't be. All my tech is destroyed or offline. As long as we don't fire anything up, they shouldn't be able to find me."

"But doesn't that mean you're stuck here?"

"'Stuck' isn't the word I would use."

A stream of words came to mind. Giddy, happy, relieved.

Free.

A small structure came into view nestled in the trees that lined the lake. Its walls were wood and the roof was hidden under an array of primitive solar panels. Antithetical to the space stations and domes where she had always lived, and yet…comforting.

She let out a sigh and relaxed against him. A feeling similar to safety washed over her. Similar, but stronger.

She couldn't put a word on the emotion until Brendan did it for her. He opened the door and stepped inside.

"Home sweet home."

Chapter Five

Brendan felt Kira slide down his back with every nerve-ending in his body. He didn't want to let her go—to stop touching her—and now he was losing his excuse.

With all the questions about who she really was and where she was from rattling around in his brain, only one kept repeating itself.

Had she heard him when he told her he loved her?

That led to more questions. Did her people even have love?

He hoped so. His heart clenched at the thought of her not being able to reciprocate his feelings.

"Thank you for helping me," she said.

He realized he was staring at her. Had been for a while.

"Sure. Of course." He shook his head and closed the door. "I'm sorry. This is a lot to absorb, you know?"

"I can imagine." She looked around the small room, curiosity lighting her features. "This is your home?"

"One of them." He wished she was seeing one of his bigger houses. Then again, after being raised on space stations and ships, maybe she'd be more comfortable in the cozier space.

The cabin had a great-room design and was built for practicality above all else. In front of them, an octagonal wood-burning stove provided a means of cooking food as well as warmth for the right half of the room. The kitchen took up the corner on the far right from the door, his desk and all his equipment filled the other right-side corner. A free-standing counter in the center of the space sort of separated it from the rest of the cabin.

He had put his couch as close to the stove as he dared, which wasn't as close as he would like. He also didn't like that it meant he would be sitting with his back to the door, but he didn't use the couch that much anyway. A fireplace set into the middle of the left wall supplemented the heat, and when he built it up, the stones would warm and hold enough heat to get him through most nights. It also helped to heat the bathroom, which was behind a door in the far left corner.

His bed was to their left. He tried really hard not to think of the bed.

"What's that smell?" she asked.

Brendan sniffed the air. All he detected was wood smoke. Well, that and his burritos.

She walked to the counter and stared at them, practically salivating.

"That's my lunch. Are you hungry? I can make you something fresh."

"No thanks. I mean, yeah, I'm hungry, but don't go to

any trouble."

"It's no trouble at all. But if you want those, go ahead. I wasn't going to eat them anyway."

She gave him a brief smile, then put her med-kit on the counter. She picked up a burrito and sniffed it, then took a bite. Her eyes rolled shut. He watched her eat another few bites, reacting as if it was the most delicious thing she'd ever tasted.

"I'm guessing you don't have burritos where you're from," he said.

"*Burritos*. No. This is delicious." She licked some refried beans from her thumb.

"Cold bean burritos. There's not even any cheese in there. What is it that you normally eat?"

"Nutrient bricks. They have everything we need in a compact package."

"Sounds like soylent green."

"What's soylent green?"

"People."

Her eyes widened and she paused mid-chew. Then she spit her food back on her plate and started wiping at her tongue.

"Relax! Relax, it was a joke. That's not made of people."

She gave him the clearest *what the hell?* look he'd ever seen. He did his best not to laugh.

She cleared her throat, then asked, "Is there a place I

can get this sand off my feet?"

"Yeah. The bathroom is right through there." He pointed to the bathroom door. "I can show you how the shower works."

"Thanks, but I think I can figure it out."

"Okay. Well, *H* is for hot water, not that there's much of it. I'll find you some dry clothes."

After she disappeared through the door, Brendan ran his hands over his face again, then just held them there. How could this be real? How could any of this be real?

Kira in his home. An alien. He didn't know which was harder for him to believe.

He heard the water start to run in the bathroom. Yeah, she was here all right. Whatever else he believed, he was sure she needed his help. He kicked himself into gear.

Fires were already burning in the fireplace and stove. He grabbed a few extra logs from the firewood rack and built up both heat sources as quick as he could.

He had just kicked off his boots when Kira emerged from the bathroom. Her eyes were wide and she held a roll of toilet paper in one hand and paper towels in the other. Nightmare scenarios played through his head. He should have made sure she understood how toilets worked.

Brendan didn't mind roughing it, but he infinitely preferred working facilities. He had no idea how Kira would adjust if she had destroyed their only toilet by filling the pipes with paper towels.

"My training covered this," she said, holding up the toilet paper.

Thank God. He let out the breath he'd been holding in a little puff.

She held up the roll of paper towels, her jaw set and a determined look on her face. Her voice shook a little when she spoke, though.

"But what in the name of the Solar Cross is *this* for?"

It took him a moment for his mind to recover. There was no disaster in the bathroom after all. And her expression… She was obviously trying not to freak out, and seeing both items right next to each other, he couldn't blame her. The thoughts that must be going through her mind.

Brendan laughed, hard. "That's for something else entirely."

She arched an eyebrow. "Care to elaborate?"

"Those are paper towels. They're for cleaning up spills and drying stuff. Like, you could use them to dry your feet, for instance. I keep a roll in the bathroom for when I get behind on laundry and don't have any clean towels. Just throw them away in the little trash can in there when you're done."

Kira stared at the paper towels for a few moments longer, as if she was deciding whether or not she believed him. Finally, she said, "Okay." Then she turned and walked back to the bathroom.

Brendan was still chuckling as he peeled off his jeans and put them on the drying rack near the stove, along with his socks. Kira should probably put her clothes on it too.

The thought of her naked was more powerful than the cold, and his boxer-briefs started to tent. He grabbed the quilt from the back of the couch and wrapped it around himself. Which was good, because when Kira emerged from the bathroom a moment later, she was completely naked.

Her long legs were bare, her hips curving and then dipping gracefully into her narrow waist. The curves just got better the farther up his eyes travelled, rounding her small but perfectly formed breasts and stalling at the dusky skin of her nipples.

Brendan dropped his eyes to keep himself from staring at her breasts, but then they latched on to the dark curls between her legs. He bounced his gaze up to her navel and suppressed a groan.

Her stomach was perfect. Flat abs faintly outlined under the smoothness of her lightly tanned skin, a gentle line flowing up from her belly-button...

And he was staring at her breasts again.

"These clothes are wet," she said. There was nothing suggestive in her tone, but that voice of hers... She crossed the room to the drying rack and draped the shirt he had given her and her undergarments next to his jeans. He hadn't even noticed her carrying them.

He snapped his gaze to hers when she turned back to him, doing everything in his power to maintain eye-contact. He bit his lips and pulled the quilt more tightly around his shoulders.

"Did you find clothes for me?"

"Hmm? Oh right." Brendan was grateful both for the distraction and that Kira would soon be clothed. "There are drawers built into the bed."

She nodded, then turned and crossed the room. Dear lord, that ass... He let out a little grunt.

Looking back over her shoulder, she asked, "You okay?"

"Yeah, I'm fine. Absolutely... Things are great." He looked up at the ceiling, then down along the walls.

Brendan had never been that great with women. Being a ginger nerd had not helped. Once he'd made his first million, interactions became even more difficult. It seemed like everyone he met would feign interest to try to get close to him, then eventually realized you couldn't fake geek. When he sold his company at just the right moment and that *m* turned to a *b*, he had all but given up on forming a genuine connection with anyone.

Kira was bringing him back to his nerdy high school days, designing robots in advanced engineering classes and exploring computer systems he really shouldn't have been getting into.

She knelt and opened a drawer. Rooting around, she

stood with one of his long-sleeved shirts. She draped it over her head, lifting her arms through the sleeves as it settled around her body. He didn't know he could be jealous of a piece of clothing, but in that moment, he sort of wanted to be that shirt.

She bent over, nearly killing him as the hem rode up to just below the curve of her ass. His shirts were long, but she was tall. His brain calculated their heights and he realized that if she braced herself on the bed, they'd be perfectly aligned for...

This was not helping. His dick was so hard it hurt. He made sure the quilt was covering him, keeping his arms out from his body enough that he hoped she wouldn't notice.

"I can grab some clothes for you too." She rifled through his shirts.

If he tried to get dressed in front of her, she'd see how worked up he was. Even grabbing the shirt from her was out of the question. He didn't want to let go of the quilt for a moment.

"I'm good."

She glanced back at him, one dark eyebrow raised high on her forehead. Then she shrugged and stood. She pushed the drawer shut with her foot before walking back to him.

"There's another quilt on the couch," Brendan said. "I recommend wrapping up and sitting near the wood stove."

Maybe he should sit far from it. Cooling off could help.

He thought about running back to the lake and diving in.

She ran her hand over the quilt, looking up at him with a shy smile. "You don't mind?"

"Of course not. What kind of host would I be if I let you freeze?"

Half a dozen sci-fi movies hit him at once that made his off-handed comment send a chill through him—stories where aliens used human bodies as hosts. He shook off the thought, but was grateful for its calming effect on his body.

His dick was already starting to calm as she wrapped herself in the quilt. He let out a sigh of relief when she was covered.

"You sure you're okay?" she asked.

"Yeah."

They walked around opposite sides of the couch and sat facing each other. The warmth from the wood stove washed over him, helping to banish the last of the chill from the lake water. He stared at her for a moment of comfortable silence.

Kira. The woman he'd talked to every day for months. That he'd laughed with, teased, offered his heart to…

She kept her head bowed a bit as she smiled at him—a shy smile, but gorgeous. Then she laughed and leaned back against the couch. His heart gave a little jerk in response. Warmth spread through his chest that had nothing to do with the quilt or the fireplace or seeing all of her incredible body and everything to do with knowing she was safe.

Chapter Six

"I can't believe you're actually here."

Kira laughed, her stomach fluttering. "That makes two of us. I suppose you'll want answers to those questions now."

"Only one matters at the moment. Are you okay?"

Of all the questions to start with… Her throat felt tight. She coughed so she could answer him.

"Yeah. I have a bit of a headache, but trust me, it was much worse for them."

"Them who?"

Right. He would need context. Kira wasn't used to talking to other people.

"The station was being boarded by hostiles. I set it to self-destruct."

His eyes went wide and his mouth dropped open. She stared at his lips again. They looked soft.

"Kira."

He scooted closer, then picked her hand up from her lap. He held it in his, tracing his thumb over the backs of her fingers.

More bumps spread over her skin. Tingling spread

through her chest and down her belly, pooling between her legs. It reminded her of *Coupling*, but felt so much better. She could feel her nipples brushing against the shirt she had borrowed from him.

She swallowed hard.

"Are you all right?" he asked again, emphasizing each word.

"I... No."

That wasn't right. Of course she was fine. She was alive, uninjured, and had secured a safe location to regroup.

"What happened?"

She shook her head. "You can't tell anyone any of this. You know that, don't you?"

"I kind of figured. Don't worry, I won't tell anyone about you. And I won't let anything happen to you."

It was such a sweet sentiment. But if the Tau Ceti or even her own people showed up, Brendan wouldn't be able to stop them. Neither would she.

He waited patiently. Ready to listen to *her*. That was new. She was in this far, and he deserved the truth. She trusted him with it.

"I am an alien," she said.

His lips tightened a bit. She noticed because she was still staring at them. She couldn't seem to look away.

"I'm part of a Coalition of planets that has—well, had —a listening station in orbit, watching Earth's broadcasts and observing your development. It was automatically gathering data and compiling it, then sending it to a committee for review until about two years ago when I was assigned to the station. I was told to start parsing the data before it was sent, which is usually a sign that a planet is nearing a tipping point."

"What kind of tipping point?"

"There are a variety. Maybe the planet was getting to a point where they were ready for first contact. Or a big event was imminent—like a war or a meteor impact—and the committee wanted someone there to get the best record possible."

"That's not reassuring."

Neither was the truth that she had pieced together. "Don't worry. I'm pretty sure in Earth's case it was something else."

"I'd worry less if you were smiling."

She smirked and shook her head. "It's a simple story of corruption."

"Again, not really helping me relax."

She took a deep breath and tried to explain everything again. "Earth is designated as a nature preserve. You have no idea how rich this planet is in resources or how rare that is. And the planetary liaison assigned to manage Earth was just arrested. I'm certain that's not a coincidence."

"That doesn't sound good."

"The head ship of the fleet—the *Arbiter*—was

involved. I'm sure everything will be sorted out in short order. Except for me. I think the liaison used his connections to have me assigned to the station so that he could filter the reports I was sending to the Coalition. When the *Arbiter* left orbit, no one contacted me. I don't think they know I'm here."

"My equipment can send a signal. You can let them know—"

"I don't want them to. I don't want to be found. I want to stay here…with you."

"Oh…" He looked puzzled, but then his face relaxed and he smiled. "Oh."

"I mean, I can figure something else out. But after all our talks, I thought—"

Brendan didn't let her finish her sentence. He released her hand so that he could cradle her face, pulling her close as he leaned toward her. Those soft lips gently brushed against hers.

Stars…

Kira melted into him. That was how it felt. His lips moved on hers slowly, gently coaxing her response.

She had used *Coupling* with other people a few times. It had always seemed more mess than it was worth. Kissing had not been involved. If it had, she might have formed a different opinion.

Rising on her knees, she kissed him back. His lips were warm and strong. They parted to let his tongue slide along her mouth. When she gasped, he pushed his tongue deeper.

She moaned against his mouth, opening herself to him, pressing her chest against his body. Her tongue tangled with his as she gripped his shoulders and pushed him back against the couch. At some point, she had shifted to straddle him and his hands had moved to her hips. She wasn't even sure when, but she loved it. She loved feeling his firm grip, the heat of his kiss, the hardness of his...

Moons, his...member...was poking her belly. Without the aid of *Coupling*.

Of course he could hold an erection without the Coalition drug. Earth mating practices were far different from what she had experienced. Giving and receiving pleasure from another person using only their bodies... Kira wanted to know what that was like. With Brendan. Immediately.

Contact, stimulation—touch and friction.

Clenching her fingers on his shoulders, she slid up his body. He hissed in a breath and moved his hands to her ass. She felt muscles deep within her responding.

The cotton of his boxer-briefs was so thin. She rubbed herself along his length, groaning as the tingling between her legs grew into a current of electric pleasure coursing through her. Nothing had ever felt so good. Not *Balance*, not *Coupling*. She wanted more.

He tilted his head to the side, breaking their kiss. That just gave her a better angle to reach his neck. She latched onto his skin, layering kisses and nips as she worked her way up to his ear.

"This is all happening kind of fast," he said. "Not that I'm complaining. But are you sure you want—"

"Yes." Stars, she was sure.

Reaching between them, she slid her hand down the hard plane of his stomach, tracing the ridges of his abs. She didn't stop until she hit the elastic of his waistband, stretching it so she could reach him.

"I've heard this called a cock," she said, wrapping her fingers around him.

He groaned and his eyes rolled shut. "Um, yeah. That's one word for it."

She applied more pressure, watching his response. Loving it. He leaned his head back against the couch, eyes still clenched shut, lips tight. He pulled in deep draws of air between long pauses, as if all of his body's attention was on her hand.

Stimulus. Simulation.

He groaned as she started moving her hand on him, mimicking mating. She imagined what he would feel like inside of her, filling her. More electricity arced through her body, this time centering from between her legs, even though he wasn't touching her there.

How could her body be doing this without *Coupling*? Without even being touched?

If they had used the drug, they would have already

climaxed by now. She wondered what else they could do in the time their bodies needed to respond naturally to each other.

"In one of the broadcasts I reviewed, a man who swore he had encountered aliens called them *cocksuckers,* as if it was a bad thing." It didn't make sense. The heat and wetness of her mouth would be an even better simulation than her hand. "Is that a bad thing?"

She watched his throat move as he swallowed.

"That's a loaded question."

"I want to give you pleasure."

He gripped her wrist and pulled her hand away from him.

"What's wrong?" she asked.

"You don't have to do this." His expression was grave. "I'll help you no matter what."

"I don't understand."

"You don't have to trade sexual favors to get me to help you."

She felt her eyes grow wide. "People *do* that? Seriously?"

"Well... Yeah." He shrugged, scowling at her.

Kira started to laugh. She couldn't help it. The idea of trading sex for anything was so...*alien* to her. That thought made her laugh even harder.

"Care to clue me in?" Brendan asked.

"I'm sorry. That's just one of the funniest things I've

ever heard."

She wiped at her eyes as she sat back so that her weight was on his lap. He picked up the quilt that she had cast off and threw it around her shoulders, keeping his scowl in place. She had a feeling it was mostly for show.

"People in the Coalition... Well, they don't really have sex," she said. "Not like on Earth, anyway."

"See, now you're just making me uncomfortable." He grinned a little, letting her know he was joking. But she could sense there was a thread of honesty woven into his statement.

"There's a drug called *Coupling* that we can use instead of having sex. It takes care of everything."

"Your people only have sex alone?"

"Not always. For some, it doesn't satisfy all their needs. Those people pair up and use it together."

"Nobody just...gets it on the old-fashioned way?"

"Gets what on?"

"Has sex."

"Oh. Not that I've ever heard. And I'm a very good listener."

She loved talking to Brendan, but she wanted to do other things. It had been too long since he had kissed her. There was too much space between them. The energy that had been building in her was threatening to turn to frustration. She wanted to go back to pleasure.

She leaned forward and brushed her nose along his

neck, then pressed a kiss there. He didn't relax into her as she'd hoped, so she pulled back again.

"What is it?" she asked.

"You've done that before, though. Right?"

"Done what before?"

"'Coupled' with someone. Used that stuff with another person. I mean, you're not..."

"I've had sex before, if that's what you're asking."

He let out a breath. "Okay. Cool. Because this is going fast and it's already complicated enough and—"

She kissed him again, pressing her lips to his firmly to make sure he received the message. She wanted this— wanted him—for no other reason than that he was himself.

Chapter Seven

For someone from a culture that didn't exactly have actual sex, Kira sure knew how to kiss. And the way she had gripped him... Every touch, every look was equal parts naivety and confidence. He didn't know how she pulled that off. His dick didn't care—it just wanted more.

He was glad his boxer-briefs were still in place. Otherwise, he'd have been tempted to just slide into her. As compatible as their bodies seemed, he wanted to make sure they took precautions.

Gripping her ass to hold her, he leaned forward, then stood. Their quilts fell away as she held onto his shoulders and wrapped her legs around his waist.

"What are you doing?" she asked.

"Taking you to the bed." He started across the room.

"Oh. Okay." She gave him another of those megawatt smiles. He had to pause for a moment to kiss her properly.

Kira in his arms. He didn't care if she was an alien or not. She was the person who knew him best in the universe. The person he loved.

He broke off the kiss and carried her to the bed, setting her down on the side closest to his bedside table. The fire he had built up chased the chill from the air, but he left her shirt on to keep her warm. There was still plenty he could do and reach.

Kneeling before her, he ran his hands up her calves then under her thighs. Her lips parted and she hissed in a breath.

"When you take that drug, do you touch each other?" he asked.

"Not like this." She shook her head, her smile faltering. "It's more like a lot of awkward hugging. That's how it always felt to me, anyway."

"That doesn't sound very appealing."

"I only tried a couple of times. I don't think—" She cut herself off, eyes widening as if she had caught herself before letting a secret slip through.

There was no point for him to try to keep his secrets from her. The technology she had demonstrated already left his *advances* centuries in the dust. No wonder she'd been able to pick up his signal—she was the intended audience.

He hoped eventually she wouldn't feel the need to keep things from him either. He wanted her to trust him fully, like he trusted her.

"You can tell me anything," he said. "I thought you knew that by now. Especially with everything you've already shared."

She pinched her lips together so tight they disappeared.

But she nodded.

"I'm not...normal."

"Oh." Maybe their anatomy wasn't as compatible as he thought. "If there are things I need to know before we go further, tell me. I can handle it. I just... I want to be close to you."

"I want that too."

She put her hands on either side of his face and kissed him again, then rested her forehead against his for a moment. When she leaned back, she had that determined look on her face that he had seen while she was programming her escape capsule to detonate.

"Coalition citizens are genetically engineered," she said. "Part of that is being designed so drugs like *Coupling* work well with our physiology."

"That's profoundly disturbing."

She let out a snort. "What's disturbing is that they don't work on me the way they're supposed to. *Coupling* is okay if I use it by myself. But *Balance* just makes me feel... weird."

"Balance?"

"It helps us maintain emotional equilibrium."

"Your government drugs you to keep you happy?"

This was the worst foreplay ever. But Kira's desire to stay on Earth made a lot more sense.

"There are septillions of people in the Coalition. *Balance* helps keep the peace. The species that can't use it are invariably the ones who initiate conflict."

His stomach started to twist. The aliens he'd thought might take him to a more peaceful society were real. And he wanted nothing to do with them or their version of peace.

Well, most of them. Kira was an exception.

"Peace at that price—" he said.

"I shouldn't have brought it up."

She leaned away, frowning, then shook her head.

"How do you do it?" she asked.

"Do what?"

"Manage all of these emotions and still function? How do you have sex when there's so much conflict? So many thoughts competing for your attention?"

"You're right. This isn't the best topic during sex."

They had plenty of time to talk later. She looked lost. He wanted to help her feel safe and at home, both in his cabin and in her own body.

"We do it by listening," he said.

That caught her attention. After being on a listening station, he thought it might make the most sense.

He ran his hands along the outside of her thighs. "We listen to what our bodies tell us."

Her smile returned—the shy yet confident look he loved.

"I am a good listener," she said.

"Then let me change the topic to something more

central to our current interests."

He slid his hands under her shirt, massaging her hips. She took in a deep breath, then let it out slowly.

"That's really nice," she said.

"I'm glad to hear it. What about this?" He brushed the backs of his fingers along her stomach and she jumped, then laughed.

"That tickles."

"Good to know."

He increased the pressure of his fingers, gripping her sides and running his hands up along her ribs till they were just below her breasts. Her smile faded and her eyes drifted shut as he cupped her breasts and gently massaged them.

"Um... I don't..."

"Do you not like it?"

"Oh no. I like it."

He ran his thumbs over her nipples. She gasped and her eyes flicked open.

Brendan smiled at her. "Do you like that too?"

She nodded. "Quite a bit."

He rose on his knees and slid his arms behind her back to pull her closer. She bent down and kissed him, running her tongue across his lips. He opened his mouth to her, meeting her thrusts with his tongue, relishing the feel of her, the taste.

Trailing his lips down along her neck, he spent a little

time there before moving farther down. He nuzzled her breasts through her shirt and she gasped. He grinned, then closed his mouth over her nipple. He ran his tongue around it, flicking it through the fabric. She let out a moan. Nuzzling her chest, he moved to her other breast to do the same.

"Brendan, I feel…"

He paused and shifted back, intending to ask her if something was wrong, but she grabbed his face again and kissed him. Her tongue delved into his mouth and she scooted closer to him. When she let him go, they were both panting.

"I feel…need," she said.

He leaned forward, cupping her sex with one hand. Her eyes went wide and her mouth dropped open. He pressed his fingers against the wetness at her core, swirling them around her clitoris.

"Moons! What are you…? That's…"

"That's me talking to your body with mine."

"Yes." She braced herself on her arms, leaning back and letting her eyes close again.

Cautiously, he slid a finger deep into her. Her breath hitched. He circled her clit with his thumb, slowly moving his hand. When he thought she was ready, he added another.

"Oh… That's…"

"Only a beginning," he said.

She opened her eyes, bright with curiosity. He smiled at her, then leaned forward.

Chapter Eight

Kira's body hummed with pleasure. Her arms tingled, her legs burned, and an ache was building between her legs that she didn't quite understand. She wanted to throw herself on Brendan, to slide her body against his until she found how they most perfectly fit together.

He had other ideas.

His fingers were moving inside her. She wouldn't have believed how good it would feel if someone told her people could do this sort of thing. And the external stimulation was even better.

He shifted his thumb aside and leaned forward. She felt her body tense at the uncertainty of not knowing what he would do next, but reminded herself that she trusted him. She trusted him like she'd never trusted anyone before. So when he bowed his head to her, she didn't pull away.

The first kiss was...remarkable. The tingling she had been experiencing seemed intense to her until the shockwave of his lips on her clitoris rippled out through her, exponentially increasing her pleasure.

Her arms trembled, but she forced herself to stay upright. She wanted to see what he was doing to her, to learn as much as she could.

Her skin was heating, almost like when she used her nanites in unorthodox ways, except there was no pain. Only pleasure. It built as his tongue made quick flicks and slow circles over her clitoris. His fingers kept moving within her, sliding in and out, over and over and—

Something deep within her broke loose. Like a dam that had been holding her back from fully experiencing her body. It vaporized in the heat of the thrumming ecstasy that tore through her.

Her head snapped back as she cried out. Still, he kept going. The stimulus threatened to overwhelm her. How much pleasure could one body take?

And yet, part of her wanted more. She wanted him inside of her, to join their bodies the way *nature* intended rather than the Coalition.

"Brendan," she gasped. She was practically panting.

He didn't pause, but looked up at her. Another wave of pleasure wracked her body. At this rate, she was going to pass out.

Or climax again.

His lips became gentler, pulling on her clitoris as he slid a third finger deep into her core. There was no build the second time. The climax hit her in every cell simultaneously. Her blood was alive, her molecules radiating energy. Everything was light and fire.

Moons, she wanted to wrap her legs around his neck

and pull him closer.

"Enough!"

He finally stopped, leaning back at her outburst.

She was going to push him to the ground and jump on top of him. But he was still wearing his boxer-briefs.

"Take those off."

He smiled and said, "Yes, ma'am."

She pulled her shirt over her head and threw it away as he complied. The air was cold to her heated skin, so she pulled back the covers and crawled to the center of the bed. When she turned back around, Brendan was standing next to the bed completely naked.

Cygnus X, that cock…

Her mouth went dry and she licked her lips. After what he'd done to her—for her—ideas cascaded through her mind of how she might reciprocate. Even those thoughts made her core clench, surprising her. If thinking about it could cause such a response, what would it be like to actually take him in her mouth?

"I can guess what you're thinking, but I wouldn't last thirty seconds right now," he said. "We have plenty of time."

He opened a drawer in the table next to his bed and pulled out a shining square packet. For a moment, dread shot through her. Did Earthlings use something like *Coupling* after all?

The change from the near-euphoria of the pleasure he

had given her made her dizzy. She took a deep breath and let it out slowly to steady her nerves.

He opened the packet and pulled out a small circle of flexible material. As she watched, increasingly fascinated, he held his gorgeous cock in one hand, then put the circle on his tip. He unrolled the material over himself till his cock was covered in a transparent sheath.

"What's that?"

"A condom. It helps prevent pregnancy and the spread of disease. We seem pretty compatible, so I figured it would be a good idea."

"That's a very good idea." And one that would never have occurred to her otherwise.

When she was assigned to observe Earth, her system had been prepared to handle the native pathogens, but she had never given any thought to preventing pregnancy. *Coupling* took care of birth control for both parties. But now that she was thinking about it...

Moons, she could get pregnant. She could carry another life within her body.

"Are you okay?" Brendan asked. "You look like you're about to hyperventilate."

"I'll be fine. Those things work, though, right?"

"Nothing is foolproof, but I've trusted them so far. If this is too much for you, we can stop."

"I don't want to stop," she said.

She wanted more. And even if his systems weren't one-hundred percent effective… The thought of a life she made with Brendan did a lot to ease her fears. She wouldn't be in it alone.

She had a feeling she would never really be alone again after this.

"Kiss me?"

He smiled and crawled toward her on the bed. "Gladly."

Then his lips were on hers and he was pressing her back against the sheets. Bliss.

He pulled the covers over them as his body covered hers. The hair on his thighs prickled against her legs as he nestled between them. She felt his cock resting just outside her core, waiting, ready to enter her.

Lifting himself up on his elbows, he brushed her hair away from her face. "Are you sure about this?"

"Absolutely."

"Thank God," he murmured, as he pressed himself deep.

The experience was revelatory.

Without the drug, she felt every millimeter of contact, even with how quickly it happened. She felt her body expand, her muscles contract around him. Her nerve-endings were already on full alert after everything he had done, and her sheath was relaxed enough to welcome him.

When he was in as deep as he could get, there was no space between their bodies. His stomach pressed against hers, their chests touched so that their hearts rested against each other. He brushed his cheek against hers, then kissed her neck, giving her a moment of stillness, a moment to just *feel* everything.

It was almost more than she could bear. She managed to whisper, "I never knew anything could be like this."

He kissed her again, and there was so much tenderness and meaning in it. What had he said about handling the conflicting emotions? Listen to her body. She could sense that there was more waiting for them and she wanted to experience it.

He lifted himself on his elbows again as he started to move within her. The entire time, he held her gaze.

She gasped as he pulled himself almost from her, feeling a spike of anxiety at the thought that maybe he was ending their union already, but then he slid back in. She moaned as he filled her again. Nothing had ever felt so good or so right.

She wrapped her legs around his and rested her hands on his back, feeling his muscles flex with his movements. She explored him, letting her fingers trace the valley of his spine and the ridges of his shoulders, watching his expression, catching every hitch in his breath that let her know when she had reached a spot he particularly liked.

It was the very best kind of listening.

Her own body was uncoiling, relaxing with each thrust. At the same time, energy was building in her again. She could feel it pooling in her belly, radiating like starlight from where they were joined.

He closed his eyes and bit his lips, his pace increasing. She sensed the build within him, echoing her own. Running her hands down along his back till she could cup his ass, she focused on the feel of the strong muscles pulling him out, pushing him deep, faster and harder until a sonic boom sounded through her body.

It thrummed and vibrated, shaking loose every tense nerve, relaxing her on what must be a cellular level. She felt his cock pulse within her, echoing the throbbing of her muscles as her body held him within her, keeping him deep.

Brendan let out a huge sigh and lowered his head next to hers. He nuzzled her hair, then moved to her mouth for a lingering kiss.

She hoped it was the first of many more to come.

Chapter Nine

It was the end for him. Brendan was sure of it. He had found his "one and only" and she was from another planet.

The reality of it hit him as he took in the wonder on her face, as he felt the ease in his heart. He'd found what he had been looking for, but on his homeworld after all.

"That was incredible," she said.

"You aren't kidding." He felt his dick slide from her body and shifted his weight so he could lie next to her.

Kira rose on her elbow so that they were nose-to-nose. She grinned broadly. "Do you think we could do it again?"

Laughing, he said, "Are you trying to kill me?"

"What? Of course not. It can't really hurt you, can it?"

She was so distressed, but it only made him laugh harder. "I'm fine. I just need to rest for a little while. And then you can have your way with me all you want."

Her smile returned. "I like the sound of that. I had a few ideas…"

Time couldn't pass quickly enough. Damn biological limitations. He grabbed a tissue to clean himself up and tossed everything in the trashcan under the bedside table.

"Do you mind if I ask you some of my questions now?

Might help us fill the time while we wait."

"Okay."

She pulled the pillow under her chin and wrapped her arms around it, lying on her stomach. Her body was putting off so much heat. He snuggled next to her, propping himself up on one elbow while he draped his other arm over her back.

"The most obvious one is, where are you from?"

"Sadr-4."

"Really? That's close."

"The galaxy is much more heavily populated than you might think."

"How come you're the only one who responded to my signal then?"

Her smile faded and she looked away. "Because I was intercepting it. That's part of my job. Well, *was* part of my job."

"That was going to be my next question. I want to know more about that listening station and what you were doing on it."

"Mostly screening broadcasts for evidence that Earthlings might be figuring out ways to prove that alien intelligence is real. The Coalition doesn't think that Earth is ready for that knowledge."

"Why do they get to decide?"

"Because they're the ones with the fleets of starships."

His stomach started to ache again. He did not like the

idea of powerful aliens making decisions for his homeworld without even letting them know a question had been asked.

Was Earth ready? Okay, probably not. But the Coalition still should have asked...somebody.

"You're upset," she said.

"Disturbed is a better word for it. And disappointed. I thought aliens intelligent enough to be capable of interstellar travel would be a little more advanced when it came to politics."

He moved on to his next question, hoping to lighten the mood.

"How is it that we're so alike? You said your people are genetically engineered. Did they design you to fit in on Earth in case you had to interact with us?"

She laughed and shook her head. "No, everyone from Sadr-4 is like me—like you. Earth was populated by a colony ship that crashed here millennia ago. They took over from the evolving hominids, but lost touch with their history when their ship was destroyed."

What the hell? *He* was an alien?

"That's...going to take me a while to wrap my head around." He searched for another question while that knowledge sank in. "You say you're all genetically engineered, though. Why haven't you made more changes to...the design, for lack of a better word?"

She looked away, her mouth tightening into a line.

Way to flatter her, Brendan.

"I mean, you are amazing, but—"

She snorted and rolled her eyes. And not in a, "Oh, go on then," manner. She really didn't believe him.

"Seriously, you're the most beautiful woman I have ever seen."

"You don't have to say that." Her voice was angry and a little hurt.

"I mean it."

She glanced back at him, expression guarded, but a bit of hope seeping in. "We didn't change the design because it works for us. What's been changing is our technology and the level of control we have over the expression of our DNA."

"That explains why you're so—"

"Stop," she said, sitting up and pulling the quilt around her body tightly. "Just stop, okay?"

He sat up next to her, wondering what had offended her so badly. Maybe the Coalition had a different view of what was beautiful. He had seen something like that on an episode of *The Twilight Zone*.

"I'm sorry I upset you," he said. "But I won't take back what I said. I do think you're beautiful."

She let out a deep sigh and rested her head against her hand. "I'm not used to hearing that sort of thing."

"Maybe you should get used to it. Because I think you're pretty great."

She let out a little laugh and shook her head. "I don't know how to take compliments. I've never been anything but average."

"If you're average, I don't want to see what passes for gorgeous among your people. My head might explode."

All that earned him was a tiny laugh. She closed her eyes and let out a soft sigh, leaning her head against his chest. He wrapped his arms around her.

After a long pause, she said, "It isn't just that I'm average."

He waited for her to continue. He could feel the tension in her body and didn't want to push.

"Sometimes the engineering goes wrong. The system glitches. That's what happened to me—what I am. A glitch."

She turned her head away. He shifted so that he could reach up and cup her chin, making them face again. Her eyes were glassy. It made him want to punch someone.

"You are not a glitch. You hear me? You're not a mistake."

A tear managed to escape her lashes and roll down her cheek. It was too much. He leaned forward and kissed her. He let the kiss build slowly, waiting till she relaxed—till she melted against him—to deepen it. He slid his tongue into her mouth, keeping his strokes gentle. When she pulled back, she sniffed and wiped her face dry.

"Thank you," she said.

"There's no need to thank me." What the hell kind of society did she come from?

"All of my test scores are average at best. That's why they installed a nanNet in me and assigned me to be an observer." She pressed herself against his chest. "I didn't really mind, though. I figured at least that way I could be useful."

"What's a nanNet?"

"It's a network of nanites that live in my brain. They help me store and parse through the data I collect."

"Hang on. They put a hard drive in your brain to make you more useful to society?"

Kira shrugged.

"That is so messed up," he said.

The irony of it killed him. She had done this so that she would feel more a part of her society, but from what he could see it had only served to isolate her.

"If someone's not born a rocket scientist or acrobat—that doesn't mean they have nothing to contribute," he said.

Kira was staring at him. He hoped he was getting through to her.

"We do things differently." Her voice was just above a whisper.

"Yeah. I see that. What about the voices of dissent?"

"Dissent?"

He took a deep breath and let it out slowly. With

everything she had told him—the drugs, the genetic engineering, making sure Earth didn't find out aliens existed—her society seemed all about control.

"Voices of dissent. The people who disagree. Who want to change society."

"There are no dissenters."

"There are *always* dissenters. How many people did you say are in the Coalition?"

"Septillions."

"And you think not one of them has a different idea of how things should be done?" When she didn't respond, Brendan went on. "Those are the voices you should be listening for."

Chapter Ten

"The only people I know of who oppose the Coalition are the Tau Ceti. And the last time I heard their voices, I blew up my listening station to avoid their interrogation tactics."

Kira didn't like much of what Brendan was saying. Primarily because it carried truth. But there was more going on than he was aware of.

"You have my complete attention," he said.

"The Tau Ceti joined the Coalition a few hundred years ago, which isn't long at all. It happened fast. Their homeworld is a swamp and has a peculiar electrical field that threw off our scanners. By the time we figured out that they were capable of extra-solar travel, it was too late to keep them pinned into their system."

"Why would the Coalition even want to do that?"

"Among other reasons, the Tau Ceti are cannibals."

"Oh. Yeah, I guess that's a good reason. No wonder my soylent green joke fell flat."

He was trying to ease the tension of the conversation, but she couldn't join him. She knew way too much about the Tau Ceti.

"Wait, they weren't going to..." His smile faded. "They wouldn't have—"

"They say they've stopped eating sentients, but there are still incidents. And after interrogating me, they would have needed some way to get rid of my body."

"Okay. Not liking the Tau Ceti. Why were they after you?"

"The only thing they could have been after is information. That's all the listening station had."

"Couldn't they have just grabbed it from the computers instead of interrogating you?"

"Possibly. My nanites were synched with the station, so they might have wanted to make sure all the data was destroyed. Whatever they were looking for, the only remaining copy is in my head."

"No wonder you don't want to be found. If tech is easier for them to find, won't your nanites be a problem?"

"Don't worry, they're powered down currently." Kira intended to keep them that way for as long as possible. "But you're right—even their tech signature would make me easier to locate with scans. I was able to grab the medkit because the tech inside is off. The only other contents are a few doses of *Balance*."

"That drug the Coalition uses to control people."

"They're not controlling citizens. It just helps people be happy."

"Tomato, tomah-toh."

"What?"

"Forget it." He shook his head again. "Why doesn't your super-friendly government use *Balance* on the Tau Ceti?"

"It doesn't work on them. Well, it works *too well*. The Tau Ceti started out as amphibian humanoids. *Balance* is applied topically. The Tau Ceti's skin somehow amplifies the chemicals and knocks them out."

"Good to know."

This would be a lot for anyone to absorb. He was handling it pretty well, so far. He shook his head, then leaned forward and kissed her. Slow, deep and wet.

When he pulled back, she asked, "What was that for?"

"You looked like you needed it. I know I sure did."

She smiled and leaned against his chest. He wrapped his arms around her shoulders.

"At least we don't have to worry about any space frogs running around on Earth," he said. "I imagine they'd really stand out in a crowd."

"Actually, one of the first things they did after joining the Coalition was to begin their own genetic engineering program to make them look more like us."

"I'm over here reaching for peace of mind, and you're just plucking it away."

"Sorry."

He was quiet for a long time. Then he asked the question she was dreading, that she hadn't even let herself think.

"Are they a threat to Earth?"

She didn't answer. He put his hands on her arms and shifted so he could look into her eyes.

"Kira, are they a threat?"

She couldn't lie to him. She wouldn't.

"I don't know."

"They want something on Earth," he said. "Otherwise, they wouldn't be here."

She wanted to argue the point, but anything she said would be grasping at straws. He was right.

"What's the Coalition doing to stop them?"

Another dreaded question.

"They don't know the Tau Ceti are involved."

He rose on his knees, pulling away from her.

"Yet," she said. "They don't know yet. I'm sure when they scan the debris field—"

"Kira, this is my planet we're talking about. My home. Everyone I love is here." He sighed and shook his head. "Do people in the Coalition even still do that? Love each other? Or is there a drug for that too?"

She understood where the hurt was coming from, but his words still stung.

"I'm sorry," he said. "I shouldn't have said that."

"I love you."

His gaze shot to hers. She smiled and reached for his hand.

"We still know how to do that at least," she said. "Love each other. We call it pair-bonding. It isn't always about love, but we still feel the urge to partner with others."

"This is hard to process. I mean, we could be having a translation issue. That word could mean something different to—"

She wrapped her arms around his neck and kissed him, let her lips linger on his. Rising onto her knees, she deepened the kiss, shifted her hand to gently trace her fingertips across his cheek and down his chest.

She paused long enough to say, "There's no mistaking this. I love you."

Kissing him again, she let her body talk for her. She trailed her fingers down his chest, then pushed him back onto the bed. He rested his hands on her hips. She could feel his tension.

Of course he was distracted. There was so much going on, so many new things he was processing. She felt it too. But they would sort everything out. Probably sooner than she wanted.

They needed to know what the Tau Ceti were after— what information was important enough to get her listening station boarded. To sift through the data in her final report, she would have to turn on her nanites. The danger that would put them in would be deadly and immediate. And if their time together was going to be that limited, she wanted to explore everything she could first.

She slid down his body, kissing his chest and stomach along the way. His cock had stiffened again. She wrapped her fingers around it and squeezed, simulating what her core had done earlier.

"Kira..."

She didn't want to start talking again. Not before experiencing this.

She wrapped her lips around him.

Brendan gasped. She lightened her grip with her hand while tightening her mouth, taking him in deeper. She could feel so many things. His heart pulsing through his shaft, his body tensing. She brushed her fingertips along his length, then down over his sac. His back arched. The change was subtle, but she felt it.

Movement, friction, pressure. Heat and wetness. She swirled her tongue around his crown before tightening her lips and sliding her mouth along his length. As she gently ran her nails over his sac, she increased her pace.

"Kira..."

His hips started to move—rising to meet her, synchronizing their movements. It was incredibly intimate, witnessing his reaction so closely. A thrumming pulse was building in him. She could feel it.

"Stop!"

He pulled her head away. Why had he stopped her? Was she doing something wrong?

"Condom," he said.

"What?"

He grabbed her arms and flipped her onto her back. For a moment, she thought he might just fall on top of her, but he held himself back. Instead, he scrambled for the drawer at their bedside and pulled out another of the metal packets. His hands were shaking.

She took it from him and smiled. He put his hands on his hips. His strong thighs were spread between her legs, his cock thrusting toward her. Maybe she'd never know what it was like to take him that way. But she'd had enough. And if this was their last chance to couple—to make love—she wanted to feel him inside her again.

She opened the wrapper, then placed the circle of transparent material on his crown. She rolled it down slowly, glancing at him as she did. He bit his lips. His control must be reaching a breaking point. When he was ready, she started to lie back, but he stopped her with a hand on her shoulder.

"No, this time it's all about you."

Chapter Eleven

Brendan dropped to his back, gripping one of Kira's thighs so he could pull her on top of him as he did. She was left straddling him, his dick resting against her slit. He wanted to thrust into her so bad he could hardly stand it. But if he did, he'd go off too fast, and she needed time to catch up.

She stared down at him with her eyes wide as if she didn't know what to do. He gripped her hips and started to move her, sliding his dick against her. She was a quick study and took over fast.

She rocked against him, swirling her hips. Even this was going to be too much if she kept that up. Lucky for him, she was more worked up than he realized. She shifted so that his dick was lined up, then lowered herself over him.

Bliss shot along every nerve-ending as she wrapped her tight quim around him. She took him in so deep—deeper than he thought she could manage. Her dark hair fell forward across her chest, brushing her breasts as she moved. She lifted herself up onto her knees, then slowly sank back down, over and over.

Brendan lifted his hands to her, brushing her hair behind her back, then lightly dusting his fingertips along the sides of her breasts. He flicked his thumbs over her nipples, letting his touch become firmer.

Her pace increased. She reached down to his hands and pulled them away from her so she could lace their fingers together. He followed her lead as she positioned his arms on the bed so that she could brace her weight on them, letting him support her. It opened them up to a new array of possibilities.

She leaned into him, making a swirling motion with her hips as she lifted herself up and then eased back down. The stroke plus the way her sex was clenching him was pushing him too close to the edge again. The pleasure was pulsing through his hips, gathering together steadily, his dick so full and ready he wasn't sure how he could last.

He thought about baseball, cold water, the stale bean burritos on the counter. Nothing helped.

Her pace increased, the frills left behind as she pumped him with her body, her hands gripping his so tight it almost hurt. He could feel her starting to pulse and let himself go, his hips rising up to meet her every time she crashed back onto him. She let out a loud cry as he felt her fall over the edge into her climax, her back arching and body pulling on him, urging him into his own.

The energy pooled in him flooded out as he came, his body spilling into her. His hips bucked and she rode him, thighs clenching him tight. His skin was on fire, a locus of energy radiating out from where they were joined.

She fell across his chest when the last waves of heat were settling in him. She made a soft contented sound as she let go of his hands. He wrapped his arms around her.

"I thought you said you came in peace," he said.

He felt her laugh as much as heard it, her body vibrating on his, humming with contentment and happiness. He wished they could stay that way forever. But he knew they couldn't. She must have felt the same.

"Kira…"

"I know." Her voice was quiet "I'm parsing the data."

"What, like now?"

"If we're lucky, the Tau Ceti are still recovering from the station exploding."

"And if we're not lucky?"

She lifted her head and kissed him. He could tell her attention wasn't entirely with him, though. He broke off the kiss and pushed them both up to a sitting position, shifting so that he could sit next to her.

"We can figure out another way. You don't have to—"

"I do. There is no other way."

He didn't know what to do, so he sat next to her and held her hand. Moments ticked by. They hadn't been vaporized, which he took as a good sign.

"I think I found something," she said.

"What?"

"A plane crash over Louisiana."

Brendan felt his stomach clench. "Yeah, I heard about that."

"Scans picked up an unusual reading. An energy burst. It wasn't long enough to run a full analysis. It could have been the Tau Ceti. But why would they take down a small passenger plane?"

"James Conroy was on that plane. He was a senator who just got elected. Is there anything in your data about him?"

"That name has come up several times. He was championing environmental issues."

"I thought you were just watching us to make sure we didn't realize aliens are real."

She shook her head. "No, my job was to make sure you didn't get proof."

Senator Conroy was all about stopping climate change. According to Paige, his first priority was convincing people that climate change was real and having a detrimental impact on Earth's ecosystems. Paige was helping him gather evidence for his reports.

"Why would an environmental activist show up in your reports at all?" It didn't make sense.

"Because of the geographical areas he was concerned with. The water sample reports the station accessed showed shifts in alkaline balance, temperature, and salinity that…"

He did not like the look on Kira's face. Her eyes snapped back into focus as her gaze met his.

"What is it?"

"They match the ecosystem on Tau Ceti-6. Their homeworld."

His heart started to pound. Aliens were real—okay. They were watching Earth. He could handle that, even them walking among Earthlings. But making permanent bases there?

"Are you saying that the Tau Ceti have changed Earth's environment to match their physiology?" He wanted to be crystal-clear on that point before he freaked out about it.

"I'm saying that they have destroyed indigenous ecosystems to make room for their own. This is worse than anything I've heard of them doing before. Raiding settlements is one thing, but this amounts to a full invasion of a preservation site. The sanctions they're risking…"

"Why would they do it? You said Earth is rich in resources, but what could they possibly be after? Gold? Gemstones?"

"The Coalition can mine asteroids. Minerals are abundant in the galaxy, and precious stones can be replicated in labs."

"What are we missing?"

"I don't know. I can't think of any reason the Tau Ceti would want to set up a permanent presence on Earth."

"They'd have to be found out eventually, right?"

"Maybe, maybe not. The Coalition is aware of the damage Earthlings are doing to their own environment. If the Tau Ceti keep their operation small enough and try to match the damage they're doing to what's already going on, they might be able to get away with it for decades."

"Shut down your nanites," he said.

She closed her eyes for a moment, then said, "Done."

The urgency he felt before at the thought of Earth being in danger coalesced into a chilling fear in his chest. Even if the Coalition figured out the Tau Ceti were involved in destroying the listening station, they had no idea what they were doing on Earth. And if the Tau Ceti managed to find Kira...

He shook his head, trying to avoid that thought. But he had to face it. If they removed her from the equation, who knew how long they could keep destroying Earth's ecosystems before the Coalition caught on.

He had no doubt his sister would fall in the line of fire eventually as well. Those water samples Kira mentioned didn't just hop into the lab on their own. Paige was Senator Conroy's main environmental scientist.

"Kira, we have to tell the Coalition what's going on."

She nodded. "I know."

Chapter Twelve

"Turning on my nanites will be nothing compared to this."

Kira watched as Brendan completed preparations to send his final broadcast. She had recorded a message that contained everything they had figured out about the Tau Ceti involvement on Earth. They would send the broadcast across a section of space that should ensure the *Arbiter* received it.

The transmission would need at least five minutes to complete and would show up loud and clear on any Tau Ceti scanners that were still functional. She was no longer just worried about the ship that had boarded the listening station. With an operation on Earth as big as they suspected, there were probably plenty of Tau Ceti waiting and watching for just such a signal. The question was whether they would be close enough to reach Brendan and Kira before they could run.

Brendan had resources. If they could reach civilization, their chances of survival would be better.

She wasn't holding out much hope.

"You ready?" Brendan asked.

She nodded, then rested her hand on his shoulder, leaning over him to watch him work. He put his hand on top of hers. They locked gazes for a moment, then he turned back to the controls and initiated the broadcast.

"There it goes."

"Are you sure they won't be able to recover any data?"

"I set up my equipment with a self-destruct. It won't take out the whole cabin, but there should be some pretty cool fireworks."

"You're kidding."

"What, you think you're the only ones advanced enough to have self-destruct buttons? Please. I worked for my government. I don't want this falling into anyone else's hands. You can't pull data from a system that's been both wiped and slagged."

"Too bad we can't time this one to take a few of them out."

The cabin was already precious to her. In only a few hours, she had built the best memories of her life there.

"Remind me never to make you mad."

She smiled, then leaned forward to wrap her arms around his shoulders and kiss his cheek. She nuzzled the soft hair of his beard. Stars, she hoped there would be time for more of that.

His smile suddenly vanished. "Part of it is an EMP. I was so distracted with everything going on, I forgot about your nanites."

"They'll be fine. They're powered down." She gave him another quick kiss. Her stomach was tightening as the broadcast neared completion. "You're not using nuclear fission for that, are you?"

Her sensors hadn't picked up anything like that near his cabin.

"There are other ways to create an EMP."

"Nothing that standard Earth-tech can make."

"Look around you. Any of this look like standard Earth-tech?"

He had a point. It was too bad Earth wasn't considered advanced enough to begin First Contact preparations. Brendan would be a perfect candidate for the preliminary committee.

His computer beeped.

"That's that." He shut down the broadcast, then keyed in the commands for the self-destruct. "We have ten minutes to make ourselves scarce. My jeep is about a five minute hike if we hustle. The EMP won't reach that far. I know you say you'll be fine, but I'd just as soon get you far from here before it goes off."

"Let's go, then."

Brendan headed for the door while Kira ran to the counter to grab the med-kit. Sunlight spread across the floor briefly, then was blocked. The hair on the back of her neck stood on end.

"Um, Kira?"

She turned around, knowing what she would see. Brendan had his hands in the air and was backing toward her. Two Tau Ceti entered the cabin.

The Tau Ceti had done their best to look like Sadirians, but there were imperfections in their process. Their mouths were too wide, faces too tall and long. And their eyes, while within Earth norms, were much smaller than Sadirians'.

One was a foot soldier, fully decked with cybernetic enhancements. As if that wasn't enough, he was carrying a laser rifle in his muscular arms. The other was tall and lanky, wearing an Earth-style business suit. His skin was pale and he had dark black hair. Somehow, the awkwardness of his features lent him an eerie sort of handsomeness. He hadn't bothered with a weapon and didn't look augmented like the other.

"Well, this is quaint." The leader's voice was low and smooth.

His soldier closed the door behind them, then took up a guarding stance.

"It isn't much, but it's home," Brendan said. "Welcome, Mister…?"

"St. John. But you can call me Horatio."

"Horatio? Okay, then. I'm Brendan. This is—"

"K-58-b7. Born during cycle 12 on Sadr-4 station 9 to batch 31. It wasn't a very good batch, I'm afraid. Full of glitches. Kira. I'm well aware."

"I'll thank you to show some manners while you're in my house," Brendan said. "Kira's not a glitch."

Brendan glanced at Kira. She shook her head tersely, but it wasn't enough to stop him from reaching for her hand. She didn't take it. It didn't make a difference. Horatio noticed.

"Uck, this compulsion you Sadirians feel to pair-bond is bizarre. It makes you vulnerable. Lucky me." His smile was nothing less than sinister. "You did a very good job concealing yourself, my dear. Didn't spare yourself so much as a laser cutter. I bet you're wishing you had a little something now, aren't you? Coalition tech can be addictive for your kind. It's a shame, really."

He walked over to Brendan's equipment, looking everything over.

Stars, don't let him notice the destruct sequence.

"Pretty sweet setup, eh?" Brendan said. Maybe he was thinking the same thing, trying to distract the Tau Ceti. "Best Earth has to offer."

"I don't know. I'm rather fond of those little robotic vacuums Earthlings have developed. But I suppose this was able to get the job done, so to speak."

"I can show you how it works," Brendan said.

No way. That would get him way too close to the equipment. Then again, maybe that was the idea. Try to take the Tau Ceti out with the self-destruct somehow? Maybe Brendan was thinking about that EMP too.

Disabling the foot soldier's cybernetics would help even out their fighting abilities.

"I'm not concerned with how it works, but rather what it was used for. The transmission was encrypted with a Coalition code we're not familiar with." Horatio turned back to them. "Let's get to business. You're both going to die. The question is how unpleasant the experience will be and who will go first. The best thing you can do is cooperate."

Even if the EMP took down the soldier's cybernetics, she wasn't sure she could take both of them. If only she had a weapon. Kira's skin was tingling with the urge to do something.

Wait, skin...

The med-kit had several doses of *Balance*. If she could splash them with it, they would be incapacitated.

She reached for Brendan's hand and squeezed it to let him know she had a plan. She only hoped it would work.

Chapter Thirteen

Horatio Cannibal Space-Frog had stepped a bit away from Brendan's equipment. He was still close enough that he was about to get a nasty surprise. By Brendan's count, the EMP and fireworks should happen any minute.

The problem was, Kira was still in the cabin. At ground zero. She was confident having her nanites powered down would protect her, but Brendan wasn't so sure. He held her hand tighter.

There was nothing they could do about that. But maybe they could learn more while they waited for the big boom.

"So…from what Kira tells me, you guys are risking a lot being here on Earth. What is it—the scenic views? Bean burritos?"

Horatio snorted. "Something like that."

Brendan looked over at Kira. "What is it with you aliens and bean burritos?"

"You know, if we're going to die anyway, I want to finish that one," Kira said. She tugged his hand and led him to the counter.

"Whatever makes you happy," Horatio said. Which was weird. "Stay on this side, if you please. I do need to keep you where I can see you."

Kira hopped up onto the counter and patted the space next to her. She was up to something. Brendan only hoped it was enough to get them out of this.

Horatio and his bodyguard didn't seem to mind. Kira picked up the bean burrito and took a bite, staring at their unwelcome visitors as she chewed.

"You don't seem very worried about the signal we just sent," Brendan said.

Horatio shrugged. "The *Arbiter* left orbit yesterday and is well on its way to Sadr-4. It'll take it at least a day to return. That gives us some wiggle room. The Sadirian wants a last meal. What about you? What would make you happy?"

"I want to know what you're up to on my homeworld." Brendan figured he might as well go for it, since the guy asked.

"I don't see the harm."

Seriously? This guy was going to spill his master plan? Had he never seen a James Bond movie?

Horatio smiled as he walked around the cabin, looking at the fireplaces and feeling the fabric of the quilts. "We're really not so bad. All we want is to make people happy."

"Why?" Brendan asked. "There's always an angle. What's in it for you?"

"Naturally occurring oxytocin, primarily. With a few other yummy human feel-good hormones thrown in the mix."

"Oxytocin," Brendan said. He looked over at Kira.

"It's the main component in *Balance*," she said.

"But you Tau Ceti guys can't use *Balance*."

"Ah, very good," Horatio said. "I see you've been learning about us already. Yes, synthetic *Balance* doesn't react well with our physiology. It's much too concentrated to be truly enjoyed. But a similar mix of chemicals in the wild…"

"Wait…" Kira set down her burrito. "You're harvesting oxytocin from humans?"

"We find it has a much smoother finish and a better buzz." He looked at Brendan and said, "You needn't worry too much about your fellows. We have a strict catch and release policy. After we feed, the human is returned to the wild. Our geneticists have worked up some modifications with the latest generation. We don't even need tools for harvesting."

Horatio leaned his head back and opened his mouth wide, revealing a pair of sharp canine teeth hanging down from the roof of his mouth. Brendan put his arm in front of Kira and leaned to the side so he was partly blocking her. Not that it would do a lick of good against that nasty looking weapon the heavy by the door held.

Horatio laughed. "You know, pair-bonding makes the blood much sweeter, the hit more…stimulating."

"Vampire space frogs," Brendan said. "You guys are

freaking vampire space frogs? You have to be kidding me."

Horatio laughed. "That's a rather apt description, I suppose. Although we've left most of our frogishness behind."

"It wasn't an improvement, from what I can see," Brendan said.

"What? All our humans are free-range," Horatio said. "It makes the chemicals more pure when we harvest them. It's too bad we can't keep you two alive. I bet you'll be tasty. But we can't run the risk of you escaping when there's a whole planet of humans we can feed from. Which brings us back to your final usefulness. I will ask only once, and then I will start removing appendages. The Sadirian knows this is not an empty threat. What was in that broadcast?"

Brendan's computer beeped. Thirty seconds.

"What was that?" Horatio asked.

Brendan shrugged. "Primitive tech. It's noisy."

He and Kira grabbed for each other at the same time, swinging themselves over the counter and onto the floor. She reached out and snagged the med-kit on the way.

His equipment let out a final beep, then he heard a crackle-bang as the explosives detonated. Sparks flew over their heads and Brendan smelled the acrid scent of burning electronics.

If all went according to plan, the EMP would have gone

off at the same time. The space frog by the door had metal devices obviously worked into his body, making him a *cyborg* vampire space frog. More fodder for the nightmares Brendan hoped he survived to endure. The grunts he heard from the direction of the door encouraged him, as did the fact that Kira seemed unfazed.

She opened the med-kit and pulled out two clear vials. She popped the lids from each and handed one to Brendan.

"*Balance*," she said. "Don't get it on your skin."

Brendan nodded. He wasn't sure what she had in mind, but followed her lead as she jumped up from behind the counter. The cyborg space frog by the door was bent double, his arms dangling heavily from his shoulders. Brendan thought maybe that was it for the guy, but he straightened and took a few jerky steps toward them.

Kira flung her vial of *Balance*. The liquid splashed onto his skin and within seconds a blissful expression covered his face. He sank to the ground, eyes closed.

"Where's the other one?" Brendan asked.

Kira slammed into him, knocking him clear as something dropped from the ceiling, landing right where he'd been. He turned and saw Horatio crouched on the floor in a stance no human could achieve. Well, not without several broken limbs.

"How many knees and elbows do you have?" Brendan asked.

Horatio grinned, then leapt at Kira.

"Look out!" Brendan shouted. His warning was unnecessary.

She dodged to the side, spinning around and landing a brutal kick into Horatio's ribs. Brendan had never seen anyone move so fast. The force of the impact propelled Horatio into the wall of the cabin. Instead of bouncing off and hitting the floor, he sort of...stuck there. He looked at Brendan with eyes that blinked sideways.

"That's just wrong," Brendan said.

Horatio launched himself at Brendan, his fangs gleaming in his wide-open mouth. Just before he reached Brendan, Kira brought both her arms down on his back, fists clenched together in a hammer of flesh and bone. This time, Horatio hit the floor.

Kira lashed out with another kick, catching Horatio under his armpit. He made a screeching noise, then collapsed. She nudged him with her foot. She was barely panting.

"That was so hot," Brendan said.

Kira raised an eyebrow at him and he shrugged.

"I'm just saying." He finally remembered the vial in his hand and flicked some of the liquid on Horatio. "Take that, vampire space frog."

When he looked back at Kira, she smiled.

Chapter Fourteen

Kira tucked herself deeper into Brendan's side as they snuggled in front of the fire. He had wrapped them both up in a quilt after making her a cup of tea. Her bare feet were pulled up next to her on the couch, and she was more comfortable than she had ever been.

The door to the cabin burst open. She and Brendan looked over their shoulders at the two Sadirians that leapt into the room. They were dressed as Earthlings, which was a bit of a surprise. Their arrival wasn't. Kira had turned her nanites back on a few times, and they let her know that the *Arbiter* was already in orbit.

Kira had warned Brendan to hold still and wait for her to explain who she was and why the signal had been sent from his cabin. Noting that the pair wore Offense bracers beneath their long-sleeved shirts made her glad for that. They were security.

The first to enter the room was a dark-haired woman with amber skin and pale gray eyes. She was followed by an extremely tall man with blond hair, blue eyes and...

"Khel?" Kira sat up straighter.

"Kira..."

Khel nodded curtly, his stance relaxing. "Stand down, Sorca. She's with us."

"Actually, she's with me," Brendan stood and crossed his arms, glaring at Khel.

Kira couldn't help but laugh at the obvious claim Brendan was staking. It wasn't just that he was half Khel's mass. From what she'd heard, Khel had always been averse to using *Coupling* even by himself, let alone with a partner. Genetically he might be a glitch, but he acted like a perfect Sadirian soldier. Her laughter cut off abruptly as General Serath walked into the room.

His hair was dark and reached the collar of his shirt. His face was half-covered by what looked like the start of a beard. That was a change from the images she'd seen. But it was definitely Serath. One eye was as green as the sunsets on Vega-3, the other blue as the sky outside.

She leapt to her feet, fighting to extract herself from the quilt. It dropped to the ground as she stood at attention. In her periphery, she saw Brendan salute.

Her stomach knotted. Why was General Serath planetside?

He stepped aside, revealing a tiny woman with blonde hair pulled back in a ponytail and huge glasses resting on her small nose. An Earthling?

As if that wasn't confusing enough, the woman reached for General Serath's hand...and he let her take it.

The room spun a bit as Kira's sense of reality adjusted

to the new data. Apparently, she wasn't the only one who had fallen for an Earthling.

"Report."

General Serath's order snapped her into her role as a Coalition soldier. *Don't think. Just obey.*

"Sir. Two Tau Cetis detected our broadcast. They've been neutralized."

Kira nodded briefly to the two bound and drugged Tau Cetis in the corner of the cabin. Sorca and Khel were already securing them with Coalition tech. Kira relaxed a bit, glad to have suspension disks to back up the *Balance* still in their systems.

"Good work," General Serath said.

"Sir?" Kira could feel her eyes bugging out of her head. Good work? It was just her duty. Why would he praise her for that? The blonde woman smiled and shifted closer.

Cygnus X…

This time, he caught Kira's stare and grimaced. "And?"

Kira cleared her throat. "We've determined that the Planetary Liaison had falsified my assignment to get me on the listening station so that he could scrub the reports before sending them to the Coalition."

"And where is the listening station?"

Moons. She stood straighter. "Destroyed, sir. It was boarded by the Tau Ceti. I initiated a self-destruct in an attempt to disable their ship and take out as many as I could while preventing them from obtaining the data they sought."

Please, let them never find out how…

"You did more than disable their ship," Sorca said. She had a grin that was nothing less than bloodthirsty. It somehow made Kira like the woman. "You destroyed it. We scanned the debris field."

Kira nodded, her stomach tight. Taking out a Tau Ceti vessel wasn't an easy feat. She had done it with a *listening station*. An odd emotion bubbled up inside of her. Was this what pride felt like?

General Serath was staring at her. She tried not to fidget.

"We also have obtained additional information," she said.

"We?"

Her stomach seemed to drop through the floor. "I was assisted by—"

"Brendan Sloan."

Brendan held up his hand, splitting his fingers in a "V" shape again. She'd have to ask him about that later—if they had a 'later'.

The woman at General Serath's side laughed and returned the gesture.

"I knew I recognized a fellow nerd," Brendan said.

"And proud of it. I'm Evelyn Chambers."

"Very pleased to meet you."

"Since Earth has different customs with introductions,

allow me," Evelyn said. "The big blond guy is Khel, second-in-command of the *Arbiter*, which is this totally amazing spaceship. That's Sorca, head of security. And this is General Serath, but on Earth, he goes by Adam Smith."

General Serath grimaced, but nodded to confirm her statement.

"Ma'am. Aliens." Brendan tapped his forehead twice in an odd gesture that made him seem he was wearing an invisible hat.

Evelyn grinned again.

He nodded toward Kira and said, "Kira made contact after her station was destroyed. She explained that she'd been monitoring a transmission I was sending into deep space and knew I had equipment that could help."

Her stomach filled with butterflies. He was protecting her again. It just might be possible that she would get out of this with all her secrets intact—talking to Brendan, her aberration, falling for an Earthling.

But she didn't want to get away with it. She wanted to stay.

"Sir—"

Everyone in the room turned to her when she didn't continue. She wasn't used to being at the center of so much attention. She took a deep breath and let it out slowly as she took Brendan's hand.

"That's only part of what happened."

Khel let out a chuff of breath and stalked to the door, leaning against the wall next to it. Sorca's eyes widened, but that grin came back.

The General—Adam—scowled.

Kira could feel her heartbeat in her throat. Adam was very likely to order a mind-wipe for Brendan. It was protocol. Being free or being in prison didn't really matter at that point. Either way, she would have lost the most important part of her life—Brendan's love.

"Permission to speak freely, sir?"

Evelyn jabbed Adam in the rib, hard. He let out a little grunt, then sighed. "I'm going to regret this. Permission granted."

Speaking her mind to one of the greatest Generals the Coalition had ever seen. Kira wasn't sure what to say, how to begin.

Brendan squeezed her hand. She looked up into his eyes, brimming with warmth and love.

"Tell him." Brendan shrugged. "Just tell him."

She took a deep breath and stared at the ground for a moment while she collected herself. "I didn't excel at anything in the pod where I was raised. I didn't...suck." She smiled at Brendan, and he smiled back. Just that simple act was infinitely reassuring. "But I didn't have anything anyone was looking for. That's why they put a nanNet in me. To make me good for something."

She felt Brendan's grip tighten, could sense the tension

coming off of him. And she knew in that moment that he still would have fallen in love with her just as she was. He would have accepted her—cherished her—without trying to change her. How could she possibly let go of this?

"I thought it would finally mean a good assignment. A ship, a crew. Colleagues. Friends."

Pain rose up from her gut, strong as a gravity well. It pulled at her, trying to draw out her hope, to crush her with the weight of the memories of loneliness. She wouldn't let it.

"Instead, they put me in a listening station. Single-unit orbiters. I have the data storage, why not. And it turned out, I was good at it. I *am* good at it. Listening. So they kept me on assignments. For four years I have been alone, orbiting worlds with sentient beings as alien to me as..." She shook her head. "As the people who raised me."

"That's not protocol," Khel said. "You should have been assigned rest-cycles for months between assignments."

"When has protocol stopped anyone from doing something that's easy?" Kira said. "I didn't speak up. I accepted the assignments, one after another, because I wanted to feel useful. I wanted to help. And then, I heard Brendan. And...I broke protocol myself. I answered him. But I had to." She looked pointedly at Adam's hand, gripping Evelyn's tight. "You of all people have to understand what it's like to finally find that person you can connect to on a...*human* level. How can I let that go, sir? Could you?"

"What are you suggesting?" Adam asked.

"I want to stay." She was surprised and gratified at how strong her voice sounded. Inside, she was shaking.

"You know what this means."

Kira wasn't sure she had heard him correctly. Was he actually thinking about letting her stay?

"Revoking your citizenship," he said. "Never being allowed to leave the planet."

She could handle that. "Yes, sir."

"And having your nanNet permanently disabled."

Her heart seized. For a normal augmented person, they might be upset to lose the extra functionality. For her, it meant losing the only companions she'd had during her long years of isolation. Before Brendan.

"No," Brendan said. "No freaking way. You're not taking that from her."

She squeezed his hand to warn him. It wouldn't make sense for her to be too upset about it. She had explained her aberration to Brendan while they waited for the *Arbiter* to return, including the danger of others finding out about it.

"It's protocol," Adam said.

"Protocol would be to give the Earthling a mind-wipe and throw Kira in jail." Everyone turned to Sorca. She shrugged one shoulder, then grinned. "I've never been a fan of protocol."

Brendan gestured to Sorca. "What she said. I'm not getting a mind-wipe, whatever that is, and Kira's keeping her nanNet. And her citizenship."

Adam arched an eyebrow.

"I'm not asking your permission to play *Little House on the Ignorant Prairie.*" He turned to Kira and said, "This isn't just about us."

Right. Kira nodded. "The Tau Ceti aren't just setting up pockets of their habitat on Earth. They're feeding on Earthlings."

"What?" Evelyn stepped forward, glancing to Adam.

"Those guys on the floor?" Brendan said. "They're vampire space frogs."

Evelyn laughed until she noted Brendan didn't join her. "Oh, you're serious."

Adam wrapped his arm around her as she shifted closer.

"They're siphoning off oxytocin and other hormones from humans," Kira said.

"So they get a hit like Coalition citizens and *Balance.*" Sorca flinched ever so slightly, glancing at the other soldiers. When she and Kira met gazes again, she knew Kira had picked up on the hidden data in her statement. Kira could see the nervousness in Sorca's eyes. Sorca didn't use *Balance,* either.

"Don't get me started on that," Brendan said. "I've learned enough about your government to have serious concerns about you making decisions for my homeworld. It ends now."

"What are you suggesting?" Adam said.

"I'm not suggesting anything. It's done." Brendan wrapped his arm around Kira's waist, mirroring Adam's posture with Evelyn. "I don't care what the Coalition thinks about Earth's level of development. We're forming the committee for pre-First Contact work. The Department of Homeworld Security. You want to make a decision about my people, you're going to talk to us first."

"I see Kira has explained quite a bit about our society." Adam fixed her with an uncomfortable stare. "But she seems to have neglected to inform you that you're not in the position to make demands."

"Oh, she didn't have to. I inferred from what she told me and set up some things while she was out of the room."

"What did you do?" Kira's heart sank. She had only left the room for a few minutes to use the bathroom. What could Brendan have set up in that time?

"I'm sorry I didn't talk to you about it first, but I wanted you to have plausible deniability."

Sorca said, "I doubt an Earthling has the resources to do anything that could possibly impact the Coalition."

"I guess I forgot to mention that I work with my own government," Brendan said. "And while I agree that they aren't ready to handle all this alien stuff, there are a few of us that can pool our resources and help to guide the

Coalition into making better choices for our planet."

"Such as?"

"Like making Kira the planetary liaison."

Kira's stomach lurched. Brendan hadn't mentioned this when they talked before.

"I'm not going to tell you what I've done, because it'd make it that much easier for you to try to stop me. Frankly, though, I'd rather we work together. These space vampires are feeding on my people and destroying our ecosystems. That has to stop."

"Agreed," Evelyn said.

Adam nodded. "Agreed."

Kira thought Adam was only referring to their goals, but then he said, "Kira will be the new planetary liaison for Earth. I'll see to it."

Kira felt her jaw drop. Her gaze met Evelyn's and the Earthling smiled so warmly that Kira couldn't stop herself from returning it.

She was going to be Earth's next planetary liaison... She could stay with Brendan, help protect his homeworld. Finally, she could make a difference. And she wouldn't be alone.

"One last matter," Brendan said. "My sister might be in the line of fire. She's an environmental scientist whose work is somehow tying her in with the ecosystems the Tau Ceti are messing with. I want a bodyguard for her. Someone who can stand up to space frogs."

Adam nodded. "Khel."

"No no no. I am not sending Thor here to watch over my baby sister." He glared and Khel and said, "Kira, *please* tell me this isn't one of the guys you used *Coupling* with."

Khel looked shocked for a moment, then launched himself at Brendan. Luckily both the couch and Adam were in his way. Adam grabbed Khel and pulled him back as Kira stepped in front of Brendan. The revulsion on Khel's face was unmistakable.

"I've never used *Coupling* in my life!" Khel said.

"He didn't understand the insult," Kira said. She tried to keep her voice level.

Brendan's eyebrows hitched up his forehead, then he grinned. "My bad. I take it back. This guy's the perfect bodyguard for Paige."

There was a moment of awkward silence, then Evelyn laughed. When everyone turned to her, she shrugged. "I was just thinking, Kira's going to be living on Earth now. That makes her a resident alien."

Brendan laughed, then turned to Kira and kissed her, passionately—in front of everyone.

"Welcome to Earth," he said.

Epilogue

This planet was vexing. Khel walked along the sidewalk observing the Earthlings scattered about the area. According to his cultural indoctrination session, those walking the same direction as him were supposed to stay on his right, while those walking toward him belonged on his left. An alarming number of humans chose to weave in and out of the pedestrian traffic, sometimes even stepping into the area reserved for use by vehicles to get around others.

Chaos.

And this was the sort of free-will that General Serath—Adam—wanted to bring to the Coalition? As Khel watched, an Earthling darted in front of an automobile, barely escaping injury. The human operating the vehicle pounded on the steering wheel, causing it to emit an ear-splitting alarm. Khel paused to cover his ears and someone ran into his back.

"Watch it, buddy." The Earthling scuttled around Khel, lifting the middle finger of one hand and pointing it at him.

Khel didn't remember that gesture from the cultural indoctrination session he'd received from Vay aboard the

Arbiter. He lifted his own middle finger of the same hand, pointing it at the human, and said, "Excuse me."

The Earthling scowled, then quickened his pace.

The sooner Khel could complete his mission and leave this bewildering planet, the better. He turned a corner, thankfully onto a less populated sidewalk. A large building dominated the area, a cut-out image of a severed arm with grotesquely bulging muscles hanging over its door.

He ran his hand over the muscles of his own arm—exposed, thanks to the Earth-style "T-shirt" he wore instead of his uniform. The stylized rendering of the arm above him was similar to his own freakish level of musculature. But why wasn't it depicted as being attached to a body?

Khel suppressed a chill. *What is this place?*

He steeled his nerves, then pulled open the door and stepped inside.

The scent struck him first, making him recoil and shake his head. He wasn't sure how to describe it, other than acrid and *stale.*

There was no one guarding the entrance, so he quickly made his way through the entry chamber, heading toward an open archway on his right. He could hear movement from within, strained grunts and the clanging of metal on metal.

The archway opened up to a large room filled with strange equipment. Some had benches or stools, as if people were supposed to sit on them. Perhaps it was some sort of interrogation area?

He turned toward the grunting noise he'd heard, only to see a prone Earthling on one of the benches, holding a metal bar above his chest. The bar had metal discs attached to each end. From the way the man's muscles pulled and the beads of sweat coating his body, it must be extremely heavy.

The bar started to drop. Khel took a step forward, intending to prevent the human from being crushed, but before the bar hit the man's chest, he pushed it back up, holding it in the air above him. As Khel watched, the human repeated the movement several times. He then set the bar onto a metal rack above his head.

The activity made no sense.

Another sound drew his attention—this one a steady drone. He gazed out over the room to see a woman with bright red hair standing on one of the pieces of equipment. She should have caught his eye immediately, but he'd been too focused on the disturbing sounds of the human closer to him.

Khel brought himself back to task. He was here on a mission, and he was fairly certain he'd just found his target. She was walking on a conveyer belt that continually moved beneath her feet. Perpetual motion with no destination. Her eyes were fixed on the blank wall opposite her with a single-minded focus that completely baffled him. What was she even looking at?

This place must be a test of one's sanity. The whole planet was beginning to feel that way to Khel. His training might not be sufficient to protect him for long. He needed to retrieve his target and get them both out of there as quickly as possible—back to the *Arbiter*.

He may have found her first, but he doubted his enemies were far behind. And if the cybernetically enhanced soldiers of Tau Ceti caught up with her before Khel could get her to safety, these odd apparatuses would seem like a recreation facility when they were done with her.

He headed toward his target, intent on one thing, one person only. Paige Sloan.

—

I hope you enjoyed *Resident Alien!* Readers eagerly awaited Khel's story, and you can read on to explore it now! I had so much fun learning more about him, as well as the take-charge Earthling that can more than handle him —but not necessarily the affect he has on her. Read on for *Business or Pleasure.*

USA TODAY BESTSELLING AUTHOR

CASSANDRA CHANDLER

BUSINESS OR PLEASURE

THE DEPARTMENT OF HOMEWORLD SECURITY

Business or Pleasure

The Department of Homeworld
Security
Book Three

Cassandra Chandler

Dedication

For my husband—it's always a pleasure.

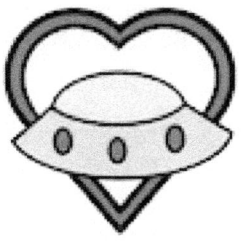

Don't miss out on any of the alien action.
Subscribe to Cassandra Chandler's newsletter at
cassandra-chandler.com!

Chapter One

At six-thirty on Saturday mornings, the gym was usually deserted. It was therefore Paige's favorite workout of the week. She had already completed a few circuits on the weight machines and was enjoying being the only person using the line of treadmills as she cooled down. After the week she'd had, she needed the break from human contact.

Her playlist abruptly switched to her brother Brendan's ringtone. Damn.

Thanks to him, all she had to do to answer was tap her right earbud. He had hooked her up with technology he'd designed himself. The earbuds included tiny microphones that could pick up her voice even if she was whispering, while filtering out ambient noise and making her hands-free talking crystal clear. The phone's reception was good enough that she wondered if he was tapping into one of the secret government satellites he worked on.

Allegedly.

The downside of the awesome tech was that she felt obligated to answer every time he called her with it. She sighed, then tapped the earbud.

"Morning, bro. What's up?"

"Hey. You're at the gym, right?"

She hesitated before answering. "Yeah."

"I figured. How are you doing?"

"I'm fine, everything is fine..."

Except it really wasn't. Jim—Senator Conroy—was dead. Today's workout was as much about grief and catharsis as keeping up with her physical health. She wasn't just sad to lose the best boss she'd ever had. Senator Conroy had been a passionate visionary. He was determined to tighten environmental laws.

Her team, which consisted of her and two ever-changing temporary interns from the local college, had been working several sites in Louisiana for three years before Jim came on board, giving her renewed hope that she could make a difference. He had been in office less than a month when his plane crashed.

Maybe Brendan was just calling to check up on her.

"I'm sending someone over," he said.

She let out another sigh, deeper than the first. "Seriously? We're not even in the same state."

"I have a...friend in the area," he said. "He should be there any minute."

"How do you even know what gym I'm at?"

"Uh..."

"Don't bother answering."

Brendan was overprotective to the point of paranoia.

She had finally been able to get him to stop hiring and assigning her bodyguards by agreeing to carry a panic button with her at all times. Brendan had designed it to look like lipstick. She wasn't sure how it worked—she just knew to press the button and it would send him some sort of signal that let him know where she was and that she was in trouble.

"I've told you before, I refuse to let your work impact my life. You want to work on top secret stuff—"

"Paige—"

"—that's your business. But I'm not going to walk around with ex-military private security goons following me just to make you feel better about your life choices."

"Paige!"

Brendan never yelled. She stopped ranting.

"This isn't about me or my work," he said. "It's about you."

"What about me?"

"Whatever you're working on has caught the attention of...unsavory types."

She let out a brief laugh. "I can't even get people to believe global climate change is real, let alone that it's impacting key ecosystems. I doubt anybody sees my work as a threat, especially now that Senator Conroy is gone."

"I wish that was the case. Listen to me very carefully. I can't speak openly right now."

She snorted. Right, Brendan couldn't speak openly on

the incredibly advanced, encoded system that he had designed. She was pretty sure the government would be pissed if they ever found out she was walking around with the tech he had given her. Brendan had assured her when he set her up with her phone and panic button that no one would know about it and his *gifts* wouldn't pose a threat to national security. The last thing she wanted was to be walking around with classified technology.

As rudimentary as he claimed it to be, her calls were still supposed to be one-hundred percent unhackable. If Brendan couldn't talk freely, that meant either he had been pulled back in by the government and they were eavesdropping using the tech he had designed for them, or the much more terrifying possibility—someone was with him that Brendan deemed a threat.

"You don't need a wormhole, do you?"

That was their code for a dangerous situation they needed a miracle to get out of—like the sudden appearance of a stable wormhole. His answer would let her know if he was safe. He laughed, and some of the tension in her chest receded.

"Not in the sense you mean. You wouldn't believe... Well, anyway, I'm in a safe spot. And I'm sending someone to bring you here. We need to talk."

"I'm glad you're safe, but I'm not leaving."

"Paige—"

"If I'm on someone's radar, that means I'm onto

something. I'm not about to drop it." Whatever *it* was.

Most people would consider her overworked, but she didn't care about the long hours. She was dedicated to helping the planet. The problem with the heavy workload was that she had so many locations and projects she was tracking, she had no clue which one had pushed someone's buttons.

Brendan's call had spooked her though. She glanced around the gym, noting that several people had filtered in while they spoke. Everyone seemed absorbed in their workouts.

"I'm not telling you to abandon your work," Brendan said. "I'm saying there's more going on here than you realize. Much more. You're going to need help, whether you want it or not."

"I don't want one of your…"

A tall man stepped into the main workout room. He was pale and blond, his hair cut short on the sides and back with bangs that fell partway down his forehead. His gray T-shirt pulled tight across the most gorgeous pecs she had ever seen. His broad shoulders perfectly offset his narrow hips and accented his V figure. Tight jeans encased his long legs, all the way down to…black boots.

She rolled her eyes. He might have been able to fool her if not for the boots. Well, and the stance. The way he walked screamed military. The question at the front of her mind became—was he Brendan's guy or someone else's?

"Tell me more about this friend you're sending."

"He's tall. Looks like Thor. Not like movie-Thor, but actual *God of Lighting*-Thor."

She grinned. "And you felt safe sending him to watch over your baby sister?"

Before Brendan had made her the panic button, Paige had seduced a few of the more attractive bodyguards he tried to saddle her with. It was a great way to let off steam, but invariably had led to them wanting more of a commitment. She was already committed to her work. Still, it worked for getting them to quit and gave her fuel to tease her brother.

"Please try to take this seriously. Khel will keep you safe and explain as much as he can."

"Kel?"

"K-H-E-L. Go easy on him. He's not from around here."

"I'll make sure he feels welcome." She purred the words, wanting to make Brendan uncomfortable. He should be for intruding in her life this way—again.

"Yeah, good luck with that. And gross." Brendan laughed as if he knew something she didn't. Which wasn't that unusual. He was quiet for a moment, then said, "I love you, sis."

"I love you, too. Be safe."

"And you."

She tapped the earbud to end the call, then turned off

her music. That had been their standard wrap up to a conversation, but there was a new tension to it. The teasing had been more strained, and that pause before his, 'I love you...'

She tried to shake off the unease and focused instead on the hottie headed her way. This guy might be enough for her to chance a fling. Her body was already tingling just from watching him approach. He was scanning the room, his brows drawn together so tight they almost touched in the center of his forehead. When he reached her, he stared at her legs.

Okay, he was a leg guy. After a few moments longer than a normal person would stare, he cleared his throat and said, "Paige Sloan. I am Khel."

He cut himself off, as if he was used to saying something more than that. Probably rank and serial number.

"Khel. I am Paige Sloan," she parroted back. He didn't pick up on the teasing. If anything, he seemed reassured by her mocking response.

"Your brother has sent me to secure your safety. We must leave at once."

"My brother is not in charge of me. Nor are you. We will leave when I'm good and ready."

His mouth dropped open, then shut, then opened, then shut. Like a giant thunder-god goldfish.

She laughed. He scowled.

Right, she was supposed to take it easy on him.

"I'm almost done with my workout. Surely the world won't end if I spend another minute on the treadmill."

He stared at her feet, then looked back over the room. She thought he was checking for threats again, but then he said, "What are you all doing?"

"We're working out."

The treadmill beeped and she hit the button to turn it off. He glanced back at her as she jumped down and grabbed her towel. She felt a bead of sweat run between her cleavage and noticed how his gaze followed it. She blotted at her neck as she stepped in close.

Standing on the floor instead of the treadmill, he was even taller than she thought. She had to crane her neck back to look at him. He had that same confused scowl on his face.

"You know," she said. "Exercise?"

Nothing.

She gestured to his physique. "How do you stay in such great shape?"

"Now is not the time for questions," he said.

Eyeing him up and down, she made her voice breathy as she said, "Then I guess you can leave it to my imagination."

His gaze snapped back to hers and his lips thinned as he pressed them together. She turned and headed for the locker room, grinning as he fell in step behind her.

"We must leave at once," he said.

"Not until I shower." She pulled out her earbuds and tucked them into the back pocket of her workout shorts next to her phone.

"This *shower* can not be more important than your safety. The longer we delay, the more opportunities our enemies will have to attack."

He sounded like one of Brendan's cosplaying friends. For a moment, she wondered if the whole thing was an elaborate charade.

"If this is Brendan playing a practical joke on me, I'm going to kick his ass when I see him."

"That is outside the scope of my orders."

She rolled her eyes and pushed open the door to the women's locker room. Khel followed her in.

"Um, Khel?"

"Yes?"

He stopped when she did, glancing around the room. If this *was* a joke, he was taking it pretty seriously. He also didn't seem disturbed at all at being in a women's locker room.

"You're not supposed to be in here," she said.

"I go where you go."

He fixed his gaze on her, clear blue eyes boring through her. She decided to have a little fun.

"Okay."

She gripped the bottom of her sports bra—the only top

she wore while working out—and pulled it over her head, smirking. His gaze flicked to her chest, then back to her face. He didn't even look like he was *trying* not to look. She wasn't used to men ignoring her body. She worked hard to be attractive. It helped her self-esteem and prevented her from having to endure lonely nights when she felt like a little company. She was *stacked* and never had trouble finding men who considered the red hair and blue eyes a bonus.

Khel didn't flinch, didn't twitch, didn't alter his expression or body language one iota. He just stared at her. At her *face*.

"Proceed," he said.

Wow. That pinged her ego. She turned around and walked to her locker.

Whatever. He wasn't into her. It had happened before and would happen again. She had to admit she was disappointed, though. He was gorgeous and it had been a while since she'd indulged in a carnal weekend with anyone.

She finished stripping and threw her workout clothes into a bag, then grabbed her toiletries and slid on some flip-flops. Khel stood at the end of the row of lockers, looking left and right. Good thing the locker room was empty.

As she walked past him to the showers, he started after her. The thought of him watching her shower with that cold stare set her teeth on edge.

"Not so fast." She turned around and planted a hand on his chest.

Heat and warmth flooded into her. His chest was rock-hard, and damn, those shoulders. She could grab onto them and do all sorts of things...

Khel sucked in a huge breath and held it. Okay. That was a response. But she wasn't into mixed signals. She pulled her hand away.

"This is as far as you go," she said.

"I am ordered to see to your safety."

"I don't care what my brother says."

He bristled. "I don't take orders from a...Brendan."

A Brendan?

She finished his original sentence in her head. *He doesn't take orders from a civilian.*

Shit. Khel was military, but not 'ex'. Brendan had told her he was taking a break from his projects. He must have been pulled back in—and somehow she was swept up with it.

Yes, technically they both worked for the government, and yes, she had received a certain level of clearance based on whatever the hell he was working on. But she had her own life, her own job, her own cause.

She would not be controlled.

Chapter Two

"I don't know who you work for, but you can tell them to go straight to hell."

This Earthling was infuriating. Khel had told her she was in danger and the first thing she had done was strip naked.

His mental programming session for going planetside on Earth had been necessarily brief. It had given him access to several languages and basic cultural functions. He must be misunderstanding the term *shower*. It was impossible that she saw cleansing her body as more important than her safety.

She turned around and walked into a room covered in small square tiles. He followed her. At least here there were fewer ambush points. She walked up to a wall with several protruding knobs, hoses, and small hooks. She hung the bag she had taken from her locker near two of the knobs, then turned them.

Water poured out from the hose above her. Her breath hitched, and she made some adjustments, then let out a sigh.

The extravagance of it... Potable water used to cleanse

their bodies? He hadn't actually believed the programming until he saw this. So many planets struggled to generate enough water to sustain life. Earthlings *bathed* in it.

As a soldier for the Coalition of planets, Khel had access to technology that made things like showers unnecessary. Between the cleansing properties of his uniform and the regen bed where he slept, his body was maintained for him. He only needed to remove his uniform for eliminations. The genetic engineers who created Sadirians hadn't been able to craft a more civilized way to deal with those bodily functions. Yet.

Paige turned to face him, a grimace pulling the edges of her lips. Leaning back, she let the water pour over her head. The bright copper of her hair changed color, darkening to a burgundy-laced brown.

She pulled a tube from her bag hanging on the wall and squeezed out a semi-liquid substance. Lifting her hands to her head, she worked the gel into her hair, creating a thick lather. She leaned her head back again, letting the water pour over her, rinsing her clean.

Her eyes were almost Sadirian in their size and shape. The similarities ended there. Her nose was short and pert, her lips full, and her cheekbones muted. The bright color to her hair was nearly identical to a shade that was popular in quadrant seven, but that style was completed with gold eyes and bronzed skin. Paige's skin was even paler than his and her eyes were a slightly darker blue.

The Department of Homeworld Security Omnibus 1

Sadirians were strong, but their muscles tended to not show through their skin. His people appeared smooth. Their arms and legs barely had variance in shape, straight lines preferred aesthetically. The same held true for their torsos.

Khel was different. He was a glitch.

Tall didn't begin to describe him. He was monstrously huge, his body reacting with the regen bed that stimulated his muscles during sleep cycles to turn him into a gargantuan specimen. The genetic engineers who created him had studied his body for years after he reached maturity before letting him begin his life as a soldier, trying to figure out where they had gone wrong.

Even without the muscles, his bone structure made him useless. Space stations and ships were often small and used every inch effectively. The *Arbiter* was one of the few ships in the fleet that had mechanical tunnels large enough for him to squeeze through.

Paige was small and compact. She could easily fit through those tight places. She was as short as a standard Sadirian, but her body seemed composed entirely of curves. Her waist was narrow and her hips broad. Her legs were heavily muscled, as was the rest of her. And her breasts were larger than any he had ever seen. He had a bizarre urge to heft them and feel their weight in his hands. They appeared soft.

She pulled another tube from her bag and squeezed out

243

more gelatinous matter. She put her hands to her breasts, massaging them as she created more lather. Trails of suds ran down her stomach, catching in the fine curls between her legs.

Something shifted in him. Heat was gathering low in his abdomen. Blood was pooling in his penis.

"For someone in such a hurry a minute ago, you sure are getting off on watching me shower." She ran her hands along her arms.

"Getting off of what?"

Turning, she massaged the lather into the supple skin of her buttocks. He wanted to touch her hips, to hold them firmly, pull her up against him—

Cygnus X, why would that even occur to him? The thought made the tightening in his penis worse, his jeans chafing. He took several deep breaths, trying to will his body to calm. It had worked the few times his body had reacted to other Sadirians.

It wasn't working with this Earthling.

She turned back to face him, letting the water pour over her shoulders. Her grimace had turned to a grin. Her hands traced the water's path down her stomach toward...

"Look out!" she yelled.

His gaze snapped back to her face. Her eyes were wide as she stared at something above him. He leapt out of the way just before a Tau Ceti dropped to the floor with a loud clang.

Cybernetic enhancements. Of course.

It looked like an average human male—light brown hair falling over its face and dressed in Earth clothing. The Tau Ceti truly were doing their best to fit in as they invaded the planet.

Khel didn't waste a moment. He lashed out with a kick that should have caught the Tau Ceti in the ribs. The strike didn't connect. The cyborg was too quick. Khel swung his fist, feinting to one side to draw it closer. He managed to land a blow to the side of its head. Better.

Before he could follow up, Paige leapt onto the cyborg's back. She wrapped her legs around its ribs and one arm around its neck. It reached toward her to pull her off, giving Khel the opening he needed.

He punched the Tau Ceti with all his strength, catching it in its side just below its armpit. The cyborg screeched as the nerve cluster undoubtedly sent waves of pain through its body. A follow-up strike should take it down.

Paige wasn't done with it, though. She had one of those tubes in her hand and squeezed its contents into the Tau Ceti's eyes before Khel could attack again.

The noise it made was horrifying. It clawed at its face, jerking from side to side trying to shake Paige loose. Moons, what kind of chemicals did humans use to clean themselves that were so easily weaponized?

Khel maneuvered behind the Tau Ceti, then grabbed Paige and pulled her off. The cyborg turned toward them briefly and hissed, revealing the set of long, sharp canines that grew from the roof of its mouth, normally hidden behind its regular teeth. It leapt over their heads, landing— and sticking—on the wall before scurrying around a corner. Khel doubted it would attack again immediately.

"What *the fuck* was that?" Paige yelled.

"An enemy. We must leave."

"No shit."

He followed as she ran to her locker.

"I want answers, Khel."

"I can explain once we've reached safety."

"Not going to work for me. Talk as I dress." She began quickly drying her body.

Her brother had been clear in his instructions. *Don't tell Paige about aliens until they reached Khel's ship.* Without proof, Brendan was convinced his sister would ignore their warning and refuse to leave. Khel hoped the Tau Ceti's attack was proof enough.

"Our attacker is from Tau Ceti," Khel said.

Paige shimmied into a pair of jeans, then pulled a dark green T-shirt over her head. "Tau Ceti, as in the star? You're saying that guy was an alien."

"Yes. And it has undoubtedly reported our location to others of its kind."

"*It?*"

"A cyborg."

"Great. A saber-toothed cyborg gecko." Her hair

dripped on the floor as she pulled on her socks and slipped her feet into a pair of shoes.

"Frog." When she glanced up at him, Khel said, "Your brother has been referring to them as *vampire space frogs.*"

She snorted and shook her head. "Sounds like Brendan."

She stood and pulled her hair back from her face, securing it with an elastic band. She stuffed everything into her backpack and closed the locker door. "And what are you?"

"I am Sadirian."

"This is so messed up." She swung her backpack over her shoulder and headed for the exit.

She didn't say anything until they were outside of the gym, the sun shining down on them and the air thick with moisture. The bright light would hinder the Tau Ceti's ability to see. Their eyes were too delicate for ocular implants and their homeworld existed in perpetual twilight.

"My apartment isn't far," she said.

She started past him, but he moved to block her way.

"That's the first place they'll look. We need to get to my ship. We'll be safe there."

"As in spaceship?" She rolled her eyes again. "Brendan must be beside himself with joy. Is that where he is now?"

"He's on the *Arbiter*. It's in orbit currently. My vessel is a smaller scouting ship. It can take us there."

"I'm not leaving the planet with you," she said. "This is insane! I can't believe I even just said that."

He grabbed her elbow, but stopped himself from urging her to walk. The look in her eyes promised violence. He couldn't refrain from admiring her confidence.

"Listen closely, Paige. The Tau Ceti want you. Not dead, but alive. Otherwise, we would both be vapor by now. And *you do not want them to capture you.* Trust me on that point, if nothing else."

She fidgeted, pressing her lips together. When she stilled, she was closer to him. He wasn't sure she was even aware of it, but *he* was. And of the softness of her skin beneath his hand.

"Why me?" Her voice was small. For the first time, she looked afraid.

He stepped closer, gripping her other elbow. If the Tau Ceti came back, he would be able to shield her better. And the proximity…was pleasant.

"Brendan believes your work is somehow threatening their plan for Earth. We've already lost a listening station over this, and they were willing to shoot down one of your planes."

"Wait… What?" Her eyes filled with tears. "What plane?"

He didn't want her to break down. They were conspicuous enough, standing still on the sidewalk as others passed them by. But he had already seen how intractable she could be.

"Senator Conroy's plane. That's how we knew that you were a target—and probably why they want you alive. As the only remaining human who worked with him in this area, they'll want to determine what you know and who you've spoken to about it."

Paige blew out her breath forcefully, and the tears he'd been preparing himself for vanished along with any sign of her fear. A muscle along her cheek twitched. The look he had taken as threatening before was nothing compared to this.

Murderous rage. If he gave her a disintegrator, he had no doubt she would use it. And the way she had attacked the cyborg, completely naked and armed with nothing more than soap...

She smacked his hands away, then grabbed *his* elbow, pulling him in step beside her.

"Where are we going?" he asked.

"We're going to my office to find out what these bastards are really after. They can't want me specifically. I don't have the clearance to be a threat to anyone. Jim—the senator—was the one with power. Like you said, what I have is knowledge. And copies of that knowledge are where I work."

"My orders are to protect you and bring you safely to the *Arbiter*."

"From what you've told me, my entire planet is in danger. How am I supposed to ignore that?"

She was putting the safety of her planet before herself. Admirable, especially considering Brendan had informed Khel that she had never received formal training or indoctrination related to protecting herself or others. She would make a fine soldier for the Coalition, if she could learn to follow orders.

It was all the more impressive that her personal choice was to risk herself to help others. And fearlessly—without the aid of chemicals to control her emotions.

What must it be like to take action based on one's own choices rather than orders or conditioning?

Khel followed his training, but didn't rely on the Coalition drugs *Balance* or *Coupling* to maintain emotional and mental equilibrium. His work aboard the *Arbiter* kept him satisfied. Work that was about to change radically.

The plan General Serath—Adam—had laid out before Khel left on his mission plagued him. Convincing the Coalition to stop using *Balance* to keep the population peaceful—giving citizens more autonomy—would cause widespread chaos throughout the galaxy.

Khel had no illusions about the violence and suffering that would result as septillions of sentients learned how to interact on their own. He understood there was corruption within the Coalition, but wasn't sure he was ready to assist with such upheaval. Surely there was another way.

His thoughts were interrupted as a large transport approached them. Paige waved at it, walking toward the street. The vehicle stopped next to them and a set of doors opened with a pneumatic whoosh. She stepped aboard and turned back to him.

"I'm going," she said. "You can come along or not. The choice is yours."

He hesitated briefly before following.

Chapter Three

Paige led Khel to the back of the bus and sat near the window. He filled the space at her side, his sheer size a comforting presence. It would be hard for any "Tau Ceti" to see her past Khel, let alone attack her.

Space frogs. *Cyborg* space frogs.

She had to be dreaming. That would explain Khel too, with his delicious physique and intriguing mix of hot-and-cold reactions to her. Stripping hadn't seemed to register with him at all. But showering in front of him…

He had watched her like he wanted to devour her. Before the stupid space frog attacked, she was getting ready to invite him to dinner.

Space frogs. *Killer* space frogs.

She shook her head, as if that would help her process things. No matter how much she wanted to not-believe, she couldn't discount the evidence of her own senses. She had seen that man cling to the tile of the locker room walls with nothing but his hands and feet. She had felt the mix of steel and flesh when she attacked him. She had seen his menacing fangs.

These aliens had crashed Jim's plane on purpose. If she

hadn't volunteered to help out with a colleague's cleanup site—which turned out to be much more involved than she was led to believe—she would have been on that plane with him. And now the Tau Ceti wanted her—alive.

She shivered at what Khel had implied earlier. Brendan wasn't the only scifi fan in the family. She had seen plenty of movies that gave her horrifying possibilities of what capture might entail. She had also seen tons of movies that showed what might happen to the planet after aliens invaded.

Not on her watch.

"I'm the project lead." She wiped at her eyes and sniffed. "And I'm between interns at the moment. Jim and I—the senator—we were talking about bringing in more full-time staff. I've been buried in paperwork for the past few weeks, trying to figure out how to bring my new team up to speed as quickly as possible with the resources I was supposed to get."

She snorted and shook her head. No team. No champion. It was just her and Khel. She reached over and put her hand on the fist he was resting on his thigh.

"What are you doing?" he asked.

"Trying to hold your hand."

He stared down at her with those cold blue eyes. She had seen the fire in them, white-hot. He would probably be amazing in bed—if he could let go of some of his repression. She pried open his fist, then interlaced their fingers and set their hands back on his leg.

"What is the significance of this?" he asked.

"Reassurance, closeness... Don't you *Sadirians* seek physical comfort from each other?"

"Our culture is different. We have moved beyond the need to obey our base instincts."

"Base instincts?" She snorted again. "That's just sad. No hugging? Kissing?"

His lips pulled into a thin line as he looked over the people on the bus again.

"No sex?"

He glanced over to her, then turned away. "Some Sadirians still seek physical pairing. Most are content to use *Coupling*."

"What's that?"

"A drug that takes the body through the stages of arousal to culmination. It's generally used alone, but some Sadirians prefer to use it with a partner."

"You only have sex while you're on drugs?"

He glared at her. "I don't use *Coupling*."

"Okay. You just made it sound like people only have sex if they're on it."

"That's correct."

"So wait... You've never... I mean..."

She couldn't even say it. It was so outlandish. This amazingly hot guy—with a body she'd love to turn into a carnal carnival—had never had sex. Even with himself.

She shook her head. "Seems like a waste of natural resources to me."

His scowl deepened.

He lifted their entwined hands and said, "Is this meeting your need?"

"What need?"

"For physical comfort."

He turned back toward the other passengers. She followed his gaze to a young couple snuggling a few seats ahead.

She was tempted to ask for more, but that would be taking advantage. Instead she said, "I'm fine."

He extricated his hand and put his arm over her shoulders. He pulled her tight against his side, surprising her with the gentleness of the gesture. For someone who wasn't used to touch, he was a pretty good side-hugger.

"Is this better?" he asked.

"Yeah. Much."

He was sitting perfectly straight. His muscles were rigid against her. Did he even know how to relax?

That was a question for another time.

"Now I understand why you were so comfortable with me getting naked," she said.

"On stations and ships, citizens and soldiers alike live in close proximity. Viewing each other's bodies is a common occurrence."

"On my planet, nudity often precedes sex. We take it a

bit more seriously."

"Noted. I'll be sure to update our base-line cultural overview to that effect."

She nestled against him, resting her hand on his thigh. He sucked in a breath and held it. Poor guy. Touch was obviously something he wasn't comfortable with. But he was doing it to help her feel better.

"Thanks," she said.

"I am merely performing my duty."

"I seriously doubt snuggling was part of your orders."

"*Snuggling.* No." He glanced at her briefly before returning to his continual survey of their surroundings.

"Tell me more about the Tau Ceti. What do they want with Earth?"

"They want something from Earthlings."

"I'm guessing this isn't an *Earth Girls are Easy* kind of situation based on what happened in the locker room."

"I don't understand."

"It's a movie about aliens who come to Earth basically looking for sex."

He let out a brief snort. So, he was capable of finding things amusing. Very good.

"Don't knock it till you've tried it," she said.

He stared at her for several long moments. She held his gaze, letting herself smirk as she cocked an eyebrow at him. If he was interested in experimenting...

"They're siphoning off hormones humans generate

when they're happy," he said.

Well, that killed the moment.

She remembered the sharp fangs in the Tau Ceti from the locker room and Brendan's nickname for the aliens. *Vampire* space frogs. A chill ran down her spine. She turned away and looked out the window as she pulled herself together.

Shit. This was real. And these things were feeding on people.

"When they...collect...what does it do to the person?"

"We aren't sure. We can only guess it disrupts the Earthling's body chemistry, leading to sadness or depression."

Great. As if there wasn't enough of that in the world already.

She took a deep breath and blew it out through pursed lips. "I still don't see how I'm involved."

"The Tau Ceti have set up at least one base of operations on Earth. We were able to intercept a record of some samples you took that match the ecosystem on Tau Ceti 6—their homeworld."

"How different from Earth's natural ecosystems are we talking?"

"Different enough. Tau Ceti 6 is warmer than Earth and covered in dense foliage and moisture. It's similar to an equatorial swamp on Earth, but there are key chemicals the Tau Ceti need to thrive. Those chemicals are not harmonious to indigenous lifeforms."

"You've got to be kidding me."

It was bad enough that she had to protect the Earth from humans, but now she had to fight to get vampire space frogs to stop messing up the environment, too?

"Where were the samples taken?" she asked.

"We weren't able to determine that."

"Well, then, let's see if we can figure it out."

The bus pulled up to the curb near the office building where she worked. She and Khel stood and made their way back out into the sweltering day. As the bus pulled away from them, she glanced around. It was creepy thinking that any of the people walking by could actually be aliens.

"Is this what you really look like?" she asked.

"What do you mean?"

"You look like an Earthling. Is it a disguise?"

"No, this is how I was made."

"Made?"

His lips thinned again. "Sadirians are genetically engineered."

"Oh wow. Please tell me everyone looks like you where you're from."

"They don't." The words were clipped and he was glaring at her again.

"Okay. Sensitive topic."

She headed toward her office building and he followed.

Somehow, she had to get Khel past Harry, the security guard at the front desk. Since barely anyone used the building on weekends, Harry was always the only one on duty. Budget restrictions.

The building didn't house anything that was deemed classified, so a single guard paid for by the building's management worked for everyone. Her group of environmental scientists had one floor, and the others were occupied by various businesses.

Nobody on Earth thought her work was important. She couldn't believe people from outer space were so interested.

"The process isn't infallible," Khel said.

He spoke so abruptly that she had trouble tracking him at first.

"What process?"

"Genetic engineering. Mistakes are made."

"Is that what happened with the Tau Ceti?"

They looked like the same species to her. Hell, all the aliens looked like humans, until they started to do things like stick to walls.

"No, the Tau Ceti are a different species entirely. Their engineers have been highly successful in crafting individuals who appear Sadirian. The Tau Ceti who attacked you looks much more Sadirian than I."

"Seriously?"

"I'm considered an unsuccessful specimen."

She laughed at that. Hard and long.

"I'm sorry," she said. "You're serious? You realize on Earth you're considered absolutely gorgeous, right?"

His scowl deepened.

"I'm not teasing. You could have your pick of partners." Hell, he could have her in a heartbeat. "That's not why you haven't experienced *Coupling*, is it?"

She wanted to know why this was such a sensitive subject for him. The thought of him being rejected because of how he looked was baffling and tragic. His society must have really different standards of beauty.

"I've had opportunities. The *Arbiter* is populated entirely by glitches like myself."

And there it was—the real reason it was an issue for him. A label conveniently marking him and others like him as being of less value. *Glitches*.

"I don't like that word," she said.

He paused briefly. "Neither do I."

She reached out and held his hand, smiling when he looked down at her. He smiled back. It was over so fast, she thought she might have imagined it. She hoped she hadn't.

Chapter Four

Bypassing the security guard was a disturbingly simple matter. He appeared to be sleeping when they arrived. They managed to slip past him unnoticed. If one of Khel's soldiers had been caught sleeping on duty...

He wasn't certain what the penalty would be. It had never happened before.

Earthlings certainly seemed to be relaxed about many things. Like Paige with her constant touches and talk of *Coupling*—sex. Trapped in a small lift with her, she once again turned to her favorite line of inquiry.

"Does *Coupling* enhance sex for the people who use it?"

"I don't know," he said.

"Right. Sorry. But you've never been curious? Even when you had those opportunities you mentioned?"

He had never been curious. At least, not aboard the *Arbiter*. But the skin of his thigh still tingled from her touch, his penis remaining half-engorged since the moment they had met, it seemed. Holding her against his side had felt peaceful, even while it set parts of him stirring. Khel was bewildered by the effect she was having on him—physically, mentally, and emotionally.

Primarily physically.

"Do you ever think about anything but sex?" he asked.

"Of course I do. But sex is one of my best coping mechanisms for stress, and in case you hadn't noticed, this is a pretty stressful situation. Plus I've read way too many books with elevator sex scenes. Even without our earlier conversation, riding in an elevator with a guy like you would have me thinking through scenarios."

A guy like him? His cheeks heated, a strange prickling sensation spreading over his skin.

How would someone go about having sex in an elevator? He was too tall to lay prone on the floor. If she took off her jeans, she could wrap her legs around his waist and he could hold her in place by pinning her to the wall...

Where in the name of the Solar Cross had that thought come from? His penis stiffened further and he shifted his weight to try to be more comfortable. Her gaze slid down his body, and she smirked at him again.

Infuriating. Exasperating.

What if she held onto the railing while he took her from behind...

A bell sounded.

"This is where we get off." She grinned and waggled her eyebrows up and down. It was strangely comical, and he laughed.

Laughing. He had done it with his comrades, of course, during late nights of games and after their many victories. This one was different. Smaller, yet deeper. It made his chest feel less heavy.

He needed to focus.

Paige threaded her hand through his arm, locking their elbows, and leaned into his side. "Let's go."

The doors opened and she led him onto a semi-lit level of the building. The dim environment would be perfect for Tau Ceti vision. He pulled himself more to attention.

"My office is this way."

He followed her to a small room lined with tables and a desk. Every horizontal surface was covered with papers. She dropped her bag on the floor.

"What is this?" he asked.

"My filing system."

"This isn't a system. This is chaos."

"Carefully contained chaos. Have a seat."

She spun her chair toward him. Khel doubted he would fit.

"I prefer to stand guard at the door."

"I don't know what I'm looking for. I need you to go over this data with me." She patted the back of the chair. Reluctantly, he scrunched himself into the seat. She leaned over his shoulder and whispered in his ear. "That wasn't so bad, was it?"

Sitting in the chair, no. Her warm breath on his neck

was another matter. He shifted in his seat again. She patted his shoulder and grinned at him.

She started to go through papers, setting stacks in front of him. "These are the most recent topographic maps. Aerial photos from the last few years. I've been focusing on the impact of climate change on nearby wetlands."

"Is any of this data available digitally?"

She shook her head. "I know it's ironic, but we haven't had funding to upgrade our systems and still rely way too much on paper. We recycle everything, at least. My interns were supposed to scan these into the computers eventually, but we were always too busy getting out in the field and collecting samples, running tests… I figured I'd get around to entering it all in the system eventually."

Khel nodded. "Then the Tau Ceti have no idea how much you know. They could easily hack your computer systems, but since you only have hard copies, they'll have to come here. They'll want to know what you've figured out."

"I haven't figured out anything. But we're going to change that."

She turned around and bent over her desk to reach some papers that were stacked on the very back corner. Her jeans hugged the curves of her backside. He was already reaching for her hips when she straightened. He quickly diverted to the papers in front of him instead. She didn't seem to have noticed. Leaning against the desk, she pulled one side of her lower lip between her teeth and started to read.

Putting his attention into their work was an excellent idea. Maybe it could push the thoughts of her out of his mind. Time passed where the only sound in the room was the rustling of paper.

What was happening to him? His thoughts kept straying back to her.

She was holding up remarkably well. He still couldn't believe she had attacked a Tau Ceti soldier. One with cybernetic enhancements. True, she hadn't known what she was fighting, but she refused to let Khel face the threat alone—even though she was naked.

Paige naked.

Their conversation had made him start to think, to question ways he had perceived the world and himself. His place in it, how he interacted with others.

He had been approached before by Sadirians interested in using *Coupling* with him. He had never been tempted in the least. The idea had frankly been off-putting. But thinking of Paige, with her soft curves and steel will—

"I think I found something."

She placed a map in front of him, then turned around and sat in his lap. He let out a grunt.

"I'm not that heavy," she said. "Sheesh."

Her attention was on the sheets of paper in her hands, which was good. His grunt hadn't been about her weight.

She was sitting snug up against his erection, that beautiful backside pressing against him. Every time she moved even an iota, he felt it reverberate through his entire body.

"Are you okay? You sound like you're about to hyperventilate." She looked at him over her shoulder. "Oh sorry. I forgot you don't like to touch."

She started to stand, but he grabbed her hips to hold her in place.

"It's okay," he grated. He stopped himself from adding, *I want more.*

The concern on her face slowly softened into something else. A slight smile, not quite the smirk she'd been taunting him with since they met. She cleared her throat and turned back to her papers, holding a bit more still, thank the stars.

"These are the numbers from the testing we did last year in some swampland we're watching closely." She held up another sheet of paper next to it. "These are the numbers from this year. I don't know how much of this you understand, but I can tell you this is really weird."

He didn't need her to explain. He could see for himself. The numbers matched the samples that Brendan and Kira had told Adam about.

"These are the samples we're looking for," Khel said. "Where did you find them?"

The look on her face was not encouraging. She set aside the papers and started pointing at the map she had placed in front of him.

"The results are the same for samples we gathered here, here, here…"

She pointed at various spots on the map. Over and over again, the range covering a staggering amount of territory.

Khel leaned forward. Without even thinking about it, he wrapped one arm around her waist to keep her steady.

The geography of the area was filled with swamp dotted by small lakes. All connected through the same waterways. He shook his head.

"This isn't a base," he said. "This is a breeding ground. The Tau Ceti are creating spawning pools."

Chapter Five

Paige didn't need Khel to tell her how bad that was. She was very aware of how destructive it could be when an invasive species was introduced. The Tau Ceti were working to gain a foothold on Earth and she had no idea how to stop them.

"We must get this information to Adam," Khel said.

"Who's that?"

"My commanding officer. Measures will be taken."

She felt the faintest glimmer of relief. It was quickly overshadowed by her experience and knowledge. Introducing another species to take out an already invading species...

"I know you're working with Brendan and that makes me trust you—partly. But I have to ask, Khel. Are you the good guys? Will you really help Earth, or are you just making room for your own people to come in and exploit our planet?"

He stared at her intently. Then he looked away. Not a good sign.

"The Coalition has designated Earth as a preserved planet. It's supposed to be protected."

"*Supposed* to be?"

"We've discovered some issues recently."

"Like vampire space frog issues?"

"Possibly worse."

Great.

"What are we going to do about it?" she asked.

Somehow, Khel didn't feel like a bodyguard. He felt like a partner. Maybe because he was actually listening to her instead of trying to control her.

"To begin, get you to my ship," he said. "Adam will need the information we've discovered to create the best course of action."

Khel rose, lifting her from his lap. He stood close, resting his hands on her arms.

"What about Earth authorities? Don't you have a secret connection to our government leaders or something?"

"That would be a very bad idea."

"This is *our* planet. We need to be able to help decide how to protect it."

"Earth isn't ready."

So much for being partners. She pulled away from him. "Why do you get to decide that?"

"Because we've seen what happens when planets as rich in resources as Earth are given a seat at the Coalition table too soon. The leaders want access to technology, and they arrange trade after trade until their planet is as barren and stripped as all the others in the Coalition."

"Then help us. Educate us. Limit us, when necessary, but at least give us a voice."

"You sound just like your brother."

She rolled her eyes.

"It's already happening, Paige. Brendan and Adam are setting it up. Not necessarily with government leaders, but we're starting to approach individuals that we think can handle it. It's early, but we're forming a First Contact council for Earth."

"Oh. Well…good."

"Brendan wants you on it to represent environmental issues."

She snorted. Yeah, right. Paige Sloan in charge of helping aliens make sure nobody messed up the Earth. Maybe even teaching them how to manage resources on the other planets in their "Coalition" and restore the environments they had stripped bare.

Wait…

"Seriously?"

A thrill of excitement shot through her. All she had ever wanted to do was protect Earth. Now she knew that there were threats to her homeworld beyond her imaginings, other planets that needed healing—and she might be able to help.

"It will only happen if we survive," Khel said. "Come on."

He opened the door to her office a crack and peered

out, then closed it again.

Paige almost bounced off his back. "I thought we were leaving."

"The guard is patrolling."

Crap.

"I didn't know he even did that."

She glanced around the small space, looking for a place to hide. Having the furniture pressed against the walls helped prevent avalanches from all the reports she had to process, but it didn't make for good hiding places. Why hadn't management stopped with all the printouts already? They were supposed to be environmentalists, for crying out loud.

"He'll be here in moments," Khel said. "I can incapacitate him."

"Absolutely not!"

Khel stared at her expectantly. She didn't know what to do. She worked plenty of Saturdays and could easily explain away her presence. Harry would probably even believe that she had forgotten to sign in. But Khel wasn't authorized to be in the building. As laid back as Harry was, he'd have to call it in.

Paige grabbed Khel by his arms and swung him around till he was standing in front of her chair. Then she pressed on his shoulders. He sat and stared at her expectantly.

Here goes nothing.

She knelt on his lap, then grabbed the back of his neck

and pulled him to her for a kiss. At least, that was the plan. He was too quick for her and angled his head away.

"What are you doing?" he asked.

"Coming up with an excuse for why you're in my office. We don't have time to explain to Harry why you're here and you don't have clearance."

"Harry?"

"The guard. If we can convince him we snuck in for a little office nookie, he'll leave us alone."

"I highly doubt—"

She pressed a finger to his lips, then ran it over their satin surface. "This is Earth. You need to start thinking like an Earthling."

His gaze bored into her, but then he grabbed her face with his strong hands, pulling her down to him. His lips brushed hers stiffly at first, but then softened as he followed her lead.

She burrowed her fingers in his hair, nipping his lips, sucking one and then the other into her mouth. He groaned and she couldn't help but smile. His hips started to move. She slid her tongue into his mouth and he froze for a moment. She explored him cautiously, giving him time to adjust. He didn't need long.

His tongue started to dance with hers, testing, teasing. He pulled her hair free from its ponytail holder and let it fall around her shoulders. He deepened the kiss, his lips massaging hers as his hands slid down to her hips. He leaned forward, pressing their chests together, his fingers tightening their grip.

"Ahem."

They both jumped at the sound behind them. Right, Harry. She had forgotten why they started making out in the first place.

"Harry! Hi," she said, shifting to sit in Khel's lap. His dick was pressing against her ass and she felt her eyes widen. "I…um…"

Right. The plan. She used her best *caught in the act* expression and did everything but bat her eyelashes.

"I just brought my friend by to show him my office."

"That right?" Harry said. "Forgot to sign in, though."

"About that… I sort of didn't want my boss to know I was here today *with someone*."

"Mmm-hmm."

She was actually sweating. Khel's body had gone rigid beneath her, and not just in his crotch. She could feel the coiled energy in him, waiting to spring. Harry was a nice guy just doing his job. He didn't deserve to be 'incapacitated'.

"Might want to use the conference room down the hall. More table space." Harry winked at them, then was all business again. "Make sure you check in with me at the desk before you leave."

He exited the office, pulling the door shut behind him. Paige let out a deep breath.

"I can't believe that worked. I mean, it always works in my favorite romance novels, but—"

She stopped when she turned back to Khel. He hadn't relaxed at all. He was gripping the armrests of her chair so tight—

Snap.

"Oops," she said.

He kept staring at her while he held up the broken piece of chair. She carefully peeled his fingers off of it so she could toss it on the floor under her desk. There was nowhere for him to gracefully rest his arm, so she planted his hand on her hip. He sucked in a breath and held it from the looks of things.

"What do I do?" he asked.

"I don't understand the question."

"To make it go away."

"To make... Oh."

Her eyes must be bugging out of her head. The thick mass of his erection was pressing against his jeans in what had to be a really uncomfortable position.

"Let me help you."

She undid his jeans to try to let things straighten themselves out on their own without realizing...he went commando.

Chapter Six

Paige wouldn't stop staring at his erection, which was making the situation worse. Khel felt her gaze like a caress. His penis jerked on its own in response. Why wouldn't his body obey him?

He closed his eyes and willed the erection to go away. Tried to think of anything but the softness of her lips on his, the warmth of her tongue in his mouth.

His penis twitched again.

"It won't stop," he said.

"I can see that. Wow, can I see that."

He glared at her. "What do I do?"

"Haven't you ever... Of course you haven't." She let out a sigh. "You've never even had morning wood?"

"Morning wood?"

"You know, a stiffy in the morning? Wake up at attention?"

"The regen bed I sleep in would address that. It maintains our bodies, scans and treats us for illness and disease, and stimulates our muscles to keep us fit and ready for duty."

"You're certainly ready for duty." She grinned at him.

"Paige! Help me."

"Sorry." Her expression softened. "No wonder you were confused by the gym. You guys could make a fortune selling those regen beds on Earth. Work out while you sleep."

She shifted on his lap, reminding him of the fullness of her hip in his hand. Her breasts would be infinitely softer. He tightened his grip as he tried to marshal his thoughts.

He should have followed orders to the letter and taken her to his ship any way he could. He had disobeyed, and now his body and mind were doing the same to him.

"You've really never had a hard-on for someone before?" she asked.

"I've had reactions, but was always able to control them. It never took more than a few minutes of quiet distraction."

But his reaction had never been this intense. He had never tried to calm his body while he had the taste of someone on his lips—the lingering memory of their body pressed against him fueling his reaction.

"I can't function this way," he said. "How do I make it go away?"

"Uh…" Her gaze dropped to his erection again and she licked her lips.

Adam had alluded to things that Evelyn taught him about how Earthlings coupled. Khel wondered just how creative they were in using various parts of their bodies to stimulate each other.

"You can always jerk off," Paige said.

"Idioms, Paige."

She sighed and took his hand from her hip. He reluctantly allowed it. Then she wrapped his fingers around his erection.

"What are you doing?"

"Showing you how to do it. You just grip yourself and...pump."

His hand felt awkward on his flesh. It was much better where her hand touched his. He wanted something, but he wasn't sure what. More of her touch, more of those amazing kisses. Thinking of it, he realized he had felt a pull toward her from the very beginning.

When Adam had returned to the *Arbiter* with Evelyn, Khel thought the General had lost his mind.

Things changed.

"Paige, I want..." He wasn't sure what. He didn't have words for what he felt.

She had seemed interested in him from the beginning as well, but he hadn't known how to respond. He still didn't. But he *wanted*. That was the one thing that was clear. He wanted her.

She sighed, then slid his hand away and replaced it with her own. The first touch sent currents of electric stimulation along his nerve endings. Every cell in his body seemed to be focused on her slight hand wrapped around him. She gripped him tight, then began to move.

"Paige," her name was a primal moan. The energy in his body was pooling low, centering on his shaft in her cool fingers.

"The regen beds have cured all disease among your people?" she asked.

"Yes." The word was drawn out as he closed his eyes and gasped.

"And I assume you've been inoculated against everything on Earth. With all your advanced technology."

"It was…thoroughly studied…"

"Yes or no, Khel."

She squeezed his penis tighter.

"Yes." His breath was coming faster. He heard a loud crack and realized he had torn the other armrest from her chair.

They both stared at it for a moment, then she swatted it from his hand. It clattered onto the floor. She slid from his lap, kneeling in front of him.

"What are you—"

Before he could say more, she leaned forward and wrapped her lips around his erection.

"Paige!"

Both her hands gripped him tight, sliding up and down along the length of him while she sucked and swirled her tongue over his crown. His body was thrumming with energy, his shaft a live-wire sending out arcs of sensation along his nervous system. The *wanting* increased. More of this, more of her.

The coiled energy burst forth, exploding into her mouth as she kept pumping him. Shockwaves of an ecstasy more intense than anything he had ever experienced crashed through him, keeping time with the pulsing of his penis.

Echoing tremors of pleasure rippled out from where they touched as she let him slide from her mouth. He was finally softening again. All he could do was stare at her.

"Better?" she asked.

"I... Yes."

She stood, and said, "You might want to put that away."

He was buzzing with energy, his awareness of everything heightened as he stood as well. The scent of her body, the heat, the dampness left on his penis as he slid it into his jeans and fastened them again.

She wasn't smiling.

"Something is troubling you," he said.

"I'm fine. We should go."

She was radiating tension. His body felt more relaxed than ever. Relaxed and yet alert. Ready to defend her, to see to her needs. Perhaps that was the issue. If she had felt half of what he did, her body must be aching.

"I can...see to your needs," he said. The idea would have revolted him just a few hours ago. Now he was excited, eager to experience more with her. The attraction he had felt since they first met had intensified. He wanted to kiss her again.

"No thanks. Deflowering virgins is not my thing. Especially since I was the only one around to help out."

She said the last under her breath, but his hearing was too keen to miss it.

"You think what happened between us was purely based on circumstance."

"Wasn't it?" She crossed her arms and glared at him.

Stars, that glare. He had over a foot on her and at least a hundred pounds, and she looked as if she was planning to take his head off. With the right training, he had no doubt she could.

"Partly. Not purely."

She rolled her eyes. He smiled, which earned him a look even more heated than the first. Anger, yes. But passion. So much passion.

"I have never met anyone like you," he said.

"What—someone who's willing to blow you while you destroy their favorite chair?"

"Someone who is alive."

"Please don't tell me you're all space zombies. The vampire frogs are bad enough."

He laughed, and her expression softened the slightest bit. Her hair was dry, the coppery waves framing her face and making him want to touch her again. Why not allow himself?

He lifted the ends of her hair with just his fingertips,

letting the strands fall feather-light across his skin. She didn't seem to mind.

"Zombies, no. But sleepwalkers. All of us. You have no idea what it's like being created in the Coalition. Existing among septillions of others without ever connecting."

"Well, now that you know what you're missing, maybe you can find a nice Sadirian and—"

"I don't want someone else. Others have approached me. But no one else has ever...captivated me. Since the moment we met—"

"Stop. Don't get your hopes up and don't pin dreams onto me because of what happened between us. I don't do relationships."

He swallowed hard, sensing that this moment was pivotal for them both. He stepped closer.

"I told you that I'm considered a glitch."

"And I told you I don't like that word."

"You aren't supposed to. None of us are. It's used to remind us of our place, that we don't belong with successful results."

Her lips pressed into a thin line. Stars, he wanted to kiss her again. He let himself lift his hands to her arms, savoring the warmth and softness of her skin.

"Even among others like me, I'm considered an outlier. The geneticists studied me for years to determine why I'm so different. All I have ever done is try to be a normal Sadirian—to fit in. The majority of our society use

Coupling alone. I didn't use it at all because I've always thought that if I could somehow exemplify what it means to at least *act* like a perfect Sadirian then perhaps I would gain some acceptance."

He was admitting the fact as much to himself as her. Deep down, he had always known he was searching for something. A sense of belonging, of value and worth. He had been trying to obtain it by being the perfect soldier, the perfect citizen. He had never let himself think that there might be another way.

Until Paige.

She lifted her hand to his face, trailing her cool fingers along his cheek.

"I accept you."

Her words struck him in the center of his chest. His breath rushed out as he bowed his head, trying to regain some control.

No, *composure*. Control was…overrated.

She sighed, then said, "That doesn't mean—"

Before she could finish her sentence, he leaned in and kissed her.

Chapter Seven

The stiffness and hesitancy Paige had noticed the first time she and Khel kissed was gone. He pulled her against his chest, savoring her lips before sliding his tongue between them. His hands grasped her waist, then moved down to caress her ass. He lifted her, and she wrapped her legs around his waist as he pressed her back against her door.

He was hard again. She wasn't as eager to help him with it this time.

Well, okay, physically, she was ready to tear off their clothes and let him keeping working his magic with his hands and lips. He was kneading her ass, rocking his hips against her in just the right places.

It didn't matter that he'd been genetically engineered. When it came to sex, the man was a natural.

But the other things he'd said, about connecting and finding acceptance… That was too much. She didn't want him to form attachments to her and then be disappointed.

Most of the guys she hooked up with took it for what it was. A one-time thing. They both walked away a little more relaxed and a whole lot happier. The few times guys had become clingy, she had shut them down quickly and fairly easily. She was committed to her job. She had never met someone who could match her passion.

Or had she?

The thought was unwelcome, but she followed it through anyway. Khel was as driven as she was. His worldview was in a tailspin, though. He had been dedicating himself to a society that shunned him and used him. And she *would* have something to say to his leaders when they finally made it to that ship.

As focused as he had been on that objective, he still had been able to have an open and flexible mind. He was realizing the problems with his society, *and wanted to do the work to fix them.* That was heady.

If she tried to shut Khel out, she didn't think he'd go quietly like the others. He would fight for her. She could tell. And it thrilled her down to her toes. Someone who could handle her, match her passion *and* her stubbornness.

It was terrifying.

She had only ever dated weak-willed guys. She could never admit it to herself before, but it was true. Khel was iron to match her steel. Her match.

No. No way.

She kissed him harder, trying to block out her thoughts. It was the situation, the craziness of it all. This was a false sense of connection based on danger, lust, and adrenaline.

He matched her intensity, his tongue driving into her

mouth to meet each parry. She ground her clit against him through their jeans, imagining what it would be like to have that huge dick buried deep inside of her, pulsing as he came.

He let go of her ass with one hand and slid his fingers up under her shirt. The warmth and strength of his palm soaked into her skin as he massaged her breast. He ran his thumb over her nipple, exploring the tight bud as it peaked beneath his touch.

With a grunt, he leaned back from her, unwrapping her legs from his waist so that she was standing again. Had he finished already? How disappointing.

She was a little dazed as he undid her pants and tugged her jeans down to her knees. He knelt before her, pulling her panties down as well.

"Khel..."

He looked up at her, blue eyes blazing with lust or... something stronger. He leaned forward, pressing his lips against the curls between her legs. His tongue lapped at her, sending threads of pleasure streaming through her body.

Yeah, he was a natural.

She shifted her legs as far apart as she could to give him better access. He must have taken that as an invitation, because he worked his hand between her thighs, sliding two of his fingers deep into her. Her core gripped his fingers, heightening the friction as he slid them in and out, her body sparking with each pull and thrust.

Her legs felt weak and the room was spinning. She reached up and held onto the coat hook attached to her door to try to steady herself. She wasn't sure she would ever truly feel grounded again after this.

After *him*.

His fingers moved within her, his lips sucking, pulling on her clit. He had to have done this before. There was no way he could hit all the right spots, match his movement with her need. There was no way they could fit so perfectly together.

Her body had a different opinion.

The pleasure he stoked in her built to critical mass as he slid a third finger deep, drawing on her clit more strongly, pumping her mercilessly.

Explosions of stimuli radiated out from where he worked her, pleasure racking her body. She felt her core clench around him, wanting more, wanting all of him. She wanted him to take down his pants and plunge into her. She had never wanted someone so badly.

The ecstasy kept on as he didn't let up, the room blacking out around them. Finally, he slowed and pulled away, leaving her panting, her body pulsing…

She swallowed a few times before she could say, "Are the lights off, or is it just me?"

"It isn't just you."

He stood, pulling her panties and jeans up. She fumbled

with the fasteners, then reached for him in the pitch blackness.

"It's the Tau Ceti," he said.

Chapter Eight

Khel had never hated anyone before. He was fairly certain he was feeling hatred for the Tau Ceti. They had interrupted a beautiful moment between him and Paige. They were threatening her life.

For that, if nothing else, they would die.

"We have to warn Harry," she said.

Harry? The security guard. Her concern was admirable, but Khel didn't think the Tau Ceti would bother with the Earthling. They had undoubtedly taken out the cameras when they shut down the building's power and wouldn't see the guard as a threat.

The total silence was eerie. No ventilation, no somewhat familiar hum of machinery built into the structure maintaining the environment. He had noticed the alien stillness the moment the lights went out.

Darkness would aid the Tau Ceti. He needed to get Paige back outside into the sun. He picked up her bag and handed it to her, then grabbed her other hand and led her from her office. Dim light filtered in from windows on the exterior wall.

"What about Harry?"

"He'll be fine," Khel whispered. "They're only interested in you."

"How do they even know I'm here? I mean, wouldn't they think that you'd already taken me to your ship?"

That was a good point. The Tau Ceti soldier that attacked her at the gym most likely followed her there from her apartment. But Khel doubted it had followed them to her office. It made more sense that the Tau Ceti were making a move on her workplace, trying to destroy the data she had collected without realizing they were too late. Well, too late if Paige and Khel could make it back to the *Arbiter* with what they had learned.

"We need to get outside," he said. "Is there another route besides the elevator?"

"The stairs." She pulled on his hand, leading him in a different direction. "Please tell me you have a stunner or something you can use against these guys."

"I had to leave everything behind. Coalition technology would show up too easily on their scans."

"And you brainiacs haven't found a way to address that?"

"The Coalition doesn't *want* technology to be easily hidden. We've had peace for tens of thousands of years. We aren't used to citizens...rebelling."

"It looks to me like the Tau Ceti are taking advantage of that."

They reached the door to the stairwell. Khel opened it

and glanced into the small space. Emergency lighting cast a washed out blue glow over the steps, leaving thick shadows in corners and alcoves large enough for a Tau Ceti to hide.

"I don't like the thought of being trapped in the stairwell with vampire space frogs clinging to the ceiling," she said.

"Neither do I. But I see no other options."

"Well, let's give ourselves the best chance."

She reached toward a small box on the wall near the stairs. It read, *FIRE ALARM PULL DOWN.*

"This will make a huge noise and cause lights to flash all over the building."

Brilliant. She looked at him briefly, smirking when he smiled and nodded.

"I hope it's on the same circuit as the emergency lighting so it still works." She pulled the lever.

Blazingly bright lights began flashing, accompanied by an ear-splitting alarm. The Tau Ceti were certain to be disoriented by it for a few moments.

"We need to move quickly," he said.

She nodded and followed him into the stairwell, both keeping their footsteps as light and soundless as possible. They started out on the fifth floor and managed to make it down three levels before Khel heard stomping steps coming toward them.

Paige pulled on his hand, leading him through the exit

to that level. She closed the door behind them as quietly and quickly as possible, then opened a small cabinet set into the wall. It held a red canister with a nozzle at its top. She made some adjustments to it as they waited for the Tau Ceti to get farther away—or come closer.

The doorknob turned. Khel tried to get in front of her, but she darted under his arm, holding the canister up between them and the door. The device must be some sort of weapon.

When the door opened, she only waited a moment before attacking. She pulled the trigger and vapor and a fluffy white substance sprayed from the nozzle. He could feel the cold emanating from the chemicals. It was a perfect offense against the Tau Ceti.

The cyborg screamed and flailed its arms, the substance making the ground beneath its feet slippery. Khel didn't waste the opportunity. He grabbed the Tau Ceti's disintegrator.

Footsteps were already coming toward them from above. He aimed the weapon at the blinded enemy and pulled the trigger. Death was instant and painless. Its body vaporized in a quick yellow burst of energy.

"What the hell was that? Did you just *kill* that guy?" Paige shouted.

Two other Tau Ceti appeared on the stairs above them. Khel aimed and fired again, hitting one. The other managed to duck out of sight.

Khel grabbed the canister from Paige and flung it across the hall, angling it so that it would clatter down the stairs. Hopefully, the remaining Tau Ceti would think it was them and follow the sound.

He pushed Paige back out of the line of sight and let the door close. She looked like she was about to say something, so he did the first thing that came to mind. He pressed her up against the wall and kissed her.

Stars, she tasted good. He struggled to keep his attention on his environment, listening for the one Tau Ceti that was left. Only seconds passed before the cyborg took the bait, following the sound of the canister's descent. Khel waited another second before breaking off the kiss and opening the door, aiming the disintegrator at the Tau Ceti just as it raised its own weapon and fired.

Khel's shot hit the cyborg in the chest, vaporizing it. The Tau Ceti hit the wall to Khel's left. The wall protecting Paige.

Panic, stark and piercing, shot through Khel's mind making it impossible to breathe. He couldn't turn his head toward her. If the wall hadn't been enough to protect her... If he looked and she wasn't there...

He felt her hands on him, pushing as if she was trying to knock him over. His breath rushed from his chest and his innards settled somewhat. When he looked down at her, the fury on her features made him light-headed with relief.

"You *killed* them!"

He didn't understand her anger.

"They would have done the same and worse to you."

"Couldn't you have—"

"What? Taken them into custody? There were three of them and we were unarmed until you helped me secure a weapon."

Temporarily, anyway. He needed to set it to self-destruct as soon as they were out of the building. He couldn't bring himself to part with it before then, but the only thing easier for the Tau Ceti to track than Coalition technology would be their own equipment.

"They are feeding on your people," he said. "Remember that. They killed everyone who was on the plane with Senator Conroy just to eradicate one target. What do you think they'd do to get what they want from you?"

Her rage faded, but she continued to scowl at him. "I don't like loss of life. Any life."

"Sometimes it can't be avoided. We have to make the best choices we can."

"Fine. But we're warning Harry."

He sighed, but nodded.

They ran down the stairs, careful of the slickness left by the weapon she had used. He would need to ask her about that eventually. After she was safely in his ship.

True to her word, when they reached the front exit she

tracked down the security guard. He was standing in front of the building.

"Miss Sloan! I'm so glad you and your friend are okay," he said.

Odd that he would already care about Khel's safety. And yet, it was strangely comforting.

"The fire department should be here any second," Harry said. "You were the only ones inside."

"That's great, Harry." Paige put her hand on the man's arm. "I can't be here when they arrive, but I need you to call this in. Listen, this isn't—"

A deafening boom sounded, the shockwave striking Khel's body as the windows in the top three floors of the building exploded. He threw himself on Paige to shield her from the glass that rained down around them.

"Shit!" Paige yelled. She looked above as flames licked out of the empty spaces, hungry for more oxygen to burn.

"Are you all right?" Khel grabbed her arms and shook her to get her attention. "Assess yourself."

"I'm fine," she said. "Harry?"

The guard's eyes were wide, but he nodded.

"We have to leave," Khel said.

She nodded. "Harry, whatever you do, don't go back in the building."

"I'm not an idiot. It looks like a gas main blew. We should all get away from the building in case there are more explosions."

"That's wise," Khel said. He released one of Paige's arms but held the other tight, leading her in the opposite direction. The guard seemed too stunned by the event to notice.

"They blew up the building to destroy my notes. My group was only using one floor," she said. "We were in this building because the work we're doing is considered harmless. There's a community college that sometimes has weekend classes here. Businesses, a charity."

"The Tau Ceti don't care what sort of casualties they cause as long as they aren't found out. Your authorities will find that this looks like an accident."

Her pace increased. "We need to get to the *Arbiter* and let your people know what's going on."

Finally. He knew better than to speak his thought aloud. Instead, he nodded.

Chapter Nine

Paige shifted closer to Khel as they rode the bus toward his ship. They had used her phone so he could give her a general idea of where it was located and they could find the best route to get there. He reached over and held her hand. He had disposed of the disintegrator already, trying to make sure they weren't tracked.

She didn't want to think about what he had done with it. Or that she sort of wished they had kept it with them.

"I still don't get it," she said. "Why does the Coalition want their technology to be so traceable?"

"They don't want our technology to fall into the wrong hands. It could be reverse-engineered, or used to upset the balance of power on a planet not ready for that level of advancement. That's one of the reasons I wasn't allowed to bring anything out of my ship. If I were to have an accident or an Earthling managed to get their hands on my equipment somehow, it could have catastrophic results."

She snorted, a joke coming out reflexively. "I managed to get my hands on your equipment, and I'd say things went rather well."

His face turned pink. "I haven't had a chance to thank

you for that. I appreciate your help."

"Yeah, they all do." She looked away, not wanting to ask her next question, but being unable to stop herself. "Is that why you reciprocated? To balance out the scales?"

"Of course not." He squeezed her hand a little tighter. "I did it because...I wanted to share that with you."

"Curiosity."

"Intimacy. I told you, I could have explored...physical interactions many times. I chose to do so with you."

Lucky me.

She might have been his first, but she doubted she would be his last. The amount of passion he had shown wasn't something he could put a lid back on. Hell, he'd probably go back to his ship and start a new trend of sex without that drug.

The thought of her lovers going on to other partners had never bothered her before. She wasn't sure why it would do so now. It wasn't like she could leave Earth to be with Khel or he could stay. She wasn't even sure she wanted that. Right?

And they weren't even lovers yet. Not really.

Yet.

"How far to your ship?" She kept her face turned toward the window.

"Not very. It's attached to the bottom of one of your highways in a section of the city that is sparsely inhabited."

"It's on the underside of an overpass in a crappy section of town. Fun." At least it was the middle of the day.

Had she really only met Khel a couple of hours ago? It seemed like so much longer. Being attacked by space frogs, having some pretty serious foreplay, and watching a building basically blow up made the time seem to dilate. That and the three people he had killed.

One had almost killed her. She would never forget seeing the wall in front of her just disappear, the Tau Ceti pointing his ray gun at her. Either he had been panicking or capturing her alive wasn't that important after all. Neither thought was reassuring.

They had killed Senator Conroy and everyone else on the plane with him. She would have died then, if it hadn't been for her micro-managing nature that kept her out in the field making sure the cleanup crew had accomplished their goals. There were always more samples to study, like the ones she had thought were off—contaminated somehow. Now she knew they weren't. The Tau Ceti were destroying Earth's ecosystems and *feeding* on humans.

She still couldn't wrap herself around the notion of killing them, though.

"When you tell your people what's going on here, are they going to kill all the Tau Ceti involved?" she asked.

"Only if necessary. The objective will be to take them into custody and send them through our tribunal process."

"That's nice I guess. How will you apprehend them?"

"Sorca, the head of security on the *Arbiter*, will come down with several teams on interceptors. They'll be armed with stunners. Her people will only use lethal force if necessary to defend themselves and others."

Paige let out a little breath of relief. "Do you have any of those 'stunners' on your ship?"

"I have two, plus a phase rifle. I was sent in a skimmer. It's a small ship with only the most basic levels of technology possible, designed for quick expeditions. I was supposed to pick you up and take you to the *Arbiter* before the Tau Ceti knew I was planetside."

"Guess I screwed that up."

"Our detour provided us with invaluable information."

"Only if we live long enough to share it."

He gently touched her cheek, turning her to face him. "We're going to make it, Paige. I won't let anything happen to you."

Then he leaned forward and kissed her again.

Heat welled up deep within her instantly. He left his hand on her cheek, his thumb lightly dusting her skin. She opened her mouth to him as his tongue slid inside, stroking her, savoring her, exploring the sensations.

She shifted closer to let as much of their bodies press together as she could manage. His free arm held her tight. She wanted to crawl into his lap and straddle him, but that would call more attention to them than was wise. At least, while they were on the bus. Once they reached his ship, everything was fair game.

"Hey, kissyfaces back there. Didn't you say you need me to stop at Third Avenue and Grand? That's coming up, and I ain't sticking around longer than it takes you to jump off the bus."

They broke off the kiss, both glaring at the driver. He glanced at them in the mirror and shook his head. A few other passengers were looking their way, grinning or scowling. Paige might have said something if the circumstances were different. As they were, she let it slide.

The bus pulled to the curb and she and Khel quickly made their way to the exit. She really hoped they had the location right. Even with his intimidating presence, she didn't want to be walking around in this neighborhood for long.

"This way." He interlaced their fingers and headed down the littered sidewalk.

His ship wasn't far, and the few people they encountered seemed put off enough by Khel's bulk to leave them alone. He led her through a torn up chain link fence toward the cement pillars that held up an overpass. Traffic whizzed by above them.

"The cloak will disengage automatically when we're close enough," he said. "I couldn't leave the ship on the ground without running the risk of someone bumping into it within the city."

"How are we going to get into it?"

He smiled down at her and her heart sort of skipped a bit.

How embarrassing.

"You'll see."

He stopped, his smile deepening. Then he looked up. She followed his gaze and gasped.

"Oh, wow."

A black ship with a crescent moon shape hung above them, clinging to the highway like a bat. It had curved wings that arced up away from them.

Though she never let herself own a car, she did indulge in admiring them. She'd always had a particularly soft spot for shiny muscle cars with sleek lines. This vehicle was even better—a masterpiece. Its lines sang like a symphony, entrancing her gaze. A hatch opened near the center of its mass, and a ladder slowly descended toward them.

"Okay, I'm pretty sure I would do you just for your ride. Wait, that didn't come out right."

Khel grinned as he guided her onto the ladder. He climbed on behind her, wrapping his arms around her and caging her against its metal rungs, presumably to keep her safe. Then again, as his hips pressed against her ass, she wondered.

The ladder began to rise. Her heart was beating fast. Heights weren't her thing. Even scarier, she realized she felt safe in Khel's arms.

And worst of all—she was starting to get used to it.

Chapter Ten

Finally, they were safely on his ship. Khel felt himself relax a bit more. He would breathe easier yet once they were on the *Arbiter*. Even though the hatch had closed, he held Paige tight against the ladder as he initiated the ship's basic systems.

"Ship, reengage cloak." He paused, listening for the familiar buzz that let him know the cloak was back in place. Now for the tricky part. "Engage artificial gravity field—level zero only."

Slowly, weightlessness settled over them. Paige was still clinging to the ladder that had folded itself into the airlock wall as it lifted them into the ship. She looked over her shoulder at him, her eyes wide. Her hair floated around her face.

He used his training to keep them in place, but couldn't help but notice how her body drifted against his. Zero-G had always been an environment to be processed and adapted to. Experiencing it with Paige made it seem like an opportunity. He imagined the two of them in deep space together, turning off the gravity field and seeing what they could accomplish.

"Lean into me," he said. "You can trust me."

Her lips pressed tight again, but she relaxed a little. She had seemed afraid while the ladder ascended. Perhaps exploring Zero-G maneuvers with her would need to wait.

He wrapped one leg around hers and lifted them both from what was normally the top of the airlock's cabin. Arcing his back while keeping her pressed against him, he brought their feet to the floor 'above'.

Relative to Earth's gravity field, they were upside-down —not that it mattered with his ship blocking that out. He twisted around using the ladder so they would be standing upright when the ship's gravity kicked in, then gave the command.

"Initiate standard gravity field."

He had never been more aware of the pull of the ship's gravity on his body. He watched as Paige's hair descended around her shoulders.

Stars, he wanted to kiss her. But she still looked distressed.

"Are you all right?" he asked.

"I'm a little stunned, I guess. Are we upside-down?"

"Only relative to Earth's gravity."

"This is so weird." She glanced around the small airlock. "I'm on an actual spaceship. In an artificial gravity field."

"Let me show you the rest of the ship."

Especially the sleeping chamber. It was located just on

the other side of the airlock wall, but there wasn't direct access. Instead, they would need to descend into the main cabin of the ship, then climb another ladder to reach it.

He placed his palm on the panel that would open the hatch to the rest of the ship. Hand and footholds were set into the wall below.

"Let me go first," he said.

He barely fit through the hatch and always found the holding spots too closely spaced. When he reached the floor, he could still touch her if he stretched. Skimmers were not designed with Khel's dimensions in mind. They were meant to be snug even for normal Sadirians, both for efficiency and safety. If the gravity field malfunctioned, they wouldn't have far to fall.

Paige stared down at him for a few moments before cautiously sitting next to the hatch and swinging her legs over the edge. She passed him her bag, which he set on the floor.

"You'll catch me, right?"

"Of course."

"I just...don't like heights. And it is seriously messing with me thinking that I would actually be falling up toward outer space."

"Then don't think about it. Come to me."

She smirked, but slid over the edge, not even bothering with the wall. He caught her easily enough.

"That was amazing," she said.

Every new experience they had shared amazed him. Even simply standing as he was, holding her with her arms wrapped around his neck, knowing that he could kiss her, touch her, and it would feel...natural.

He lowered her to the floor so she could look around. Following her, he tried to imagine his ship from her perspective.

The main cabin of the skimmer was like all Coalition ships. The design was minimalistic, with controls built into the walls identifiable only by etchings in the otherwise smooth metal. Once activated, readouts and command options would illuminate on the displays.

Grooves in the walls at various stations acted as hand-holds and places to connect safety straps that extended from their uniforms in the case of sudden gravity loss. He should probably change back into his uniform, but found Earth clothes to be quite comfortable. Plus he already associated them with extremely positive experiences.

"Is there a way we can see outside?" she asked.

He walked to the appropriate controls and opened the screens that covered the ship's viewports. He wondered what she thought of seeing the world upside-down. As he hoped, she smiled as she approached.

"That is trippy. It really feels like we're the ones who are right-side up."

"Space travel is one of the most important cornerstones of the Coalition. Addressing the issue of artificial gravity was a necessary early step in the development of our society. It was worked out millennia ago."

"Before things became peaceful and you guys stopped inventing things."

He didn't have a response to that. He couldn't deny that the Coalition hadn't been making many technological advancements lately. Like in the last few centuries. Even genetic engineering advancements were simply fine-tuning the process to perfect the desired results and minimize glitches like him.

"So you can cloak your ships but not your weapons," she said.

"Portable tech is too small to contain cloaking generators. Otherwise it wouldn't be an issue."

"I still think the Coalition should work on that. At least blocking scans, even if the stuff isn't completely cloaked. Maybe build in a self-destruct sequence if you don't key in a unique identifier within a specified timeframe or something."

That could actually work, if any of the decision-makers still cared enough to try to improve procedures. "I'll relay your suggestion as soon as we get to the *Arbiter*."

"I guess we'll be heading out soon, then?"

"Actually, we need to wait until nightfall. There's always a chance that the cloak will fail. Protocol dictates that arrivals and departures in urban areas of non-Coalition planets happen at night. That's also why skimmers have dark hulls."

"Can we at least send them a message with what we discovered?"

"I think we should wait." He could have insisted, but knew she would appreciate being part of the decision. He *wanted* her to be part of the decision. "The first Tau Ceti that attacked us escaped. It's undoubtedly informed its superiors that I'm in the area. Since the three that attacked your office building didn't return, they must know we haven't left yet. They'll be scanning for us actively. We should send the transmission right before we leave."

"I guess that makes sense. It won't be dark for hours, though." She smiled up at him. "What would you like to do to fill the time?"

He smiled back, putting his hands on her waist and pulling her closer. "There's one more section of the ship you haven't seen yet. The sleeping chamber."

She wrapped her arms around his neck. "I'm not tired."

"I am very glad to hear that."

He bent down to kiss her, memorizing the softness of her lips, the velvet feel of her tongue. Slowly, he walked them back to the recesses that acted as hand and footholds set into the wall that led to the sleeping chamber. He lightened his kiss and reached out to press his hand against the access panel for the hatch above. She pulled away as it slid open, glancing up.

"I'll be right behind you," he said.

She nodded, then turned and started up the wall. He helped her find the places to put her hands and feet, letting his grip linger on her backside as she climbed. When she reached the top, she disappeared over the edge. He followed her quickly.

The sleeping chamber was even more cramped than the main cabin. Khel bent over a bit to avoid hitting his head on the ceiling. Paige had no trouble standing upright in the small space.

"Cozy," she said. She angled her head toward the regen bed. "Do you even fit in that?"

"Barely." He was using Adam's skimmer, which had a specially crafted regen bed that was larger than most. Adam was a few inches shorter than Khel, but the bed had been made with extra room for his comfort. Khel's toes touched one end while his hair brushed the other.

"The floor looks pretty comfortable," she said. "And it's a lot more spacious."

"I sometimes use it for rest." He rolled out the mat he had brought along for that purpose.

"Nice."

She pulled her shirt over her head and tossed it on the floor. Khel lowered himself to his knees to better watch her. She smiled as she kicked off her shoes and reached down to pull off her socks. Then she undid her jeans and slowly slid them down her legs. She stepped out of them and tossed them away.

The undergarments she wore were a matching pale blue. He hadn't really noticed that before. He had seen stars a similar shade. The fabric looked soft, with intricate designs woven into it. He wondered what it would feel like against his skin.

"I'm getting way ahead of you, Khel. Might want to catch up."

He drew his shirt over his head and cast it aside, then shifted to sit so he could take off his boots and socks. Undressing in front of her, he felt oddly vulnerable. She had been graceful in her movements, making it a sensual dance. He couldn't even stand up in the room.

"Hold on a moment," she said. "Could you kneel for me again?"

He happily did as she asked.

"We have plenty of time," she said. "I want us to enjoy ourselves."

She knelt in front of him, then placed her hands on his hips and guided him to rise up on his knees. Then she undid his jeans for him, as she had before. This time, her soft smile alluded to pleasures he could barely imagine. He was trying, though.

He thought of resting above her, his penis buried deep in her warm, pulsing core. Or with her on top, her breasts rubbing against his chest as she moved on him. He was glad he had forced himself to study the logistics of sex, even though he had never planned to use *Coupling*.

He still never planned to use it.

She reached into his jeans, gently running her fingertips over his rigid shaft. Arcs of pleasure ran through his body. She continued the feather-light touches for a few more moments before wrapping her fingers around him and gently moving her hand up and down.

"Paige," he moaned.

"Yes?" She increased the pressure of her grip. His eyes rolled shut.

"*Coupling—*"

Her hand stopped moving on him, but she didn't let him go. "I have no interest in trying out your space sex drug."

His eyes snapped open and he laughed. "That isn't what I was about to suggest."

"Oh. Well, good." She started moving her hand again and he groaned.

"*Coupling* prevents pregnancy. My people are still fertile, even though we're genetically engineered."

"We don't have to worry about that. I have an IUD. It prevents pregnancy."

"Excellent." The word came out like a purr and she laughed.

"And we already covered the whole disease thing," she said. "I know you said you're inoculated against Earth stuff, but I do get tested regularly and have always used condoms before."

"What's a condom?"

She laughed. "Some day I'll show you one. Might be fun to change things up."

She paused again, her brow furrowing for the briefest of moments.

"What is it?"

"Nothing." She shook her head and smiled, but it seemed a bit forced. "I want to focus on this moment. Let's not think of anything else. Just you and me and right now. Deal?"

No thoughts of duty or the Tau Ceti or the *Arbiter* awaiting them. Only Paige, and her cool touch and warm heart. Her passion.

He could do that.

"Agreed."

"Excellent." She grinned as she mimicked his statement from earlier. Then she bent her head to him and drew him into her mouth.

So much pleasure. Warmth and wetness cascading along his nerve endings as she swirled her tongue around his crown and flicked it over the length of his shaft.

He wanted to touch her. He buried his fingers in her hair, gently encouraging her, trying to keep himself from plummeting over the edge into the ecstasy she promised. He felt himself getting too close, and just before he said something, she stopped.

"Lay back for me," she said.

Unable to form words, he simply obeyed. How could

she read his body so well? She pulled his jeans from his legs, then reached behind her back to unclasp her bra. Rising, she slid off her panties, then stood with one leg on either side of him.

Was she contemplating falling on top of him and letting him plunge into her immediately? His penis jerked at the thought. But he wanted to give her the same pleasure she had been giving him.

He sat up, which brought him perfectly in range to reciprocate. Her legs were long enough the he only had to arch his back a bit to press a kiss to the softest folds of her flesh.

He brought his hands first to her buttocks, kneading her flesh and tracing their curves. She moaned as he pressed deeper with his tongue, flicking her clitoris as she had done to his shaft.

Resting one arm behind her to help stabilize her, he used his free hand to delve into her with first one, then two fingers. Her body took him in eagerly. He added a third, and she gasped, stiffening and pulling away.

"Too soon," she said. "I want the next one to be together."

He nodded, though he had no idea how to achieve that objective.

"Tell me what to do."

She put her hands on his shoulders, pushing him to the floor and joining him, knees on either side of his hips. She kissed him with a tenderness and passion that left him breathless. Then she shifted her kisses along his chin and jaw, making her way to his neck just below his ear. Goosebumps rippled across the surface of his body. Her voice was a breathy whisper.

"We just need to listen to our bodies and share what we're experiencing, especially when we're getting closer to the edge." She nuzzled his ear. "It's like electricity humming just above your skin, leaving you wondering when the lighting will strike."

Chapter Eleven

That lightning was already gathering in Paige's body. Khel had almost sent her over the edge with his unexpected and amazing foreplay. She was glad he seemed as worked up as she was. But she wanted to make sure they were in synch.

She lowered her hips to his, pressing his shaft into her slit. Sliding over his length, she brought herself back toward that edge, letting her body wet him and help them both be ready for him to enter her. His dick was huge, and she wanted to enjoy every second of him without a moment of discomfort.

His breath was hitching and his eyes were closed, his fingers clasping her ass and squeezing as she moved. Yeah, they were probably both ready. Still, she hesitated.

She had never let a man into her body without a condom before. Beyond knowing that there was minimal risk of physical consequences, the intimacy they were about to share was something she had never allowed herself with anyone.

Khel isn't just anyone.

She pushed the thought out of her head. They weren't

supposed to be thinking—just experiencing. Focusing on each other and the pleasure they were sharing. Everything else could wait.

With one last long glide along his shaft, she lined up his crown and began slowly inching down over him. He was thick, spreading her flesh, making her feel tight. She let out a slow breath, willing her body to relax, to expand to welcome him. She had to back off a few times, sliding him most of the way out before easing him back in. Finally, she sat back, taking him in fully, his dick filling her.

She didn't dare move. If she did, she would go off. Judging by the look on his face, he was in the same boat. His eyebrows had drawn together so tight, they were forming a single line across his forehead. The idea almost made her giggle, which was good. It helped her to cool off, to gain some distance.

"Take a deep breath and let it out slowly," she said.

He complied without opening his eyes. The wrinkles between his eyebrows lessened infinitesimally.

"Good," she said. "Now talk to me. Tell me what you're feeling."

He shook his head.

"It might help you last longer."

He swallowed hard. "I don't want...this to end. Ever."

She smiled, then slowly inched up along his shaft. The friction was setting off spirals of pleasure that echoed through her, resonating along her skin.

"We can always do it again." She slid back down, taking him all the way in. "And again, and again."

He finally opened his eyes. So much passion. Such intensity.

It scared her.

"Not the sex," he said. "You. Being with you. I don't want—"

She kissed him before he could say anything else. Her heart was hammering in her chest.

She didn't do commitment. She wasn't that girl. She answered her body's needs, had the occasional fun romp, and always—*always*—walked away.

But with Khel...she didn't want to.

These thoughts were unwelcome. She shifted her focus to her body, to the ecstatic feeling of his dick filling her, pulling against her flesh. She tightened the muscles of her core, milking him, pushing him closer to the edge as she increased her pace.

Sitting back, she felt him rock into her, his hips pumping, grip tightening. The sensations were swirling around where they connected—*were* connected. Physically. Just physically.

Electricity scattered across her nerves, building until the lightning struck, branching through her body, filling every cell until she felt herself radiating energy. He cried out, his back arcing and his hips bucking against hers, pounding his dick into her as he came. She felt every pulse, her body echoing it, pulling on it, wanting more.

She wanted...more. More than this fleeting pleasure. More than a one-night stand.

His eyes were wide as he stared at her. Dammit, he was feeling it, too.

It had to be an illusion. The adrenaline of the situation, being thrown together. Feelings this intense didn't happen so quickly. Not real feelings.

This wasn't love.

"That was..." he said. "I've never..."

"That makes two of us." She smiled as she let him slide from her body, feeling grateful for the distance and missing the connection at the same time. She wanted to run away, screaming. Instead, she made herself lie next to him and tried to relax.

"Listen, you should know that sex can make you feel an artificial sense of connection," she said.

"You feel it, too," he said.

Oh crap.

"I feel... It doesn't matter. Stressful situations can make people feel closer. And adding sex to that can make it worse."

"You're trying to dismiss what I feel—what *we* feel. Calling it 'artificial'. Nothing about this is artificial. Are you truly going to tell me to ignore my emotions after everything you've said? Everything we've done? Did it only apply to *physical* feelings?"

Honestly, that's what she had been focusing on. But damn Khel with his drive and his passion and his amazing body. He was the total package. She just wasn't looking to buy.

"It doesn't matter," she said again. "You guys don't even have real sex. I highly doubt you have partners or marriage or—"

"We pair-bond. My people still decide to partner with others. It can be a mutually beneficial arrangement, or because of mutual attraction. We still fall in love."

She rolled away from him and sat up. "But not in half a day. Nobody falls in love that fast."

"From what I understand, falling in love is a process. Who is to say how it begins or will proceed?"

He sat up next to her, but didn't reach for her. She wanted him to, and cursed herself for it. Of all the people to fall for—or start to fall for, as he pointed out—an alien?

"This isn't a passing thing for me," he said. "I am forever changed. Not from the coupling or the threat of the Tau Ceti. Because of you."

And that was the problem. He had changed her, too.

Chapter Twelve

Pair-bonding had always seemed an archaic and unnecessary social construct. Now, Khel was wondering what would be involved in formalizing a relationship with Paige.

He didn't really care about paperwork. He just wanted to be with her. From everything she'd said and done, it didn't seem one-sided. Then again, he was new to this.

Paige grabbed her undergarments and pulled them up her legs, then started shimmying into her jeans. "Infatuation isn't love. Admittedly, the sex has been great, but we'll get over it in a couple of..." She paused and glanced at him. "Months."

She didn't look convinced, which encouraged him. He stood, hunched over, but didn't bother with his clothes. She dug through the pile and pulled out her bra, struggling with the straps in her haste.

As she sorted her clothing out, she repeated, "We'll get over it."

Khel was silent as she dressed. He waited until she'd pulled her shirt back over her head to speak.

"Do you want to?" he asked.

"Want to what?"

"Get over me."

Her mouth dropped open and she paused in the middle of pulling on her shoe. Before she had a chance to answer, the gravity field failed. There was no shift through Zero-G. Up was suddenly down.

Khel was inches away from the ceiling. He felt the first tug of Earth's gravity and launched himself at Paige, trying to catch her before her head struck the hull. He barely made it in time, curling himself around her and altering her trajectory so that she wouldn't injure her head, neck, or spine. They ended up in a pile on the ceiling, his sleeping mat and clothes strewn over them.

"What the hell was that?" she asked.

"I don't know. Ship, report." Nothing. "Ship—"

The light in the chamber was coming from the small viewport in the sleeping chamber. He had left the screens open after Paige requested a view.

No power. That meant no defenses and no cloak. At least they were still firmly attached to the highway overhead.

A rending sound tore away that small comfort. The hull groaned, and the screech of metals grinding together rang in his ears as something attached to the ship and pulled. He scrambled to the viewport. Paige hurried after.

A large transport with an Earth-style exterior was parked right beneath them. It looked like a large semi truck, but the top of the trailer was open, revealing technology the likes of which Khel had never seen. Part of it included a grappling arm that had attached to the skimmer. There were two other arms with some sort of sonic cutters at the ends, the beams slicing through the wings of his ship.

"Khel…"

He didn't have time to reassure her. The force of the grappling arm attached to his ship had to be impacting the highway overhead. If the stress grew too great, it would pull the busy pathway apart, endangering scores of Earthlings.

He pushed Paige toward the hatch that led below. She grabbed his clothing as they went. Lifting her, she crawled up into the ship's main cabin area. She had to be filled with questions, with fear. But she was trusting him and following his lead. The thought fortified him for what was to come.

He lifted himself through the hatch, then ran to the manual release for the docking clamps. He pried off the cover for the lever and pulled on it with all his strength. With any luck, the skimmer would be too heavy for the grappling claw and would crush the Tau Ceti beneath them.

He felt the clamps start to give and shouted, "Brace yourself!"

Instead of the sudden drop he had hoped for, the ship

only shuddered. He heard a rending sound—most likely the wings coming off. Metal scraped metal as the remains of his skimmer descended. They stabilized at a slight angle, no doubt so the ship would fit into the vehicle. Through the viewport, they could see the light slowly vanish as the top of the trailer closed.

No power. No cloak. No weapons, propulsion, shields...or communication. How had the Tau Ceti managed to disable his ship? How had they found him in the first place? And most importantly, how was he going to protect Paige?

A light appeared in the inky darkness. Paige's phone.

"You said we'd be safe when we reached your ship," she said. There was no accusation in her tone. Her voice was flat and calm.

"I thought we would be. I'm so sorry."

"Save the apologies. Right now, we need a plan."

He wouldn't let either of them fall into Tau Ceti hands. The only plan he could think of involved a well-placed phase rifle set to overload and a final kiss—if he could even get his weapons to work. The ship had been thoroughly neutralized.

"Your silence is not encouraging."

"This is unprecedented," he said. "The Tau Ceti have disabled my ship. Without power, there's nothing I can do to protect us."

"I'm not going down without a fight. Where do you

keep your weapons?"

He led her to the panel for the weapons' locker and opened it. Everything on the ship was meant to control enemies, not kill them. He grabbed a stunner and tried to power it up. Nothing.

"Okay, then." She turned her phone toward her face, working on the screen. "I'm not getting a signal, so they're probably blocking me. But I still have power. Why would that be?"

"They must only be targeting Coalition technology. The ship's hull blocks transmissions. It's part of the design. Only the communications array built into the ship will relay messages."

"And the Tau Ceti have shut that down. Which is good for us."

"What?"

She glanced toward him, grinning. "They think they have us beat because they've taken out your ship. But they've underestimated our Earth technology."

"They know about phones. I doubt we'll make it off the ship without them commandeering it."

"But will they bother trying to block its signal? Will they even be watching for one from me?"

"I don't know."

"Would you?"

He thought for a moment, then shook his head. "No. Earth technology is rudimentary. There aren't any signals worth blocking. Taking your phone would be enough for me. Besides, anyone on the planet you could try to call for assistance would be completely outgunned."

"*Anyone on the planet.*" She started using the light from her phone to look around his ship. "But if I can get a signal to orbit—"

He shook his head. "Your cell phone won't be able to reach Brendan, if that's what you're thinking. And, as I said, they'll most likely commandeer it immediately."

The light from her phone crossed her backpack. She quickly ran to it. "That's not what I'm thinking."

She dug around in her bag, then pulled out a small plastic cylinder. It looked completely unremarkable.

"What is that?"

"A panic button. It's made to look like lipstick. The signal it emits is supposed to be untraceable."

"There is no Earth technology that is untraceable."

"Yeah, and the Tau Ceti can't see through your cloaks, either. If this can send a signal even for a few moments, Brendan might be able to pick up on it."

He knew she was grasping for hope. Hope he tried to share.

"You might be ready to give up, but I'm not," she said. "This is our best shot. I'm going to take it."

He wished she was half as interested in keeping their relationship alive. If so, they would stand a chance. He was further aggravated that her zeal only made her that much more attractive.

Shaking aside his thoughts, he set his priorities straight. First, fight the Tau Ceti…after getting dressed. And if they survived, he would fight for a chance with Paige.

Chapter Thirteen

"There has to be something around here we can use as a weapon." Paige was racking her brain, trying to come up with anything else that might give them an edge.

She was the first to admit—if only to herself—that the panic button was a longshot. Though she suspected Brendan had it hooked up to satellites, she couldn't be sure. He had always denied it when she asked.

Even if it could reach Brendan, the Tau Ceti might scan her and find the signal. They might have a general jamming device wherever they were taking her and Khel.

Then again, they might not. If she'd learned anything about these aliens, it's that they were cocky bastards. The Coalition had been coasting for so long, it sounded like they were falling to entropy. And the Tau Ceti thought of Earthlings as walking snacks, not cunning adversaries.

Even if the Tau Ceti took away her bag, the panic button would keep emitting its signal. Brendan would eventually find it—find her. She only hoped it would be in time.

She shook aside the dark thought. They were going to get through this. And afterwards…

Afterwards, she'd have to give Khel his answer. As much as she would prefer not to.

She *didn't* want to get over him.

The thought of following this new relationship through to its natural conclusion scared her more than facing the Tau Ceti. When she let herself think of where she and Khel were headed, she actually imagined them as weathered from time. Did his people age the same way as Earthlings? She had never considered growing old with someone before. She shelved that question for later.

"Maybe we can use the rifle as a club," she said. Or chuck the ray guns at the Tau Ceti.

She shook her head at her own ridiculous thought, but then another popped in. A possibly viable one.

"You said your tech is programmed to self-destruct. Is there any way we can bring that system back online? And if we did, would it be powerful enough to take them out or cause a diversion?"

"It would be, but they'll be on guard for that. Kira used the self-destruct sequence for the listening station where she was assigned to observe Earth. She took out a fair number of the Tau Ceti when she did so, along with one of their ships."

"Remind me to thank her, whoever she is."

"Your brother's partner."

"Partner?"

"Yes. She broke protocol and began conversing with

him several months ago. Apparently, they fell in love. They've gone so far as to enter their pair-bond into Coalition records."

What the hell? Her ears started to buzz.

Everything going on around her, and this caused her to freak out. "Brendan got married and didn't tell me? I'm going to kill him!"

"There were and continue to be exigent circumstances."

"Still... The guy is at the forefront of communication technology on Earth. He could have called."

"It's been less than a day."

Right. Everything was happening at light speed. She leaned against the wall, closing her eyes for a moment and taking deep breaths to try to center herself. Khel's soft touch on her cheek didn't startle her. She had felt his warmth as he approached.

"I can't promise you that everything will be okay," he said. "But I will die protecting you."

She let out a brief laugh. "I don't want you to die. I want both of us to live. So cut it out with that kind of talk. I'm just trying to find some balance here."

"Balance?"

"Emotional equilibrium. Or don't you super-advanced aliens need to worry about that anymore?"

In the dim light from her phone, she could see him thinking.

"The Coalition provides a chemical for that. It's even

called *Balance*."

"That's the first thing you've told me about the Coalition that reassures me. I'm glad they're using their advancements to help people with imbalances in their brain chemistry."

"There are no imbalances in brain chemistry. The regen beds take care of that. *Balance* is for all citizens, to keep them content and maintain peace."

"You've got to be kidding me. They're prescribing happiness? Does the Coalition allow its citizens to experience *anything* that's real?"

His silence said more than any words could. She was getting close to the limits of what she could take. Vampire space frogs were bad enough. But the more she learned about the Coalition, the more turning to them for help seemed like an, 'out of the frying pan' situation.

"Brendan and Kira weaponized *Balance* against the Tau Ceti," Khel said.

Now he had her interest. "How?"

"Sadirians apply it topically. The Tau Ceti have sensitive skin. *Balance* helps Sadirians feel well adjusted. For the Tau Ceti, it makes them euphoric and then knocks them out."

"What are you suggesting?" she asked. "That we palm some and try to shake everyone's hands?"

"There isn't much on board. But if we use it at the right moment, we might be able to escape."

They didn't even know where they were being taken. For all they knew, the Tau Ceti were just moving Khel's ship to a less conspicuous spot before vaporizing it and everyone on board. Except the Tau Ceti still wanted to know what she knew. From what Khel had said, she had a feeling vaporization would be preferable to their questioning techniques. She hoped to avoid both scenarios.

"I have specimen containers in my bag," she said. "If we transfer this chemical into them, the Tau Ceti will be less likely to take it away."

"Brilliant."

They worked together to get it done. They were just finishing when she felt the truck carrying the ship slow to a stop. She reached into her bag and hit the panic button, then buried it at the bottom, keeping the specimen containers full of *Balance* near the top.

Khel quickly hid the empty *Balance* vials in one of the panels in the ship's walls while she slid her backpack's strap over her shoulder. He came to stand at her side, finding her hand and interlacing their fingers.

The ship lurched, and they grabbed onto each other more tightly. Light filtered into the ship as the top of the vehicle carrying them opened. She could see trees covered in sphagnum moss through the viewport and prayed the Tau Ceti weren't planning on dumping them in the swamp to drown or starve.

The ship began to turn. The ceiling they were standing

on became a ramp as they slowly spun back to an upright position. Khel held her waist, helping them slide safely to the wall and then land on the floor when the ship settled.

More sunlight illuminated the ship as a ramp in the flooring opened. Two Tau Ceti cyborgs marched aboard. She was beginning to recognize the clunking sound of their steps. Advanced technology, yet they hadn't bothered to try to make them light on their feet. It was just another symptom of how individuals seemed to be devalued in both cultures.

A man wearing a white hat and suit walked up the ramp. His bow tie was a thin black ribbon. His eyes were large and protruded from his head in a very frog-like way. His lips were thick and his face gaunt.

"Good evening," he said, in a thick Southern accent.

Okay. She wasn't expecting that.

For some reason, it made him even creepier. He was an alien. He was supposed to sound alien, not like one of the locals.

"My apologies for the accommodations during your trip. I'm afraid there's one further formality before we can move forward."

He gestured to one of the cyborgs. Paige put up a little resistance—mostly for show—as they took her phone. The guy patted her down, then Khel. He handed Paige's phone to the guy in the white suit.

"Thank you for leaving the screen unlocked," he said.

After messing with it for a moment, he put it in his pocket. "Your battery's looking a bit low."

"It's not meant to be used to light up a spaceship," she said.

"Again, my apologies. Let's head outside and enjoy some fresh air and refreshments."

Was he kidding? He bowed slightly and turned, walking down the ramp. His two goons stepped forward menacingly. Yeah, he wasn't kidding. Khel took her hand and walked next to her as they left his ship.

The heat and humidity struck her senses. She looked around, trying to figure out where they were. All she saw was swamp. She remembered the maps they had focused on at her office. This could easily be one of those locations.

The guy—space frog—in the white suit led them along a narrow trail that opened up onto an immense and immaculate lawn. A huge mansion sat fifty yards away. He led them to a gazebo instead.

Trees towered above, casting the spot in perpetual shade. The space frog trotted up the stairs and sat at one of four chairs around a circular table, then gestured for them to join him.

She cast a glance at Khel as they followed. When he nodded, they both sat. Someone she presumed was another Tau Ceti brought a tray of what looked like lemonade and small sandwiches.

The Tau Ceti who had greeted them on the ship took off his white hat and set it on the table. "I'm Norm. Would you care for something to eat or drink?"

"No thanks," Paige said.

"Whatever makes you happy."

She snorted. "What, so we'll make a tastier snack later?"

Norm smiled, then took a sip of lemonade. "I've read all about you, Paige Elizabeth Sloan. Crusaders have a bitter finish. Too much adrenaline."

"What can I say? I love my job—and my planet."

"We have that in common. Well, the part about loving the planet. Earth is amazing. It's become a very popular retreat."

"Yeah. I see you Tau Ceti guys are really making yourselves at home."

Norm laughed. "You must expand your thinking, Ms. Sloan. It's true that we've carved out a little territory for our own recreational activities. But the Coalition's umbrella falls over hundreds of thousands of sentient species, each with their own environmental needs—not that the Sadirians really stop to think about that often."

He cast a brief glare at Khel before resuming his friendly expression. "Earth is truly one of the most amazing planets we've encountered. Such varied ecosystems. It's capable of supporting so many different forms of life."

Paige's stomach knotted. She thought they were only dealing with the Tau Ceti. What he was alluding to was much worse.

"You know, this doesn't have to end badly for you," he said. "Your expertise could be quite beneficial for myself and my colleagues."

"Set up your own damn spawning pools," she said.

His eyebrows hitched up his forehead and he smiled. "See? That's exactly what I mean. Even the planetary liaison we've been working with hadn't figured out what we were up to. Mostly because he didn't care. But you care, Ms. Sloan."

He leaned forward and closed his eyes, inhaling deeply through his nose. When he sat back and opened his eyes, his gaze was predatory. "It's written all over your scent."

She lurched forward, grabbing the pitcher of lemonade and getting ready to club him with it. Khel grabbed her arm and held her still. She looked past Norm to the two armed cyborg guards who had leveled weapons at her.

Norm was just smiling. He gestured to the guards to stand down and they did. Khel gently guided her hand to set the pitcher down, then they both eased back into their seats. He squeezed her wrist lightly before letting her go.

"Earthlings," Norm said. "So passionate. So many delicious emotions. I myself have been cultivating a taste for any number of the chemicals associated with each. I bet you're spicy."

She took a deep breath. "Do you want me to throw this lemonade at you or not? Because you're really sending a clear message. *I am an asshole. Please throw this drink at me.*"

Norm laughed. "I'd rather not mess up my suit. But you're right, I should be more clear. You have limited options. I originally thought to torture you to find out how much you know. You've already told me you know about our spawning pools, and that's really all I need."

He paused to let that sink in. She was no longer necessary. They could kill her at any time.

"How do you know I haven't shared my knowledge with others?" She hoped she was buying time for a rescue and not roping herself into an interrogation with him.

"If you'd been able to send a signal to the *Arbiter*, the place would be crawling with Sadirians," he said. "And I doubt your friend here let you share anything with other Earthlings."

So much for stalling.

"I could still torture you for the fun of it," he said. "It would be interesting to see how the taste of your blood would change if I killed your partner, since it's obvious you've pair-bonded." He paused and smiled at her, giving her a chance to process just how much power he held.

"Do all Tau Ceti have this kind of flair for the dramatic, or did you pick it up from being on Earth too long? Because, you know what they say—you are who you eat."

Norm laughed. "Oh, I do hope I don't have to kill you. You're one of the more entertaining humans I've encountered."

"I'll be sure to add that to my resume. 'Entertainer for vampire space frogs'."

He laughed again, which was perfect. If she could keep him talking, that would give Brendan time to get to them.

"I'm afraid the only way I can justify keeping you alive is if you prove yourself useful—beyond your wit and tendency toward violence."

"What do you have in mind?"

"If you truly are unwilling to assist with our spawning pools, perhaps you could help out some of our colleagues. We're not the only ones facing challenges in acclimating to Earth. They're loving the cold, but I hear the Centaurans are having trouble adjusting to the oxygen levels in the Himalayas."

She really, really wanted to smash the pitcher into the side of his face. But then they would kill her. And Khel. She still wasn't ready to give up hope that the signal would reach Brendan and he could... She didn't even know. If he was with Khel's commander on the *Arbiter*, surely there would be something they could do.

"Death or cooperation," she said. "Like that's actually a choice."

"I knew I had you pegged as a crusader." Norm shook his head, then grinned and gestured to his goons. She spoke quickly.

"I have some questions before we start working together."

He blinked a few times, then smiled and leaned back in his chair, waving off his lackeys. She had surprised him. Good. She wanted him off-balance...before she put him on *Balance*.

She smiled.

"Well, this is a most pleasant surprise," he said. "What do you need to know?"

Chapter Fourteen

There was no way that Paige was considering collaborating with the Tau Ceti. And the Centaurans? Cygnus X, how had they managed to set up a base on Earth? The problem was so much worse than Khel had thought. And it went beyond this one planet.

The Tau Ceti had learned how to thwart not only the cloak for his ship, but they had shut down all systems— even the failsafe self-destruct. Whatever technology they had developed, it posed a serious threat to the Coalition. Possibly a fatal one. Adding to that the fact that the Tau Ceti were working in concert with others...

Strength in numbers had been on the Coalition's side. They had colonized most of the Milky Way, setting up bases and building new planetary populations. They had fleets of ships and outnumbered any other single species that was allied with them.

And *every* new species discovered allied with them. The Coalition didn't offer a choice.

But if other planets started banding together, if they were making advances like the Tau Ceti had demonstrated... The Coalition didn't stand a chance.

When Adam approached Khel with his plan to try to bring more freedom to Coalition citizens, it had seemed insane. The disruption it would cause to their society... Was nothing compared to what they were truly facing. He still couldn't believe that no one had discovered what was going on.

He could only hope that Paige's panic button was transmitting and that Brendan would pick up its signal. If the Tau Ceti had taken Khel and Paige to their spawning pools, they were far enough from settlements that Adam could order interceptors to the surface. All they needed was more time.

"Tau Ceti and Centaurans," Khel said. "Are there any other Coalition 'allies' here that will face the tribunal?"

Norm laughed. "You'd be surprised how many of us have been unhappy under the Coalition's rule. Even among your own citizens."

Khel couldn't bring himself to respond. His teeth ground together. Earth's planetary liaison working with the Tau Ceti was bad enough. The corruption that had been exposed as Khel dug into his smuggling operation was appalling. And that was before he knew about the Tau Ceti *and Centauran* settlements.

"When was the last time anything changed in the Coalition?" Norm asked. "What you have isn't peace—it's stagnation. Trust me, I come from a planet that's a swamp. I know these things. This is the beginning of the end for the Coalition."

"Yeah, yeah," Paige said. "Let's finish with the posturing."

She lifted her backpack to the table and stood. The guards shifted forward, but Norm gestured for them to stand down again.

"Khel's told me enough about the Coalition that I already know I don't like them. If you guys are setting up shop and willing to let me in, I can at least stop you from totally messing up the planet while you're putting down roots. Especially since it's going to happen no matter what."

She opened her bag and pulled out several empty specimen containers along with the ones holding *Balance*, then said, "Take me to your spawning pools."

Norm smiled and stood. "Excellent. A most reasonable choice."

"I want to keep Khel, though." She turned toward Khel and ran her fingertip along his jaw. "No vaporizing him, no matter how annoying he can be."

Something in her gaze, an intensity that he recognized, told him that it was a ruse—it had to be a ruse. And part of a plan. He trusted her.

She turned back to Norm and said, "I'm assuming you have a lab for me to work in and someone who can explain your technology?"

"Absolutely. But you don't have to get started right

away."

"I'd rather get it over with." She fiddled with her specimen jars and swung her bag over her shoulder. "Make Khel walk out front."

"So my guards can keep him in check?" Norm asked.

Paige shrugged. "I just like watching his ass while he walks, but that, too."

Norm laughed and she smiled. It made Khel's stomach churn. But he believed in her. Believed she had a plan and knew what she was doing.

She had said they underestimated Earthlings and that was their best chance to escape. Walking behind the guards with Norm gave her an opening. And she had the *Balance* in her hands.

Khel glared at them, trying to look betrayed and angry. He barely resisted as the guards turned him around and pushed him forward, listening closely as Paige talked to Norm behind them all.

"My coworkers have always told me it's weird that I never go anywhere without specimen vials. Joke's on them."

Khel could hear her fidgeting, her clothing rustling as she moved.

"Crap. These are already full from that drainage ditch I was testing yesterday. Could you hold this one for me?"

"Certainly," Norm said. "I'm happy to help."

Khel smirked as he imagined Norm taking the small

cylinder. He was sure Paige had figured out a way to get some *Balance* on the outside. He counted down in his mind. *3-2-1.*

Norm's body barely made a sound as it impacted with the soft earth. Khel dropped and kicked out with his legs, sweeping the guards' feet. One leapt clear, but the other was caught and fell.

Jumping back up, Khel struck the one that was still standing. In his periphery, he saw Paige swing her arm, liquid spraying the guard on the ground.

They hadn't had a chance to sound the alarm. If they could take out this last one—

The cyborg dropped its weapon and lifted its arms in the air. That was odd.

Paige's eyes were wide and her mouth had dropped open. Then she smiled and nodded.

"I guess not everyone in the Coalition is too complacent to take action," she said.

Khel looked over his shoulder at *four* interceptors blocking out the sky above the trees. He laughed, relief flooding his body.

Paige opened another vial of *Balance* and splashed the last cyborg, then watched him fall. She nudged all three prone Tau Ceti with her foot and nodded. When she turned to Khel and smiled, his heart started to pound. They had done it.

She stepped over the guards and jumped into his arms,

kissing him passionately. He crushed her to his chest, devouring her mouth with his. She wrapped her legs around his waist, bringing their bodies even closer together.

Three of the interceptors broke away from the group, fanning out over the area. No doubt, they were searching for more Tau Ceti, building a sensor web that would hopefully detect any who tried to escape.

Or they simply couldn't stomach Khel's display of affection. He was amazed to realize that he didn't care.

The voice that projected from the remaining ship's communications relay as it landed was one he recognized, but it wasn't Sadirian.

"Ugh, stop it! That's my sister!"

Paige broke off the kiss and shouted, "Shut up, Brendan!"

She pressed her forehead to Khel's and they laughed.

"Come on," she said, sliding down his body and lacing their fingers together as she stood next to him. A ramp was opening beneath the main interceptor and she pulled him toward it, squeezing his hand. "I want to see where this takes us."

Chapter Fifteen

Two spaceships in one day. Paige could barely believe it. But the interceptor sat in front of her, its chrome hull reflecting the trees around them. The ship had the same sleek lines as Khel's skimmer—before the Tau Ceti had snapped it in pieces—but was a complete circle rather than a half-moon. Panels had unfolded from the bottom of the ship to hold it up off the ground.

Cylindrical mechanisms protruded from the outer ring of the ship at regular intervals. Some rotated around as if they were scanning the area. Others very obviously had weapons attached, the design a larger version of the phase rifles she had seen.

The Sadirians weren't messing around with their interceptors.

She'd probably be more comfortable on board than staring at its guns. Before she could set foot on the ramp, Brendan ran out of the ship. He grabbed her up in a huge bear hug the likes she hadn't experienced since High School.

A dozen people—aliens—marched down the spaceship's ramp after him, carrying phase rifles and stunners. They were all wearing shiny silver one-piece uniforms. The belts at their waists had a few items attached to them of various shapes and sizes. She could only speculate about what they did. Their faces were concealed in featureless chrome helmets, and they wore thick gloves and boots.

Some disappeared into the foliage, while a few remained to deal with the Tau Ceti she and Khel had taken down. She focused on her brother.

"I'm so glad you're okay," he said.

Dammit, her eyes were tearing up. She squeezed him back just as hard, trying to shake it off.

"You think cyborg vampire space frogs can take me down? Please."

He laughed, then set her back on her feet—but he kept one arm around her shoulders. He extended his hand to Khel and said, "Thank you. For keeping her safe."

Khel clasped Brendan's forearm in what must be the Sadirian version of a handshake. He set his other hand on Brendan's shoulder.

"No thanks are required. And in truth, she aided me much more than I aided her. Paige is an incredible warrior." Khel glanced down at her, his cheeks turning pink. "You should also know, we—"

"I shouldn't know anything. I got enough of an eyeful already." Brendan shook his head, clenching his eyes tightly shut for a moment. "What I should have done was warn you. Paige is…outgoing. I thought you'd be immune to her charms. I should have known better."

"Underestimate me at your peril," she said. "And talking about me as if I'm not present will earn you consequences."

She stuck her fingers between a pair of Brendan's ribs where she knew he was incredibly ticklish and he leapt about a foot off the ground.

"Paige!" He rubbed the spot and glared at her.

She grinned, then stepped forward so she could stand next to Khel instead. She tucked herself against his side and wrapped her arm around his waist.

"What are you wearing?" She hadn't noticed before, but Brendan was dressed in a silver catsuit just like the Sadirians. Well, his didn't have the shiny chrome helmet or gloves. The outfit made his red hair look extra coppery.

"You look like something out of a science fiction movie from the 50s," she said.

He glared at her. "It's a Coalition uniform. We have to wear them on the *Arbiter*."

"I look forward to seeing you in one of them." Khel grinned down at her. She could get used to that grin.

"I look forward to seeing you *out* of one." She put her hand on the back of Khel's neck and pulled him close for another kiss.

Brendan groaned in the background.

"I see you're keeping the human safe."

Khel jumped at the booming voice, his body stiffening in ways that weren't nearly as much fun as earlier in the day. He turned to face the trio of people Paige only just realized had been hanging around close by.

One was a man almost as big as Khel, with dark hair and thick stubble covering his jaw. He was flanked by two women—a blonde and a brunette. The brunette was also tall. Her thin, wiry build and ready stance screamed 'soldier'. Definitely Sadirian.

Brendan walked to her side and she reached for his hand without seeming to think about it. Was that Kira? Her new sister-in-law...

Paige would deal with that later.

The blonde, though, was picking at the collar of her uniform and shifting her weight from foot to foot. Her hair was pulled up in a messy bun, and she kept reaching to her face as if she was adjusting invisible glasses, then letting out little sighs. That one had to be human.

"General Serath," Khel said. "I mean Adam. Yes, Paige Sloan is in excellent health."

"Apparently." Adam leveled a stare at them, one eye a rich green and the other a deep blue.

"Whoa, that's a cool design," Paige murmured. "Nice to see you guys are capable of creativity."

"Adam is a gl—"

Khel stopped himself from finishing, and it was a good thing. Paige was pretty sure she could make him jump, too, if he dared to use that word again. The blonde woman was glaring at him as well.

"An unexpected result," Khel said. "What you see is nature, not science."

"I like to think he's a little of both." The blonde woman hooked her arm in the crook of Adam's elbow, and waved at Paige with her free hand. "Greetings, fellow Earthling. I'm Evelyn."

"Hi." Paige smiled at her, then nodded toward the brunette. "I'm guessing that makes you Kira."

Kira nodded curtly. "That's correct."

Paige smiled and cocked her head to the side as she moved her gaze to Brendan. "And that makes you a dead man. Mom's going to go nuts when she finds out you got hitched without telling her."

Brendan shook his head. "Neither of us will be telling her for a while. We have other priorities. Besides, it was important that Kira and I formalize our relationship. Being pair-bonded to an Earthling will give Adam a stronger case for appointing her as the new planetary liaison for Earth and should also help with them recognizing the Department of Homeworld Security."

"The what?"

"Earth's First Contact committee," Kira said. "That's what Brendan's calling it."

Paige snorted. "Of course he is."

Evelyn shrugged. "I don't know. I think it's kind of

catchy."

"So, the three of us get to decide the fate of the planet?" she said.

The idea was insane.

"We're working on that." Kira nodded toward Adam. "Adam still needs to return to Sadr-4 and present the case to the Coalition High Council. Until the First Contact Committee—"

Brendan cleared his throat.

Kira sighed, then said, "Until the Department of Homeworld Security is recognized, they'll continue making all decisions regarding Earth."

Paige's stomach seemed to fall to her feet. Three humans determining the fate of their planet was a hell of a lot better than a bunch of aliens who didn't have any stake in their homeworld—especially given what she knew of their society.

"How likely are they to recognize our sovereignty?" Paige said.

Adam and Kira exchanged a glance. Paige could feel Khel stiffen beside her.

"That bad, huh?"

"We'll do our best," Adam said. "But there are other matters we need to bring to the High Council. The Tau Ceti must be dealt with for exploiting Earth's resources."

Khel shook his head. "It's much worse than that. They weren't just trespassing. They were setting up spawning pools."

Kira's jaw dropped. Adam hid his surprise a bit more effectively, but it was still there.

"Norm—their leader—also told us the Centaurans are here, looking to set up a permanent presence," Paige said. "And they're not the only ones."

Adam wrapped his arm around Evelyn and pulled her against his side.

"General, Earth has not been properly managed." Kira's voice was strong. Whatever shock she had experienced, she was over it, and ready to take action.

Paige liked that.

"There is a very strong case to bring in a First Contact committee at this point, given this information," Kira said.

"Agreed." Adam leveled a stare at Khel again. "If we can prove it. But that proof will also bring the Coalition into the first real war we have experienced in thousands of years."

"The war has already begun," Khel said. "The Tau Ceti were able to completely incapacitate my ship. They've developed new technologies that will bring the Coalition to its knees if we don't stop them."

"That's not possible." Kira stepped forward, her hands curling into fists.

"Anything is possible," Paige said. "All of us standing here together is proof of that."

Khel wrapped his arms around Paige's shoulders,

pulling her against his chest. She let herself lean on him. She had a feeling she'd be doing that a lot in the coming days.

Adam shook his head. "These matters are better discussed aboard the *Arbiter*. Sorca has been dispatched to retrieve the fourth prospective member of the First Contact committee."

"Department of Homeworld Security," Brendan said.

Adam barely glanced at him before continuing. "As soon as she returns with Eric, we can convene the inaugural meeting and determine how to proceed."

Paige wanted to protect her homeworld, but the thought of all those planets stripped bare, their inhabitants left to the mercy of the Coalition... She couldn't let that pass.

She stepped away from Khel, and said, "This has moved beyond the needs of Earth. Whatever we decide, it has to be in the best interest of all the citizens of the Coalition. From what Khel has told me, we have an incredible opportunity to assist your people. If we work together, we can help each other. Maybe repair some of the damage done to other worlds by overharvesting resources."

Adam's lips twitched into an almost-smile. "Brendan was right about you being an excellent candidate for the First Contact Committee."

"Department of Homeworld Security," Brendan said.

Paige rolled her eyes. "We get it, Brendan."

Adam ignored him. "I want to hear more of your ideas for regenerating our stripped planets. Pairing Earth's resources with Coalition technology could go far in easing the transition we will be proposing to the High Council."

A thrill of excitement shot through her. Protecting her world and healing others... Paige was surprised at how much those other planets mattered to her already. She wanted to help. Wanted to do something.

"We have much work ahead of us." Khel moved to stand beside her and took her hand in his.

As long as they kept working together—as partners—she had a feeling everything would be okay. She had to believe it.

With Khel at her side, it wasn't that hard.

She gave him a brief smile. "Then let's get down to business."

Epilogue

Sorca ran through the skimmer's pre-launch sequence for a final time, her mind still buzzing from Vay's cultural indoctrination session. The materials were already blurring, but Sorca didn't care. She just wanted to get planet-side as quickly as possible.

"Sorca."

She turned toward the open hatch at the sound of the familiar voice. Ari was standing to the side of the ramp, his bald head and silver-clad shoulders sticking into the ship due to his formidable height.

"Ari?" she said. "Why are you holding around in the hangar bay?"

"I think you mean, 'hanging around'."

Hanging around? What would he be hanging? But then, 'holding around' didn't make much sense, either.

She shrugged.

"You don't have to go," Ari said.

Sorca let out a sharp laugh. "You heard General Serath's orders. I am to retrieve the Earthling Eric Peterson and bring him back to the *Arbiter*."

"Khel has already been sent to retrieve Brendan's sister.

It makes more sense to send a lower-ranking soldier after Eric."

"Protocols allow for Khel and I to both be off-ship at the same time for important missions. Besides, Serath is back on the *Arbiter*. The command structure is secure."

Ari shook his head. "Earth had a strange effect on Serath. I mean 'Adam'. Until we know why, or the extent of that Earthling's influence on him—"

"*That Earthling* is his bondmate. And her name is Evelyn." Sorca quickly cycled through the last of the checks, then crossed the ship and squatted down next to Ari. "What is this really about?"

"This planet is…unsettling."

That was one word for it. Sorca would have gone with exhilarating, exciting, dangerous, or even *new*. It was a change, and the High Council—along with good soldiers like Ari—viewed change as a threat. So did Sorca.

The difference was, Sorca liked threats. She chose to view them as challenges.

"This planet is primitive and diverse," she said. "Both of those things are uncommon in the Coalition. Steel your nerves and embrace the opportunity."

"Opportunity? For what?"

"For victory!"

She swatted him playfully on the chest. At least, she'd intended to. The force of her "swat" knocked him back hard enough that he hit his head on the hatch. For a moment, he disappeared from her view.

"Apologies." She started to swing herself down over the ramp to reach him more quickly, but he popped back up, rubbing the back of his head.

"I'm okay," Ari said. "This is the exact kind of thing that makes me think perhaps I should go instead."

"The first injury was unintentional. The next will not be."

Ari's gold-hued skin paled at that.

"I mean no offense," he said.

Ari was one of her most trusted security officers, but she would not have him question her abilities. The fact that he was doing so in the first place... Vay must have said something about the cultural indoctrination session. Shared that Sorca's mind was rejecting too much data.

"Your concern for your fellow officers is one of your strengths," Sorca said. "But in this case, it is unnecessary. I assure you, I'm up for the task."

She winked at him, closing both eyes briefly while giving him her most reassuring smile. He opened his mouth as if he was about to speak, but then shut it again and shook his head.

"Of course." He bowed low. "We'll be standing by, just in case you should need anything."

"I know you will." She stepped back into the main area of the ship, then pressed the control that closed the hatch.

Her team would be standing by, but she'd be certain

that she didn't need them. Earth was gloriously unpredictable. For her, that meant fun. But for the others—like Ari—that meant danger she would rather they not face.

They weren't super-strong, extra-resilient, or somewhat immortal—with quirks. Better to keep them on the *Arbiter*, and save this mission for herself.

The space-side doors of the hangar bay opened, revealing a gorgeous view of the planet below. Blue and white and green. For a moment, she was stunned by the simple beauty of it.

The skimmer beeped, reminding her of her mission.

"Eric Peterson," she murmured. "You have no idea what you're in for."

She grinned as she pressed the command to launch.

—

Brendan needs people he can trust in his newly formed Department of Homeworld Security, and there's no one he trusts more than his handler, Eric Peterson. When he asks Adam, aka General Serath, to send someone to bring Eric to the *Arbiter*, Sorca, the head of security is assigned the mission. And when she and Eric meet... Well, it puts a very different spin on alien abduction! Read on as the adventures continue in *Tied up in Customs!*

CASSANDRA CHANDLER

TIED UP IN CUSTOMS

THE DEPARTMENT OF HOMEWORLD SECURITY

Tied up in Customs

The Department of Homeworld
Security
Book Four

Cassandra Chandler

Dedication

For Holly A.—an awesome Earthling.

Don't miss out on any of the alien action.
Subscribe to Cassandra Chandler's newsletter at
cassandra-chandler.com!

Chapter One

"What is Brendan getting me into now?"

Eric mumbled the words under his breath, scanning the diner as he pretended to read his menu. He made a mental note of the access points of the room—doors, windows—possible lines-of-sight for snipers, items that could hide threats. Everything was cataloged.

Booths lined the seating area, and the central space was filled with a maze of tables. He had asked for a spot near the back wall, where he could easily see all the entrances and exits, as well as the patrons and staff.

The diner didn't use tablecloths, which helped his survey. And it wasn't a place he visited often enough that it would be easy for anyone to predict him being there. Brendan had been very specific that he wanted to meet in this place, but had hedged about why. Which meant he was up to something.

Once, he had roped Eric into being part of a zombie walk. Only once.

Even though Brendan had made Eric swear he would be unarmed when they met, he'd still nearly dislocated a civilian's shoulder trying to protect Brendan from what

Eric perceived to be an attack. Brendan had thought it would be okay because zombies "weren't real" and Eric "should have known it was just for fun, since it was his day off…"

For a genius, the guy could be an idiot. Much like Eric was starting to feel.

This was going to be another zombie walk. He just knew it. Especially since Brendan had once again made Eric swear to come unarmed. But if that's what it took to get Brendan back to work on the communications array, so be it.

Honestly, Eric kind of thought Brendan's weirdo play-acting games were…fun. Not that he'd ever admit that to anyone.

Eric was looking forward to this entirely too much. Maybe he did need to take more time off. He could even try to find someone who shared his interests.

Let's see, that would be protecting people, maintaining peace, finding a way to improve everyone's standard of living without compromising what each specific country has achieved, understanding that I'm absolutely dedicated to my job…

At least, he used to be.

He and Brendan had been talking about Eric's single-minded dedication to his job way more than an asset and handler should. Eric chalked it up to building a good rapport with Brendan, but they had come dangerously close to crossing into friend territory.

Crap. They were totally friends.

Eric should ask for a reassignment. Hell, maybe he should retire, like Brendan was threatening to. Find a job in the private sector. With the way his superiors were handling Brendan's project, he might even be able to do more good there.

Eric tossed the menu down on the table just as the door opened. His train of thought stopped when he saw the woman who entered the diner.

Her skin gleamed a rich gold and her dark brown hair fell past her shoulders in thick locks. She was wearing an unbuttoned red-and-black checkered flannel shirt with the sleeves rolled up. Her forearms were corded with muscle. She had on a nondescript gray T-shirt underneath that was tucked into crisp jeans that hugged equally muscular legs. Her hips and chest looked soft and full, though.

Eric shifted in his seat a bit, his mind already primed to be looking for...something. Even from across the room, he could see that her eyes were pale gray, clear and piercing.

Her gaze landed first on the door to the kitchen, then slid across the open space between the dining area and the chefs, where they handed out food to the wait staff. Her glance briefly paused on the entrance to the hall that led to the bathrooms and again on the rear exit.

She was surveying the room, like Eric had just been doing. She wasn't even trying to be subtle about it, though.

Eric leaned back in his chair, resting his hand in his lap for an easier draw—then remembered that he didn't have a weapon.

Shit.

At least he had his handcuffs.

She scanned the crowd, her gaze latching on to his with laser focus. And she smiled.

Eric felt a tightness build in his chest. Not quite dread, but definitely anticipation.

God, she was beautiful.

She started to weave her way toward him, passing waitresses carrying plates filled with eggs and bacon. She stopped suddenly, her eyes going wide as she…sniffed the air. Outright sniffed it, like a hungry animal might.

Beautiful and *strange.*

Eric strained to make out her words through the jumble of noise in the busy diner as she spoke to a waitress.

"What is that?"

The waitress looked irked as she said, "The number seven special."

"Number seven special."

"It's on the menu." When the woman didn't make any sign of moving out of the way, the waitress said, "Do you mind?"

"If I minded your presence, I assure you that you'd know." A near-feral smile twisted the woman's full lips as she watched the waitress back away, then turn and take a different route to her destination.

After a few moments, the woman headed toward Eric again, eyeing the plates of the other customers along the way. She stopped fairly close to him, standing in the empty pathway between the tables, hands at her sides.

It would have been an innocuous pose, except for the way she kept her knees slightly bent and her weight evenly balanced on the balls of her feet—which were encased in black combat boots. From that stance, she could easily spring in any direction she needed.

She held her fingers straight, palms toward him as if she was showing him that she was unarmed. It seemed an almost subconscious gesture, which unnerved him even more.

His gut and his observations told him two things about her right away. She was dangerous and she was not local.

"Eric Peterson," she said.

He waited a few moments before responding, trying to analyze how the situation might play out. He didn't have enough data to form any theories. She obviously knew who he was, so he nodded.

"And you are?"

Her lips twitched up in a mysterious—and somehow taunting—smile.

"Sorca."

"That's it? Just Sorca?"

Instead of elaborating, she lifted her arm and picked at

her sleeve. "This is Brendan's shirt. I wear it as proof of my...friendship with him."

What has Brendan roped me into this time?

"And where is Brendan?" Eric asked.

"Elsewhere. He wanted me to tell you that he's safe."

"Why would he feel the need to let me know that?"

"He said you would worry otherwise. I think he was also afraid you might eventually attack me if you were concerned for his safety." She cast that feral smile at Eric, as if the idea delighted her. And waited.

"I'm not... I'm not going to attack you in the middle of a diner," Eric said.

Her face fell. Was she insane? What kind of game was Brendan playing at, and who the hell had he invited to play?

Sorca shrugged, and said, "I am also to give you this."

She started to reach for the pocket on the front of her shirt. Eric's pulse spiked, his body tingling with adrenaline as he prepared to react, thinking of how to protect the civilians in the diner if she should draw a weapon.

Even though he hadn't moved, she froze, fingers extended again in that, "I come in peace" gesture, despite her seeming eagerness to fight. She kept her arms held out to her sides as she leaned forward.

"Perhaps you would feel better if you retrieved the item yourself. It is in the left pocket of Brendan's shirt."

Eric let out a sigh, a small bit of his tension leaving

with it. He still kept himself absolutely ready for an attack as he carefully reached two fingers into her pocket for the piece of paper he could see within it. He did his best to ignore the heat from her body or the closeness of his hand to her breast.

He pulled out the note and flicked it open, keeping her in his line of sight. The message was short and unhelpful.

Eric, this is Sorca. I am safe, but our planet is not. Do as she says and she'll bring you to me.
Brendan
P.S. Brown foxes like boxes more than oxes.

Eric would have dismissed it immediately as one of Brendan's games, except he ended it with one of the codes they had developed for covert communications—an official code meant to let each other know the message was authentic.

Brendan knew he could only use this one once. Why would he waste it on a game?

Talking to Sorca while she was standing next to the table was both awkward and drawing unwanted attention from the nearby patrons. Eric gestured to the empty chair across from him.

"Will you join me?"

One of her dark eyebrows hiked up her forehead. She stared at a plate sitting on a nearby table and licked her upper lip. Slowly.

The tingling coating Eric's skin turned from pre-fight adrenaline to a blasting heat that coalesced in his groin. If this had been part of a regular assignment—part of a mission—things could get very interesting between them. But this was one of Brendan's games. Probably.

Eric shoved away the physical reaction, not letting himself fully register the thoughts that were behind them—thoughts he couldn't seem to stop, at least as long as he was looking at Sorca. Eating would probably help take his mind off of her .

He slid his menu across the table to her as she sat, and said, "What'll you have?"

Her brow furrowed as she looked at the menu, cocking her head to the side. The smirk vanished from her lips as she studied it—holding it upside-down. Was she pretending that she couldn't read?

With a laugh, she shook her head and tossed the menu back across the table. "Whatever you plan to eat will be fine with me as well."

He flagged down a waitress, and said, "Two number sevens, please."

"Sure thing, handsome." The waitress winked at him before walking away.

"Her eye is spasming," Sorca said. "Is she injured?"

"That was a wink. She's fine."

Sorca's brow furrowed as she stared at him.

"What?" he said.

"You confirmed that you are Eric Peterson."

"I am."

"Then why did that woman call you 'Handsome'?"

"Ouch."

Eric chuckled and Sorca joined in—a few moments late.

Pretending she couldn't read *and* that she didn't understand the word "handsome"? He decided to roll with it.

"It's a descriptive word," he said. "It means she likes how I look."

"How you..." Sorca's brow furrowed again as she glanced around the restaurant before her intense gaze settled back on him. "Your physical appearance. She appreciates your physical appearance."

"That's one way of putting it."

Sorca leaned back in her chair, one eyebrow cocked as she cast her smirk at him. He had never been the subject of a brazen stare before. It was more unsettling than he expected.

He sorted through the rules of the game. Sorca was acting the part of someone unfamiliar with local idioms and customs. There was an odd cadence to her speech—which seemed overly formal—but she didn't have an accent that he could place. In fact, she didn't seem to have any accent at all.

She seemed eager to test herself against him physically. The combat boots and stance warned him not to underestimate her. And the muscles on her arms... He'd never seen such definition on a woman.

Brendan had used one of their codes. Maybe this was some sort of military simulation game? He was heading into dangerous territory by bringing Sorca into it, if she *wasn't* military. She could be someone from an associated project that Eric hadn't met yet...

A strange thrill jolted through him at the thought—half dread, half excitement. He needed more information. And the only way he was going to get it was to play along. He stared across the table at the mysterious woman with the devil-may-care smile.

"You have hair on your face," she said.

He felt his jaw drop open. He snapped it shut, started to speak, then shut his mouth again.

He had training to cover any number of cultural differences. He knew six languages, twenty ways to take down an armed opponent without hurting them, many more ways to do so with...different results. But none of his scenarios, none of his experience, came anywhere close to this woman. The energy she put off was completely alien to him.

"Brendan also has hair on his face," Sorca said. "And another male I know who has been staying in this area for a time. Is this considered handsome?"

Another "male"?

"It depends on your taste," Eric said.

"Hmm. I think I like it." She leaned an elbow on the table, craning her neck to look at the rest of his body. Her gaze heated. "Handsome, indeed."

"Thanks." Under his breath, he added, "I think."

If this was her idea of flirting, it was the strangest, most aggressive conversation he'd ever had.

Flirting... Oh, no.

His stomach sank. Was Brendan trying to set Eric up on a date?

It didn't matter if that's what it was. That was not happening. Even if Sorca was the most gorgeous woman he'd ever seen. Who also gave off an aura of being able to handle herself in a fight. Maybe even combat. She could be *ex*-military...

Her behavior was too bizarre for her to be a foreign operative. But there was definitely something not local about her. Like really not local.

She wasn't among the list of Brendan's eccentric friends that Eric had read about during Brendan's background check. Someone new, then. And this was someone Brendan thought would be a good match for Eric?

That theory seemed to be the most plausible. He would have to find a way to let her down easy.

Chapter Two

Such a fascinating Earthling.

Sorca gazed at the *handsome* male sitting across from her. His eyes were brown with a gold tinge, his hair much the same, but his facial hair was darker.

She struggled to call up the words for facial hair. A... bear and mustache. Yes, those were the words. Probably.

Her cultural indoctrination session had been interesting. Vay, the *Arbiter's* cultural programmer, had worked with Sorca for hours, trying to load the proper protocols and translations into her memory. The effort had been tiresome.

How can Vay even call herself a soldier when she's more interested in making friends than waging battle?

There were deeper impulses woven into the very fibers of Sorca's being that would not be overwritten. Her brain was rejecting more and more of the Coalition's subconscious programming, rebelling against the intrusion. Or maybe she'd been cloned so many times that her brainwaves were getting tired of the constant overwriting.

She seemed to lose a little more of herself each time her

mind was mapped onto a newly grown body—after her previous one was killed. She wondered if the most recent batch of genetic engineers would keep trying to make more of her or just finally let her be purged.

The mental blocks to their programming might be tied to the extreme physical strength her Cygnian DNA gave her. She'd never know at this point, and didn't really care to spend additional time learning more about herself.

But this human... She would like to learn more about him.

The waitress had already taken their order, and returned with plates bearing foods unlike anything Sorca had ever seen. Two white nebulas with burning orange-star centers. They were beautiful. Triangles made up of some sort of compressed sand sat next to them, along with strips of a wavy brown substance that gave off the most amazing scent she had ever encountered.

She leaned over her plate and took a deep breath through her nose, breathing out through her mouth to keep the scents in place before taking another long breath. Her eyes rolled shut, the aroma even twining around her tongue, making her salivate.

"I take it you like brunch," Eric said.

She realized she was not behaving the way the Earthlings surrounding her were. In fact, when she glanced at the nearby tables, several humans were laughing, while others stared at her, their eyes as wide as if they'd seen a mated pair of Lyrians propagating.

She snorted at the image, turning her gaze back toward Eric. He didn't seem shocked. Or amused. He just looked...confused.

And handsome.

"Why hands?" Sorca said.

Eric's dark eyebrows rose on his forehead. "Pardon me?"

"What are hands in relation to 'handsome'?"

"I don't know the etymology of it," he said. "You should ask Brendan."

"I will, when I see him next." She gestured at Eric's plate, and said, "Begin."

If he ate first, she could mirror his actions to avoid further unusual behavior on her part.

"I... Uh..." Eric shook his head. "Okay."

He picked up a silver device with several parallel prongs that would make a fairly effective stabbing weapon, and another that looked like a metal stick or some kind of useless knife. The edge was blunt and the hilt had no guard to keep his hand safe should he try to kill something with it.

Eric stabbed one of his white nebulas with the pronged tool, then used the not-quite-functionless knife to cut off a section, which he lifted to his mouth.

"Interesting," she murmured.

"Me eating eggs is interesting?" He let out a short

laugh.

The white nebulas were called eggs. She made a mental note, even though she knew it was unlikely she would ever encounter this delightful food again.

He pointed at her plate with his knife, and said, "If you think that's interesting, you should poke one of the yolks with your toast and see what happens."

She looked at her plate, trying to figure out which thing was "toast" and which was "yolk". Perhaps "toast" was the word for the silver pronged item. He'd used his to stab his egg segment and lift it to his mouth. But then, what was "yolk"?

She picked up the silver toast and held it in a killing grasp, quickly striking the triangles on her plate. At the last moment, she remembered to hold back her blow. She didn't want to harm the implements of eating, nor was she ready for Eric to witness her strength.

The metal toast impaled the compressed-sand yolk, a shower of tiny granules breaking off from it as it split in half with a satisfying *crunch*. Sorca looked up at Eric, beaming at her accomplishment.

He still looked confused.

"That's not... Here." He set down his toast and knife, then picked up a piece of his yolk, and said, "Toast."

"Oh."

The compressed-sand triangles were "toast"? Then what was "yolk"? And why would she poke anything with a piece of food?

He pointed at his plate, toward the bright-sun centers of his eggs. "Yolks."

He gently poked the circle of orange with his toast. Thick fluid burst forth, running over the white segments of his eggs.

She sucked in a breath, her gaze darting to her plate. She didn't bother with the toast, but jabbed a finger into the yolk.

It offered little resistance, the somewhat slimy coating giving way beneath her fingernail. The fluid within was hot. More of it gushed out around her finger, flowing over the nebula-white eggs.

She lifted her hand, laughing as the viscous orange goo dripped onto her plate. She darted her finger into her mouth, eager to taste it.

Words failed her, at least in the primitive language they used on this planet. She had no sensory experience to compare with the yolk's smooth texture or the solar storm of its *taste*. Her tongue seemed to come alive for the first time. Prickles of sensation flooded along her arms, the fine hairs standing on end as the follicles beaded.

She pulled her finger from her lips, sucking every last molecule of yolk from its surface. More. She wanted more.

The sound of metal clanging on ceramics brought her attention back to Eric. She opened her eyes to see him leaning back in his chair with both hands over his face. He dropped his palms to the table and shook his head.

"Listen, I don't know what Brendan's up to," he said, "But this... I'm not into this."

She set her hands firmly on the table, mirroring his posture. "What do you think 'this' is?"

He took a long breath and let it out slowly, his gold-brown eyes staring at her intently. "Brendan has been after me to do more R&R. My job doesn't really allow for that."

"Arenar? What is that?"

"Rest and relaxation. R and R."

"Rejuvenation cycles. I see. And you think he has sent me to you to assist with this 'R and R', yes?"

"Didn't he?"

She smirked at him, then picked up a segment of toast and dipped it into the delicious yolk. She thoroughly saturated what she now understood to be the edible carrying mechanism before bringing it to her mouth and slowly taking a bite.

The toast crunched. The sound was immensely satisfying. And the flavor of the yolk was heightened by another smooth substance that had been spread on the toast. There was a saline element to it that countered the thickness of the orange fluid, much like the crisp texture of the toast countered the yolk's smoothness.

She let the bite partially dissolve on her tongue, breathing in deeply through her nose so the aromas of the surroundings could heighten the experience. When the flavors had begun to fade, she finally chewed and swallowed.

Eric stared at her the whole time. He kept his lips shut tight, but she noted how his pupils dilated.

"Rejuvenation is vital in maintaining optimal performance," she said. "If Brendan believes you need assistance with this, I am happy to cooperate in a variety of ways."

A muscle began to flex along his cheek beneath his bear. Was that the right word? It didn't feel quite so.

Regardless, she wanted to run her fingers along his jaw, to feel its strength. Instead, she ate more of her excellent brunch.

This male was strong—a naturally occurring specimen, generated completely at random who held excellent attributes. Fascinating.

He narrowed his eyes at her. "How exactly do you know Brendan?"

"We are recent acquaintances. One of my colleagues trained with his bondmate."

"Bondmate?"

"Yes." She knew there was a word for it in this region, but couldn't remember it. "Brendan has recently developed a physical and emotional relationship with her."

"That's funny. He never mentioned anyone to me."

Brendan had informed them all that Eric was part of a group that enforced law. It was absurd to her that this fell outside of the military. Why have multiple groups within a society who had overlapping skills when one unit could be trained to fulfill both functions?

Earth could greatly increase the efficiency of their operations if they had access to the genetic engineering techniques of the Sadirians. They could tailor each individual to the task they would be assigned. Although, for a natural specimen, Eric seemed very well suited for the cultural function he had selected. He reminded her of many of the soldiers she served with aboard the *Arbiter*.

She was fairly certain she had raised Eric's suspicions. Her assignment was to bring him to the *Arbiter* so that he could join Earth's newly formed Department of Homeworld Security—or receive a mind-wipe if he refused. Brendan most likely wanted Eric in good condition when he arrived. His cooperation would assist with that.

While she parsed through the scenarios going through her mind, she lifted one of the wavy sticks of...fabric? Eric had eaten a bite of his, so she assumed it was edible.

The smell rising from it sent another thrill through her body. It was even better than the eggs and toast. She took a small bite, the texture requiring her to chew the substance more than the others.

The explosion of flavors shook her. She let out a groan, then shoved more of it into her mouth, chewing rapidly.

"What is this?" She covered her mouth to keep any of

its contents from falling out while she spoke around the incredible food substance.

"Bacon."

"Bacon." She practically purred the word, holding another strip between both hands and snapping it into two pieces.

Her meal was nearly finished, and Eric's suspicions were fully engaged. Daylight would keep her from leaving the planet until nightfall—unless she wanted to break protocol and risk being seen by Earthlings should her ship's cloak fail. Which she didn't.

Originally, she had planned to simply approach Eric, lure him to a secluded spot, and secure him for transport to her ship. She'd imagined it would involve striking him in the head with just enough force to render him unconscious, then carrying him back to her ship.

Now... Now, she had other ideas. She had seen the way General Serath—Adam—and his Earth wife, Evelyn, displayed their bond through touch.

Wife. That was the word she had been looking for when speaking of Brendan's new lifemate.

Sorca had been curious, observing both couples share their affection through light touches and kisses when they thought no one was watching. She had rarely seen them *not* touching, in fact.

She hadn't seen the appeal. But this was just the *food* that Earthlings ate, and the stimulus was beyond anything she'd ever experienced. Outside of combat, anyway.

She had hours to explore more of the environment before she'd be able to fly the skimmer back to the *Arbiter*. She now intended to make good use of them. The opportunity to explore the customs and delights of a planet with preservation status was unlikely to ever come to her again. All that remained was for her to determine how to gain Eric's cooperation.

Chapter Three

Watching Sorca eat was much better than having his own brunch. Eric had never seen someone enjoy their food on such a primal level. The way she was looking at him made him wonder if she was thinking of having him for dessert.

Brendan had strange friends.

Eric still wasn't sure about the point of this whole exercise, though. Was it a blind date? Some sort of weird roleplaying scenario? Both? And where was this woman from that she'd never encountered bacon? There was no way she could have faked that reaction to it.

He'd asked about some of Brendan's pastimes while trying to forge a bond that would keep Brendan working on the project. They'd talked about cosplaying and... Harping? No, larping. Live action role-play.

If that's what this was, Sorca seemed to be going all-out in her role.

Whatever Brendan hoped would come of this, Eric had one objective—get Brendan back to work on the project. Eric could tolerate the weirdness of the whole situation. And honestly, spending time with Sorca wasn't that bad.

Definitely strange, but not unpleasant.

Without looking at her plate, she picked up a piece of egg white, dripping with yolk, and slid it into her mouth. She sucked her finger clean, holding him with that sultry smile for a few moments as she chewed.

"We should copulate." She didn't bother to lower her voice. In fact, she made the proclamation louder than her earlier words had been.

He felt the gazes of several people nearby snap to their table and heard a few gasps. Sorca turned her head in the direction of one of the more scandalized sounds. She leaned toward an older woman sitting at the table next to them.

"You have a strong opinion on the matter," Sorca said. "What is the protocol when you wish to establish a physical relationship with someone?"

Glaring at Sorca, the woman said, "I have no comment."

Her word choice struck Eric as odd—but then, what about today wasn't? She cast a quick glance at him from the corner of her eye. It was probably just the weirdness of the situation, but something about the woman was setting off warning bells in his head. Before he could examine it further, Sorca drew his attention again.

"Eric Peterson." She pushed back from the table, then stood and held out her hand to him. "Come with me."

Letting her down easy wasn't going to be an option. At

least if he followed her out, he could avoid making a scene in the diner. He threw a few bills on the table and stood, but didn't take her hand. She didn't seem bothered by that at all. Or by the few cheers or clapping that broke out around them.

He was about to tell the cheering squad to calm down when Sorca lifted her arms in the air and yelled, "Victory!"

He was supposed to keep Brendan safe and focused on his work. After this, Eric might kill Brendan himself.

Eric followed Sorca out of the diner, trying to get his thoughts in order. She walked right into the street, stopping with her hands on her hips and feet spread in a strong stance. A fighter's stance, that seemed again to be second nature.

"Sorca..." His voice trailed off as he realized a truck was bearing down on her. She was standing in the middle of the street. "Sorca!"

He sprinted for her just as she noticed the vehicle. She turned toward him and leapt from the street, hitting him in the ribs and knocking the wind from him. He swore he was off his feet for several seconds as she carried him back toward the building, fast.

The next thing he knew, the brick wall of the restaurant was abrading his skin through his thin shirt—and Sorca was pressed against his chest, one arm wrapped tightly around his waist. She was muscular, but tiny. He hadn't realized how short she was until they stood side-by-side. Well, face-to-chest.

He was panting from the adrenaline, a dull ache in his ribs where she'd impacted. She merely looked up at him and smiled.

"That's an interesting transport," she said. "Its mass and velocity make it dangerous. You must not risk yourself for me. You aren't replaceable."

"And you are?"

She laughed, as if the brush with the truck had been nothing. "You would be surprised."

What did it take to rattle her? When the people in the diner were judging her, when the waitress tried to intimidate her, even the cheerleaders for her victory shout, she didn't seem to care at all. Eric couldn't imagine what it must be like to live like that.

"It'll catch up with you eventually," he said.

"What will?"

"Living like you've got nothing to lose."

"Perhaps. But what a race it will be to the end." She laughed, bringing her free hand to his face to run a finger along his jaw. "Now, come with me. I have things to discuss with you that are not for others' ears."

What the hell? It was all part of the game, and he really did feel that he needed to find out what was going on. At least she'd stopped talking about "copulating". Not that the idea was off-putting *per se*…

"Fine," he said. "Take me to Brendan."

She stepped up on her toes, sniffing Eric's chest as she did. Her nose grazed his collarbone, setting off a chain reaction of goosebumps. Her arm was still wrapped around his waist, her body pressed against his.

She let out another of those self-satisfied purrs, but this time it was all about *him*. The attention was unsettling in the best and worst ways at once.

She might not be talking about copulating anymore, but he was pretty sure she was still thinking about it. Unfortunately, so was he.

"Eventually," she said. "I wish to experience more of the pleasures your homew— Your home has to offer."

For the first time, she'd stumbled over something, actually stopped herself instead of acting on whatever whim seemed to catch her fancy. She glanced around, as if checking to make sure no one had overheard her.

"Home-" something. What had she been about to say?

She stepped away from him, but grasped his wrist and pulled him after her. "There is a park nearby. It will give us privacy for our conversation and…rejuvenation."

"Rejuvenation?"

Her gaze slowly passed down his body before returning to his eyes. "Arenar is important to maintain peak efficiency."

He let her pull him away from the wall. "Why do I have a feeling I'm going to regret this?"

"Your feeling is inaccurate. I promise you pleasure. There will be no regrets."

He let out a laugh as he fell in step beside her. He couldn't help himself.

"Are you always this confident?" he said.

"It is well earned."

After they had walked for several minutes, she turned from the sidewalk onto a walking path that led into a forest. A wave of misgiving passed through him. No one was nearby, and the trail probably wasn't heavily used this time of day. It would be a great place for an ambush.

When he hesitated, she said, "You have nothing to fear from me. I am sworn to protect you."

That was a change from what he was used to. He was always the one cast in the role of protector.

He snorted, remembering that it was all part of the game. He started walking again, certain Brendan was somewhere in the woods, waiting for them to arrive. Eric just hoped there were no costumes involved. That would be awkward.

"Sworn to Brendan?" Eric asked.

She laughed. "Of course not. Sworn to my commanding officer, General Serath."

"When did Brendan get the promotion?"

"I don't understand."

"I was making a joke. I assume Brendan will be playing the role of General Serath?"

"Playing the role?" Her eyebrows hitched up her forehead and her mouth dropped open. She started to laugh. And kept going, until she'd doubled over.

"Brendan could never pass for..." She struggled to catch her breath. "I mean..."

"Now *I* don't understand," Eric said. He felt like he should be irked, but her laughter was so pure, he felt himself smiling instead.

She shook her head as she straightened. "You will when you see Serath."

"I look forward to it."

"I suppose I should be calling him 'Adam', since that is the name he has now chosen for himself. I don't know that I will ever think of him as anything other than Serath."

"Have you worked with him for long?"

"I have."

There was warmth in her tone when she spoke of this "Serath". Maybe she did care about something. Odd that Eric felt a bit of a twinge at the thought of her caring for another man when they had *just* met and he was still fairly convinced that she was crazy.

The trail branched off, one path a gentle slope, and the other heading up at a steep angle. Sorca headed for the steep path. She was leading him deeper into the forest. The hike quickly went from pleasant to annoying as sweat trickled between his shoulder blades. She still didn't seem winded at all.

"No one's around," he said. "Why don't you tell me more about what's going on here?" He needed to know the rules of the game if he was going to play.

"You know Brendan has been trying to contact an advanced alien species."

Oh, here we go...

Aliens. He should have guessed it when Brendan's note mentioned the planet being in danger. When she'd stopped herself earlier, he would bet she'd been about to say, "Homeworld".

"Everybody needs a hobby," Eric said. "What of it?"

"He succeeded."

"Of course he did."

"You're not surprised?" She glanced over at him, a puzzled look on her face.

"He's a genius, especially with communications systems. If anyone could make contact with aliens, it would be Brendan."

"Your faith in him is encouraging. But a knowledge of technology will not be sufficient for him to lead Earth's First Contact Committee."

"First contact? Oh, right. With the aliens." Eric managed to keep himself from snorting.

Brendan and his...friend...had obviously put a lot of thought and effort into this. Sorca was absolutely throwing herself into the part. She sounded and acted like she believed every word she said. Every crazy word.

"So, are you one of those aliens he contacted?" Eric asked.

"I am."

"Convenient that you happen to look like an Earthling."

"It is." She nodded, taking the comment totally seriously. "Being able to move about freely with most Earthlings none the wiser will assist us in protecting your planet."

"From what?"

Even though it was a game, Eric still felt a tremor of misgiving flow through him. He lived every day with more knowledge of the precarious balance of human existence on Earth than most people had to deal with. The thought of aliens joining the mix—with their own ways, needs, and agendas—was unnerving.

"Brendan and Serath will provide you with the details," she said. "But first…"

She stepped off the trail into a small clearing. The grass had actually been mowed. It grew thick where the trees didn't block the sun overhead.

"Nice park," he said.

She smiled at him over her shoulder, walking deeper into the field. "Kira told me about this. 'Blades of grass'. I wish to experience it."

"Experience it how?"

Sorca sat and untied her boots, then pulled them off and tossed them aside. Her socks quickly followed. Digging her toes into the greenery surrounding her, she let out a long sigh. The acerbic remark he'd been about to make stuck on his tongue when she smiled up at him. It was such a genuine look of happiness.

Damn, she was a good actress.

"Join me," she said. "The blades are cool and do not cut."

"I'm aware. This is my planet, remember?"

She laughed as she stood. "What is an everyday occurrence for you is something I have never experienced." She looked down at her feet, lifting one then the other slowly, almost as if she was kneading the ground. "It tickles!"

For a fraction of a second, he wondered if this really was a game. Her joy seemed so authentic. He couldn't read any signs of deceit in her expressions—and he'd been trained to detect them.

But that would mean she *was* an alien. That would be crazy.

"Join me." She reached her hand to him.

This was all part of the game. Brendan was going all-out to help Eric relax and have some fun. He might as well enjoy himself.

"What the hell." He pulled off his shoes and threw them on the pile she had created.

"And the fiber covering," she said.

"Fiber covering? Oh, you mean my socks."

"Socks. Yes."

"You really are thinking of everything."

"It's a simple matter. You will enjoy the grass more if it comes in direct contact with your skin. And I did promise you pleasure."

Heat coursed through him again. There were all kinds of pleasure he could think of that he would love to enjoy with a strong, beautiful woman. Even if she seemed a little…off.

Because she was an alien.

Right.

He pulled off his socks and tossed them on the pile. The grass was cool beneath his feet, blades prickling along the sides. It did feel good, and some of his tension eased.

Sorca let Brendan's shirt slide to the ground. Maybe she wanted to feel the wind better or—

Eric's thoughts froze as she pulled her own shirt over her head and dropped it on the growing pile of clothing. The sun seemed to caress the smooth skin of her back, highlighting the lines of her muscles and shoulder blades. She turned, her arms stretched toward the sun, giving him a glorious view of her full breasts.

"Stars, this feels amazing," she said.

Eric stammered for a moment, only finding words when she started to unfasten her jeans. "Sorca, what are you doing?"

"Removing my clothing. You should do the same."

"Wait, what?"

He had thought she was kidding with her talk of copulating and pleasure. But then, she certainly did look extremely happy—even with something as simple as feeling the grass on her feet and the sun on her skin.

She pushed down her jeans and stepped out of them. Instead of standing again, she dropped to the ground and stretched.

"What the hell are you doing?"

"Enjoying the grass." She propped herself up on one elbow. "What are you doing?"

Honestly? He was enjoying watching her enjoying the grass.

The sun gleamed along the line of her side and hips. He wanted to trace it with his fingers, to feel the mix of strength and softness he could see with his eyes. He wanted to roll her over in the soft grass and…copulate.

Chapter Four

Earth was even better than Sorca imagined. She hoped she would make it back to one of the recording pods in a reprogramming center before she inevitably met up with something that killed her. She wanted to keep these memories in the next body the Coalition grew for her.

And she wanted to make more memories. With Eric.

She stood and slowly approached him.

He let out a nervous laugh and shook his head. "Look, if this is all part of the game—"

"Everything is." The words came out sharper than she'd intended, emotions that she needed to suppress roiling beneath the surface.

She had lost count of how many versions of herself she'd been. With the way her mind was rejecting even the simplest of cultural programming sessions like the one that prepared her for Earth, she had a feeling there wouldn't be many more.

His smile faded as she drew near. When she was close enough to feel his body heat, she stopped.

"You are unlike most of the sentients I have encountered," she said.

"So, you want to have sex with me because I'm an exotic Earthling."

His tone did not sound eager or excited. He seemed... annoyed. Perhaps if she flattered him...

"You are strong and hairy," she said. "I like your bear."

"I truly have no idea how to respond to that."

"Your bear and mustache."

"*Beard* and mustache," he said.

"Beard and mustache," she repeated. She struggled to find the right words, then remembered what the waitress had said at the diner. "Handsome. You are handsome."

He snorted and one eyebrow arched up his forehead. "Thanks, I guess."

"Do you not find me handsome as well?"

He outright laughed, his smile crinkling the corners of his eyes. "That isn't the word I would use."

Her chest felt tight, her heart suddenly beating faster against her ribs.

How could she be able to feel disappointment about this still? The muscles obviously visible beneath her skin made her a freakish specimen among her kind. Those who were intrigued by her physicality saw her only as a curiosity—especially when they learned of her Cygnian DNA.

Eric had seemed so different from those people. She had hoped he would be different in this regard as well.

She did her best to discard the useless emotions. The...

longing.

She wanted to beat on something—to smash it beyond recognition.

"I see," she said. "Among my people, my musculature is also considered unattractive."

She started to step away, but he grabbed her arm. His grip was firm at first, but gentled when she looked up at him.

"You're the most beautiful woman I've ever seen."

"*Beautiful.* I know this word." It was a high compliment among his kind. "Are you certain you're using it correctly?"

He laughed. "Yes, I'm sure."

He brushed her hair past her shoulder, letting his thumb trail along her cheek. The touch was shockingly gentle. She grabbed his wrist and pulled his hand away.

"I'm sorry," he said. "I thought you wouldn't mind, since you said you wanted to…"

"Copulate." She remembered the phrase he had used. "Have sex. Yes."

"Touching is generally involved in that."

"Of course."

Perhaps with Earth-sex.

The Coalition provided everyone with a drug they called *Coupling* to handle their biological urges. Most citizens used it alone, but some preferred enjoying the experience with a partner. Since the drug handled all stages of arousal, including culmination, there wasn't much interaction required.

Sorca had always found using *Coupling* unsatisfactory, even with a partner. Her body chemistry seemed to resist its effects. She had an even worse reaction to *Balance*—the drug used to maintain emotional equilibrium among the populace.

She released Eric's wrist, wondering if he would touch her like that again, his fingers as light as breath against her skin.

"I'm not saying we're going to have sex."

She smirked at him. "Your pupils are extremely dilated and your breath rate has increased."

"Sorca…"

"What is your preferred protocol?"

"My 'preferred protocol' doesn't usually involve a woman being absolutely committed to playing her role as an alien looking for an Earth hook-up."

"Hook-up?"

"Sex, Sorca." He shook his head. "This is really weird."

"Are you interested in copul—in having sex with me or are you not?"

He let out a sigh, and said, "Yes."

A thrill of victory sparked along her nerves. She leaned in closer, till the fabric of his shirt whispered across her flesh.

"Whether you believe I'm an alien who is profoundly

interested in sharing this pleasure with you or that I'm a woman playing a role, it would seem you have only one decision to make."

"Which is?"

"Whether you want to play along."

He laughed briefly, but then lifted his free hand to her shoulder. He still held her arm in a gentle grip.

"You really want this?" he said.

"The pleasures of Earth. I wish to experience them with you. To share them."

He shook his head. "What the hell."

He leaned in and pressed his lips against hers. A kiss, like Sorca had seen Serath and Evelyn exchange.

Eric's lips were a bit dry, but soft. He moved them against hers like his thumb had caressed her cheek. He ran his hands down her arms, then around to her back, pulling her close.

The embrace locked them together. She didn't like the idea that she would have to use her strength to break his hold. To even the battlefield, she wrapped her arms around his neck, drawing him closer. Now they both held the other captive.

Perhaps her action had a hidden meaning, because he let out a small groan and slid his tongue across her lips. She gasped at the strangeness of the feeling, and he thrust his tongue into her mouth.

She would have thought it would be appalling to have

someone else's tongue in her mouth, but instead warmth spread through her. One of his hands slid down to her buttocks, gripping her firmly and pushing her against his erection.

They were having sex with their mouths. She hadn't known such a thing was possible. But the movements of his tongue, her body's response to his presence within her...

She ran her fingers through his hair, grabbing a handful of the dark strands and tilting his head to the side—carefully. The last thing she wanted was to injure him. He groaned again, but instead of deepening the kiss, he shifted his face so that his lips were pressed against her neck.

More warmth. More tingling sensations as the follicles of her skin drew to attention.

Slickness was gathering between her legs. As if he sensed it, he...moved his hand there. She gasped as he pressed his fingers within the folds of her flesh, parting them, delving deeper until—

"Stars!"

He was within her again, in a way she had never imagined. Spreading her, moving inside and out. His fingers pumped like a piston while his thumb circled a nerve cluster she hadn't known she possessed. All the bodies she had gone through, all the lifetimes, and she had never experienced this part of herself.

At some point, she had released his hair, and was now

half-wrapped around him. She wasn't sure when it had happened. She only knew she must be careful with him.

She wrapped her arms around his shoulders—positioning her body so that she wouldn't hurt him too badly if she forgot herself again. Something was building within her, and she had already lost awareness of herself once.

His pace increased, his fingers flexing deep in her core, stretching her, spreading her slickness. The energy he was building intensified. Warmth and tingling, sparks and plasma bursts, until it coalesced in a white-hot explosion that fired out from his hand at her center, through her entire body.

She screamed, barely registering the answering calls of startled birds that leapt from the trees into the air. He grunted, lowering her to the ground and kneeling between her parted legs.

"I didn't hurt you, did I?" he said.

She was confused at first, hearing the words running through her own mind spoken by him. Why would he think he had hurt her?

The physical sensations he had generated within her were joined by something deeper, stronger. An emotional resonance she hadn't anticipated.

He cared. He cared if he hurt her.

"You didn't cause me pain," she said. "You gave me pleasure unlike anything I've ever experienced."

He was panting, his hands fisted on his thighs as he gazed at her. His eyes held hunger.

"I promised you pleasure," she said. "That I would share this with you."

Eric nodded as he rose on his knees. He unfastened his jeans and shoved them down his thighs. His member jutted at her, the tip glistening.

She had never seen this part of a male so close. When she had used *Coupling*, she had barely had time to bring her partner into her body before the drug completed their mating activities for them.

Eric was glorious.

He reached into his back pocket and pulled out the small folded bit of fabric where he kept his currency. He opened it and pulled out a small square of metal. No, not metal, from the way he tore it open. Something she hadn't encountered.

He pulled a small circle of pliable material from the shiny square. After pressing the circle to the tip of his erection, he rolled it down, covering himself.

When they were finished, she'd have to ask what it was. For now, she was more interested in action than knowledge.

"Are you sure you want to do this?" he said.

She laughed. "How can you even ask?"

"I always ask."

"Then here is your answer, Eric Peterson. Yes."

He dropped his body onto hers, pressing against her core. She could feel the strain thrumming through his body, mirrored in her own. Red clouded her vision as he entered her—for once, not battle rage. Something else. Something new.

It was like flickering plasma running over her skin— energy that didn't burn or hurt, but made her feel alive in a way she'd never felt before. She wanted more of it, wanted to grab him and pull him closer, deeper. And she was afraid if she did, she'd snap him right in two.

As he pressed himself into her, he groaned. "God, you're so tight. My cock's going to go off any second."

"Your what?"

"My dick. You just...feel too good." His eyes were pinched shut and he held himself completely still, as if he was struggling with his own self-control.

She tried to piece together his meaning. "You're about to orgasm."

Her body was pulsing, preparing for its own release.

He let out a laugh and shook his head. "Yes, if you want to be specific about it. Thanks for the distraction. It's helping."

"I will assist you in prolonging this experience."

For once, she had no idea what action to take. Among the Sadirians, she was considered to be bizarrely attuned to her body. Her physicality was what made her of greatest use to the Coalition, after all. In battle, she always knew what to do. But this was an entirely different physical experience.

Eric was taking slow breaths, still not moving. She could feel a deep throb from his dick resonating within her.

Finally, she admitted her ignorance. "I don't know what to do."

He opened his eyes as he let out a snort. "Be less beautiful? Less soft and strong at once. Less confident and sexy and…oddly vulnerable."

"I can't change those things—"

"I was kidding. I wouldn't change anything about you."

"Nothing?"

"No. Not even your bizarre personality."

"There must be something you would improve upon."

While they were working on Sorca's hybridized DNA, the genetic engineers in the Coalition had tried repeatedly to improve upon her abilities and form, often with… unfortunate results.

Several times, they had implanted her memories and persona in those forms. Sometimes, she would survive long enough to be sent to a recording center and update her mental imprint. She suppressed a shiver, pushing the thoughts away.

She didn't want this memory to be tainted by the past. Eric started speaking again, drawing her attention back to the moment.

"I want to say I'd make your pussy have less firm of a grip, but that would be a lie. I've never felt anything so good."

Slowly, he pulled his hips back. The movement was distressing at first, until the friction struck her nerves, making her gasp. She grabbed at his back, instinctively trying to keep him close. At the last moment, she remembered to only take hold of his shirt.

He sank back into her with a rocking motion. She gasped at the waves of stimulation pulsing through her body, the odd heaviness in her limbs and fullness in her chest.

"Stars…" she said.

"Damn…"

"This can not end."

He kissed her neck and held his lips close to her ear. "We can always do it again."

"Can we?"

"As many times as you want."

"I wish to do this *many* times."

"I better pick up more condoms, then."

"Condoms?"

"You don't have to keep pretending to be an alien. This activity is absolutely entertaining enough for me."

"I never said I was pretending."

He laughed and shook his head.

Again, he lifted his hips, pulling his dick from her. And

again, he slid back in, as deep as was possible. She felt him filling her, pushing against the muscles of her core as they gripped him.

He repeated the motion a few times, increasing his speed. The pulses moving along her nerves intensified, pleasure beating against her senses. He lifted himself on one elbow while he reached with his other hand to grip her thigh and pull her leg up along his side.

"Wrap your leg around me," he said.

"I can't."

"Sure you can. You don't have to be that flexible."

"It isn't that. I don't want to hurt you."

He laughed, pausing in his movements. He took a few deep breaths, perhaps trying to calm his body.

Sorca didn't want to calm her body. She wanted to experience what was just on the other side of the waves of energy rippling through her from where they were joined.

"You don't have to worry about hurting me," he said.

"I always have to worry about hurting those near me," she said. "Especially during this."

His brow furrowed as he thought on her words. He had yet to see her strength.

"I'm not like you," she said.

"Because you're an alien?"

She nodded. The plasma waves were ebbing, and for a brief moment, she wondered if she did want them back. Perhaps it would be better to just walk away now, before she completed their coupling—*sex*—knowing she would never experience anything like it again.

He tightened his grip on her thigh, holding it tight against his side, then pressed his chest against hers, crushing his hips to hers. The nerve cluster reawakened with a cascade of plasma bursts throughout her body.

No, she should definitely complete this encounter.

Eric grabbed the back of her neck, bringing them as close together as was safely possible, then he rolled over, pulling her along with him while they were joined. He let out a grunt as she instinctively adjusted her weight, straddling him.

Her muscles were denser than a standard Earthling or Sadirian. It increased her effectiveness in battle, but made her heavier than someone her size would normally be. She wouldn't crush him, but didn't want to make him uncomfortable.

She raised herself on her elbows as he released her thigh, bringing his hands to her hips. He was smiling at her.

"I don't understand why you performed that maneuver," she said.

"You seemed worried about my safety. Worry isn't very good when it comes to enjoying yourself. I figured if you take over, you'll feel better."

"How do I—"

She leaned back and the motion pushed him even

deeper into her core. Her spread legs opened her slit so that the nerve cluster he had so expertly stimulated earlier was pressed against his pelvis. More bursts of plasma. Heat pulsed along her skin with each touch and gyration.

"Cygnus X…"

"I'm guessing that means you like it?" Eric smirked up at her.

"Yes," she groaned.

"And this?" He pressed his thumb into her slit, rubbing the nerve cluster. Her body thrummed like a phase rifle powering up to full.

"Eric…" Her eyes drifted shut, all her senses pulling inward, to where they were joined.

"Move on me, Sorca. It's okay. I promise."

She kept her hands at her sides, gazing down along her body to where she could see him buried deep inside, and smiled.

"Earthling, you have no idea what you're in for."

Chapter Five

Eric had maybe five seconds to ponder that "I-know-something-you-don't-know" smile of hers. Five seconds of holding his breath before she took his advice and started to move.

She rose up on her thighs, the movement pulling along his dick in a stroke that nearly ended him. Then she cautiously lowered herself back down, her body pressing against his shaft, all softness and strength and heat.

If he hadn't been wearing a condom, he wouldn't have lasted ten seconds with her. As humiliating as that experience might be, he was more tempted to try it with her than with anyone else he'd ever had sex with.

Her dark hair fell across her chest as she became more confident in her strokes. He brought his hands to her breasts, lifting them and kneading them. When he gently pinched her nipples between his fingers, she gasped and increased her pace.

How could anything feel so good? Gooseflesh spread over his arms as the energy building in him crested.

She threw her head back and let out a primal scream, her core pulsing, coaxing him to his own climax. It hit him like a sonic boom, vibrating in every molecule of his body. She kept pulling on him, pumping him, her body not giving him any escape from the pleasure cascading along every nerve ending.

It was hard to breathe. His vision dimmed around the edges as his orgasm went on and on.

Finally, she slowed, then stopped, barely panting.

"Are you all right?" she said.

"I'm not sure."

Physically he felt...amazing. Almost like their bodies had fused where they connected. The afterimage of the pleasure they had shared was so intense he didn't even mind the thought. Which *did* bother him.

He couldn't afford to get that wrapped up in anyone. He had a job to do, people to protect.

Sorca lifted her hips. Normally, he would have slid from his partner at that point, but with her, it was just a continuation of what had come before. He felt every millimeter as their bodies...disengaged, for lack of a better word.

Damn, he'd really been sucked into the whole alien thing.

She rose and took a few steps away, stretching her arms to the sky again. He sat up, gauging how weak his legs would feel when he stood. Her core was right at eye level. Even after that amazing sex—or maybe because of it—all he could think about for that moment was grabbing her by her ass and pulling her to his mouth.

"You have an angry look to you, Eric. Was our sex not satisfactory?"

He was angry, but with himself. He'd never let himself get so carried away with something like this before. He wasn't even sure what "this" was.

"Satisfactory isn't the word I would choose."

She actually looked a bit concerned, her face bearing no trace of her sultry smile and the slightest crease appearing between her eyebrows.

"Did I err?"

"What? No, you didn't do anything wrong. You did everything right, in fact."

Very, very right.

"Then why do you look upset?"

"Because that was spectacular. And you have ruined me for Earth women forever."

Slowly, she smiled. Eric felt it like a blow to the chest. The edge of mischief was missing. Instead of looking amused, she looked *happy*. Fulfilled. And he had helped her to achieve that—in the most pleasurable of ways.

He was in trouble.

"I want to learn more," she said. "When can we have sex again?"

Deep trouble.

"Sorca, I—"

She held her hand to him, as if to help him up. He

figured he'd humor her, and took it.

The next thing he knew, he was on his feet. He might have even been *off* his feet for a moment, just like when she'd leapt out of the way of that bus earlier. How strong was she? She didn't seem to notice his confusion, and kept right on with the conversation.

"You enjoyed it, correct?" she said.

"Well, yes."

"Then why should we not couple—I mean have sex—again?"

Couple? More odd phrasing. And she said it so naturally.

Eric had been trained to notice when people were lying. He'd assumed that she was so into her part that she wasn't giving any tells. But now, he could see what it was like when she was experiencing a genuine emotion. He'd seen it in that smile.

She hadn't broken character at all. So that meant… what? That she really was an alien?

He laughed at himself internally as he tried to think of anything but sinking into her heat again.

"For one thing, I only had the one condom," he said.

"Condom. You mentioned this before."

He pulled out his handkerchief, then peeled the condom off of his dick. He briefly flicked his wrist in a, "this" gesture. There weren't any trashcans around, so he wrapped it up and put it in one of his front pockets.

"What is its function?" Sorca's excitement hadn't diminished. And she *still* hadn't broken character.

The more emotion she showed, the more holes he should be seeing in her game. But instead, she seemed more sincere. A weird feeling of misgiving started to grow in him as he fastened his jeans.

"Can we quit with the games?" he said. "I mean, after…"coupling", I'd kind of like to know the real you."

A bit of mischief sparked in her smile again. "I will answer your questions if you answer mine."

"Fine. Within reason. But first, you have to get dressed."

"All right."

She gathered up her clothes and dressed with surprising speed and almost military efficiency. Eric shook off the thought, his misgiving growing.

When she was dressed, she turned to him and said, "What is a condom for?"

"Oh, for crying out…" He shook his head. "It prevents pregnancy and the spread of disease."

"Aha! Then we don't need them for sex. I am free from any Earth-borne pathogens, and will be purged of anything I'm exposed to from our encounters after my first sleep cycle in a regen bed when I return to my ship." She grinned at him, fists on her hips in a victorious stance.

"Sorca, come on." He let out a sigh.

If Brendan had expected them to become a couple, he'd

picked a very strange woman for this bizarre blind date—
and that was what it felt like to Eric at this point. Sure, on
the one hand, things were going great physically, but
emotionally and mentally, how was he supposed to
connect...

"Wait, what about pregnancy?" he said. "Why doesn't
that worry you?"

"The genetic engineers sterilized me during my design.
There are specific laws which govern the DNA they used
in my creation. They can't risk it being spread, stolen, or
manipulated outside of their labs. My body even has a
self-destruct and will disintegrate me should either my
heartbeat or brainwaves end."

Cold chills rocketed down his spine at the thought. He
actually shivered, until he reminded himself that this was
all just a game.

Eric had a natural instinct to protect people. And even
though this was all a messed up fantasy scenario, he still
felt something in him reaching toward her, wanting to
protect her.

"I don't know what's more disturbing," he said. "That
your fantasy involves such a fucked up system or that
you're pretending you don't have a problem with it."

He really was in it too deep. But not so deep that he
was okay making light of such a serious topic. Apparently,
she took it pretty seriously too, because when her smile
faded, it was replaced by a menacing glare.

"I am a soldier for the Coalition of Planets," Sorca said. "Chief of Security for the fleet's flagship, the *Arbiter*, under command of General Serath, who has enforced peace in this galaxy more effectively than any officer in Coalition history."

"I get it. So you serve the very monsters who created you."

"I was *created* to serve."

The world she was describing was horrible. He shook his head, as if that could clear it of the civilization she'd described.

"I don't understand why this distresses you," she said. "Everyone in the Coalition has all they need. Every citizen has purpose."

"Purpose is not the same as meaning. Why am I even playing along with this?" He took a few steps away before turning back to her. "Truth, Sorca. I wanted *truth* when I asked my questions, not more games."

"I have only spoken truth to you, Eric Peterson. And to say otherwise insults my honor."

"That's enough. I'm out. Tell Brendan I'll contact him tomorrow about—"

As he walked past her, she grabbed his arm, freezing his chain of thought. Freezing it because she was holding him in place—*with one hand.*

Cautiously, he pulled against her grip, just to test out how bad of a mess he'd gotten himself into. She didn't budge. Instead, her grip tightened enough to send arcs of pain up his arm.

"Brendan has requested your presence on the *Arbiter*." Her voice was low and her lips curled up in a near snarl. "I am under orders from General Serath to bring you to the ship. Know that I speak the truth when I say, I *will* bring you to the ship. I do not fail in my missions."

His stomach felt leaden. Was she insane? And if she was, had she done something to Brendan?

Eric knew several ways to break her hold on him— ways that would counteract her strength. But it might be better to play along. Maybe he could get her to take him to Brendan, since that's what she seemed to be so focused on.

Her expression softened as she seemed to shake herself. She looked at her hand on his arm and loosened her grip so that it wasn't quite as painful. When she spoke, her voice was gentler as well.

"I'm sorry. I don't want to hurt you. The amount of reprogramming I've had is having unforeseen effects on my capacity for emotional control."

"Reprogramming? So, what, are you an android now?"

"Of course not. Androids are much too expensive to create and maintain."

"So, the Coalition just creates *people* to serve it. Disposable people."

Her only response was a tightening of her lips.

"I'm torn right now, Sorca. Because I really don't want

you to be crazy. But if you're telling the truth…"

That thought was so much more frightening.

She stepped close to him, running the fingers of her free hand along his cheek. "I will protect you, Eric. As much as I'm able. But I have to follow orders."

"And if you're ordered to kill me?"

"It won't come to that. At worst, you'll receive a mind-wipe and forget all that's passed between us. But I'll remember. Even through death."

Yeah. She was crazy.

Before he had a chance to say more, she ducked down and hefted him in a fireman's carry, draping him across her shoulders. He was so surprised by her speed and strength that he didn't even have a chance to react.

How the hell was she carrying him? *Effortlessly.* She headed back to the trail, without a single hitch in her stride.

"Sorca, put me down."

"I'm sorry it has to be this way. I think it will be safest for you if I carry you to my ship. Once you see it, you'll know I'm telling the truth. And there's so much more you need to know."

"Such as?" He looked around for anything he could use to help himself get free. She had that grip of steel on one of his arms, but he could strike at her with the other.

"Earth is being invaded by hostile aliens," she said.

"Like ones that abduct you after the most amazing sex

of your life?"

He couldn't believe he'd already had sex with her. But he hadn't known that she was… Crazy? An alien? Neither option was appealing.

"I'm pleased you enjoyed yourself so much. It was also my most pleasurable experience. Even better than bacon."

He snorted despite his situation.

Aliens. Right.

He saw a flash of gray fur in the brush next to them and his heart picked up in response. Craning his neck for a better look, he saw that it was just a deer. A weirdly pale, not-bothered-by-humans deer, but still just a deer.

He was definitely letting this all get to him. How the hell was she still carrying him, though?

"I'm not your enemy," she said. "The *Arbiter* is here to assist. General Serath fell in love with an Earthling during his shore leave here. Earth is now special to him and he will do everything in his power to protect it."

"Great."

"Brendan needs your help to sort out how to handle the situation."

"And how did Brendan get involved?"

"He made contact with the soldier who was operating our listening station."

"That makes as much sense as anything else, I guess."

He needed to keep her talking while he figured out a plan for what to do next. If she'd done something to

Brendan, Eric couldn't kill her. Not until he found and retrieved his asset.

The thought tugged on his heart with surprising strength, like the woman carrying him. He didn't want to have to kill Sorca. And he wanted Brendan to be okay— not just as an asset, but as a friend.

"And I'm sure Brendan won him over with his charming personality," Eric said.

"*Her*. Kira is the woman Brendan has pair-bonded with. They fell in love while conversing using his encoded communications array."

Fuck.

How the hell did Sorca know about that? *She should not know about that.*

Eric wasn't the only one in deep water. Brendan was way out there, too—surrounded by sharks. If he'd shared information about the classified projects he was working on… There was nothing Eric could do to protect Brendan.

Eric revisited the possibility that Sorca was an enemy agent. And immediately dismissed it. The entire situation was too bizarre.

Sorca kept on talking, not winded by carrying Eric's weight while walking uphill. His feet were almost dragging on the ground.

"Apparently, Earthlings have quite an effect on Sadirians," she said. "Since Earthlings are initially of the same species, I suppose it makes a bit of sense."

"The same species?"

"A colony ship crashed on your planet millennia ago. The Sadirians who survived lost touch with their origins as they assimilated with the environment and took over from the evolving hominids."

"Of course they did."

The ground bounced along below, the trail left behind as she ventured into the brush. She managed to avoid most of the low-hanging branches that might have hit him, and the foliage seemed to be thinning.

She wasn't bothering with trying to restrain him as she carried him. Either she didn't know any better or—the more alarming possibility—she didn't see him as any kind of threat. He kept running through various scenarios of ways he could get free, with different levels of physical ramifications for her.

"You're like a glimpse into the past," she said. "Back when Sadirians actually interacted on a more intimate physical and emotional level. I must say, having now experienced this myself, I understand the appeal. I was curious about whether something similar would occur between us when I received the assignment."

"Wait, you mean falling in love? Because sex in a park isn't the same as falling in love." Even super hot sex.

"Don't be ridiculous. My duty is to my ship and to General Serath."

"And the Coalition."

She shrugged, accidentally digging her shoulder into his stomach. He let out a grunt and she stopped.

"Did I hurt you?" she said.

"Yes."

She set him down, negating his need for any of the plans he'd been working on to escape her clutches. Well, to a point. She still had a grip on one of his wrists. He looked around at where they'd stopped, trying to get his bearings.

The trail was long gone. They had emerged from the trees at the top of a cliff. There was only a narrow space a few yards wide with sparse grass between the forest and a sheer drop-off.

What the hell did she plan to do next?

Chapter Six

"Nice view," Eric said. "Do you mind if I get a better look?"

"Proceed." Sorca didn't see the harm in Eric exploring his surroundings. She would be curious as well, if their roles were reversed.

She let go of his wrist, but walked at his side, just in case he should try to run. He didn't seem like the running kind, however. A thrill shot through her as she wondered if he was the type who might issue a challenge to her instead. She'd felt his body tense a few times while carrying him, as if he was considering an attempt at breaking away from her hold.

They stopped near the cliff's edge and looked out at the hillside. Sharp rocks dotted the ground at least a dozen meters below them. It would be best not to fall.

The skimmer was close. She'd flown it in over the cliff, landing in a large clearing they could easily reach by walking along the space between the trees and the drop-off. When it was time to leave, she'd have a clear path. And the ship was also far enough out of the way that it was unlikely Earthlings would accidentally discover it.

"Protocol dictates that we leave at nightfall," she said. "That way, if the ship's cloak fails, Earthlings are less likely to notice the skimmer."

"Let me guess. Your ship is right next to us, but it's cloaked."

"No, it's meters away, in a larger cleared area. If it were that close, the cloak would have disengaged after sensing my proximity."

He laughed and shook his head. The light caught in his hair. She hadn't truly tested it to see if it was as soft as it looked. She hoped she would still have a chance.

Something in the way he was standing made her tense. There was a quiet readiness to him, an ease that belied impending action.

"I caution you against trying to attack me," she said, even though the thought of it sent another wave of excitement through her.

Their physical interactions had already been intense beyond anything she'd experienced. The idea of having the opportunity to face him in combat was…stimulating.

"If I try to leave, will you try to stop me?" he said.

"I will not try. I will succeed."

He snorted and shook his head. "Damn, you're cocky."

In case he did try to escape, she needed to be certain that he knew exactly what he was entering into. He had already glimpsed her strength, but there were more complex aspects to issuing her a challenge.

"There are specific laws which govern combat with me."

"I can't wait to hear about this." He lifted his arms briefly, then dropped them to his sides. "Enlighten me."

"Anyone who defeats me in hand-to-hand combat becomes my bondmate."

"Bondmate?"

"We'll be pair-bonded under Coalition law."

"What does that mean. Like married?"

"That's a simplification, but an apt one. The laws are part of the agreement between the High Council and the people of Cygnus-1 who supplied the specialized DNA used in my creation. They are a warrior culture, and the Coalition must honor their customs. Pair-bonds are created through martial challenges."

"So if I try to leave and we fight—"

"I will defeat you."

"Or, we'll end up married," he said.

"I will defeat you." She smiled as she imagined how much fun it would be for him to try to best her in battle. "I will also be required to log you among the many who have faced me in combat. It only seems fair I should let you know the ramifications of what you attempt."

He shook his head and turned back to the cliff, his hands on his waist. A small part of her—a ridiculous part —wondered what it would be like should he prevail. The thought was quite distracting.

She almost didn't notice when he quickly shifted his weight away from her, only to bring his arm around in a vicious, back-handed blow. She let the hit partially connect, gauging his strength as she staggered back a few paces.

Unlike most of the Sadirians—and even some challengers of other species she had faced—there was purpose behind his blow that added to his innate strength. He was attuned to his body in a way that most of her challengers had long forgotten.

This was going to be fun. She just needed to be careful not to hurt him.

"Human, you have no idea who you're challenging."

"If you think I'm going to keep playing along with you without a fight, you're mistaken."

"It's you who are mistaken, if you think you stand a chance against me."

"I'm the one who landed the first blow."

"And I shall land the last."

She lashed out with a quick kick, aiming to knock the breath from him to facilitate his recapture. He dodged to the side—which she'd expected. Even at the most basic training level, Sadirian soldiers knew to do their best to avoid getting hit.

As she followed up with two quick punches, he feinted to her right, leaning back so that her attack met nothing but air. An interesting move.

"I've never seen this fighting technique," she said. "What do you call it?"

"A little bit of this, a little bit of that."

Brendan had warned her that Eric was some kind of Earth soldier. She still couldn't believe their military had such variety on the planet—even among each geographically-based community. "Countries", they were called. And combat training wasn't reserved for soldiers. They permitted their *citizens* to learn.

Foolish.

There was no way that Eric could stand against her strength and durability. She was being cautious, but eventually, she would land a blow that would make him concede. The skimmer was close enough—with its regen bed and med kit—that she was confident she could repair any damage he might sustain. And that was where she needed to get him anyway.

He blocked another kick, but somehow managed to grab her ankle. Instead of trying to hold on to her, giving her leverage she could use in any number of countermoves, he twisted and released it, forcing her to twirl her body in the air to avoid damage to the joint.

She staggered a few paces away when she landed, regaining her balance. What sort of maneuver was that?

Eric stood still, regarding her calmly. He had yet to attack her. Not since that first strike.

She launched herself at him, again with her fists.

Perhaps he would get a *little* bit hurt. Except, once more, he stepped to the side—this time striking out and landing a blow to her back that sent her stumbling.

Fun. Yes.

Also infuriating.

She wheeled around, letting go of her control even more. When he deflected her punch, he grunted, shaking his hand as he quickly backed away. Now he was aware of her strength, her speed, and her increased density.

He was getting closer to the trees, but she didn't think he was trying to run. Perhaps he was trying to maintain a safe distance from the cliff's edge behind them.

"Concede," she said. "Before you're injured."

He rubbed his forearm. "Tell me where Brendan is."

He wasn't running because he was concerned for his friend. An admirable sentiment, and one she could perhaps use to end the conflict.

"I already did," she said. "He's on the *Arbiter*, waiting for you."

"I don't believe you."

The statement shouldn't have riled her like it did, but her vision blurred red around the edges. She had never lied to him. Not once. And he continued to insult her honor by saying otherwise.

She charged him, swinging around in a kick that had little control, but ample strength. He dodged it, his eyes wide as her foot connected with the tree behind him. The trunk fragmented in a satisfying explosion of force, sharp pieces of wooden shrapnel flying through the air.

He barely managed to stumble away as the entire thing fell over. It was still partially attached to its base, leaving it at an angle between them.

At least he was on the side nearer her ship. If she could herd him there and get close enough, the cloak would deactivate and he would see it. Perhaps that would be enough to convince him she spoke the truth.

She could have leapt over the trunk, but she wanted him thoroughly convinced that she was not of his world. Bending down, she put her shoulder under the tree and lifted.

The connecting fibers were stronger than she anticipated, but couldn't match her. With a yell, she tore the tree from its base, lifting it above her head just enough that she could hurl it over the cliff.

She turned back to him, panting, and was gratified by the look of shock on his face.

"You see, Earthling. You are no match for me."

He lifted his arms before him, hands fisted, elbows bent. He widened his stance, weight evenly distributed between each foot. A fighting stance.

She felt her lips pull back from her teeth in a smile. This was a challenge. A full-challenge.

Yes...

"I'm not looking to be your match," he said. "I'm

looking for Brendan."

"Then let me take you to him." That would end the chance of Eric being hurt, even if it meant ending their battle.

"I'm not going anywhere with you."

"How can you still not believe me?" She gestured to the furrow in the ground near where she'd thrown the tree. Tightness was building in her chest, confusing emotions rising in her that made her want to break things.

"There are drugs that can make people strong. The tree could have been rotted. Hell, it could have been a fake made of balsa wood. Brendan has the resources to arrange it. This whole thing has been a setup from the beginning."

"A setup?"

"A trick." He shook his head. "Why am I still explaining this to you? No more games, Sorca."

"This has never been a game for me," she said. "Not truly. I haven't tricked you, and to accuse me thus taints what we've experienced together."

"Would you give it a rest already?"

The tightness in her chest erupted in a primal yell as she ran at him. Not holding back, she struck again and again. Each time, he deflected, dodged, or sidestepped her attack. Somehow, he was using her strength against her.

"Sorca, stop. You're out of control."

Why should he care? She screamed again, spinning around with a kick that shattered another tree. This one was much larger than the first, and as it fell, she couldn't escape its low branches.

It didn't matter. She could lift it from her as soon as…

Her thoughts scattered as her body flooded with warning. The ground was moving beneath her. No, the tree was pulling her. Pulling her toward the cliff.

"No," she screamed, clawing at the earth. "Not before I've imprinted!"

She kicked at the tree to try to untangle herself from it, but it was moving too fast. They both went over. As it fell free of her at last, she barely managed to catch her fingers on the edge of the cliff.

Eric stood above her, panting. Blood trickled from a scratch along his cheek. She didn't know if it was from the tree or her attacks. All she remembered was the rage. The despair.

Soon, she wouldn't remember that. Her vision blurred at the thought of the loss of him. Of what they had shared.

"I wanted to remember you," she said.

The earth gave way beneath her grip.

Chapter Seven

Eric threw himself to the ground, grabbing Sorca's wrist as she fell from the cliff. He started to slide over with her, and dug his fingers into the ground as far away from the edge as he could. The earth had been loosened by the *second* tree she had somehow smashed with a single kick.

He hoped he would have time to think about that later. At the moment, he turned all of his focus toward keeping them both from falling onto the rocks below. His shoulder felt like it was dislocating, but he ground his teeth against the pain and pulled, keeping his body as close to the earth as he could.

Please... Please...

He repeated the phrase in his mind until her head was above the edge, then her shoulders. As he rolled over, pulling her on top of him, he finally let out a breath.

Damn, she was heavy.

She would probably kill him now. He was vulnerable, his shoulder was sending arcs of pain through his body. With her unbelievable strength, all she'd have to do was punch him hard enough and that would be it.

Instead of picking up the berserker rage that had so

clearly taken her over earlier, she straddled him, pushing herself up with her hands on his chest. Gently, thank God.

Finally, she was panting as well. Now he had an idea of what it took to wind her. He wasn't sure if it was adrenaline, fear, or exertion. He was betting on the first. Her eyes were wide and her full lips parted.

"You saved me," she said.

"Yeah."

He struggled to catch his breath. Maybe she wasn't going to kill him after all. She could still be planning to drag him back to her spaceship.

Christ, was he really thinking that was possible? He didn't know what to believe at this point.

"You *risked yourself* to save me."

"It's becoming something of a habit."

She snapped her mouth shut, eyes blazing with intention.

Here it came. What the hell would it be this time?

"I concede," she said.

He wasn't sure he'd heard her right. She had him at a complete disadvantage—at her mercy. Feeling her legs on either side of his thighs, her hips pressing down against his dick, for a brief moment, that didn't seem like the worst thing in the world.

He shook himself internally, remembering the stakes. Either Brendan had been flipped by enemies pretending to be aliens, or...

Or there were aliens invading Earth. One of which—a completely gorgeous one of which—was straddling Eric and gazing down at him with the most intense sense of wonder he'd ever seen.

Shit.

"I'm not marrying you." He spoke mostly to distract himself from the terrifying thought of hostile aliens taking over his planet.

Sorca shook her head. "It's done. You knew the stakes when you challenged me."

"But I didn't defeat you."

"You did. I would be dead if not for you. According to Coalition law, we are pair-bonded."

"Great."

At least she wasn't planning to kill him. At the moment.

"You're disappointed," she said.

"What? No. I mean…" He shook his head, trying to ignore the heat where their bodies touched.

His system was still flooded with adrenaline from the fight. And the sex.

Damn, he had really stepped in it. Way worse than he'd thought earlier, especially now that he was actually considering that everything she'd told him up to this moment had been the truth.

Apparently, he was crazy now, too. Maybe they *were* a pair.

"As your bondmate, I can assist you with your

interactions with the Coalition," she said. "I will either resign or retain my commission, depending on what you deem most beneficial."

"Hold on. First, I would never ask any partner to give up something they love for a relationship—and I sure as hell wouldn't make the decision for them. Second, we aren't bondmates."

"We are," she said. "I don't understand why the idea upsets you. I'm considered very valuable—"

"Stop. Just stop. Do you even realize how that sounds? You are your own person, Sorca. No matter where you're from or who...made you."

Genetic engineering. Forced sterilization. And she had mentioned 'remembering him through death'. What the hell did that mean? What kind of life was she leading on that ship? Suddenly, the idea of them being married wasn't looking so bad to him, if it meant he could help get her away from that.

"Marriage is a big deal on my...homeworld," he said.

It felt ridiculous to say those words and mean them. At the same time, thinking back on everything that had happened since they met, it was starting to sound more real—to *feel* more real.

"I won't stand in the way of you...marrying... according to your traditions," she said. "We're only pair-bonded in the Coalition. And many citizens actually enter into a multi-bond with others. Those are usually more business-oriented mergers, but I imagine they sometimes lead to physical and emotional attachment. You're free to marry whatever Earthling you wish. I do hope that we can occasionally meet to have sex, however."

He would love to have sex with her way more than occasionally. But the rest of what she was saying set his teeth on edge.

"That isn't how we do things on Earth."

"You don't bond with multiple mates or partners?"

"Well, some Earthlings do, but not me. I want a life-partner. One. Someone I can laugh with and care for. Someone who will support me and that I can support. Who understands my need to protect others or maybe even shares it. Someone who understands that there are greater needs out there than our own."

Even as he was saying the words, he realized the truth. The truth she'd been telling him all along, but that sounded too impossible to believe.

With a beaming smile, she said, "I believe I can fulfill all of those criteria."

"Oh, hell."

He grabbed her wrists and pulled her against his chest, then rolled both of their bodies a bit further from the edge of the cliff. His intention had been... He wasn't sure what. But once he was on top of her, seeing her smile up at him with what looked dangerously like hope mixed with excitement, his brain stopped cooperating.

Maybe that tree she dropped on his head had given him a concussion. Maybe this whole thing was some sort of nervous breakdown from working too much.

Work. Right.

He pulled out his handcuffs. With her not resisting him, it was probably the only chance he was going to get to stop this weird situation from spiraling any further into crazyland. He rose so he was straddling her, then pulled her hands into his lap.

"Oh, excellent." She reached for the fastener of his jeans.

"That's not what—"

He let out a sigh, then snapped the handcuffs on her wrists. She held them above her face, cocking her head to the side as she examined them.

"They're beautiful." She beamed up at him. "I accept your gift."

"Those are handcuffs."

She stared at him.

"I'm detaining you. Until I have a better understanding of what's going on."

"So, we're not having sex again?" She sat up so that their chests pressed together, looping her arms behind his neck. "Because these could make that interesting."

His dick jerked at the thought, wanting to be buried in her heat again. Damn, it was tempting. But he needed answers.

"I have questions," he said.

"Ask me whatever you want." She nuzzled his neck. "If it's within my power to answer and won't endanger you, I'll respond."

"And if it betrays the secrets of your people? Of your rank and role on the *Arbiter?*"

"Telling you military secrets of the Coalition without authorization would absolutely endanger you. It would necessitate a mind-wipe." She leaned back and smiled at him. "But if you return to the *Arbiter* with me and join the Department of Homeworld Security, I have no doubt that General Serath will share ample information with you."

"The Department of what, now?"

"Homeworld Security. That's the name Brendan has established for Earth's first contact committee."

Eric let out a laugh and shook his head. "You do realize how impossible this all sounds, right? It's like something out of one of Brendan's sci-fi books."

"Sci-fi. I have heard him say this word repeatedly, as well as General Serath's Earthling-wife, Evelyn."

"Yeah... You might want to get used to it."

The urge to kiss her was strong, but so were other urges. If he started them down that path, he didn't know if he'd have the willpower to stop.

Reluctantly, he extracted himself from her embrace and stood. He offered her his hand to help her up—not that she needed it. She could uproot full-grown oaks and hurl them like javelins, for crying out loud. And this was his...wife?

He could practically hear Brendan's voice teasing him in his head. *"Your* space-*wife."*

Eric growled internally at the thought.

As soon as she was on her feet, she stretched, pulling her hands apart. The chains connecting the handcuffs broke, some of the links flying into the grass.

"What the hell?"

"I'm so sorry, Eric." She looked at him with a deep frown on her face, holding her arms out for him to see the dangling chains. "I've broken your gift. I didn't think they were so fragile and my body is still filled with residual adrenaline."

"It's okay," he said, though he was actually reeling.

Part of him was still in denial. Part that broke along with those handcuffs. She hadn't even been *trying* to break them. How strong was she?

"I wanted to use them the next time we had sex." She sounded genuinely disappointed.

He let out a half-laughing, half-choking sound. "I can always get another pair."

"Excellent." She smiled, then took his hand in hers.

This entire situation was absurd. But he couldn't deny what he'd seen with his own eyes. She was an alien. And that meant...they were married.

If he'd thought for a moment that she could possibly be telling him the truth, he would never have challenged her, knowing what was at stake. And yet—since he was too far down the rabbit hole to turn back now—being married to a member of the alien race that was supposedly allying itself with Earth had to be a good thing for his planet. Right?

He would do his best to ensure it was. With a sigh, he shook his head, and then said something he never dreamed he would say.

"Take me to your leader."

Chapter Eight

Delight surged within Sorca. Eric was accepting her—accepting the truth about her mission. He *believed* her. Or was starting to.

"I'll take you to my ship, but we must wait until nightfall to depart," she said. "The protocols exist for a reason, and will help to keep us safe."

"Safe from what?"

"As I said, Earth is being invaded by hostile aliens."

"Right. Where are they from?"

"Tau Ceti."

"And you?"

"I am a product of Sadr-4, genetically engineered to serve as a soldier."

"Is that why you're so strong?"

She shook her head. "Not entirely. I'm a Cygnian hybrid—made from Sadirian DNA combined with that of the sentients of Cygnus-1. The Cygnians have incredible strength and durability due to gravity fluctuations on their homeworld."

"Gravity fluctuations?"

"It's near the black hole Earth scientists call Cygnus

X-1."

"I'm having trouble wrapping my head around all of this."

She was having her own difficulties believing the reality of her new situation. When he could easily have ended her life during his challenge, Eric had endangered himself to save her. That was *twice* that he had done so in the brief time since they had met. She wondered if there was something in his genetic makeup that compelled him to help others.

And he was her bondmate. A thrill of excitement raced down her spine at the thought. She knew she met his criteria for a fully pair-bonded partner—a wife. All she needed was time in which to convince him.

He didn't believe things easily. He was wary of his opponents and his circumstances. Now that she had more at stake, she might have to give that a try.

Death had never seemed like a big deal to her. But this could be the last physical form she inhabited. She doubted the Coalition would provide Eric with a new version of her if she should die before him.

And if they did create a new version of her, but didn't let her update her imprint beforehand, she would forget Eric and his challenge. Everything they had shared would be lost.

Suddenly, the cliff edge seemed too close.

"Come," she said. "We need to reach my ship as

quickly as possible."

"Why? I thought we couldn't leave until tonight."

"That's true. However, I need to log your victory immediately."

"Listen, Sorca—"

She grabbed his wrist and pulled him into step beside her. "It's better for your world." Eventually—she hoped—she could prove that it was the best for him as well.

"This is a cultural misunderstanding."

"It's Coalition law. I'm considered Cygnian, even though the Sadirians created me. Part of the pact between my people and theirs that enables them to use our advanced DNA is that they honor our customs—and the martial challenge is our most sacred tradition. The High Council won't go against this outcome once it is officially logged."

But *only* if it was officially logged.

"Transmissions are currently restricted," she said. "But the ship can be set to automatically send the signal as we depart this evening."

"I haven't agreed to go with you."

The skimmer wasn't far from where they had fought. The space between the cliff's edge and the trees widened, forming the clearing where she had landed.

"You asked me to take you to Brendan." She stepped closer to her ship, setting off the proximity sensor. "This is the only way to reach him."

The cloak fell away, revealing the sleek lines of her personal skimmer.

"Holy…" Eric's voice trailed off.

Sorca let out a breath that purred in her chest as she looked at her ship. She couldn't help it.

In the dark void of space, the black hull of the skimmer was nearly invisible, even without its cloak. On Earth, sunlight gleamed along its surface. Green trees and blue sky reflected on its polished hull.

The curved shadow it cast on the ground would make a pleasant resting space. She wondered if Eric would be willing to have sex with her again now that they were pair-bonded. It seemed an inviting place for it…

"I hope that this addresses any doubts you may still have." She turned to Eric, her smile faltering when she saw him.

His eyebrows were drawn together on his forehead, several furrowed lines between them. A muscle twitched beneath his beard and up along his cheek. His lips were pulled down in a grimace.

She tried to name the emotions flitting across his features. Rage. Fear. Determination.

"Everything you've said is true," he said.

"Yes. I told you that."

"I have questions. Many, many questions."

Sorca nodded curtly, a form of almost-salute she had only ever used with Serath. In that moment, Eric was so like her commanding officer, she couldn't believe she'd not seen the similarities before—primarily the force of will both men seemed to project.

But instead of stalking toward her ship, as Serath would, Eric deferred to her. He gestured to the ship and waited for her to approach first. She walked to the skimmer and pressed her hand against the control that would lower the ramp, watching Eric's expression darken further. This time, she was the one who gestured for him to go first.

Without hesitating, he walked up the short ramp that led to her small vessel. She followed quickly, leaving the ramp open to allow them fresh air. All of the viewports on the ship were open as well.

Eric's gaze scanned every surface of the ship—the controls at each station along the walls, the ladder and hatch leading up to the compact sleeping quarters above, the edges of the rectangular lockers where supplies and weapons were stored.

He looked at the trees through the main viewport. She left him to it, quickly accessing the communications station and setting it to transmit the change in her status as soon as possible.

His silence became unnerving.

"I don't understand why seeing my ship has upset you so," she said. "It proves to you that everything I've said is true. That Brendan is safe."

"He's safe for now. But the fact that you've been telling me the truth also means that my entire planet is in horrible danger."

"The Coalition will protect Earth from—"

"The Coalition *is* the threat," he nearly yelled. He shook his head, and said, "I'm sorry. Tell me more about your government. Please."

Not their weapons. Not their technology. She was so surprised, she wasn't sure how to respond.

Navigating Eric's cultural mores was proving to be more challenging than she'd anticipated. For once, she actually wished she had spent more time with Vay during the mission's cultural indoctrination session. It might have helped Sorca understand how to communicate with him better.

"Could you narrow your parameters?" she said.

"You said you were designed by your government to be a soldier. Do they design everyone or just the military?"

"Everyone is the product of genetic engineering, designed for a specific societal function."

"Are the results always what they expect?"

"No. Occasionally, citizens don't meet their intended specifications. We call them glitches."

He winced at the word, and his expression hardened. "Are these individuals assigned new roles in your society?"

"Based on their scores on the ability tests we all take

after emerging from our maturation chambers, yes."

"How old are they when they emerge?"

"By Earth standards, you would consider them in their early teens."

"Shit," he muttered. He ran a hand over his face briefly. "What happens after they emerge?"

"Everyone continues their development and begins training on basic functioning and societal protocols. Their scoring determines where they're assigned. Most often—especially in cases where their appearance or physicality is not considered within norms—glitches are placed in the military."

Eric's eyebrows hiked up his forehead and his mouth dropped open. He shook his head, and let out a harsh laugh.

"Let me get this straight. Your government takes all the marginalized citizens in your society, and puts them in the military?"

Sorca shrugged. "Specific ships can be designed to accommodate larger people. If a citizen can't properly maneuver in the limited space allowed in the standard Sadirian space station, ship, or dome-world, it isn't possible for them to live among civilians. They serve our society by acting as our peacekeepers and enforcers."

"So, they're your police as well as your military?"

"It's more efficient to have only one segment of the population with this training and equipment."

He shook his head. "I've dealt with many kinds of governments. Democracies, dictatorships—the corrupt, inept, and just plain evil. I have never encountered outright stupid, though. And that is the dumbest thing I have ever heard in my life."

She felt an emptiness within her. Her conditioning mandated that she defend her government, even if the words felt hollow.

"The Coalition has existed for thousands of years," she said.

Existed. Not thrived.

"Your Coalition has devalued an entire segment of its population by labeling them as *glitches*—and then given them access to their most powerful weapons and training."

"Do not underestimate the High Council, Eric. They will do anything to make sure the Coalition remains in control of the galaxy."

"The *galaxy?*" he said. "How many people are we talking about?"

"Including all fully assimilated species—septillions."

"Only septillions?"

"I don't understand."

"The galaxy is a huge place. Why aren't there more people in the Coalition?"

"More aren't needed."

He looked as though she'd struck him. His breath rushed from him as he covered his face with his hands.

"I don't understand your reactions," she said. "Why create more people than you need? Why waste resources?"

He wheeled around and dropped his arms to his sides. His voice boomed off the walls of the small space they shared. "Because, Sorca, people aren't just resources. They're *people*."

He included everyone in that word. She could feel it with sudden and shocking clarity.

He would consider the needs of Sadirians equal to those of Lyrians, Centaurans, Antareans, Cygnians. Even the loathsome Tau Ceti. She could feel the strength of his words, that he would include all sentients in that one powerful word.

People.

Chapter Nine

The room—ship—was starting to spin. At least, that was how it felt to Eric.

What the fuck kind of messed up society was Sorca from? And these were the "good guys" out to protect Earth?

Yeah. Right.

The enormity of it made him sick to his stomach. His planet and everyone on it was in even more danger than he'd ever imagined. The differences between the people of his homeworld seemed so small compared to this.

And what about Sorca? If her ultra-controlling government found out that she had bonded to an Earthling, what kind of retaliation could she expect? Eric didn't believe for one second that they would just let her walk away.

They'd already put a self-destruct system inside of her. Who knew if they had a way to trigger it remotely? The thought made his heart pound. He had to protect her.

"Don't send the transmission," he said.

"What do you mean?"

"You can't tell your government that we're pair-bonded."

She bristled, and he reached out to her, grasping her arms and pulling her closer in the near-claustrophobic tightness of the ship. He was going to say something, to explain that he wasn't fighting her bizarre combat-based mating ritual.

Instead, he kissed her.

It wasn't slow and it wasn't gentle. He knew she didn't need those things, and he needed…her. Immediately.

He crushed her against him, hands pulling on her clothes, tongue driving into her mouth. It only took her an instant to match his frenzy, her hands burrowing into his hair and holding him locked against her.

He felt her kick off her shoes and followed suit. Then their clothes practically flew off their bodies, ripping in their haste. He was overwhelmed with the need to touch and keep touching her. He needed more.

The moment they were naked—except for the remains of his handcuffs—he picked her up, relieved that she finally trusted herself enough to wrap her legs around his waist. There was a mostly smooth patch of wall near the ladder that led to a hatch in the ceiling.

He swung her body around toward it, hoping he wouldn't press her up against a control that would be activated by contact with her bare skin. He'd seen how she entered commands into the ship by tapping on what looked like etchings in the walls.

As soon as her back was braced against the metal, he pressed his dick to her core. He was already hard, but her muscles were so strong that it took much more force than he was used to using to drive himself into her.

"Tell me," he gasped. "Tell me if I hurt you."

"You won't hurt me, Earthling."

He let out a tiny chuckle at what was becoming her pet name for him. Then he pushed himself into her, deep.

Every millimeter of flesh that parted for him felt like fireworks erupting through his body. Her core was so wet and tight and...perfect.

To him—for him—she was perfect.

He let himself go, his dick sliding against her flesh in frenzied thrusts, her moans and gasps spurring him on. Her nails dug into his back, pain ringing out and joining into the deafening chorus of *being*, of everything he was feeling, physically and emotionally. Pain and pleasure. They faced them together. At least for this moment.

"Eric," she gasped.

Her back arched off from the wall with enough force to nearly knock him back. He grabbed the ladder to keep himself stable, to give him better leverage to intensify his thrusts. He had never fucked anyone like this before, so wildly, abandoning the veneer of civility to share the primal ecstasy of another's flesh.

He pinned her against the wall, grabbing her thigh to keep them connected safely. Her body clenched his dick hard, her strength flowing through every part of her like a drug. He wanted more.

He hammered his hips against hers. Her core pulsed around him, milking him, pushing him over the edge into the purest sense of abandon he'd ever experienced.

"Yes!" Her scream echoed from the walls.

His vision exploded into stars as his climax joined hers. "God, Sorca," he yelled.

He kept on pounding into her, pulling every ounce of pleasure possible from their connection, keeping them both in the epicenter of bliss for as long as he could until it finally started to fade. At last, he stopped, pinning her to the wall, feeling their bodies' rhythmic communication— their heartbeats pulsing where they were joined.

"That..." She licked her lips, her chest pressing against his in sporadic gasps. "That was amazing."

He hesitated a few moments, but then pulled himself from her body before daring to speak. "You can't send the transmission."

Her smile faltered. Dammit, he wished he had more time, but this had to be settled immediately and there was so much to do. So much ahead of him.

Her gaze grew fierce and he knew he was in trouble. She shoved off from the wall, as he'd expected. The force of it knocked him on his ass. She followed immediately, pushing him down and grabbing his wrists, pinning him to the floor of the ship.

"It isn't that I don't want you," he said.

Her grip on his wrists loosened.

"You said you might relinquish your position in their military. What would happen to you if you did? I don't trust them to let you go."

She sat back on his hips, their bodies comfortably pressing together. She pulled his arms down as she moved, so that his hands rested on her waist.

"The High Council won't risk violating the agreement with Cygnus-1," she said. "If they do, they know they'll never receive new samples of Cygnian DNA. Besides, they only have to wait until I die due to an Earth ailment or age or my own..."

"Impulse control issues?"

The scenarios she presented were hypothetical, but he didn't like even thinking about it. Still, when she grinned this time, he felt as if he was part of the mystery behind the smile. His chest felt full at the realization—knowing it would only make it that much harder for him to walk away.

"*I* am the one who has bonded with you. Once I die, the Coalition can clone me again and reprogram my mind with the latest imprint they have on file from before this assignment. They risk nothing by giving me a single lifetime with you."

He sat up, fast. So fast that they nearly conked heads.

"Clone you *again?* Reprogram you? Holy shit, Sorca, is

everybody—"

She covered his lips with her fingertips. "It's only the Cygnian hybrids, as far as I know."

"How many of you are there?"

"I don't know. They don't let us meet."

Of course they didn't.

"I still don't understand how such an oppressive government controls so many people—so many cultures. And you say they maintain peace?"

"*Balance* helps."

He knew he was going to regret asking, but he did it anyway. "And that is?"

"A drug that regulates the mental and emotional states of most citizens. Hence it's name—'balance'. It's meant to maintain equilibrium and keep everyone functioning at maximum efficiency. But it also...dulls the will."

He covered his eyes as she spoke, shaking his head. "I should have guessed."

He dropped his hands back to her hips, preparing to argue further. He doubted Sorca would just go along with him. She was too determined, too passionate for that.

"If they even suspect that they can't replicate you, there's no way they'll let you go." He opened his eyes to hold her gaze with his. "Do you understand? That's why you can't tell them we're pair-bonded."

"I understand your concerns, but it's too late. The transmission has already been logged in the ship. There's no way to stop it."

Chapter Ten

"That doesn't mean I can't help you." Sorca let Eric nudge her aside so that he could rise. She stood with him, trying to make him see reason. "For however long I have —"

"Stop. You don't get it." He paced a few steps away, putting as much distance between them as he could on the small vessel.

"Get what?" She wasn't sure what he was planning to withhold from her. Or why it should matter enough that her breath was catching in her chest.

He let out a deep sigh. "You say we're married according to your ways. I'm not going to try to get out of that."

She couldn't believe his words. Was he actually accepting her as a bondmate? Fully?

"It was my error in judgment that put us in this situation," he said.

"Error." Her heart felt leaden. Her vision grew red around the edges as the extreme sways in emotion took their toll.

If he thought their pair-bonding was a mistake, there

was no way he would ever truly accept her. She would be a tool for him, just as she'd been for the Coalition all of her life. At least it was a familiar role.

"Then tell me how I can be of greatest use to you." The sharp edge to her tone was new to her ears.

"Partners don't use each other, Sorca. That's what I'm trying to tell you." He crossed back to her, gently gripping her arms. "I don't want to use you. I want to help you."

"*You* want to help *me*? But, I'm supposed to—"

"So am I. I can see it in you. It's what we both do. We serve. We protect. But have you ever stopped to think that maybe you need protection as well? The Coalition has exploited you. Exploits all of their populace from the sounds of it."

"It's all we've known." She couldn't begin to imagine another life. Except...

Except, she already had. She had already been creating scenarios where she remained on Earth with Eric. She could find a way to contribute—especially with their shared abilities and military training. She would ease his life with her presence. They would spend their days together bringing peace to his people, and their nights sharing their bodies, bringing peace to each other.

The idea of it was frivolous and dangerous. It could only bring disappointment, such as she was feeling in that moment. There was no way she could attain that life.

"I don't want to use you," he said.

"Then you do not wish to be my bondmate."

"I didn't say that."

"Then what *do* you want, Eric?"

He stared at her, the muscle along his jaw twitching again. "I want my planet to be safe. I want my people—all of my homeworld's people—to find a way to get along. And I don't want to be at the mercy of a soulless dystopian government for its survival."

She shook her head. "I can't give you any of those things. But as long as you strive for them, I can promise to be at your side."

"Is that what *you* want? If you could do anything in the world—anything in the universe, I should say—what would you do?"

No one had ever asked her that question. No one asked anyone that question in the Coalition.

"If you knew that you had *time*, Sorca. If you weren't so okay with being...replaced with an exact duplicate. What would you want?"

"I would want to spend that time with you."

"You've only just met me."

"I believe I've learned a great deal about who you are in that time. You've risked yourself to save me multiple times. You've gone along with what you thought was a game—first to support your friend, I suppose, and then to try to help him. You're both playful and serious, and can be as impulsive as I, while never abandoning your mission."

The more she considered it, the more traits they seemed to share. The physical compatibility alone would have been enough for her, but she believed they could eventually forge a true emotional connection. Like the one between Serath—Adam—and Evelyn.

"I think we're a good match, Eric Peterson. I will make your mission mine and protect Earth at your side. I will protect those who you care about and...hope to someday be counted among them."

"You already are."

Her heart seemed to swell in her chest, her ribs enduring a pressure unlike anything she'd experienced. She felt...full.

"You're talking about giving up the galaxy to stay here with me," he said.

"It's not that much of a sacrifice."

He laughed and shook his head. His eyes darkened as his pupils dilated. Was the thought of staying with her that stimulating to him? She shifted a bit closer, tilting her lips toward his.

When he spoke, his tone was serious again, his breath warm on her skin. "I need to talk to your commanding officer. And I need to know that Brendan is okay."

"I swear to you that he is safe."

"I believe you. I'll just feel better when I see him with my own eyes."

"Night will fall shortly. I can answer more of your questions in the meantime."

"Let's start with these 'hostile aliens' invading Earth. You called them the Tau Ceti?"

"Yes." She tried to mask the disdain she felt for them from her voice.

"What do they want? Territory? Resources?"

"So far, all we have determined is that they are... feeding on the populace."

His eyes widened. "They're eating people?"

"Not all of them."

"Not..." He sputtered. "What parts are they leaving behind?"

"I'm being unclear. Their genetic engineers have altered the base physiology of the Tau Ceti so that they are capable of biting a human and drawing out blood, siphoning out chemicals that give the Tau Ceti a feeling of wellbeing, and returning the blood to their target."

His expression was oddly devoid of emotion. He looked almost as though he'd been stunned. Perhaps he still didn't understand. She struggled to find words that would assist him.

"Brendan has been calling them, 'vampire space frogs'."

"Vampire space frogs," Eric repeated. "I'm just...going to give my subconscious some time to work on that. How are the humans affected by the attack?"

"Most likely they suffer from chemical imbalances afterwards. And the Tau Ceti must perform some sort of mind-wipe on them, which would be disorienting at the least."

He let out a breath. "Like we don't have enough problems already. Why don't the Tau Ceti just take that drug the Coalition is using to control the rest of the populace?"

"The Tau Ceti are one of the few sentient species whose physiology is incompatible with *Balance* and *Coupling*," she said.

"*Coupling*—the other drug... I probably shouldn't ask, but what does that one do?"

"It takes the body through the stages of sexual arousal through climax."

He snorted and shook his head. "Drugs instead of sex."

"Or in addition to. Many citizens choose to take *Coupling* with a partner to increase its effectiveness in providing emotional fulfillment. Having now experienced..." She struggled again to find the best word to express her thought.

"The real thing?" he suggested.

She smiled. "Indeed. Having now experienced 'the real thing', I can state that it's not at all effective in providing a true sense of emotional or even physical connection."

"And what will the High Council do once others in the Coalition start to hear rumors about what Brendan and his…bondmate have experienced? Or this General of yours and his Earth partner? Are we going to be overrun by Sadirians looking for Earth mates?"

She had to laugh at that thought. "Not at all. Earth is a designated preservation planet. It's exceedingly difficult to gain authorization to come here, and there must be a compelling reason to do so."

At least, there should have been. With the arrest of the planetary liaison and the presence of the Tau Ceti, she had a feeling that perhaps more was going on planetside than even General Serath knew.

The crease appeared between Eric's brows that she had noted correlated with his experience of strong emotion. This time, he seemed deep in thought as well.

After a few moments, Eric said, "With how controlling the High Council is about everything, how is it they didn't know about the Tau Ceti presence?"

"We have recently discovered that Earth's planetary liaison was corrupt. At the very least, he's been smuggling items offworld to accumulate resources—most likely with the help of the Tau Ceti. Several high-level members of the Coalition have been arrested in conjunction with our investigation."

"Has anyone questioned this liaison yet?"

"I have. I'm the head of security for the Coalition's flagship, remember?"

He smiled at her softly. "That's right, you are. It sounds

like an important position."

"It is."

He was still holding onto her arms and began rubbing his thumbs back and forth across her skin, causing the follicles to stand on end in that stimulating way. The motion seemed instinctual to him, as if he didn't even have to think to provide her with pleasure and comfort.

"You're offering to give up a lot to help Earth," he said.

"To help *you*. But yes, Earth will benefit as well."

"Did you discover anything useful from the liaison?"

"When I was questioning him, my priority was to find conspirators within the Coalition. I wasn't thinking of your world or people. If Serath allows it, I'll question the liaison again with this in mind."

"Do you think Serath will let me be present?"

"That depends on whether you join the Department of Homeworld Security or not."

Eric let out a little laugh. "Brendan must be having the time of his life with this."

"Actually, he takes the entire situation quite seriously. He's convinced the matter is more serious than we know, and has theorized that any number of your...'urban legends' are actually rooted in extra-terrestrial activity on the planet."

"Alien sewer-gators. Great."

"He hasn't mentioned 'sewer-gators', but he has speculated about beings known as Grays, the Yeti, and

Bigfoot."

Eric lowered his head. His shoulders trembled, as if these names had frightened him.

"Don't be afraid," she said. "I'll protect you from any alien incursion—"

He started to laugh, lifting his face to hers with a tense smile crossing his features. "I'm sorry. The absurdity of it all is just getting to me."

"There is nothing to apologize for. You've assimilated a great deal of information quite well in an extremely short period of time."

"I'm glad you feel that way, because I think I need a little time to let my brain process this all."

"Understandable. If it would assist you…" She leaned even closer, until her breasts brushed against his chest. "I'd be happy to engage in a distracting activity."

His smile softened as he lowered his lips to hers, and murmured, "Bondmates with benefits."

Chapter Eleven

Outside of the ship, the view was amazing. Eric gave himself a few moments alone to watch the sunset and try to get his thoughts in order while Sorca prepped the ship for departure. He was about to leave the planet. *The planet.*

Part of him still wondered if this was part of some elaborate hoax that Brendan had put together. He had the money—and motive—to build the ship. He could have created replicas of trees rigged to look like Sorca was knocking them down during the fight. But Sorca herself...

She's what had convinced Eric that it was all true. She was just too real.

There was a rawness to her that he had originally mistaken for instability. Now that he knew more about her history and her culture, he understood better.

If he had died repeatedly and been recreated as the product of cloning and memory implants—and had more of the same to look forward to... He wasn't sure he'd be handling that as well as she was. She was even stronger than he'd realized.

Earth was in danger. It was a huge responsibility to be

one of the few people who knew about that. But Sorca was in danger, too. And the threat to her felt much closer. The need to protect her was a hell of a lot more immediate and tangible than invading aliens he had yet to see.

He heard rustling behind him. Sorca was in the ship— on the other side of the clearing. The hair on the back of his neck stood on end as he slowly turned, his thoughts of aliens making his imagination run wild.

A deer was standing at the edge of the treeline. Just a deer.

He was about to laugh, but he still had that feeling of misgiving. The deer took a step closer. Its hide was pale. Was it the same gray deer from earlier?

Eric had asked Sorca about the Tau Ceti's appearance. Apparently, they had engineered themselves to look like Sadirians, which meant they also looked like a regular human. Well, right up until they snapped down the fangs embedded in the roof of their mouths before feeding.

She hadn't mentioned anything about aliens that looked like deer. This was probably just a wild animal, which was dangerous enough on its own. He took a step back, then remembered that the cliff's edge was a few feet behind him, along with a sixty-foot drop that ended in jagged rocks.

"Easy," he said.

The deer stepped into the clearing, its head low to the ground. It seemed docile enough. Far more docile than it had any reason to be. It glanced over at the ship. Maybe there was something about the skimmer that was making it behave strangely?

It sped up as it approached Eric with more purpose. What the purpose was, he had no idea. He stayed still, arms out to his sides in what he hoped was a reassuring gesture.

The deer stopped right in front of him. It was bigger than he'd expected. Hunting animals wasn't something he'd ever had an interest in, so his experience was limited. He had enough of tracking things down in his work.

"Easy," he said again.

He held his breath as the deer cocked its head to the side, staring at him. Its pupils were dilated, entirely obscuring its irises. Now that he thought about it, its eyes seemed bigger than they should.

"This is just too weird."

The deer's lips quirked up, almost like it was amused. Eric must be worse off than he thought.

It lurched up on its hind legs. Eric lifted his arms to defend himself. He'd seen videos of deer attacking hunters before, and expected it to start lashing out at him with its forelegs. Instead, the deer started to glow.

"What the hell?"

Through the silver light emanating from it, he saw its eyes grow bigger—still entirely black. Its head shortened and rounded, its ears retreating into its scalp. Its limbs and torso lengthened to slender, sinuous reeds.

Holy shit.

The transformation happened so fast. It looked like a Gray—the alien most commonly described by humans Eric *used* to think were crackpots. He would never discount a report of a UFO sighting again.

Partially blinded, he didn't see when the thing lashed out with one of its oddly moving arms, wrapping its long fingers around Eric's neck and squeezing. He couldn't breathe, couldn't call for help. He grabbed the Gray's wrists, trying to break free, but the thing wouldn't budge.

Still glowing dimly, the Gray lifted Eric off of the ground, pulling him closer. Its mouth was a thin slit in a vaguely featureless face, but he swore the corners of the lipless gash twitched up in a smile. With its free arm, it pointed at Eric's face, its sharply pointed finger getting closer and closer.

Please don't probe me...

It grabbed the edge of Eric's mouth, sliding its finger along his cheek and teeth, like it was doing a DNA swab test. If he could have moved his neck in the thing's iron grip, he would have bitten it, but he was too busy holding himself up, trying to suck in any amount of air so he didn't black out.

The Gray pulled his finger from Eric's mouth, then... licked it. It cocked its head to the side, like the deer had done.

What the fuck?

The light grew brighter again, and Eric could feel the thing's hand changing shape around his neck. It shrank down to a more average human size. The moment Eric's feet touched the ground, he dug his thumb into its forearm in a spot that would cause a human to reflexively open their hand.

The Gray dropped him and he rolled as he hit the ground. Eric wasn't sure if he'd escaped or the thing had released him. All he cared about was the fresh air burning its way across his bruised windpipe and into his lungs.

Gasping, he looked up to see the woman from the diner that Sorca had tried to talk to about copulation protocols. The woman's eyes were completely black and her features half-way between the Gray's and a human's.

As he watched, its features shifted again, losing the definition they had just gained. Then, it swelled larger as it coalesced into a familiar shape and face—*his*. The light dimmed, and Eric was left staring at an exact duplicate of himself.

With all the classified projects he'd worked on, he could think of dozens of reasons that someone would want to copy and replace him. But he had a feeling this alien was after something less Earth-based.

The Gray grinned at him, then reached down and started dragging Eric to his feet with inhuman strength. He doubted it was a compassionate gesture. This close to the cliff's edge, it was almost certainly just trying to push him over before he regained his voice.

Eric pretended to wobble on his feet, coiling his strength and "stumbling" closer to the Gray. As soon as he was in a good enough position, he launched his shoulder into the thing's chin with all his strength.

The Gray was taken by surprise and staggered back from the blow. Eric was about to press his advantage when he heard Sorca call out from the ship.

"Don't move," she said. "Either of you."

He turned to see her standing at the end of the ramp with what was obviously some kind of high-tech rifle braced against her shoulder—and aimed in his direction. In unison, he and the Gray raised their hands.

"Sorca, it's me," the Gray said. Its voice perfectly matched Eric's.

"No, *I'm* me," Eric said.

"I don't know what that thing is. It attacked me and somehow turned into me."

"It's a Gray," Eric said. "I don't know what you call them, but that's their name on Earth."

"Sorca, you told me the only aliens on Earth are the Sadirians and the Tau Ceti," it said. "What *is* this thing?"

Shit, how did it know that those were the only aliens Sorca had told Eric about? Unless it had been following them and listening in on everything.

He'd noticed the weird deer while Sorca was carrying

him to the ship—when she'd started telling him about the dangers Earth faced. And if it *had* been the lady from the diner, it could have been following them the whole time. It could have seen the results of their fight, and heard them talking afterwards.

"Sorca, please trust me," it said. "I'm your bondmate."

And there it was. This thing was after Sorca.

Chapter Twelve

"Describe what you saw." Sorca kept the phase rifle pointed at the two Erics in front of her. Not many sentients could alter their appearance. The situation was bad. She just wasn't sure *how* bad.

"It was tall, thin, and gray-skinned," the Eric on her left said.

Right-Eric chimed in as well. "And had dark black eyes. Huge eyes. And slender limbs."

Cygnus X. The situation was dire indeed.

"You're describing a Scorpiian. They're bounty hunters and deadly assassins." She watched both Erics' reactions. Neither flinched at being identified. Both looked equally surprised.

But what was a Scorpiian doing on Earth?

Though she hadn't sent her transmission yet, her ship was receiving data from the *Arbiter*. Apparently, Khel had already returned to the ship with Brendan's sister, Paige.

They'd sent an emergency transmission to her ship to let her know that the Tau Ceti had been setting up spawning pools on Earth—a scenario Sorca would never have imagined.

The Tau Ceti were facing extreme sanctions for these acts, but the information she received hinted at some kind of new technology they'd developed that must have made that prospect less upsetting for them. It also made them a much greater threat to the Coalition—and Earth.

She hadn't told Eric yet, but there were supposedly Centaurans on Earth as well. Who knew how many other sentients had invaded the planet or what their plans for it might be. She needed to determine which of these Erics was *her* Eric and dispatch the Scorpiian so they could get to the *Arbiter* as quickly as possible.

"I'm guessing you mean someone from one of the Scorpii systems," left-Eric said.

Some*one*, not some*thing*. The probability that left-Eric was the true Eric increased.

"She sure as hell isn't talking about the bug," right-Eric said.

Hmm. The humor on that one…

"Sorca, if that weapon can stun us, shoot us both. It's the only way we can assure your safety," left-Eric said.

"Unless it wants you to do so," right-Eric said. "What if there's more than one and it's trying to get you alone?"

Right-Eric was both displaying his concern for her and his ignorance. Scorpiians always worked by themselves. That way, they didn't have to share their bounties when they captured their targets.

But what bounties could it be seeking on Earth? If it

tried to collect on a bounty, it would have to admit to trespassing on a preservation planet. Unless it was a covert bounty or…

Or sanctioned at an extremely high level. Perhaps even by the High Council itself. Which would mean that they were already aware that Earth was being invaded.

She set aside that truly disturbing thought. It was essential that she navigate this situation successfully. She had to warn General Serath. And she had to save Eric. Whichever one of these versions was truly him.

"Scorpiians are immune to the stun function of this phase rifle," she said. "As one of you well knows. Stunning you both would make an ambush that much easier, and remove my only support personnel."

"Support personnel?" right-Eric said. "I thought I was more than that to you."

Her heart gave a little lurch. Before she could respond, left-Eric spoke out.

"It knows everything that's passed between us. *Everything.* Including the fact that we're pair-bonded. It's after you. It wants to use you, through our bond."

That was a terrifying thought. If she ended up with the Scorpiian without knowing it, it could use her position and status to its own ends. Scorpiians were masters at manipulation.

"Lock us both up in the sleeping chamber of the skimmer," left-Eric said. "Surely the people on the *Arbiter* can tell us apart when we get there."

"How do you know so much about her ship?" right-Eric said.

"Because she told me, dumbass."

Sorca grinned. Both had humor. Both looked exactly like her Eric. But which one was he?

"It would be much too dangerous to bring a Scorpiian aboard the *Arbiter*," she said. "We'll have to resolve this between the three of us."

"Great." Right-Eric rolled his eyes.

"How does the Scorpiian know so much about us?" she said.

Right-Eric replied first. "It's been following us in the form of a deer—a common woodland animal in this area. I saw it while you were carrying me up the hillside, but I didn't say anything because I didn't think it was important."

"And it saw me see it," left-Eric said. "But it did a piss-poor job of imitating a deer, because its hide was way too *gray*."

Left-Eric was trying to goad right-Eric. The tactic seemed to be in line with what she knew of her new bondmate. Right-Eric didn't show any reaction to the insult.

From what left-Eric said, there weren't many questions she could ask to establish his identity. She didn't know much about him yet. She was determined to get through this and have the opportunity to learn more.

"This will get us nowhere," she said. "If the Scorpiian has truly overheard everything, there's no way that talking can determine who is the imposter and who is truly Eric."

"Do you have something else in mind?" left-Eric said.

"Only one person has ever bested me in combat. If we fight, I'll know who the real Eric is."

"No, no, no," right-Eric said. "That's way too dangerous."

Left-Eric shook his head. "I agree. There has to be another way."

Sorca locked the rifle and set it down on the ramp. "There is no other way. And be advised, I will only be able to identify you correctly by not holding back. I expect you both to do the same."

"Sorca," left-Eric said.

There was no time to waste, with the sun setting and stars knew how many hostiles planetside. She looked from one of them to the other and grinned.

This was going to be fun.

With a battle cry, she ran toward the pair of them, attempting to backhand the one on the left while spinning into a kick aimed at the right. Both men leapt out of range, as she expected. They mirrored each other's stances perfectly.

Scorpiians were feared for good reason. They were masters of infiltration, getting close to their bounties before springing their attacks. She couldn't let her guard down. At the same time, she didn't want to hurt the real Eric.

She followed up her attack first with the Eric who had started out on her right. Kicks and punches that he parried easily enough. Despite what she'd said, she was holding back, which probably wasn't the best course of action to determine who was the imposter.

She increased the force of her blows. Right-Eric was still able to block them. He even managed to land a few hits that she'd be feeling when the adrenaline rush of the battle was over.

During her attack, she had left her back open. Left-Eric hadn't taken advantage of that. Then again, the Scorpiian could easily have predicted that Eric wouldn't be eager to fight her.

She sprinted toward left-Eric, but instead of engaging with her, he...ran away. Not far, but all he did was try to stay out of her reach.

He hadn't seemed the type to run before. Perhaps this was the imposter.

"I won't fight you, Sorca," left-Eric said. "I'm not the Scorpiian."

"That's exactly what it would say." She closed the distance between them and swung at him—still holding back her strength and speed. Which one *was* he? "Engage me. It's the only way I can know for certain."

His lips pressed together in a thin line.

She swung at him again, but this time, he stood his ground, deflecting her blow with that curious fighting technique he'd used before. Yes, this could very well be her Eric. A few more tests would be necessary.

Before she could attack again, the other Eric came up behind him and struck him in the back of the head with the rifle. Left-Eric crumpled to the ground.

"What are you doing?" she yelled.

"I was trying to help you," right-Eric said.

She grabbed the rifle, easily jerking it from his grasp. Her vision clouded with red. What if that was the real Eric bleeding at her feet? But what if *this* was the real Eric?

She dropped the weapon and leapt at him, grabbing his shoulders and pulling him forward so that she could strike him with her forehead. He staggered back from the impact, and she let him, releasing her hold.

Another punch—that she successfully landed. A kick that sent him sprawling to the ground. As soon as he regained his feet, she was on him, no longer holding back.

There were no graceful dodges, no redirecting the energy of her attack. Just the brutal force of her strength and speed pummeling him into a bloody...

No blood. There was no blood.

She looked back at left-Eric, who was struggling to get to his feet, using the rifle to prop himself up. Blood ran down his temple and into the collar of his shirt. Red, human blood, not the quicksilver that ran in a Scorpiian's veins.

How injured was he?

Her skin prickled with fear. She needed to get him to the regen bed.

"Look out!" he yelled.

She turned back to the Scorpiian, just as it morphed its hand into a sharp spike. Dodging it with nanoseconds to spare, she grabbed its arm and pulled it off balance in a clumsy approximation of one of the real Eric's techniques. She caught the Scorpiian before it could fall to the ground, hefting it into the air. The inertia of its attack actually made the process much easier. There was definitely something to this Earth combat.

With another battle cry that drowned out its shrill scream, she ran toward the cliff and tossed it over the edge. She turned back to Eric just as he managed to get to his feet. He took a few wobbly steps in her direction, falling into her arms as he reached her.

Smiling, he said, "Remind me never to piss you off."

Chapter Thirteen

The forest was spinning wildly around Eric as Sorca drew his arm across her shoulders, supporting most of his weight. He felt nauseated and his vision was blurry. Not good. He still managed to keep his grip on the space rifle that his evil twin had cold-cocked him with, though.

He probably had a concussion. At least the Gray—the Scorpiian—was gone.

"Are you okay?" he asked.

"You're the one who can't stand, yet you ask if I'm okay?"

Eric half-shrugged. "That thing hit you pretty hard a couple of times."

"I'm more durable than that, as you well know. I'm more concerned for you. The regen bed in my ship can address your injuries."

"Wait a minute." Something was nagging at the back of his mind—swirly as it was. "The Scorpiian. Did you hear it hit the ground?"

Sorca looked up at him, her eyes wide. She mostly carried him to the edge of the cliff.

The rocks below weren't splattered with carnage, as

he'd expected. In fact, there was nothing on them at all.

"Eric."

He followed Sorca's gaze to the treeline beneath them, a hundred yards or so from the bottom of the cliff. The Scorpiian stood there, in its tall, Gray form, with folds of near-transparent skin connecting its arms and legs illuminated by the setting sun.

"Did that thing just glide to safety after being thrown off a cliff?" He wanted to be sure he wasn't imagining things.

"Scorpiians are feared for good reason."

"At least it doesn't look like me anymore."

"Come." She turned them back toward the ship, moving at a fast pace. "We must leave the planet as quickly as possible."

"The sun hasn't quite set yet."

"I want you healed before we board the *Arbiter*. You'll need to be at your best."

"Why do I feel like there's something you're not telling me?"

"Because you're observant and intelligent. And there are several things I haven't told you yet."

A wave of nausea washed over him as he wondered what else could go wrong.

As soon as they were aboard, she closed the ship's ramp. Lights along the ceiling and floor began to glow, immediately replacing the sunlight that had just been cut off. Sorca pressed a control, and a bench slid out of the wall. She set him on it and knelt beside him.

"Are you in much pain?" she said.

"Not really." His head felt like it was cracked in half, but he could deal with that.

"I don't believe you."

She smiled, tracing her fingers over his forehead. He could feel her gently pulling hair free that was sticking to his skin.

"I warned you that you would be injured if you persisted in trying to defend me," she said.

"You're worth it."

Her eyes widened and her mouth dropped open. For a wrenching moment, he was afraid she might start to cry. But not his Sorca. *His* Sorca.

He cupped her jaw, tilting her head up to his so that he could claim her mouth. He delved into her, caressing her tongue with his, feeling her rise up and melt against him. The room was still spinning, but possibly for a much more pleasant reason when they finally parted.

"I'm glad you figured out it was me. And not just because I wouldn't have stood a chance of surviving being chucked off the cliff like that."

"Even in the battle, I could tell you were trying to protect me. It truly is hardwired into your DNA."

He laughed and shook his head. He couldn't deny it. As far back as grade school, he'd felt compelled to help people when they were being picked on. Too bad that sentiment hadn't been passed on to the Scorpiian when it took his shape.

Sorca picked up the rifle and carried it to its storage rack, snapping it into place. The wall slid closed over it, making the weapons locker nearly invisible.

"I think I'll feel better once you teach me how to shoot one of those things," Eric said.

"That time will come sooner than you think." Her hands flew over the etchings on the wall, bringing systems to life throughout the ship.

Lights flickered on the walls, and a gridline superimposed itself over the viewscreen. He could hear things powering up and feel the vibration of engines through his seat.

"Does this thing have seatbelts?" he said.

She turned back to him and smiled. "Our uniforms have safety harnesses built into them that we can attach to the walls in case of sudden gravity loss. We'll want to change before we board the *Arbiter*. It's standard protocol."

"Far be it from me to stand against standard protocol. Are you going to tell me that news before we get there, too?"

"I was going to wait till you were out of the regen bed."

"I'd rather not."

She sighed, then crossed the small space and sat next to him. "The Tau Ceti are much more invested in Earth than we thought. General Serath sent a coded transmission to alert me to the danger. They've been setting up spawning pools—altering Earth's environment so that they could make a permanent home here."

His stomach lurched again. Maybe he *should* have waited till her regen bed fixed his probable-concussion. He rubbed his eyes, trying to clear his mind.

"So what? Sanctions? Arrests? I can't see the Coalition going to war for a planet that's not even one of their members."

"If they go to war, it will not be over this. In fact..."

He'd only seen her censor herself once. What was she holding back this time?

"We're bondmates, remember? And to me, that means we're partners. I want—I *need*—to know what we're dealing with."

She nodded, then said, "I have grave concerns. The fact that there is a Scorpiian bounty hunter operating on Earth leads me to believe..."

Her voice trailed off, a furrow appearing between her eyebrows. He reached over and stroked her cheek.

"Sorca..."

She took a deep breath and let it out slowly. Here it came...

"Scorpiians often work for the High Council. They don't pursue bounties that won't pay out for them. There are no bounties on Earth that they could be seeking that aren't sanctioned, even if they're covert."

"I don't understand."

"I believe that the High Council is aware that there are other sentients trespassing on Earth. They may even be the ones behind the Scorpiian's presence. And if that's the case, they may have been aware of the planetary liaison's actions as well. They might not think there's a problem on Earth at all."

The room spun faster as he processed her words. If their government was aware of its citizens breaking their own laws, and was using secretive ways of dealing with it instead of facing it in the open... Earth faced an even greater challenge than he'd realized.

"Let's get me to the regen bed," he said. "I need to talk to Serath."

Chapter Fourteen

Back aboard the *Arbiter*, Sorca experienced the strange sense of detachment that usually only accompanied adjusting to a new body. She supposed it was a reaction to the knowledge that this was most likely among the last times she would walk these corridors. The adjustment was easier with Eric walking at her side.

"I feel ridiculous," he said.

Another crewmember paused to let them pass, pressing his back to the wall to give them room. The *Arbiter* had larger corridors than most ships in the fleet, but the Coalition still understood that space was to be used as efficiently as possible—just as they used their people.

That knowledge had never chafed as it did now. Earth truly did have a transformative effect. Or at least its inhabitants did.

Eric shook his head. "I can't believe your uniform is a silver catsuit."

"I don't know what cats have to do with it, but our uniforms have been designed to provide maximum protection while utilizing the fewest resources."

"Uh-huh." He walked a bit closer to her when they

were alone again, and said, "I do have to admit, you look gorgeous in it."

She grinned at the compliment. "As do you."

He chuckled. "Thanks."

She wished she could wear the special bracelets he'd given her underneath it, but he had convinced her to leave them back in her quarters. Perhaps she could have one of the mechanical engineers aboard the ship repair and reinforce the chain that had connected them...

"I really like the look on your face right now," Eric said.

Grinning, she pressed the control panel that gave her access to Serath's main meeting room. The door slid open, revealing the relatively large, circular space. Eric followed her inside.

Her next-ranking security officer, Ari, stood on the far side of the room, his dark eyes taking in everything. He nodded curtly at Sorca, his bald head nearly brushing the ceiling of the chamber.

Vay stood next to him, her gaze darting around the room. She needed to be trained to be more discrete in her environmental observations.

That task will fall to Ari now...

Brendan was standing on the near side of the oval table that filled most of the chamber. He and Eric walked briskly toward each other and clasped hands, also grasping each other's shoulders.

"I'm glad you could make it," Brendan said.

"Your friend here didn't give me much choice." Eric grinned at her over his shoulder. "She carried me to her ship when I tried to leave."

Brendan took a deep breath and held it for a moment before blowing it out. Visibly attempting to be calm, he said, "Sorca. The next time I ask you to go get someone, please don't *abduct* them."

She shrugged. "Next time, give clearer orders."

"I'm glad she insisted," Eric said. "From what I've learned, things are pretty bad."

"They are much worse than any of us knew." Serath's commanding tone echoed across the room.

He entered with his bondmate, Evelyn. Khel followed with a woman who had the same red hair as Brendan. Sorca guessed this was Paige.

"Please sit," Serath said. "We have much to discuss."

Sorca led Eric around the table so that they could sit across from Brendan and Earth's new planetary liaison, his bondmate, Kira. Everyone's expressions were grim—even the normally cheerful Evelyn's.

She tucked a lock of her blonde hair behind her ear and tried to push a pair of glasses that she was no longer wearing up her nose. After her first sleep in a regen bed, her eyesight was perfect.

Wearing anything on one's face was dangerous on board. If the ship suffered decompression, the helmet built into the collars of their suits would unfold to cover their heads and seal the uniform. Evelyn's glasses would have obstructed the process, but she still seemed to mourn their loss.

Sorca understood a bit better now why Evelyn had yelled at Serath afterwards about not being consulted before her body was altered.

"Kira," Serath said. "Speak."

Kira looked a bit surprised. Her gaze flitted to each person seated around the table. When her eyes locked with Brendan's, he smiled at her and nodded slightly. She immediately looked more comfortable, straightening in her chair

She spoke in a strong voice. "The Tau Ceti very nearly set up spawning pools on Earth. They've been feeding on the population for an undetermined amount of time. There are also Centaurans somewhere on the planet. The previous planetary liaison is in custody on board. We've determined that he was running an extensive smuggling operation that was supported by several very high-level members of the Coalition."

"Sorca," Serath said. "Your report."

He glared at her with his mismatched eyes—one bright blue and the other green. His presence dominated the room. She noted that everyone started to fidget in their seats. Even Eric was affected, sitting straighter in his chair and not taking his eyes off of their leader.

Serath had told her once that she was the only one who seemed to be unaffected by him—which was part of why he valued her so much as his chief security officer. Undoubtedly, he was not happy to know of her pair-bonding.

He'd get over it.

"The High Council itself was most likely aware of the smuggling operation," Sorca said.

"What?" Khel's shout echoed in the room. He had always been extremely loyal to the Coalition. Sorca wondered if his new relationship with the Earthling, Paige, would alter that.

Paige set her hand on his shoulder, and said, "Easy, there. Let's hear her out."

"Present your evidence," Kira said.

Sorca grinned at the new liaison. The woman had a voice like steel. It seemed to match her temperament. Earth was in good hands there. Sorca hoped it would be enough.

"Eric and I were attacked by a Scorpiian," Sorca said.

Most of the Sadirians in the room gasped. Serath's glare darkened.

"How in the name of the Solar Cross are you still alive?" Kira said.

"Um, excuse me?" Evelyn raised her hand tentatively, as she often did when she had something to contribute. "Scorpions aren't that dangerous. Even really big ones.

You can just stomp on them. I don't get why it's such a big deal."

Brendan and Paige turned to Sorca, obviously as confused by the statement as Serath's bondmate.

"Not the bug," Eric said. "Aliens from one of the solar systems in the constellation Scorpii. They look like your standard movie Grays. And they can shapeshift."

"Grays are real?" Brendan's face actually lit up. So did Evelyn's.

Ari shook his head and Vay had turned ashen. She wove a little in place, as if she might topple over any moment.

Serath reached for Evelyn's hand and entwined their fingers, resting their arms on the table. He understood the danger of the situation.

"Scorpiians are assassins," he said. "They can take the form of any being whose DNA they've sampled. And they are nearly impossible to kill."

"The High Council uses them to collect bounties on individuals who are deemed extremely dangerous to the Coalition," Sorca said.

"I think it started out following me to try to get to Brendan." Eric spoke with confidence, even in such novel circumstances. Sorca's estimation of him increased yet again. "Probably due to his work on the communications array or his link to Kira."

"The Scorpiian changed targets after it learned that Eric had defeated me in combat," Sorca said.

"He… He what?" Khel leaned back in his chair, his eyes wide as he stared at Eric.

Eric just shrugged. He smirked at Sorca. "Technically, the tree is what took you down."

"I refuse to be pair-bonded to a tree. And you're the one who spared my life instead of ending it. The victory is yours."

"Pair-bonded." Kira shook her head. "I don't understand."

"That makes a bunch of us, I think," Evelyn said.

Serath's scowl-creased brows formed a single dark line across his forehead. "Sorca is a Cygnian hybrid."

Kira glanced over with raised eyebrows. To her credit, she looked away quickly instead of indulging her curiosity with the long stares Sorca was more accustomed to when her true nature was revealed.

"Anybody want to clue the Earthlings in on what that means?" Brendan said.

"The Cygnians are a warrior race," Khel said. "Their prowess is legendary. They have incredible strength, skin like stone, and can—"

"Enough." Serath's booming voice made everyone jump in their seats. Evelyn grasped his arm in what Sorca now recognized as a reassuring gesture. He looked at Kira. "Explain."

After a few moments of silence, Kira spoke in an even voice. "Cygnian DNA is highly sought after by Coalition geneticists. The Cygnians consider any hybrids created to be their citizens. Part of the agreement in supplying us with their DNA is that the Coalition respect their customs."

"Okay," Brendan said. "So, how does that make them married?"

"Cygnians pair-bond through martial challenges," Kira added.

Brendan and Evelyn both said, "Oh," at the same time. Paige merely shook her head and smirked.

"Sorca has officially logged Eric as the victor in his challenge," Serath said. "The Coalition has no choice but to recognize their partnership. To do otherwise risks losing the cooperation of all the Cygnians among us and destroying relations between Cygnus-1 and the High Council."

The strain in his voice tugged at Sorca's heart in a way she wasn't sure she'd have been capable of even a day ago. Serath was the closest thing to a friend that she'd ever had. She didn't like the thought of bringing him difficulty or...pain. From the look on his face, perhaps he felt the same way about her and didn't want to see her leave his command for personal reasons, as well as due to his station.

"It is not yet certain whether I will relinquish my position," she said. "Eric will decide—"

"Excuse me." Eric leaned forward in his chair so that he

could crane his neck around and hold her gaze. "*We* will decide. I'm not making any of these decisions alone. We're partners, remember?"

She smiled at him and nodded. Warmth flooded her chest. It was so strange to not see herself as a tool.

She hoped Serath would understand. Victory in combat or not, she *wanted* Eric.

"I am...pleased to see that you have partnered with someone who shows you such respect," Serath said. "We will all need to support each other if we are to navigate the future successfully for Earth and the people of the Coalition."

The "people" of the Coalition? Not the Coalition itself. Sorca sat up straighter.

She had served with Serath for decades. She knew how he thought—or at least, she *had* known. Before he went to Earth and came back changed.

Was Serath planning on challenging the High Council? If so, she wanted to be part of that. Very, very badly.

"The Tau Ceti have access to new technology that threatens every sentient in the galaxy," Serath said. "We need to determine the source of this technology. There are also issues we need to address with the High Council, and even more that remains to be done on Earth."

"Brendan and I are ready to assist, sir," Kira said.

The corner of Serath's mouth twitched up for a brief moment. "I'm glad to hear it. You have quite a bit of work ahead of you. In light of Sorca and Eric's revelations, we will need to leave a larger contingent on Earth. The problem is more widespread than we originally estimated."

"Thank you, sir," Kira said.

Serath turned to Sorca, his glare back in full force. "Who will remain?"

"Vay, Ari, and Rin, for a start," Sorca said.

Vay's smile seemed to brighten the room even more than the lighting panels. Sorca had never seen someone look so excited. Ari leaned forward, as if he was about to argue, but then he let out a sigh and remained silent. Sorca doubted her next suggestion would pass without argument.

"And Khel," she said.

She didn't want to separate Khel and Paige. But if he and Sorca both remained on Earth, that would mean that Serath would lose both of his top officers in one reassignment.

"Khel and Paige are coming with the *Arbiter*," Serath said. "They've logged their pair-bond to enable her to join us and assist with our petition to the High Council for official recognition of Earth's first contact committee."

"Um, Department of Homeworld Security," Brendan said.

Serath let out a sigh, but went on. "I'll need a list of names. At least a dozen."

"A dozen?" Sorca couldn't hide her surprise. Serath was allocating an unusual amount of resources to Earth.

"I considered it a cultural exchange as well as a military assignment. Paige has expressed interest in helping planets who over-allocated their resources when they joined the Coalition," Serath said. "If she can help to increase their autonomy, it will decrease their burden on the Coalition."

"Are you sure the High Council actually wants that?" Eric said. "They seem pretty keen on keeping everyone under their control."

"We can only present our case," Serath said. "Much will be determined by their…reaction."

Sorca had a feeling he wasn't only thinking of the High Council giving new orders. If they ruled against Earth, how far was Serath willing to go to protect his bondmate's homeworld?

"Being pair-bonded to Sorca…" Eric said. "Does that mean I can join you as well when you present your petition to the High Council?"

Serath nodded. "It can be arranged."

Eric turned to Sorca, grasping her hand under the table and squeezing it. "We can be there and see their reaction ourselves. I want to meet the people who hold the fate of my world in their hands. Are you okay with that?"

"Yes."

"Sorca, think about this for a minute. What do *you* really want?"

She had never in her many lives been asked that question before Eric. The answer was as clear as the feelings growing in her heart for this amazing Earthling.

"It's what I want, too. I want to help your planet, and to fight for it by your side. And...I want to help my own people. They need to understand that they don't have to keep living this way."

She turned back to Serath and smiled. "Our attempts to change our culture will very likely get all of us killed. But we'll die in good company."

"And on that cheery note..." Brendan said.

"We're going to make it." Evelyn spoke calmly—her voice quiet, but stronger than Sorca had ever heard it. "The fate of our homeworld and the entire the galaxy is at stake. We'll succeed. We have to."

"Then we have our orders, from Serath's bondmate herself." Sorca lifted her arms over her head, dragging Eric's up with hers. "Victory!"

"What the hell." Eric shook his head, then yelled, "Victory!"

She grinned broadly.

This was going to be fun.

Epilogue

Sorca had pair-bonded. Vay still couldn't believe it, even after reading the entry five times. Sorca had logged the challenge in the official database for the Coalition of Planets, as well as the victory of Eric Peterson. There was no legal way around it.

First General Serath—now known as Adam Smith—had pair-bonded with Evelyn Chambers. Then the new planetary liaison, Kira, had logged her pair-bond with Brendan Sloan, the Earthling who'd formed the Department of Homeworld Security. And even Khel, the last Sadirian Vay would have ever thought capable of forming an emotional attachment to another, had fallen in love.

She shouldn't get her hopes up, but…

"What is it about this world?" Vay stared up at her monitor, the blue and white planet slowly spinning below, oblivious to its power over her people.

The Coalition was a virus. A blight on the free will of the galaxy. It devoured entire planets' resources, destroyed their cultures, and for what? The promise of technology that would extend sentient beings' lives and protect them from physical suffering, all the while drugging them into happiness and forcing them to spend their longer years in servitude?

A workstation behind her pinged and Vay jumped in her seat. She plastered a smile on her face as she glanced all around the empty room, even though she knew she was alone.

Nothing to see here. Just doing my job…

Thank the stars that the Coalition couldn't read minds. Yet. Vay at least had that last freedom—her own thoughts.

Still, she needed to be careful.

Earth had a strange potential. Humans were changing her people, and Sadirians hadn't really changed for thousands of years.

Vay wished she could get a closer look. She needed to talk to Earthlings, to figure out what they were doing that was having such a profound impact. If she could understand it, maybe she could leverage it to make some *real* change. Change beyond one ship, one crew.

With the help of Earth, they could change the galaxy. If she could find like-minded people who would help her, they could set everyone free.

She knew she shouldn't get her hopes up. But it was too late for that.

Staring intently at the blue planet in her view screen, she smiled again. A real smile this time.

"I *will* figure you out," she said.

—

That Scorpiian isn't done with the Department of Homeworld Security yet. It would be great if a tough Coalition soldier like Ari could get the drop on it—but that would be too easy. Enter Vay, the very combat-inexperienced cultural programmer assigned by General Serath, aka Adam Smith, to help everyone learn to get along. Don't worry, Vay. We believe in you. Read on to see how they deal with this new threat in *Entry Visa!*

USA TODAY BESTSELLING AUTHOR
CASSANDRA CHANDLER

ENTRY VISA

THE DEPARTMENT OF HOMEWORLD SECURITY

Entry Visa

The Department of Homeworld
Security
Book Five

Cassandra Chandler

Dedication

For my book club—thanks for waiting.

Don't miss out on any of the alien action.
Subscribe to Cassandra Chandler's newsletter at
cassandra-chandler.com!

Prologue

"A Homeworld Holiday"

Christmas Eve

"Who in their right mind spends two hours tracking down a fruitcake on Christmas Eve?" Henry spoke under his breath, even though no one was nearby. "Oh yeah. I forgot. I'm not in my right mind."

He ran his hand through his hair, knowing it would make his brown curls stand on end and not caring. Finding an open store was something of a miracle. Now if only it had what he needed to fulfill his family's tradition—even though his family didn't exist anymore.

He shook his head, as if the movement could keep the dark thoughts from taking root in his mind.

There were beautiful lights all around him. He focused on the colorful strands, looking at the lavishly decorated holiday aisle. His gaze landed on a single brick of fruitcake sitting in a large display basket.

"Bingo!"

He practically leapt at it, his fingers closing over the prize just as another hand reached for it. Reflexively, he pulled back, cradling the fruitcake against his chest.

His heart beat fast, his hindbrain reminding him of close calls he'd had with rattlesnakes and other bitey animals in the woods. But it was winter, and the snakes were all hibernating. Plus, he was back in civilization surrounded by people. One of whom he'd probably just offended.

"Sorry, I…" His words stuck in his throat.

He was staring into the biggest, deepest blue eyes he'd ever seen. They were open wide, the woman's lips parted and her dark eyebrows hitched up her forehead. The red and green stocking cap she wore couldn't quite hide the blonde hair that stuck out from underneath it, barely brushing her shoulders.

She was almost as tall as him, which put her at nearly six feet. With the impossibly perfect symmetry of her features, she could easily be some sort of supermodel. Except for her quirky, definitely not mainstream fashion-sense.

She was wearing jeans and an incredibly ugly sweater under an overstuffed coat. He could make out antlers on what was probably supposed to be a moose. It was hard to look at the pattern of her sweater with all the different colors on it fighting for his attention—or maybe trying to blind him.

"Wow," he said. "I mean, 'hi'. And this is the last fruitcake. You should have it. Here."

Her lips curved into a huge smile as he offered it to her. Her front two teeth stuck out just the tiniest bit more than the others. It was adorable.

She shook her head. "No, it's yours."

"But there aren't any more." He looked back in the basket, as if he might have missed one in the obviously empty container.

She laughed. Henry felt color flood his cheeks at the sound.

"I'll survive," she said.

"Coffee can help with that." He would absolutely need some to make the drive back to his parents' cabin. *His* cabin now.

"Coffee?" One eyebrow arced and her smile turned into a smirk.

"It's a hot beverage that helps you stay awake. Or so I've heard."

She laughed again, even though his joke was utterly lame. Her smile broadened.

"Let me get you a cup. Since you're being so gracious about the fruitcake."

What was he doing? It had been a while since he'd spoken to anyone...other than himself. And here he was asking out a total stranger. An absolutely gorgeous stranger.

Plus, it was Christmas Eve. She had to have better things to do than hang out with an itinerant, aspiring cryptozoologist.

But she shrugged and said, "Okay."

"Okay?" His forehead nearly cramped from his eyebrows spiking up. He cleared his throat and forced his expression into the closest thing to neutrality he could manage. "Okay."

They walked to the cashier together, and she watched with open curiosity as he paid. Strangely, it reminded him of his biology classes—how they'd been taught to observe wildlife. He shook away the thought as absurd, and vowed to never be away from civilization for that many weeks again.

"Shall we?" He gestured to the door.

"We shall."

He laughed as he followed her into the snowy night.

The sidewalks were clear, but drifts lined the street and hugged the walls where the snow had been pushed away. Wreaths and bright snowflake decorations made of lights alternated on the streetlamps over their heads.

"I'm Henry, by the way."

"Henry." She nodded, then held out her hand to him. "I'm Vay."

He slipped the fruitcake into his coat pocket and shook her hand. "Vay? That's an unusual name."

She shrugged, still pumping his hand up and down. "You're the first 'Henry' I've met."

"Really? I always thought it was a ridiculously common name."

"Depends on where you're from."

"Do they shake hands this long on your homeworld?"

She gasped and pulled her hand back like he'd stung her.

"I'm sorry," he said. "That was just my pathetic attempt at humor."

"Oh. A joke."

He tried to recover and figure out what had set her off. If nerd humor wasn't her thing, getting coffee with him was going to be an ordeal for her.

"I guess I should also mention that I'm kind of a huge nerd. I make obscure science fiction references and tell weird jokes that probably only I find funny." Although, she'd laughed at a couple already. That was part of why he'd had the courage to ask her for coffee.

"I see. I have a friend like that. Do you also make puns?"

"'Make puns'?" He laughed at her odd word choice. "Yes, I do make Earth human puns."

She snorted and stuck her hands in her pockets, her smile returning. "Well, where do you get this Earth human coffee of which you speak?"

"That would be at the all night diner. We have many on

our planet." He started walking again, his pace picking up as she fell in step beside him. When they reached the door, he held it open for her and said, "Welcome."

She ducked into the warmth and light of the restaurant, still smiling at him. Another Christmas miracle.

Her eyes broadened as she looked around, taking in the ceiling tiles, grubby carpet, booths, and long bar that ran along the side of the space. A bedraggled Christmas tree stood nearby, covered in lights and ornaments that looked like they were homemade. Vay walked over to it with a rapt expression on her face.

"Would you like to sit here?" He gestured to the booth next to the tree—specifically to the seat that would let her stare at it while they had their coffee.

"Is it okay?"

"Sure."

They slid into their booths, staring at each other. He wasn't sure how such a beautiful woman managed a goofy smile, but he was pretty sure his matched.

A waitress showed up with two cups of coffee and a carafe. "You want something from the kitchen?"

"I'm good," Henry said. He looked over at Vay. "You?"

"This is fine, thank you." She smiled at the waitress as the woman walked away, then leaned over her coffee and inhaled deeply, her eyes closing briefly. "This smells amazing."

"Diners often have the best coffee."

He picked up some sugar packets and flicked them back and forth to get all the granules in the bottom, then tore them open. Vay watched with that same keen interest as she'd had at the store, then followed his example. She waited for him to pour them in his coffee before doing the same, and even picked up her spoon after he did. It was like watching a time-delay alternate reality mirror.

Why was she mimicking him, though? It was almost as if she'd never made herself a cup of coffee before. He tested the thought, watching her as he picked up some creamers and poured them into his coffee. Sure enough, she did the same.

There were several types of hot sauce on the table. He picked one up and shook it, pretending to prepare it for his drink.

She looked at the bottles, then grabbed one that resembled his.

"Okay, hold on a minute." He put the hot sauce back in place. "You've had coffee before, right?"

Her eyes grew wide again and her mouth dropped open. "Uh…"

"You've never had coffee?"

She set down the bottle and wiped her hands on her jeans. "Maybe this wasn't such a good idea."

She slid toward the edge of the booth seat, setting her hand on the table as she prepared to leave. Henry reached out and grabbed it. She stared at his hand on hers, as if that was yet another thing that was new to her.

"Wait." His heart was pounding.

He didn't want to be alone. Not tonight. And even though Vay was turning out to be…really weird company, he liked her. She laughed at his jokes, and had a kind of vulnerability about her that made him want to help her, even though she didn't seem to need it.

"Please stay," he said.

She took a deep breath, then nodded and slid back onto the seat. She turned her hand over in his and held on.

"Thank you," he said.

Her smile was more hesitant. "I don't really know much about this area. I saw the lights and…I just had to stop by and see what it was all about."

"You're from someplace that doesn't have Christmas?"

The drawn expression returned to her face, and her fingers tightened on his hand. It wasn't too strange to think of her not celebrating the holiday, but she seemed completely ignorant about it. He squeezed back, trying to find a way to put her at ease.

"Right," he said. "I forgot for a moment that the ways of my homeworld are alien to you."

She cast another suspicious look at him. He smiled, hoping to draw on the common sense of humor they seemed to share.

"I mean, even on Earth, Christmas is one holiday

among many," he said. "There are tons of holidays around this time of year that I know nothing about. I'm just following my family's traditions."

A sharp stab of pain passed through his heart and his vision blurred for a moment. Vay tightened her grip on his hand again. She must have noticed.

"My friend who plays with words like you do is visiting her family. I thought she was celebrating someone's... 'birthday'?" Vay said the word as if she was unsure of herself—or uncertain of its meaning. "Now I wonder if I misunderstood her."

"Why?" His heart felt tight. He was getting better at reining in his emotions, even if his imagination was playing tricks on him. It had to be. Who didn't know about birthdays?

Vay smiled and shook her head. "She spoke of celebrating Hana...something. Hana is a common name where I'm from."

"Hanukkah," Henry said. "She was probably talking about Hanukkah. It's another holiday celebrated around this time of year. We Earthlings are a diverse bunch."

Vay smiled at him, as if she really enjoyed playing along with his joke. "The commonalities are stronger, from what I've observed. Otherwise, you would have destroyed each other long ago."

"Oh, really?" He took a sip of his coffee, daring to rub his thumb over the backs of her fingers.

A flush rose to her cheeks and she stared at their entwined hands. She cleared her throat and glanced at him briefly, then turned to look out the window.

"You join together with your families in the darkest, coldest part of the year. You celebrate with lights and... proximity." She looked back at their hands. "Lights in darkness. Togetherness in the cold. As a...space-faring wanderer, that is something I can understand."

Her smile broadened again. Henry's stomach was full of butterflies.

Not just playing along—she was expanding on the game.

"Where have you been all my life?" The words slipped out before he could stop himself.

"Lots of places. Too many." She shook her head and said, "And unfortunately, I need to get back."

"So soon?"

"My ride is waiting for me."

"Oh."

"But thank you for the coffee." She pulled her hand from his, picking up the mug and taking a sip. Her eyes widened and she made a terrible face, sticking out her tongue and scrunching her eyes shut. "Cygnus-X, this is terrible!"

Henry busted out laughing. Vay kept shaking her head and even wiped her tongue on her coat sleeve. That only made him laugh harder.

"Sorry," he managed, though tears were streaming down his face. "I know I shouldn't laugh."

"How do you drink this vile substance?"

"It's an acquired taste, I guess. Some people don't like it."

"I'm among their number." She gave her head one last shake, wiping her tongue on the roof of her mouth. "I do appreciate you procuring it for me."

He wiped his eyes dry, regaining control. "Any time. In fact, I would love to do this again. Only with a substance less vile."

She grinned at him. "I would like that, too."

Henry pulled out a pen and wrote his number on a napkin, then handed it to her. "Next time your travels bring you near, give me a call."

She picked up the paper and stared at the numbers, then folded it and tucked it inside her coat. "If it is at all in my power, I will."

Henry downed his coffee while Vay made yuck noises and smiled at him. He managed not to choke laughing. He put enough money on the table to cover their drinks and give the waitress a really nice tip.

They slid from the booth and stood. Wherever Vay was from, they had differing ideas of personal space. She was only inches away, smiling up at him.

"I know you're new to the ways of our Earthling holidays, but there's another fairly common thread that runs through most of them this time of year," Henry said.

"What's that?"

"Gifts." He picked up one of her hands, then pulled out the fruitcake and placed it in her grasp.

"But you wanted this."

"Honestly, I don't even like fruitcake. I was just trying to hold on to..." He shook his head. "Something that's passed. I want you to have it."

"I have nothing to give you in return."

"You gave me your company. Your time. And at this moment, that is worth more to me than I can say."

If he kept thinking about that, he was going to tear up again. It was time to start moving on. Somehow, he felt that would be a little easier after this chance encounter.

"Thank you." She held the fruitcake against her chest, staring at it as if it was something precious.

He put his arm around her as they headed for the door. He hadn't meant to do it, but it felt natural and she didn't object.

"You should know that a lot of people don't like fruitcake, either," he said. "But it could be a great paperweight or doorstop."

"It's heavy and solid. It would make a good projectile weapon." She grinned up at him.

"Well, don't go throwing it around on your spaceship. It'd probably go right through your windows."

She paused at the door and laughed. "Our viewports are

a bit stronger than that."

"Good. Because I don't want anything getting in the way of our second date."

"Date?" She cocked her head to the side.

"It's a custom among our people. We tend to pair off when we like each other to spend time and…"

She leaned in a bit closer. "Enjoy proximity?"

His mouth went dry. "Sometimes."

He cleared his throat, not knowing what to do. She had to leave, she had his number. If anything was going to happen between them, it was up to her now.

Well, maybe not entirely.

"There is one more Earth holiday tradition I could introduce you to," he said. "If you're interested."

"What's that?"

He pointed above the door, to the mistletoe hanging over their heads. "Mistletoe. When you're standing beneath it with someone you like, it's customary to…kiss them."

"Oh." She smiled. "That sounds pleasant."

"Wow." He couldn't hide his surprise. But before either of them could think themselves out of it, he pressed his lips against hers.

She leaned into him, her lips moving softly in response to his, almost tentatively. When he pulled back, her eyes were wide with wonder.

Never having tasted coffee he could believe. Never

hearing of Christmas... Okay, that was harder. But this being her first kiss... That was impossible. Right?

She blinked a few times, then looked away and laughed.

"I like this tradition," she said.

"Me, too."

As much as he wanted to hold on to the moment, he couldn't think of another reason to keep her. He opened the door and walked into the night, feeling a warmth in his chest that the chill air couldn't touch.

"I expected you back before now."

Ari's booming voice rumbled through the small shuttle as Vay strapped herself into the seat next to him at the pilot's console.

"My expedition was more fruitful than anticipated." She held up the gift Henry had given her and beamed at her pun. Vay would have to tell Evelyn about it when she returned from celebrating with her family.

Ari arched an eyebrow at the treasure in Vay's hands. "What is that?"

"Fruitcake."

"It looks like a nutrient brick."

Vay nodded. "That's what drew my attention. Its form and shape are like the food we're used to from the *Arbiter*.

But look at all the colors within it. Like the lights these Earthlings have used to decorate their town. We should share it with the others when we arrive at Homeworld Security headquarters."

"If you wish."

"I hear it's an acquired taste, though."

"You hear? From who?"

"I met a helpful Earthling."

"Most of them seem to be," Ari said. "It's an extraordinary planet on many levels."

He engaged the cloak that would obscure the vessel from the eyes of any curious Earthlings. Like Henry.

Ari paused in his launch preparations. "With you being our cultural programmer, I can justify stopping here to let you explore this town. But it was still unscheduled and we'll have to answer for it."

"I know," Vay said.

Ari was silent for a moment, then said, "Did you find what you were looking for?"

The lights had drawn her to the small town as they flew overhead. There was something almost magical about them. She'd had no idea what she was looking for when she asked Ari to make his stop. But she was absolutely sure she'd found it.

"Yes." Vay hadn't stopped smiling since she'd left Henry. Since he'd kissed her.

Ari smiled as well. "I'm glad. Then let's go."

Vay looked at the gift in her lap, then out the viewport. Her reflection beamed back at her in the transparent material, the bright, colorful lights illuminating the town below shining through.

Chapter One

A few weeks later…

"This is crazy." Vay repeated the statement as she walked toward the office of Earth's new planetary liaison, K-58-b7. Or, more simply, Kira.

Kira's bondmate, Brendan, stepped into the hallway. Vay quickly plastered a smile on her face. Hopefully, he hadn't heard her talking to herself.

"Hey, Vay." He used the same rhyming greeting every time they interacted.

"Hey, Brendan. Is Kira in her office?"

"You're in luck. She just returned from the Himalayas." His ever-present smile widened. "I still can't believe you can get from Asia to Montana in half an hour."

"Coalition shuttles are a good bit faster than anything you've developed on Earth," Vay said.

He chuckled. "Maybe a little."

She grinned, happy he was playing along with her understatement. "Is she alone?"

"Yeah. She dropped off Ari and Rin to look for the Centaurans. We may finally have a lead on where their base is located."

"Centaurans don't have bases. They're nomadic, even on their own homeworld."

"No wonder we're having trouble finding them. Kira's lucky Adam left you behind to help out with the search."

"Thanks, but I don't think he was actually planning for me to help hunt down the rogue sentients invading Earth. Having a cultural programmer around was probably more about setting up Earth's First Contact committee."

Brendan arched an eyebrow at her.

"Oh, right," she said. "I mean, 'Department of Homeworld Security'."

He stepped around her, walking backward up the hall so that he could maintain eye contact. "See, that's what I like about you, Vay. You respect our culture."

"That's what I'm here for." Vay turned as well and took a few steps backward, trying to mirror his motions, but bumped into a table. She twisted quickly and managed to catch a vase that had started to tip toward the floor.

Brendan chuckled. "See you at dinner."

"Yeah." Vay cautiously stepped away from the table as he disappeared down the stairs at the end of the hall. "Maybe."

Hopefully not.

Her stomach was churning. What was she doing? She wasn't a soldier like the others. Okay, technically, they were all soldiers in the great fleet of the Coalition of

Planets, but she was a scientist. A cultural programmer—one of the lowest ranking, most often denigrated positions in their entire society.

On a professional level, she found her fellow sentients' dismissal of her function fascinating. On a personal level, it "sucked ass", as Brendan would say.

The populations of new planets adapted to the Coalition's ways when they joined. It was mandatory. The only exceptions were the sentients who were physically incapable of imitating the dominant culture. And, if she was honest with herself, nobody in power cared about them.

The only Sadirians who cared about other cultures were the cultural programmers. And their job was supposed to be making life easier for the High Council and others in positions of power, not help the people being ruled.

"Why is this Antarean clicking at me? Is it an insult?"

"No, sir, that's just the noise their mandibles make when they're trying to form sounds in our language."

She was a facilitator, not a hunter. But Kira had limited resources, which presented Vay with an opportunity that she couldn't let pass by. She walked down the hallway with a more determined stride—being careful not to bump into any more furniture.

The door to Kira's office was open. Vay's heartbeat sped up. She had hoped she would have a few moments to build up her nerve to make her request, but Kira had probably heard her approach a mile away.

It was just an assignment—one that Vay desperately wanted. There was no harm in asking. Right?

"Are you just going to lurk in the hallway all day?"

Vay jumped at the low, strong voice echoing down the hall. There was no more time to second-guess herself. She quickly entered the office, hoping to appear confident instead of unprepared.

"Hi," Vay said. "I would ask how you heard me, but you did spend all that time running 'listening' stations." She made air-quotes around the word, the way Brendan had taught her.

Kira quirked up an eyebrow at the joke. And was that a hint of a smile?

Her dark hair was pulled back in a disheveled ponytail and there was a faint, yet distinct flush to her tanned skin. But then, Brendan had just been visiting, and Vay doubted he would have left without a kiss.

A strong pulse of excitement shot through her system at her own memory—a single kiss shared with a special Earthling on Christmas Eve that had changed Vay's world forever.

Suddenly fortified, she said, "I wanted to talk to you about the signal we detected today."

"What about it?"

"It's really close. Minutes away by shuttle. It's weak and didn't last more than a few seconds, but I think we should still investigate it."

"Yes, and if I had anyone to send, I'd have already—"

"Send me."

Kira's eyebrows shot up on her forehead. "You?"

"I can handle it. Like I said, it's only minutes away. It's probably nothing. A small-time operation or maybe just a signal that escaped from a sentient passing through that area."

"What if it's the Scorpiian bounty hunter that we know is operating on Earth? We still haven't tracked it down."

"I can send a distress call."

"You wouldn't get a chance. You'd never see it coming." The determined gleam that seemed to live in Kira's eyes was back. Vay felt her opportunity slipping away.

"It's probably nothing," Vay said.

"But it *could* be something."

Desperate, she reached for any way she could reassure Kira enough to send Vay to investigate. "A Scorpiian wouldn't have made the mistake of letting a signal be detected."

"No one is perfect. And even if the signal is from another rogue sentient, the Scorpiian might have picked up on it and be headed there to hunt whatever bounty is on the trespasser."

"Which makes it all the more important that we act quickly. We can track it down and—"

"There are too many unknowns." Kira shook her head. "Of all the assignments I've given out so far, this is the most dangerous. It makes more sense to wait and send Ari."

"I've received the same training, even if my skill set was weighted toward more diplomatic resolutions. Maybe that will work in my favor."

"Scorpiians aren't known for their love of diplomacy. They're more known for their ability to conceal themselves, get close to their targets, and kill them."

"I'm aware of that, sir. I also know that Scorpiians blend in to reach their targets, stalking and studying them so they can fool even the closest of friends. They don't just murder anyone who gets in their way—it would bring too much attention to them. And they wouldn't make the mistake of letting a signal like this slip through, no matter how faint it is. Like you said in this morning's meeting, it's likely just a false alarm. Why wait and send Ari to confirm that, when you can send me now?"

"What if it *is* the Scorpiian and it isn't following their standard cultural protocols? What if it's not a false alarm?"

"Then I'll gather intel—from my ship, flying cloaked and at night—and let you know what's going on. I can run passive scans during the day while my ship is safely hidden in the forest of the region. And if it is a Scorpiian, I'll turn around and come back here immediately. It'll never see me leaving."

Kira snorted. "You've been spending too much time with Brendan. His sense of humor is rubbing off on you." She fixed her dark eyes on Vay, all sense of amusement vanishing. "Why is this so important to you? Really?"

"I can't say, sir. But it is important to me. I've studied Earth customs enough to walk among them if necessary. I can be there and back in a couple of days."

"Vay, if this is about how many of us have pair-bonded with humans—"

She laughed. "I can honestly say that I'm not asking for this assignment in the hopes that I'll run into an Earthling and feel some sort of magical connection that I'm compelled to act on, falling hopelessly in love."

It was true. Because that had already happened. With a tall, somewhat gangly, brown-haired, brown-eyed Earthling.

Henry had the greatest smile. He'd made Vay laugh, even when she could tell that he'd been dealing with something that weighed on him. And he'd shared something of himself with her—the ways of his people, and his own kin. He'd made her feel part of something beautiful and special.

She hadn't had a chance to ask him what was bothering him at the time. Ari had been waiting for her in a shuttle nearby. They weren't supposed to make the stop, but she'd been drawn to the festive lights decorating the small town and wanted to understand what was happening.

Luckily, Kira had been forgiving of the little side-trip, especially when Vay spun it as a cultural observation sub-mission. And it seemed luck was helping Vay out again. Henry lived very close to the signal's origin.

He'd given her his phone number. She could use that to triangulate his position. Maybe she could see him again, even just one more time. But only if she received the assignment.

Vay did her best not to fidget under Kira's intense stare. After a few more moments, Kira shook her head.

"Go. Report in every hour when you're not in your rest cycle."

Vay was stunned. Was she really being allowed to go?

"Standard procedure is every three hours."

Kira raised an eyebrow at her.

"But I'll report in every hour," Vay said. "Yes, sir. Thank you, sir."

She turned and practically ran from the room before Kira could change her mind.

Chapter Two

"This was a bad idea."

Henry stared at the ceiling of his parents' cabin, his gaze absently following the grain of the wooden beams. They had built most of the place with their own hands, using repurposed or other environmentally friendly materials. The cabin was filled with memories.

He couldn't sell it. He couldn't leave, either. Imagining it sitting empty in the forest was too…lonely.

"And I know something about that." He sighed and rolled onto his side. "Hence the talking to myself. Because there's no one else to talk to."

Maybe he could leave the cabin alone for a little while. Just until he'd had more time to grieve properly—around other people.

He wished he'd thought about the effects of being isolated while dealing with this before quitting his job. He hadn't been thinking clearly at the time.

All he'd thought was that his inheritance would be enough for him to live on for years and he could always find another high school that needed a biology teacher. And he'd had something in mind to keep him busy.

"Get going, Henry." He spoke in his best imitation of his dad, imagining his advice. Moving into their cabin so Henry could look for evidence of a Sasquatch probably wouldn't be among it.

He deepened his voice again. "If you're going to look for Bigfoot, go look for Bigfoot. Get off the damned couch."

Henry laughed, almost feeling like his dad was with him again. He sat up and stretched.

"Cryptozoology is tangentially related to biology," Henry said. "So it's kind of like work."

Dad wouldn't necessarily have agreed, but he would have been amused and supportive. He'd have joined Henry on his walks through the woods, looking for evidence of cryptids—lifeforms that may or may not exist outside of legend. Henry smiled as he stood and walked across the room to grab his coat from the peg where it hung by the door, glad that he'd remembered it this time.

"Get going, Henry," he said, in dad's voice. "Something great is just on the other side of that door."

Cold swept over him as he opened the door. Something great *was* on the other side. Well, some*one* great.

"Vay?"

Her blue eyes were wide as she stared at him, one hand poised as if she'd been about to knock when he opened the door. Her short blonde hair stuck out from underneath the same silly Christmas hat that she'd been wearing the night they met—Christmas Eve. And she had on the ridiculous, eye-jarring moose sweater in half a dozen clashing bright colors.

All of that came to him from his peripheral vision, because he couldn't look away from her face. Those beautiful eyes and perfect features. Pert nose, gently curved lips.

Soft lips… He knew from their experience under the mistletoe. His skin was suddenly tingling, and not from the cold.

"Hi." A wisp of a smile pulled at the corners of her mouth.

"Hi. Hi," he repeated, shock giving way to enthusiasm.

Vay was here. Here!

Before he could think better of it, he stepped forward and picked her up in a huge hug, swinging her around in a circle and laughing. He couldn't believe how much he had missed her. She wrapped her arms tightly around his neck, her laughter merging with his and ringing through the trees.

As he set her down, she smiled at him. It warmed him better than any coat would. He loved her smile— especially how her front teeth stuck out just a tiny bit more than the others. It was the one imperfection to her features that made her beauty that much more real.

"I'm not imagining you, am I?" he said.

"No. Unless I'm imagining you, too."

He shook his head. "Not that I'm aware of. What are you doing here?"

"Working up the nerve to knock on your door?"

They both laughed again.

"I happened to be in the neighborhood, and you'd extended that kind invitation..." she said.

"Of course! Come in."

He stepped back into the cabin, drawing her in after him. He closed the door, then helped her take off her coat. There was a rug inside to deal with the snow crusting her boots, some of which had already fallen onto his coat that was lying on the floor. He didn't even remember dropping it. He picked it up and hung it on a hook next to Vay's.

For a moment, he was stunned, looking at their coats next to each other on the hooks. He wanted to keep seeing them that way with a need that made it hard for him to catch his breath—and also was completely ridiculous. How could he have such strong feelings about her after spending less than an hour in her company?

He knew he'd been smitten with her the night they met. It had felt like more than infatuation, though. It still did.

Thinking about her gave him the happiest moments he'd experienced in months, even when he'd thought they would never see each other again. She'd left him with the distinct impression that her life was too busy to give her room for socializing. But now she was standing next to him and it felt...right.

Her gaze drifted from the kitchen area to the rustic furniture, fireplace, and loft above. Her lips were slightly parted and her eyes were wide. He hoped that meant she liked it.

The stones surrounding the fireplace were still warm from last night's fire and the potbelly stove near the kitchen was full of chunks of burning wood. The cabin was pretty cozy. Or it would be with a few quilts. And thermal underwear.

Henry and his parents had worked hard to make the space inviting and beautiful. It was just as gorgeous from the outside, with two-story timber walls and a wood-shingle roof covered in snow. He'd strung solar-powered Christmas lights all around it after he and Vay had met. Their battery charged up all day so they could shine through most of the night when the light sensors kicked them on. The place was like a postcard, inside and out.

"You live here?" she said.

"I do."

"It's lovely."

He laughed, remembering the running gag from their first conversation. "Not bad for a primitive planet."

"What?" She looked genuinely shocked—and a little scared, which was strange.

"Sorry, I was just doing a call-back to Christmas Eve. Remember, I kept making jokes about you being from another planet because you'd never heard of Christmas?"

Or birthdays. Or tasted coffee.

He still hadn't figured out how she was so sheltered, but he had a few ideas. The most probable theory was that she'd been raised in some sort of cultist compound. His favorite idea was that she actually *was* an alien. He felt his smile broaden at the thought, but managed not to tell her about it.

"Right. The joke." She let out a nervous laugh.

He tried to shift the conversation toward something that would help put her at ease, but barreled right into probably the least safe topic.

"How long are you in town for?"

Please say, 'forever', he chanted in his mind.

"A few days."

"Oh." He tried to hide his disappointment. He wasn't sure how successful he was.

Vay took his hand in hers. "But I'd like to spend them with you. If that's okay."

"Okay? That's great."

He was relieved when her smile became more relaxed.

"I can make us hot cocoa," he said. "I promise you'll like it much more than coffee."

She made a face and laughed. "That wouldn't be hard. I tried to develop a taste for coffee, like you said people do, but still haven't managed."

"If you hate it so much, why bother?"

"It reminded me of you."

She must have seen how stunned he was at her admission, because she said, "What?"

"It's nothing. I'm just glad to know you thought of me since Christmas."

"You made quite an impression," she said.

"A good one, I hope."

"You could say that."

She was here, after all. How had she even found his cabin? Maybe she asked around town. He didn't want to look too closely at this...miracle.

"My work takes place mostly at night," she said. "But I should have a few hours in the afternoons and evenings."

"That's fine. You can take naps here." He gestured to the couch and the loft upstairs. Warmth flooded his body at the thought of her in his bed—even alone.

Or not...

"That's sweet, but my superiors probably wouldn't approve of that. I need to check in with them frequently."

"Right. That makes sense." Sort of. His theory about her being in a cult was gaining traction. "Have you eaten? I could make us something."

"I'm not hungry, but thanks." She angled her head toward the couch and shrugged one shoulder. "Could we sit and talk?"

"Sure."

No matter what she needed or why she was here, he was grateful to be with her again. And if this was all they could have—just a few days—he'd gladly take any and every moment she could share with him.

Chapter Three

Vay let out a huge yawn as she flew in yet another widening circle over the forest. She'd only managed to get a couple of hours in her regen bed and she couldn't have cared less. Her cheeks were tired from laughing, making her that much more aware of the smile that seemed to be permanently installed on her face.

She'd spent the day with Henry. Almost the entire day. Aside from dodging a few uncomfortable questions about how she had found him, she had even managed to be mostly open and honest with him.

She'd had to be careful that he didn't figure out the truth about her. The last thing she wanted was for him to receive a mind-wipe.

Somehow, knowing that he was thinking about her and had fond memories of their time together on Christmas Eve made her feel a warmth deep in her body unlike anything she'd ever experienced. It was like happiness, only more intense. And it was systemic.

She wriggled in her chair a bit, as thinking about him made her belly fill with tingling energy. Energy that spread lower, making her ache in a way she hadn't been able to work up the nerve to explore. Yet.

It was new. Everything with him was new. And she wanted to experience whatever she could in the time they had.

If only there were more of it.

A light flickered to life on her command console. Not from the scans she was running, searching for that errant signal, but from the communications array. She'd forgotten to check in.

"Crap."

Kira was going to be unhappy. She might even pull Vay back to the mansion where the First Contact committee was headquartered.

There was no way she would leave without saying goodbye to Henry. But she wasn't ready to do that yet.

She would just have to talk Kira into letting Vay stay. She tapped on the control to open the connection, feeling her smile fade to more normal levels.

Instead of her commanding officer's angular features filling the com-screen, she saw a man with a strong chin and narrow eyes. His complete lack of hair was helpful in jarring her out of her surprise.

"Ari? I thought you were in the Himalayas."

"I am. And I see where you've been assigned."

Double-crap.

Ari had been piloting the shuttle when Vay insisted on making the stop in the nearby town. He'd risked getting a reprimand by indulging her curiosity.

"I forgot to check in," she said. "I need to send my 'all's well' code."

"I sent it for you. I know that Kira is holding everyone to extremely high standards in following protocols."

He was covering for her. Again.

"Kira's not that bad. She's new to being planetary liaison, and doesn't want to do anything that will endanger us making our case to the High Council on behalf of Earth."

General Serath—Adam—and his Earthling bondmate Evelyn were en route to Sadr-4 to try to convince the leaders of the Coalition to establish a First Contact committee on Earth. It was much earlier than was standard procedure, but the circumstances were highly unusual.

For one thing, the previous planetary liaison was in General Serath's brig awaiting trial. And for another, the growing number of Earthlings who had learned of the alien operations on Earth had already taken matters into their own hands, forming the Department of Homeworld Security.

Two of the Earthlings on Earth's ad-hoc First Contact committee had joined Serath to both observe and help make their case—Brendan's sister, Paige, and his government liaison, Eric.

Paige was an environmental scientist, and planned to offer her skills and knowledge of Earth's incredible resources to help restore the ecosystems of planets that couldn't support life without domes anymore.

Eric was going along to negotiate on Earth's behalf and offer a less overt boon to the Coalition. He and Sorca were pair-bonded, as baffling as that still was to Vay. And Sorca planned to leave the fleet to stay on Earth with Eric if the Department of Homeworld Security wasn't officially recognized.

Given her cultural assessment of the High Council, Vay doubted it would be enough to have Earth's First Contact committee approved. All the more reason to enjoy her time with Henry while she could. If she had any more.

"You can relax. This transmission has been encrypted so that no one can listen in," Ari said.

"How did you manage that?"

"Brendan. His understanding of our communications technology is impressive."

If only Henry had a skill like that to offer. Maybe he could join Earth's First Contact committee as well. He wouldn't need a mind-wipe then. They could be together, like the others and their bondmates.

"Vay, we can't do anything that might hurt the chances of Earth's First Contact committee being recognized."

Ari's booming voice was stern. Almost like he was giving her a warning. He couldn't know about Henry, could he?

"I want Earth to be safe," she said. "I won't jeopardize

that."

"Good." He let out a long sigh. "The last time we were in this area and we made that stop—"

Triple-crap. He knew something.

"Ari, don't."

Brendan might have helped Ari encode their communication, but she still wasn't comfortable with them coming out and talking about Henry openly. There was no such thing as a completely secure system.

"Listen to me," Ari said. "You came back changed. You'd found that…celebratory fruitcake. Maybe no one else noticed, but you and I have been stationed together since we were first assigned to the fleet. I know how much of an impression that fruitcake made on you. Earth fruitcake is appealing. I get that. The pretty colors, the flavors—"

"I didn't eat it," she said.

"What?"

"I couldn't bring myself to. It's too pretty. I put it in a stasis pod."

That she kept under her pillow back in her room. Ari didn't need to know that.

She knew she'd derailed his metaphor. She wanted him to stop talking about it—to stop talking about Henry. But Ari was stubborn.

He ran a hand over his face. When he looked at her again, his eyes were full of sympathy. Maybe even pity.

"A stasis pod is a good place for it," he said. "You can think about it and remember whatever fun you had finding that fruitcake. But you can't take it back to the *Arbiter* with you. You can't hold on to that fruitcake forever. Eventually, you're going to have to let it go. The sooner you do, maybe the less it will hurt."

"I appreciate you looking out for me. I really do. But this is my decision. If I want to experience more fruitcake, that's my choice."

He shook his head and mumbled, "What is it about this planet?"

"Ari?"

"Yeah?"

"Thank you."

He let out a little snort and smirked. "Just looking out for my team. Watch your back, okay? Earth isn't all fun and fruitcakes. And with a Scorpiian running planetside, we all need to be careful."

"I will be." She thought of an Earth expression that matched very well with Ari's mission tracking down the Centaurans he was after. "Good hunting."

He snorted again, his smile widening. "Safe journeys."

The transmission ended. Vay felt a lump form in her throat.

Whatever else was happening on and with Earth, this assignment was bringing the people she was stationed with closer together. It was making what they did more meaningful somehow. She hoped that would last when they all were inevitably reassigned.

Chapter Four

"Brachiation. That would explain it." Henry looked up at the bare trees surrounding him. "If they get around by swinging through the trees, they wouldn't leave much evidence behind."

The fog from his breath puffed around his face in a billowing cloud. Once again, he'd forgotten his scarf. And hat. And gloves. At least he wasn't planning to stay out long.

"Except they're famous for leaving footprints." He returned his gaze to the snow-covered ground. "Big footprints—hence the name. But even that evidence isn't too common, so maybe... Maybe I should stop talking to myself."

And save his voice for Vay. She'd be at the cabin in a few hours. He hoped whatever work she'd done the night before had gone well and that she was getting some rest. He couldn't wait to see her again.

They had talked all day yesterday. All day, and he never once became bored or tired. He realized the newness of their relationship was contributing to how well things seemed to be going. They'd also spent a lot of time talking about his favorite topics, like scifi movies and books—which seemed to absolutely fascinate her. But even the lulls in the conversations had been companionable.

He loved spending time with her. He'd never clicked with anyone like he did with Vay. It was amazing.

A stick cracked loudly ahead of him, pulling him out of his thoughts and back into his surroundings. The hairs on his arms stood on end. He should have been paying more attention.

Aside from the recent cold snap and thick snow, the winter had been relatively mild. The black bears in the region had been known to leave their dens throughout the winter when the oak trees had a good crop of acorns. Like the trees he was walking through at that moment.

"Please don't be a bear."

He looked up into the dark eyes of a black bear.

"When I thought climate change was a threat to my existence, this is not what I pictured."

The bear let out a low growl.

"Easy, fella." Henry tried to remember what to do. His thoughts were scattered. "When a bear attacks, I'm supposed to try to look big, right? And make a lot of noise?"

The bear charged him.

"Oh, crap."

Henry started waving his arms above his head and jumping up and down. He yelled as loud as he could, making gibberish sounds that grew more desperate by the second.

The bear suddenly skidded to a halt only a few feet away. It turned around, and with a startled roar, it ran away.

Henry stared after it, wondering what had just happened. Then he started to laugh.

"I can't believe that worked."

His skin still felt electrified from the adrenaline. He let his head drop back, eyes closed and face pointed toward the sky. Relief washed over him as he took deep, steadying breaths—until he felt warm breath flow over his face in return.

"I'm going to open my eyes now," he said. "And I am not going to see a bear about to drop on my face."

He slowly turned around as he opened his eyes, looking up at whatever was in the tree above him. Only it wasn't in the tree. It was standing, hovering over him.

Henry stumbled backward, tripped over his own feet, and landed hard on his ass. His brain struggled to process what he was seeing.

"Oh my God."

He was staring at a seven-and-a-half foot tall Sasquatch. A Sasquatch!

Its face had a flat nose and broad mouth surrounded by bluish-tinged, wrinkled skin. Most of its head and all of its body was covered in a thick coat of white fur. Its eyes were bright blue, with horizontal pupils that almost bisected its irises.

"Gorilla," he muttered to himself. "It's like a giant, albino gorilla. Except for the eyes... Blue, not pink."

The Sasquatch planted two of its arms on its hips...and crossed the other pair over its chest.

Four arms. Four. Arms.

Henry's throat was so tight, it hurt to swallow. The creature leaned forward and exhaled another huge breath from its nostrils, blowing Henry's hair away from his face.

"An albino gorilla?" Its deep voice sounded remarkably...huffy. "That is offensive."

Henry let out a high-pitched laugh. "It can talk. Of course it can talk. Because this is a delusion. I've obviously gone insane."

"Excuse me, but I'm not an 'it'. I'm male."

The Sasquatch stood up and fluffed the fur around its cheeks. At least, it *looked* like fur. Until it sharpened into stiff quills that quivered like a defensive porcupine's.

"I'm sorry," Henry said. "This is kind of new to me. I've never met a Sasquatch before."

"A what?"

"A Sasquatch. You know—Bigfoot? Yeti? Gigantopithecus?" He always looked to the fossil record first to explain cryptids.

It—he—the Bigfoot rolled his eyes. It extended one of its arms to the ground to balance as it lifted a foot, and pointed at it with yet another arm. "Do my feet look big to you?"

"Uh, proportionally? I guess not. But I don't know what else to call you."

"How about 'Craig'?"

"Why would I call you that?"

"Because it's my chosen Earth name."

"Earth name..."

Henry's heartbeat sped up. He'd always dismissed the possibility of cryptids being of extra-terrestrial origin. But seeing 'Craig' in the flesh, it made a hell of a lot more sense than this lifeform evolving from something native to Earth.

"You're an alien," Henry said.

"I'm a Lyrian. Educate yourself." Craig huffed out another big breath through his nostrils. "But I suppose that would be futile. If you did learn anything about us, the Sadirians would swoop in and erase your memories. You can't throw a tnergog without them trying to give somebody a mind-wipe."

The Sasquatch... Lyrian... *Craig* made an offhanded gesture with one of his arms.

Henry didn't know how to respond to Craig's statement. He was having trouble forming coherent thoughts. To make things worse, his nose started to tingle a moment before he let out a huge sneeze. He managed to turn his head to the side at the last instant.

Craig pounded two of his hands into the ground on either side of Henry's legs and let out an ear-splitting roar that sounded like a cross between an angry bear and a constipated elephant. Henry caught a glimpse of teeth as he fell backward—so many teeth—like the inside of a Great White's mouth.

"Please don't eat me," he yelled. "It was just a sneeze."

"What is 'sneeeeeze'?" Craig drew out the word.

"It's an involuntary reaction to being exposed to allergens, bright light, or cold." Henry recited the definition like he was back in front of his class. "It's just how the human body clears out its sinus passages and nostrils."

Craig glared at Henry for what felt like a long time. He wasn't sure if he should be trying to make eye contact or avoid it. The last thing he wanted to do was make Craig feel challenged.

After a few more moments, Craig sat back on the ground. "*Sneeze* is weird."

"Yeah." Henry stifled another near-hysterical laugh. He didn't know what might set Craig off.

"This whole situation is kind of weird to me, too," Henry continued. "But I promise, I don't want to hurt you."

Craig's lips twitched up on one side. A smirk? Henry wondered if it meant the same thing to a Lyrian.

"Not that I could if I tried," Henry said. "But I wouldn't

try. I'm not that kind of person."

"And what kind of person are you?"

Henry sat up, very slowly. "I'm a biology teacher. I study the lifeforms on my planet and teach children about them."

"A noble task." Craig's eyebrows rose. He looked sincerely impressed.

Henry couldn't keep himself from letting out a little snort of derision. "I wish all the other Earthlings felt that way." When Craig cocked his head to the side, Henry added, "Many of the people where I'm from don't actually value teachers much."

"That's foolish," Craig said.

"Tell me about it. I'm Henry, by the way. That's my name."

"Henry."

They sat on the ground, Craig staring intently at Henry, while Henry did his best to only make occasional eye contact. The ground was freezing, and the cold started to get to him. He pulled his coat around himself more tightly.

"You lack fur," Craig said.

"Yeah. For the most part." Henry laughed, then ruffled his hair. "I have this, at least."

"That is insufficient."

"Well, I forgot my hat and scarf at home. And my gloves." He dropped his hands onto his lap just as his stomach let out a loud gurgle.

Craig was on him again in an instant, teeth bared as he knocked Henry backward onto the ground.

"It was just my stomach growling," Henry yelled.

Craig kept hovering over Henry, but seemed to relax.

"Is it angry?" Craig asked.

"What? No." Henry let out a little laugh, more relief than amusement. "It means I'm hungry. I sort of forgot to eat breakfast this morning, too."

Craig exhaled sharply. "Earthling, where are your parents?"

Even if Craig wasn't an alien, he couldn't have known how his question would hit Henry right in the gut. He almost preferred when the Lyrian was getting in his face. Terror was easier to handle than the weight of his grief.

When he'd been talking to Vay, it was the first time that Henry had felt anywhere close to normal in as long as he could remember. He'd been careful to avoid the topic of his parents—which was probably part of why he hadn't learned much about her own upbringing.

"They died a couple of months ago," Henry said. "Car accident."

Craig's eyebrows rose again, his jaw going slack so that his mouth hung open. "You're an orphan?"

"I guess so, technically. But I'm self-sufficient."

"You ventured into a cold environment without proper coverings and neglected to feed yourself."

Henry shook his head and laughed. "Well, when you

put it like that..." He wished Craig would give him a little more space "I'm dealing with it. I'm twenty-six, I can—"

"Twenty-six? As in twenty-six Earth solar cycles?"

"Yes." Henry didn't like the way Craig was looking at him. Was that pity? Concern? "Which means I'm an adult. I can take care of myself."

"Obviously not." Craig puffed out another breath, looming even closer. He slid two of his arms under Henry's back and picked him up with no apparent effort.

"What are you doing?"

"Taking you someplace warm where there is food."

Craig wrapped even more of his arms across Henry's body, holding him close to his chest. His fur was unbelievably soft and warm. It was like being carried by a giant kitten. A many-armed, bizarrely protective kitten.

"This isn't necessary," Henry said.

"Of course it isn't."

It might have been Henry's imagination, but he thought there was a bit of a purring noise coming from Craig's chest as he spoke. The condescension came through loud and clear, even if it was intended kindly.

"I'm glad you see it that way." He waited for Craig to put him down. Instead, the Lyrian kept walking, his stride carrying them quickly through the forest. "Um, Craig?"

"Yes, Henry?"

"You can put me down now. Like I said, I can take care of myself."

Craig chuckled. "Your mental acuity seems to be suffering. Perhaps you need sleep as well."

"I don't need sleep."

If Henry fell asleep—which was never going to happen while he was in the care of an alien—he might miss his time with Vay later. The fact that his mind immediately went to her when he was being carried through the forest by an alien Sasquatch told him how far gone his heart already was.

"I am a full-grown adult," Henry said.

"Nestlings are so cute at this stage. They've just grown their first pair of arms and think they can take on the world."

"I don't want to take on the— Wait, did you say *first* pair of arms?"

Craig ignored the statement.

"I've been watching you roam around the forest for a while now," he said. "What were you looking for?"

Henry let out a defeated sigh. "You."

"Well, then. Congratulations."

"Thanks."

Chapter Five

After another reduced cycle in the regen bed, Vay knew she should be feeling tired. Instead, she was invigorated. She couldn't wait to peel off her uniform and put on her Earth clothes.

She'd only brought along the one outfit, though. If she had packed more, it might have raised suspicions. Kira was being a bit overprotective and had checked several times to make sure Vay had everything she needed for the assignment. And Vay wasn't supposed to leave the ship unless absolutely necessary.

She was also supposed to be spending her "down time" in the afternoons and evenings going over the data she was collecting both on her nightly patrols and during the stationary scans her ship conducted each day. Technically, she did review everything as soon as she ended her rest cycle. It just didn't take that long. There hadn't been any more anomalous readings.

She grabbed a nutrient brick and sat at the console, staring at the scrolling information. Her stomach rebelled at the once-familiar substance.

Ari's warning came back to her with jarring force. She

shouldn't get attached to anything on Earth. They'd have to go back to Sadr-4 eventually—and the space stations, ships, and dome-worlds. Her future was filled with nutrient bricks.

No more pancakes. No more fuzzy sweaters. No more Christmas lights or fresh air.

No more Henry.

Her eyes blurred. She couldn't even wipe them clear on her uniform. The material was hydrophobic, and would just sort of smear her tears around. Instead, she blinked rapidly until her vision improved.

Too many of the Sadirian soldiers who had visited Earth were pair-bonding with Earthlings. Even if Henry eventually fell in love with Vay, there was no way to know if she'd be permitted to stay.

The High Council found it hard to believe that anyone would give up access to their technology to remain on a relatively primitive world, and required an incredible amount of investigation, interviews, and testing to allow it.

If they granted her request, it would mean her Coalition citizenship would be revoked and Vay would be banished to Earth forever. That would be a dream come true. But she had to be honest with herself. It was very unlikely to happen.

It would be much easier if Henry decided to come with her to live aboard the *Arbiter*—or wherever else she was stationed. The Coalition could find something for him to do, and they were much more understanding of someone from one of those "primitive planets" wanting to improve their circumstances by bonding with a Coalition citizen. Less bureaucracy to navigate, but a much bigger sacrifice. She wouldn't let Henry give up Earth to be with her—even if his feelings for her ever became strong enough for him to make the offer.

She pounded on a disposal port to open it, then dropped in the barely-eaten remains of her nutrient brick. At least it wouldn't be wasted. The tiny shuttle she was using would sterilize and recycle it into her next meal.

Maybe Henry would offer to cook for her again.

She should just be happy with the time he was giving her. And she was actually learning so much about Earth's cultures from talking to him through the game they'd accidentally begun. He thought she was playing along when he spoke to her as if she was from another planet. If only he knew the truth.

She was sure he wouldn't freak out if she told him. He would accept her for what she was.

She hoped.

Maybe she could convince Kira to request that Vay be permanently reassigned to Earth. Most of the sentient species that the Coalition had discovered were already integrated into their culture. They didn't need many cultural programmers anymore, which she was actually glad for.

The High Council usually waited for a planet to have a single, homogenous culture before approaching them about joining the Coalition. They said it made it easier for them to adapt, but Vay knew the truth. It wasn't about adaptation—it was about conquest. Her predecessors had assisted in the obliteration of countless cultures.

They'd provided the High Council with reports and ideas on how best to get other sentients to adapt to the ways of the Sadirians, who held most of the power in the galaxy through their much more advanced technology. Surely some of those cultural programmers had hated what they were forced to do as much as Vay did.

Being assigned to the *Arbiter*, Vay was able to study the few sentients who couldn't—or wouldn't—conform. She provided information on how to help them adapt that was…not exactly helpful. She made sure her data was just good enough to keep her on the *Arbiter*, but didn't give the Coalition anything that could actually help them destroy those cultures.

She didn't see the harm in preserving other ways of life. Earth was a perfect example, with so many different sub-cultures within each culture even. If they could make that work and actually help each other, which many Earthlings did, surely the Coalition could as well.

The Antareans, with their intricate hive societies, could teach Sadirians about caring for their communities. Lyrians could teach them about familial bonds, which they formed with a speed and passion that was only matched by their formidable tempers.

Every sentient had worth. Why couldn't the High Council see—

A flashing light finally snapped Vay out of her thoughts. Moons, she knew she had a tendency to get caught up in her own head, but she'd blanked out on screens and screens of data. Luckily, she'd programmed the computer to double-check her work and notify her of anomalies. Like the one blinking on her screen.

"What is that?" She pulled up the data and looked at the screen more closely.

Another anomalous reading. It looked like residual energy left from another sort of scan—one she wasn't familiar with. She compared her earlier readings of the area, fine-tuning the shuttle's systems to look for that particular signature. They were faint, but she could see a definite pattern.

Something had conducted a scan in a broad circular area using a technology she wasn't familiar with—that *her ship* wasn't familiar with. And her shuttle was equipped with the most advanced Coalition tech available.

This was new. It was powerful. And Henry's cabin was within its field of scrutiny.

"Crap."

There was no time to change into her Earth clothes, and her shuttle was grounded. The area was somewhat remote, but popular with campers and hikers. She couldn't risk her ship being detected. If she took off in the middle of the day—cloak or no—Kira would pull her back to headquarters immediately.

Vay wanted to grab a phase rifle to take along, but there were too many unknowns. If she dropped it or someone managed to take it from her, everyone would be pulled from the Earth assignment and Serath's chances of getting the First Contact committee recognized would be ruined.

Her wristband had a built in weapon as well as a shield. It would have to be enough.

She hit the control to close her helmet. The segments clicked rapidly into place, then fused. For a split second, the opaque metal left her in complete darkness, but then the internal screens flickered to life, giving her a view of her surroundings along with additional readouts and her uniform's functional levels.

Within moments, she was outside in the forest, running toward Henry's cabin. She would make a quick pass to confirm that everything seemed okay, taking care that he didn't see her in her uniform, then investigate more of the scan area she'd detected.

"Activate bio-sensor."

A grid appeared in her field of vision—tiny specks of light showing her where small animals were located outside. If anything bigger drew near, her uniform would warn her before she was close enough to be seen or heard.

"Everything's going to be fine," she said. "Henry is fine."

He had to be.

Chapter Six

"If you've been watching me all this time, how did I never notice you?" Henry couldn't believe he was adjusting to being carried by a giant fur-covered alien. "You're not exactly inconspicuous."

Craig chuckled. "Lyrians are masters of disguise. Our coats can change to match our environment, see?"

He seemed to disappear into thin air as Henry watched. He felt Craig's fur ripple where they touched, and could see a vague outline where he knew Craig was, but that was it. After a few seconds, Craig became opaque again.

"How did you do that?" Henry said.

"My spines are able to bend light. It's useful for eluding capture, but makes more sentients interested in catching us."

"I don't understand."

"We don't have to be in our skins for our spines to work. Our pelts can be made into the ultimate camouflage uniforms."

Henry was stunned. His stomach started to cramp up as he thought of the implications. "I can't even imagine someone being capable of doing that. Are you safe on

Earth?"

"I appreciate your concern." Craig glanced down at him and smiled, that small purring sound rumbling in his chest again. "We're as safe here as anywhere in the galaxy."

"Wait... We?"

"My mate, Barbara, is here as well."

"Craig and Barbara?" Henry laughed. "How do you have such ordinary names?"

"Our language isn't biologically compatible with your species."

"As in, our anatomy can't pronounce it?"

Craig snorted. "More like, if exposed to it for prolonged periods of time, your eardrums might rupture. Plus, it tends to carry, and would make us easier to detect. We selected Earth names to use for the duration of our mission."

"That's...great."

Henry had so many questions. About their physiology, where they were from, what life was like on their planet— and on others, if they knew about them. But there was one answer he needed before he satisfied his scientific curiosity.

"What is your mission on Earth?"

"Don't worry, we're here as collectors, not conquerors."

"I'd feel a lot better about that if you weren't carrying me to an undisclosed location."

Craig laughed, a loud, rumbling sound that made Henry

smile despite his worry.

"We're collecting seeds. Some we gather ourselves, and others we trade for."

"Trade with whom?" Henry tried to imagine what that exchange would look like. For some reason, he pictured Craig wearing a giant raincoat and Fedora, like in the movies.

"There are a few open-minded humans who have agreed to assist us in exchange for certain materials and equipment that assist them in their research."

Humans working with aliens for scientific research? Henry wanted in on that. Well, as long as Earth wouldn't suffer for it.

"Are you sure that's safe? I mean, what are those humans even using your stuff for?"

"We don't ask." Craig sniffed. "That would be rude."

Henry hesitated to ask his next question, but felt he had to. "And what are *you* using *our* stuff for?"

"Once we have enough seeds that can be modified to fit in with various ecosystems, we'll replicate them in our lab so we can distribute them to those in need."

"That doesn't sound so bad," Henry murmured.

"It won't negatively impact Earth in the slightest, and will greatly improve living conditions for several sentient species who have been victimized by the Sadirians." He sneered as he said the word.

"You mentioned them before. I take it you don't like

them very much."

"They are evil, Henry. All they care about is control. They come in offering technology that can improve life for everyone on a planet—at a price. They start small, making trades that seem completely reasonable. But once the sentients are addicted to their technology and think that's all they need to survive, the Sadirians strip the planet of resources. The population becomes completely dependent on them for survival."

Henry shivered. He wasn't sure if it was from the cold or the idea of such a cruel civilization.

"Don't worry, nestling," Craig said. "We're well hidden from the Sadirians who are on Earth."

"I'm not a nes— Wait, did you say 'on Earth'? As in, there are Sadirians on Earth right now?"

"Among others."

"Others…"

Henry was having trouble wrapping his mind around the concept of Earth being filled with different kinds of extraterrestrials. How many cryptids might actually be from other planets? How many were threats?

"The Sadirians aren't invading, are they?" he asked. "Or planning to offer Earth their technology?"

He had no illusions about Earth's ability to resist such an offer. Human greed was already damaging the planet. If the Sadirians were everything Craig said they were, they would only make things worse.

"Honestly, I'm not sure," he said. "But Barbara and I will protect you. Don't worry."

Before Henry could yet again explain that he didn't need to be protected and could take care of himself, the forest around them vanished. It just disappeared, replaced with smooth walls made of some sort of greenish metal. Lights blinked here and there, and he could hear the hum of machinery around him.

"What just happened?" Henry said.

Craig grinned. "Welcome to our home."

"Craig, sweetheart, the new samples are—" The new voice sounded much the same as Craig's. If anything, it was a little deeper. Barbara?

Craig pressed Henry closer, partially covering Henry's body with the spines of his chest.

"Before you get angry," Craig said, "let me explain."

"Explain... What is that you're carrying?" she said.

"You know that Earthling I've been watching?"

"Yes." She dragged out the word.

"He was attacked by a bear, so I—"

Barbara let out a sigh deep enough to ruffle Henry's hair. She must be standing right next to them. Henry tried to crane his neck to look at her, but Craig was holding him too close.

"So you ran to the rescue," she said. "Why in the name of the Solar Cross did you bring him back to our ship? You're risking everything."

"You risked the same when you decided to help that Earthling Carol and her son."

Henry could feel the low vibration of Craig's growling voice through his chest. He did not want to be in the middle of a fight between two space-Sasquatches. Wriggling out of Craig's four-armed embrace didn't seem feasible, though.

Barbara's voice held an answering growl. "That was different. She needed help creating medicine."

"Henry needs help, too," Craig said. "He's an orphan."

Henry blew the spine-fur out of his mouth so he could speak. "Pheh. Pheh. I am not. I mean, technically, I am, but I'm an adult."

"He's cold and he's hungry and he's all alone," Craig said.

Cold and hungry, yes. But not alone. Not since Vay had shown up on his doorstep. But then, Craig probably didn't know about her. He might not have followed Henry back as far as his cabin while "observing the human in the wild".

Craig leaned closer to Barbara and lowered his voice, as if he thought he could whisper quietly enough that Henry wouldn't hear him. "And he's only twenty-six Earth cycles old."

"Twenty-six?" There was a catch in Barbara's voice.

Here we go.

"Twenty-six is considered mature for my species,"

Henry insisted.

Barbara brushed Craig's fur away from Henry's face, giving him a chance to finally see her. She pretty much looked exactly like Craig, except the fur around her face was much shorter, revealing more of her ears. They were shaped sort of like bat wings. They even moved like wings as she studied him.

"Cool…"

Henry shook himself, gently pushing away from Craig's chest. Now was not the time to be studying Lyrian physiology.

When his feet were on the floor of what must be their spaceship, he could see an opening behind Craig that led to the forest. Henry had been in this area dozens of times recently and seen nothing out of place.

"Is your ship invisible?" Henry asked.

"Yes." Craig puffed up his chest and smiled. "Lyrians are at the forefront of cloaking technology. Not that anyone knows, thanks to Sadirians stealing all the credit."

Barbara's lips peeled back from her teeth and she hissed at Craig. A second row of teeth protruded from inside her mouth.

"Darling, let's be civil," Craig said. "You're scaring Henry."

"I'm fine." Henry did his best to hide his fear—and keep from losing control of any bodily functions—while Barbara calmed down.

Once her teeth were back in a more familiar configuration she exhaled sharply like Craig often did. She glared at Henry, making his palms sweat.

"He looks like a Tau Ceti," she said.

Craig smiled, as if that was a compliment. Henry tried to follow his lead.

"Thanks?"

The corner of Barbara's mouth quirked up. He hoped that was a good thing.

She turned back toward the archway where she'd come from. "I knew I should have agreed when you asked to breed more nestlings."

As soon as she was gone, Craig pulled Henry into a crushing hug while ruffling his hair.

So many arms…

"She likes you," Craig said.

"Really. How could you tell?"

Craig let Henry go and shrugged. "She didn't tear off any of your arms."

"Ha ha." Henry followed Craig deeper into the ship. "Wait, you were joking, right? Right?"

Chapter Seven

"Stop freaking out." Vay repeated the words over and over again, not that it was helping.

Henry wasn't at his cabin. But the energy signature she'd been tracking was.

It was so faint, if she hadn't known what to look for, she wouldn't have noticed it. But there were definite traces of energy all over his home. Her heart hadn't stopped pounding since she'd left.

She wasn't sure how or why, but she was certain it was the Scorpiian. For a single, crazy moment, she wondered if maybe it and Henry were one and the same. Disguising itself as a human would be exactly the kind of thing it would do to blend in and get close to its target. But she just couldn't believe that was true.

Henry was kind and warm. He was loving and gentle.

Scorpiians were cold assassins. She would have picked up on that while they talked, she was certain. At one point, he had even wrapped his arm around her as they sat close on the couch.

No. Henry was human. He was an Earthling.

But the Scorpiian had most likely been in his home.

She'd thought through all the angles of why it would be there. There was no reason for it to be interested in Henry. He didn't have power or influence.

The only thing that she could figure it would be looking for there was her. From her readings, she knew that it had been there after she'd visited with Henry and not before.

If it had managed to find samples of her DNA—which was pretty likely, since she and Henry had eaten a meal together and she'd probably shedded hairs on his couch— the Scorpiian would be able to take on her appearance.

Gaining access to the Department of Homeworld Security would endanger everything they were working for on Earth's behalf. And if it managed to get aboard the *Arbiter*, she shuddered to think of what it could accomplish by taking on the form of the right person at the right time.

It had already tried to manage both of those tasks before, but had been stopped by Eric and Sorca. Kira's team had been on high alert ever since, but had yet to encounter the Scorpiian again—that they knew of.

Vay's ship was locked down, so it couldn't gain entry to it. Plus, it would want to eliminate her before taking over her form. She needed to get back to her ship, but had to know that Henry was safe before she called in and told Kira...

Honestly, Vay wasn't sure what she was going to tell Kira.

But she would make it back to headquarters to tell Kira something. The scans from Vay's uniform were on maximum power and—

A blip of light appeared on her uniform's viewscreen. That couldn't be right.

One moment, there was nothing. The next, there was a human-sized lifeform a few dozen meters away. How had someone appeared so close to Vay without her sensors warning her?

Brendan called their uniforms "silver catsuits". They weren't exactly inconspicuous in the woodland setting. And there was no place for her to hide. Apparently, it was a moot point. Whoever it was had spotted her.

He immediately took off running. She wasn't sure whether she should pursue, but then her target yelled, "Hey, Sadirian. The Tau Ceti started settling down here before you. Find a different planet to exploit for resources."

A Tau Ceti? Here? She took off in pursuit. The sentient was far ahead of her, leaping over brush and ducking behind trees.

A Scorpiian might be more than she could handle, but a single Tau Ceti...

Wait. Why would a Tau Ceti be alone in a forest with no human prey nearby to feed on?

Vay needed answers, and the only way she would get them would be to catch this...whatever he was. Lucky for her, he didn't seem very coordinated.

He kept catching his coat sleeves on branches. The long white scarf he wore trailed behind him, snagging on tree limbs. One caught hard, jerking him to a stop. He made a choking noise as his legs kept going forward from his momentum, then he fell onto his back.

A huge amount of snow from the branch above dropped onto him. She reached him just as he was digging himself out, flailing as he reached the surface. She slid the power level of her wristband to its mid-range, so the blast would only stun a Tau Ceti. She could question him when he revived.

"Pheh. Pheh." He spat out snow, wiping it from his face. His eyes widened when he saw her, but probably not as wide as hers did behind the screen of her helmet.

Long straight nose, full soft lips, big brown eyes... It was Henry.

By all the stars in the void, how had they managed to run into each other again? Out here?

He looked at her wristband and raised his hands in a gesture she knew indicated surrender.

"Don't shoot," he said. "I'm an Earthling. Just an Earthling."

She opened her hands and slowly lowered them to her sides, hoping to calm him down. His chest was heaving, and his lips pulled down in a deep frown.

"How do you know about the Tau Ceti?" she said.

"I…uh… Just made it up." His gaze darted around, as if he was looking for a way to escape. "Tau Ceti is a close system. I think it's on the list of the ones who might have habitable planets."

He turned his attention back to her. "And you... You're obviously some sort of crazy person dressed up in a shiny silver catsuit. A very flattering catsuit."

He shook his head and looked away, his frown deepening.

"You called me Sadirian," Vay said.

Henry shrugged. "Just another nearby system?"

"It's not that close."

"I'm a biologist, not an astronomer." He laughed as if he'd made a joke.

"This is serious, Henry."

She saw his throat work to swallow beneath the fluffy white scarf, then he let out a foggy breath.

"How do you know my name?"

Her chest felt tight and her eyes burned. If he'd had contact with alien sentients, he would need a mind-wipe. Protocol was absolutely clear on this, and to deviate would bring down sanctions from the Coalition.

Since establishing a First Contact committee was such a high priority, Kira wouldn't risk upsetting the High Council by letting a loose end like Henry wander around Earth.

Who had been talking to him, though?

That was Vay's opening. They needed to find out what he knew and how he'd learned it. Who better to gather that information than Kira's cultural programmer? Especially since Vay had a link to Henry.

It would give her time to figure out what to do. How to protect him.

He leaned away from her, as if he was trying to escape through the earth itself. He looked terrified.

"I won't hurt you." She extended her arm to him. He stared at it for a moment, but then took it and let her help him up.

As soon as he was on his feet, he dropped her hand and started inching away. "That's nice of you to say, but it would be a lot more reassuring if I wasn't staring at my distorted reflection in your very fifties-scifi-movie-looking helmet."

"Just... Don't freak out."

"That is actually a very unsettling thing to hear from...a fellow Earthling dressed as an alien in a remote area of unpopulated forest."

She laughed and he cocked his head to the side as if she'd surprised him. With a deep breath, she tapped the side of her helmet. Its seams split open, the segments folding up on each other and nestling into the storage compartment built into the neck of her uniform.

His eyes widened. "Vay?"

She smiled and lifted her hand in a half-hearted wave.

"Hi, Henry."

"Hi." He said the word with wonder, his mouth stretching into the broad smile she was used to seeing from him. "What are you doing here?"

"I was in the neighborhood…again?"

"In a skin-tight silver catsuit." His eyebrows furrowed, but he was still smiling.

Part of her wanted to play it off as a game—to return to the banter they'd shared the day before and when they first met. But the joke was over. It was too late to go back.

"Actually, it's my uniform."

He nodded, his smile fading. "Right. Because you actually *are* an alien. Which is why you didn't know what birthdays were or Christmas or coffee or fruitcake. Or kisses."

"I actually knew what kisses were," she said. "I'd just…never participated in one."

Which it sounded like he'd noticed. She wondered if she'd done something wrong during their one and only kiss under the mistletoe. She wished that she had kissed him again yesterday, when things were simpler between them.

The wind picked up and her nose started to run. She sniffed, wishing she had some tissues or something. She didn't relish the thought of wiping her nose on the crinkly fabric of her uniform.

He quickly took off his scarf and wrapped it around her

neck. It was incredibly soft and warm.

"Here you go."

"Thanks."

His hands lingered on her shoulders. They were standing so close, she would only need to lean in a little bit to kiss him again.

Was it possible that he was okay with her being an alien? She didn't understand how he wasn't freaking out.

Something rustled in one of the bushes nearby and Henry jumped. Maybe he was internalizing his reaction. He looked past her before wrapping an arm around her shoulders and urging her to walk in the direction of his cabin.

"It seems we have some things we should probably talk about," he said. "Let's get back to the cabin where it's warmer."

"Okay." She tried to look behind them, to see what had spooked him, but didn't notice anything.

He picked up the pace, making it impossible for her to keep walking without tripping if she didn't watch where she was going. Her stomach churned with misgiving.

He knew about Sadirians. He knew about the Tau Ceti. What if he knew more? What if he *was* more? The Scorpiian.

No. There had to be another explanation. And she was going to find out what it was.

Chapter Eight

Life, in general, was weird. Being a biology teacher, Henry was aware of this. He observed it, studied it, and taught others to do the same. But his life? It had become absolutely bizarre.

He'd been adopted by a pair of space-Sasquatches from the Lyra system—who refused to take no for an answer. It was hard to be upset about that, because they were teaching him all kinds of things about the universe. Plus they were making him feel like part of a family again.

And he was walking through the forest with Vay, who had just magically reappeared in his life. And who was also an alien. An *evil* alien, if Craig and Barbara were to be believed.

"I think somebody needs to pinch me," he said.

"Why?"

"I just feel like I'm dreaming."

"I don't see how pinching you will help with that."

"It's an expression we have here on Earth."

He'd meant it as a joke at first—falling back into their "she's from another planet" game, but then realized that it was actually a perfectly reasonable thing to say.

He continued in a much more serious tone. "When someone thinks they're dreaming, they ask to be pinched so that the pain will either wake them up from the dream or prove to them that they aren't actually sleeping."

She laughed. "I'm not going to pinch you."

"It's probably for the best." After a brief pause, he said, "But you *are* Sadirian."

"Yes."

He still couldn't believe it. Not that she was an alien—hanging out with Craig and Barbara for most of the day had accustomed him to the idea of extra-terrestrial sentients walking around on his homeworld. But they had also painted a terrifying picture of Sadirians.

When her helmet had started to open, Henry knew that the person inside would look like a human. But seeing Vay's face...

Her voice pulled him from his thoughts.

"Henry, I have to ask. How do you know about us?"

"Let's wait till we're inside the cabin."

If Craig happened to be out on a walk and saw them together, Henry didn't know what would happen. He wasn't sure he could keep Vay safe, no matter how much his new—very weird—"foster parents" seemed to like him. They *hated* Sadirians.

Luckily, the cabin wasn't much farther. He hurried forward when it came into view.

The things they had said about Vay's people made

Henry's heart ache. They couldn't be true. At least, not about her. Henry needed to hear her side of things.

Once they were inside, he said, "I'll start a fire."

He hurried to the large stone fireplace that made up the entire wall to the left of the front door. Before leaving, he'd set everything up so all he had to do was strike a match and place it in a few strategic places to get the blaze going. He had wanted to be able to focus on Vay and have the cabin comfortable for her as soon as she arrived.

This wasn't what he'd pictured.

"It smells like coffee in here," she said.

"Yeah. Sorry about that." After starting the fire in the big fireplace, he headed for the potbelly stove that stood between the kitchen and living room area.

She followed him a little distance behind. "It's okay. I still like the smell."

He placed some logs in the stove. Some tea or cocoa would help calm his nerves and maybe help him feel a little more grounded. The match gave him some trouble as he tried to get it to light. Flames burst from it, catching his thumb a little too closely and burning him. The match fell harmlessly onto the stone flooring surrounding the stove.

"Are you hurt?" she asked.

"What?" He stared up at her, shaking his hand. "Oh, this. It's nothing. I'm just...trying to get the fire going." He stepped on the match to make it go out, then picked it up and threw it in with the logs before squatting down and getting out another.

"Let me help." She knelt next to him, holding up her arm.

Most of her uniform seemed to be made of a flexible fabric, but there were a few places with formed metal sections. The housing for her helmet that ringed her neck was one. Another was the wristband she was pointing at the wood in the stove.

She tapped on what looked like some etchings on the metal, then drew her finger up a line running along the side of the wristband.

"You might want to sit back," she said.

"Why?"

A bolt of light shot out of the end of her wristband as she made a fist with that hand. Henry was so startled, he fell onto his ass. The wood burst into flames.

"Are you okay?" she said.

"Yeah, I'm fine."

Except he wasn't.

Craig and Barbara might be giant, spine-fur covered, four-armed aliens, but they didn't walk around with rayguns. And Henry was betting that Vay hadn't dialed her wristband up to the maximum setting just to start a fire.

The Lyrians' ability to camouflage themselves seemed a very inadequate defense. Still, Henry didn't doubt for a second that they would attack Vay on sight. And lose.

He really needed to keep them apart. Or disarm Vay, but

in a way that would keep her safe, just in case Craig swung by the cabin and saw them together. Henry didn't want her getting hurt either.

If Craig thought Henry was entertaining another Earthling, Craig would stay out of sight. But that meant that Henry needed to get Vay out of her uniform.

"I'll make us cocoa." He scrambled to his feet, contemplating his options.

If he spilled something on her uniform, maybe she'd take it off. The cabin was still cold and the water from the reservoir on the roof would be freezing. Even a little bit of a spill on her uniform would make it uncomfortable to wear. Unless it was water-resistant.

He didn't have any better ideas. Of course, the moment he committed himself to the plan, his imagination showed him Vay slowly peeling off the skin-tight fabric.

He remembered the soft feel of her body next to his as they'd sat on the couch and talked for hours the day before. His world had seemed so much more normal then.

Letting his imagination run a little felt safer than thoughts of alien rivalries and his planet getting caught up in the middle of it.

She would need something to wear afterwards. He could picture her long legs stretching out from beneath one of his soft flannel shirts. His hands tingled at the thought of touching her. Blood started pooling in places…he really didn't want it to at the moment. He needed to focus.

Water. Cocoa. Keep Vay and Craig and Barbara safe.

The kettle sitting on the stove already had fresh water in it from the morning. He opened the cabinets above the sink and pulled out a pair of mugs, then the hot cocoa mix.

"I didn't get around to making you any yesterday," he said, "But I promise you'll like hot cocoa much more than coffee."

"I've actually already tried it. And I do."

"They have cocoa on your mothership?"

"Mothership?"

"You probably don't know that term." He poured a bit of water in the mugs, planning to offer her something to drink while he made the cocoa and maybe "tripping" as he handed it to her. "We Earthlings tell stories about extra-terrestrials. Sometimes, we reference the ship they travel on as the mothership."

"Why?"

"I'm not really sure." He'd never thought about it before. "Maybe because it takes care of the people living on it and brings them to new worlds?"

She laughed. "That's something we Sadirians would never think to call it."

"Why is that?" He was more focused on his plan than his question.

It was now or never. He started walking toward her, both mugs in his hands.

"Sadirians don't have mothers. Or parents of any kind."

Henry tripped. For real. His feet seemed to forget how to work together to carry him toward her. She reached out to catch him, bumping his arms and spilling the icy water all over both of them.

Chapter Nine

Vay reached out to catch Henry. His mass was too much for her to manage gracefully. The water he was carrying splashed out of his mugs, drenching them both. It beaded on her uniform, running off harmlessly, but it soaked through the front of Henry's shirt. It might have even hit him high enough to wet the shirt she could see underneath.

"Cold! Cold!" He set the mugs down on the counter as quickly as he could, then pulled the fabric of his shirts away from his chest.

"We need to get those off of you," she said.

Earth clothes couldn't come close to the protective qualities of her uniform and the cabin was still chilly. He had to be profoundly uncomfortable. At least the fires were starting to put off some heat.

She grabbed his elbow and pulled him toward the large fireplace just past the couch. As soon as they were in front of it, she started unbuttoning his flannel shirt.

"How do you not have parents?" he said.

"We're genetically engineered—created from genetic material from either donors or DNA banks. I guess if the donors pay to have a child created from their DNA, technically they'd be considered that citizen's parents. But even those offspring are grown in maturation chambers."

"People pay to create children in petri dishes?"

It took Vay a moment to remember what a petri dish was. "Maturation chambers are much more complex than a petri dish."

"You get what I mean, though."

She had his shirt unbuttoned and tugged it up out of his jeans, then down his arms. The white T-shirt underneath was wet all along his neck and down the front of his chest. It looked like he had on another long-sleeved shirt as well under that.

"How many layers of clothing are you wearing?" she said.

"Lots."

She pulled the T-shirt loose, then lifted the hem as far as she could. When he didn't lift his arms to help, she gave it a firm tug, glaring at him a little. He grabbed the bottom of his shirt and pulled it over his head himself.

"I'm trying not to judge your society before knowing more, but that sounds awful," he said. "Is it?"

The final layer of clothing—she hoped—was made out of thermally insulating fabric. Brendan had purchased cold weather clothing for everyone stationed on Earth to assist with the Department of Homeworld Security. The insulating layer was usually worn closest to the skin. Which meant that he was naked under it.

Her stomach started to tingle. The sensation spread quickly, dropping down through her abdomen and pooling between her legs.

If he took off this last shirt, he might get cold. She glanced at the nearby couch, noting a fuzzy blanket that was tossed over the back of it. She could wrap him up and keep him warm. And the shirt did look a little bit damp. He should take it off. Just to be safe.

She gripped the bottom of his shirt and started to tug it free. Her gaze seemed magnetized to the latch of his jeans, and she couldn't help imagining the soft fabric of his shirt sliding against his skin.

Not all Earthlings wore undergarments. Henry might be among them. Pulling his shirt free might be stimulating his

—

"Vay?" He grabbed her hands, stopping her.

"I'm sorry."

She must have overstepped. Yes, they had shared that one kiss, and enjoyed proximity the day before, but that could have been about sharing warmth. He might not be as interested in her physically as she was in him.

At least, she assumed that was what all of these sensations flowing through her meant. It was all so new to her. He made her body respond in ways she'd never experienced before, awakening urges she wanted to explore.

"Was it awful?" he said. "Being grown in a tank and

then… What happens when you're done 'maturing'?"

"Oh."

He hadn't even been paying attention as she stripped him. She definitely hadn't made the same impression on him as he had on her.

"It was fine," she said. "Like I said, it was all we knew. Before Earth."

"But there are other sentients who still have children naturally. You have to know about those."

Who had he been *talking* to?

Even if he'd come across a rogue Tau Ceti, there was no way they would share this kind of information. Plus, their breeding program would have to strike Henry as much worse than how Sadirians made new citizens. At least with her people, there was no cannibalism of their broodmates involved.

"I don't know how you found out about all this," she said. "But it is very dangerous for you to have this knowledge."

"Dangerous for whom?" His mouth was pulled in a stern line.

"For you. If my people find out that you know all of this, they'll—"

"Order a mind-wipe. I know about the Coalition and their protocols."

She gasped. She couldn't help herself. This was so much worse than she thought.

Henry took a deep breath and let it out slowly. "But I want to hear it from you. I want to know your side of the story."

"What story? You shouldn't know any of this."

"But I do know. And since I'll probably get a mind-wipe if you report me, what's the harm in at least giving me the peace in this moment of knowing—" He clamped his mouth shut.

"Knowing what?" she said.

"Knowing that you aren't one of the bad guys."

Her heart seemed to freeze in her chest. "I'm not."

When he turned away, she reached up and gently gripped his face to try to get him to look at her again. He stared at the shining material of her gloves, his mouth forming that line again. She wanted his smile. The openness that he'd shared with her the night they met.

She stepped away from him, tapping commands into her wristband as quickly as she could. As soon as she heard it release, she snapped open the compartment for her helmet, then unsealed her uniform.

"What are you doing?"

"I'm showing you exactly who I am."

She had her uniform off in seconds. Gloves, boots, all of it. She wadded it up in a ball and tossed it behind the couch, leaving her standing in front of Henry in just the black mini top and form-fitting shorts the Coalition provided female soldiers to wear beneath their uniforms.

Even that was too much—a link to them she couldn't stand. She started to peel off her undergarments, but Henry stepped forward and grabbed her wrists, stopping her.

"Vay."

The room was blurry. Her eyes had filled with tears. She pulled her arms free from him and wiped them away.

"This. This is who I am. V-21-b3. Twenty-first embryo of batch three from the V unit. Cultural programmer. One of the most valueless functions in our society. They don't call us anthropologists or social scientists. I'm a cultural programmer. Do you know why we're called that?"

"No." Henry's voice was barely above a whisper.

"Because we don't study cultures to learn ways to improve our own or even simply for the sake of expanding our knowledge and understanding of each other like you do on Earth. We study them to figure out the best ways to destroy them. To *program* them so that they follow Coalition law. That was my entire reason for existing before I came to Earth."

"And what is it now?"

"I've been tasked with learning more about how so many different cultures exist on Earth simultaneously. How they manage to interact and deal with differences. We're hoping that we can present a case to the High Council that will show them there are other ways—better ways—of ruling the galaxy."

"Why do I feel like there's a 'but' coming?"

"If they don't listen, my colleagues and I will most likely face disciplinary action for overstepping our orders. Maybe even be mind-wiped ourselves. They'll put us into reprogramming pods and turn us into whatever kinds of soldiers they want us to be."

She started to tremble, thinking of that very likely future. "Henry, I don't want to go back to that."

He grasped her face firmly and pulled her toward him. Liquid fire seemed to pour along her skin as his lips touched hers. The kiss wasn't tentative like their first had been. He claimed her mouth, his tongue sliding along her lips until she opened for him.

She wrapped her arms around his waist, pulling him closer. His warmth seeped into her, bone-deep. Stars, she'd never felt anything like it.

Slowly, he ended the kiss and shifted back a bit.

"Sorry," he said.

"For what?"

"Losing control."

"Never apologize for kissing me. Especially like that."

He chuckled, running his hands lightly down her arms. "Vay, I don't understand everything that's going on. But I'm going to do my best to help you."

"I know."

It was strange to be so sure of him already, but she was certain he would help in any way he could. She just had to be sure he didn't endanger himself by trying.

Chapter Ten

"You must be freezing," Henry said.

The fires were starting to heat up the cabin, but there was no way the tiny strips of fabric Vay was wearing could be keeping her warm. His slightly-damp thermal shirt was barely keeping him from shivering.

He led her to the couch, wrapping her in the blanket he always kept there.

"Thanks." She pulled him down next to her, holding onto his hand tightly.

"We're going to figure this out."

"It's not your burden. I'm sorry I was so upset a moment ago, but I can handle it. Really."

"I believe you. But you don't have to handle it alone."

"I'm not alone. There's a whole team assigned to Earth at the moment."

"I don't know if that's reassuring or not." He shrugged, and said, "At least they're friends of yours. That says something about them."

"Something good, I hope." She gave him a tentative smile.

"Yes."

"We're setting up a First Contact committee with several Earthlings on it. We hope to establish good relations between our people."

"Any chance they need a high school biology teacher with an interest in—" He stopped himself before saying, 'cryptozoology'.

As much as he hated to admit it, letting her know about that side of him could endanger Craig and Barbara. Bigfoot was the most well-known cryptid. He didn't want Vay to figure out his source of information was a Lyrian.

"I'm not sure," Vay said. "I would ask, but if they find out about you..."

"They'll probably insist on a mind-wipe."

"If I don't tell anyone, maybe they won't discover you. But you'd have to promise not to tell anyone what you've learned."

He laughed. "Who would believe me?"

She arched an eyebrow at him and frowned.

"But more importantly," he said, "I won't tell anyone anything in the first place. I promise."

Her lips quirked back up into a smile. Lips he had recently kissed. And she had kissed him back.

It was hard not to think about how little she was wearing under the blanket.

"Are you sure you don't want to put your uniform back on?"

She shuddered. "No, I'm fine."

"You don't seem fine."

"I'd rather be cold than wear that. I hate it."

Henry was surprised at the vehemence of her words.

"It's not that bad," he said. "I mean, it's a little 1950's scifi cliché, but—"

She broke in before he could finish his thought. "Do you know how often we have to wear our uniforms? Always. That's the kind of existence I have to look forward to when I go back. The only time we can take them off is for bodily eliminations. And those only happen every couple of days, thanks to the regen beds and the specially formulated 'food' they make us eat." She made sarcastic air quotes when she said the word. "With all the development effort they put into our nutrient bricks, you'd think they would have some flavor or texture, but they don't."

"At least it's not—"

"Please don't make a Soylent Green joke."

Henry let out a short laugh. "How do you know about Soylent Green?"

"My commanding officer's husband, Brendan, is a self-proclaimed geek."

"Husband. So, you guys get married. And sometimes to Earthlings, unless you also have geeks among your kind."

She grinned at that. "Several of my colleagues have fallen in love with Earthlings and pair-bonded with them."

A sharp spike of dread hit his system. Her life sounded

terrible, and he could imagine her trying to escape it by any means necessary. He was trying very hard not to be suspicious of her interest in him.

She was gorgeous, smart, funny... He wasn't used to someone like her being attracted to someone like him.

"Vay, I have to ask. You aren't looking for some Earthling to...pair-bond with so you can—"

"Please don't make a 'Gray card' joke. And that's not what this is about."

He felt his eyebrows rise up his forehead and had trouble bringing them back down. "Brendan again?"

She shook her head. "Evelyn. She was the first Earthling to pair-bond with one of us. She told me she initially had similar concerns about General Serath's interest in her. But with Scorpiians—what you call Grays —operating on Earth, I'd rather not joke about them."

"Grays are real? And on Earth?" His forehead was going to cramp at this rate.

"It's not a good thing. They're shape-shifting assassins who can take on the form of anyone whose DNA they've sampled."

"Cool," Henry said.

She arched an eyebrow at him.

He feigned a stern expression. "I mean, that's terrible. Very frightening."

It actually was, if he let himself think about it. He wanted to keep his focus on Vay—on this moment they were sharing.

She looked away briefly, then said, "I was actually a little concerned for about a nanosecond that maybe you were…"

"What, a Gray? Me?" He laughed and shook his head. "I promise I am not a shape-shifting alien assassin. Or an alien of any kind. At least, as far as Earth is concerned."

"Actually…"

His heartbeat picked up. "Vay. I'm not an alien. Right?"

"Technically, you kind of are. I mean, your people have been on Earth for so long, the Coalition considers you Earthlings, but humans are actually descended from a Sadirian colony ship that crashed here millennia ago."

"But that… The fossil record…" His brain stalled.

Craig and Barbara hadn't mentioned any of this. But then, they probably wanted to distance Henry from the Sadirians as much as possible in their minds.

"The hominids evolving at the time were following a very similar path," Vay said. "Certain planetary environments tend to favor similar results."

He could think of several examples of that on Earth— birds that evolved forms best suited to their ecosystem that were almost identical to different species in other regions. But thinking about that sort of thing on the level of humanity made his brain stall again.

She leaned forward and kissed him, and his thoughts stopped altogether. It wasn't like the tentative kiss they'd shared on Christmas Eve. Her mouth moved against his, assertive, demanding. She buried her fingers in his hair.

Whatever else was going on, there was something happening between them. A spark that neither could deny. He gave in to the pleasure rippling through him, pushing her back on the couch and covering her with his body. They were the same species. Which meant they were biologically compatible—hopefully.

He should probably check.

Shifting his lips to her neck, he trailed a line of kisses toward her ear, then said, "We can do this, right? Earthlings and Sadirians?"

"Yes." Her voice was a breathy moan. "Just tell me what to do."

That was weird. Surely she knew what would be involved. Unless she'd never...

He pushed himself up on his elbows, a different kind of pleasure warming him as he saw her flushed cheeks and heavy-lidded eyes.

"You've done this before, right? Maybe not with Earthlings, but with other Sadirians?"

Her eyes became a bit more focused—and shuttered. "I have. But we do things differently."

"Different how?" All sorts of scenarios ran through his head. He tried to tame his imagination before it completely extinguished his ardor.

"When Sadirians have sex, we use a drug called

Coupling. It handles pretty much everything for us. Arousal, climax, aftereffects."

"That sounds like…no fun at all."

She laughed. "It's a *little* fun. But not like this. I stopped using it with a partner years ago. It has about the same effect solo."

"You even use it by yourself?"

"*Most* Sadirians use it by themselves. It's designed to satisfy our biological urges. Interacting with a partner while using it is sort of looked down upon."

He laughed and shook his head. "That's kind of the opposite of a lot of Earthlings. But if you've never…'explored yourself', how do you know what you enjoy?"

"I was kind of hoping to figure that out with you."

Oh boy.

Meeting Vay and being with her like this already felt like some kind of miracle. What she wanted to experience with him, though—her first real physical intimacy—was sacred ground.

He rose from the couch, pulling her after him. He grabbed the blanket and wrapped it over her shoulders.

"I don't understand," she said.

"It sounds like that drug put your body on autopilot. I want to be sure that you can focus on this experience completely."

"Okay."

He led her to the fireplace, where the stones were already radiating heat. Swallowing hard, he took the blanket from her and laid it on the floor. Then he slid his fingertips under the hem of her sports bra and lifted it over her breasts.

He tried not to stare as she shimmied out of it. He really tried.

Her breasts were perfect. Full and round, with rose-colored nipples that he couldn't wait to taste.

But he would.

He turned her around and lifted her hand to the mantel. "Hold onto this."

She did as he asked, looking back at him over her shoulder. The trust she was showing... He would live up to it. He was going to help her, no matter what it took. Starting with this. An introduction to her own body.

"Many Earthlings explore their bodies to learn what they do and don't like," he said.

"Explore how?"

He stepped up behind her, his heart pounding. He was already so hard. His balls were aching. He took a moment to adjust himself and her eyes widened.

"Don't worry." He smiled at her. "This time I'm keeping the focus entirely on you."

"I don't know what that means."

"Then let me show you."

She smiled at him, then turned back toward the fire. He

heard her let out a nervous breath. A soft orange glow bathed her skin. He wanted to see more of it. And it would help him to help her.

He hooked his fingers in the waistband of the tight shorts she was wearing, then slid them down her long legs. When they'd reached her ankles, she stepped out of them. He was at eye-level with her ass. He could imagine standing and grabbing her hips and driving himself into her.

But not yet. Not. Yet.

He ran his hands up her legs as he slowly stood, then along her sides. When he reached her breasts, he cupped them firmly, kneading their softness. She sucked in a breath and jerked back, but he was right there to keep her steady. He pressed her firmly against his chest, massaging her breasts the entire time.

"Do you feel that?" he said. "The weakness in your knees. The fluttering in your stomach. Anticipation. Desire."

She leaned against his chest, nuzzling his cheek. "I feel it."

He rolled her nipples gently between his fingers, till they tightened. Vay arched her back, pushing her ass against his dick.

This was going to be harder than he thought. He wanted to thrust against her. But he didn't want to distract her from what she was feeling from and within her own body.

"Cygnus X. That feels so good."

"So good you're thinking about a black hole?"

She laughed. "It's a phrase that indicates strong emotion."

"We're only getting started."

"What are you going to do?" Her voice was breathless.

"What are *you* going to do. I'm only here to help."

Her hair was short enough that he could move it aside by nuzzling her neck, and as soon as he'd bared her skin, he nipped it gently. She pressed back against him, shifting her ass in a maddening way. He placed his left hand next to hers on the mantel, then lifted her right with his and set it on her stomach.

He pressed his dick against her harder, felt it start to pulse a bit. He couldn't believe how worked up she was getting him. It was time to return the favor.

He guided her hand down her stomach, till they reached the soft curls at the apex of her legs. He sucked the skin of her neck, tonguing her flesh as he lined up her fingers with her slit.

Apparently, kissing had excited her more than he thought. She was already slick. He entwined their fingers, circling her clit, flicking it, rubbing all along the length of her.

"Henry..."

She moaned, spreading her legs to give them better access. His heart was hammering in his chest. He had never wanted anyone so badly. If he wasn't careful, he was going to go off in his pants.

He had plans, though. So many plans. Things he'd imagined doing to and with her during the time they'd been apart. But he had to last through this for them both to experience even more.

He pressed his dick against her ass, trying to focus completely on her as he pushed on her hand, guiding her fingers deeper, into her core. She gasped, but he didn't let up. In and out, rhythmically pumping her hand with his— slowly, letting her savor every impulse from her nerve endings. She took over for him, alternating between deep thrusts with her fingers and quick swirls around her clit.

"That's it," he murmured in her ear. "It's your body. Figure out what you like."

And then hopefully she'd let him do the same to her.

"I don't know what... I don't know how to climax on my own." She looked over at him, eyes soft with pleasure, lips still full from their kisses.

He covered her hand with his again, pressing her hips harder against his swollen dick. Imagining what it would be like to part her flesh and bury himself in her. The thought almost set him off again. Maybe it would help her too.

"Imagine me buried inside of you."

He whispered the words against her ear, then nipped it as he started to thrust against her. Pulling her fingers up to her clit, he moved them in a few quick circles until she had taken over on her own.

"Only I'd be going deeper." He slid one of his fingers into her core, pumping it as he thrust against her.

"Faster." He slid a second finger in.

She let out a groan and rose up on her toes, as if she was trying to position his dick to plow into her. He was throbbing so hard, about to go off any second. He wanted this to be about her, but his body was reacting as if everything he was saying was true.

"Harder." He slid a third finger in deep, pumping them relentlessly, thrusting against her in time with his movements.

He felt her core spasm around his hand, pulling on his fingers, milking them. He pressed against her clit with the heel of his hand as he kept going, wanting this climax to be one she would never forget.

She threw her head back and screamed, "Stars!"

He pressed himself to her as hard as he could, fingers still buried deep as her body calmed against him—willing his own to calm as well. He wanted this moment to last.

And then he wanted more. More moments like this.

He wanted more time.

Chapter Eleven

Vay was still reeling from her body seeming almost to unmake itself through the searing orgasm Henry had shared with her. The knowledge that her body was capable of giving her more of this pleasure without the assistance of Coupling was incredible. And if it felt that good on her own, she couldn't imagine how much better it would be with a partner.

"Henry—"

She could still feel the fullness of his member pressed against her ass, but he'd let go of his hold on her. He was moving around behind her, getting something out of his pocket.

"I forget my hat, I forget my gloves, but I always have my wallet with me, even when hiking through the forest."

He tossed his wallet on the floor, finally shifting back from her. She heard him unzip his pants, and the rustle of fabric as he pulled them open. Was he not going to undress?

Part of her wanted to experience his skin against hers. Another part wanted him inside of her immediately. The latter desire increased in strength as the velvet skin of his shaft rubbed against her hip as he moved.

She craned her neck to glance at him over her shoulder. He was holding a small metal packet between his teeth. He tore it open and pulled a small piece of plastic or something from it. He unrolled the material down his shaft.

A condom. She remembered reading about them. He grabbed her hips, pausing when their gazes met.

"Are you sure you want to do this?" he said. "I mean, with me?"

She wrapped her arm around his neck, pulling him close for a kiss. She could feel him prodding against her flesh.

"Absolutely," she said.

He let out a sigh, then kissed her again, his tongue sliding between her lips. One of his hands found her breast again, while the other delved between her legs, as if he hadn't gotten his fill of feeling her in that intimate way.

He shifted his hips, angling them beneath her as he released her mouth. She could feel the tip of him pressing against her core. Turning back to the fire, she gripped the mantel with both hands to steady herself.

Henry slid into her, slowly, his fingers digging into her hips as he let out a low groan. A matching sound escaped from her chest. He was stretching her, filling her.

Heat and the purest experience of *sensation* flooded her body, generated from where they were connected. Finally, she felt his pelvis pressing against her ass.

All of him was within her. All of him.

The thought sent another wave of tingling stimulation over her skin. He leaned back, releasing her hips, but keeping himself buried inside her, then pulled his shirt off and tossed it away.

"I want to feel more of you." He leaned forward, so that his chest touched her back.

Henry's warmth seeped into her. More of him—his energy—soaking into her. Then his hands were on her again. Kneading her breast, circling her clitoris. She felt a deep pulsing throb within her.

"Was that your climax?" she asked.

"What?"

Henry laughed, and she could feel the vibration through their body. They were connected everywhere, it seemed.

"No," he said. "I'm trying to calm myself down before moving—to *avoid* my climax. Well, put it off for a bit, at least. There's so much I want to experience with you."

A pang shot through her that nearly equaled in pain what he was giving her in physical pleasure. There was so much she wanted to experience with him, too. So much they would never have time to explore together.

She needed to be distracted from those thoughts. She needed more of him, of this.

"Henry, please…"

His hands moved to her hips, his grip strong. Slowly, he

pulled himself from her almost completely, then slid back in. The friction sent shooting tendrils of pleasure through her, like sparks lighting up every nerve-ending. Again, he pulled himself out, then thrust back inside of her. As he'd promised, he started to move faster, landing harder. She clenched her fingertips onto the mantel to hold herself up. His pelvis slapped against her ass as his pace increased, his body ramming into her like a piston.

The sparks along her nerves started coalescing into a flame that burned white-hot, filling her body, flooding through her. Her heart seemed to stop for a moment, everything stilling, until it burst through her awareness in a cascading torrent of sensation. The flames coursed through her body, energizing every cell, every molecule. She'd never felt such a pure connection to another.

Henry cried out her name as his pounding thrusts reached a frenzied level. She felt his shaft pulsing within her, resonating with the aftereffects of her own climax and keeping her in that blissful state for that much longer.

He finally stopped, buried as deeply within her as he could reach, his chest pressed against her back and his hands wrapped around her waist. She felt him rest his head on her shoulder, a shudder passing through him.

"That was incredible," she said.

"I wholeheartedly agree."

"Thank you."

"You are most welcome."

He laughed and she felt him slide from her body. The absence was disorienting. She tried not to think about how his absence would affect her when he was gone from her life entirely.

He turned her to face him, pulling her against his chest. The fire was warm, as was he.

"How long do we have?" he said.

So, he was thinking along the same lines as she was. It was hard to ignore the reality of their situation. But she could try.

"We have today. Maybe tomorrow."

He sucked in a quick breath, and his eyes seemed to glitter in the firelight. He pulled her close and pressed his lips to her forehead. For a long moment, he left them there.

"Let's not waste it," he said. "Any of it."

She nodded, her throat too tight to speak. He lifted her chin so that he could look into her eyes.

"Vay. Every moment with you is a gift."

She let out the breath she hadn't known she was holding, then wrapped her arms around his neck and held him tight.

There had to be a way they could share more of this. She could start the arduous bureaucratic process that would enable her to stay. But that might endanger General Serath's efforts to have the First Contact committee recognized.

She could ask Henry to come with her. He might just

agree, if he felt even half as strongly toward her as she felt toward him. But she cared about him too much to ask it of him.

She could fake her own death...

Her ideas were getting more desperate—and ridiculous. She'd never be able to pull it off. She'd be found, disciplined, and Henry would receive a mind-wipe.

Her mind was still reeling, eating up the precious time she had in Henry's arms. She needed to focus on what she had in each moment. And maybe while she was doing her scans back at her ship she could figure out a way they could be together.

Chapter Twelve

The light streaming in through the windows was starting to gain a tint of orange. Normally, Henry loved the sunset views from the cabin.

His life had become anything but normal.

The sun setting meant that Vay would be leaving soon. She should be back at her ship before dark. Her uniform would probably keep her warm and help her see, though. Maybe they could have a bit more time together.

He'd do anything for more time with her.

Her people valued love. They had to if it was possible for them to pair-bond with Earthlings. And if others could do it, why couldn't they?

It might have seemed sudden from an external view, but it wasn't. His feelings for her had been building since their chance encounter on Christmas Eve. This was the real thing. He was sure of it.

His dad often talked to Henry about how he and Henry's mom became a couple. It was love at first sight on dad's part. His dad had winked as he said, "You mother took a little convincing." But he explained that their future together had been worth fighting for.

Henry would fight for his future with Vay. Even if it was complicated by the fact that she was an alien.

Unless that could make it easier...

She seemed to hate her life with the Coalition. From how controlling they sounded, Henry doubted that they would just let her go. But maybe she could escape. All she'd need was a little help. And he happened to know a pair of Lyrians who were adept at avoiding the Coalition. He just had to convince them to use their skills on Vay's behalf.

Sure, because they love Sadirians so much.

They might not love Sadirians, but they seemed really taken with Henry—a feeling that he couldn't deny was mutual. It was the weirdest thing, but hanging out with them and talking and laughing had felt like family. Craig had even said as much, and Barbara had called Henry "nestling" before he left.

Vay shifted closer against him under the huge pile of blankets he'd heaped in front of the fireplace screen. Her legs were entwined with his and her arm draped over his chest. He kissed the top of her head, and she let out a contented cooing sound.

If he was Craig and Barbara's family, then so was Vay. Henry had to convince them to help her.

He wasn't actually sure she'd welcome their help. The Lyrians' hatred of Sadirians might not be one-sided, and knowing that in advance seemed like a good idea. Coming at the matter head-on didn't seem wise, so he started with a different line of questioning.

"Tell me about the Tau Ceti."

Vay laughed. "I thought you already knew about them, from your mysterious source of information."

"I want to hear your perceptions of them."

"Okay." She was silent for a moment, her fingertips trailing soothing circles over his chest. "They're amphibians. They evolved from something similar to frogs. Their genetic engineers modified them to look more like Sadirians and they can now stay away from water for a long time. The best specimens are difficult to differentiate from us, but most have telltale characteristics that set them apart. Narrow eyes, wide mouths."

"Great."

And Craig had said that Barbara comparing Henry to a Tau Ceti was a compliment?

"You know why they're on Earth, right?" she said.

"No."

Craig and Barbara had covered so much ground with Henry. Since he didn't really know much about all of these new species in the first place, he didn't know what questions to ask. The galaxy was much more populous than he'd dreamed.

When Vay didn't continue, he prompted her. "I take it from your silence that it isn't a good reason."

"It isn't. But they're not killing anyone, at least. That

we know of."

A chill swept over him. "The fact that you're opening with that is not as reassuring as you might be going for."

"Sorry. The Tau Ceti have modified their forms further so that they have retractable fangs that they use to siphon blood out of humans. They strip the blood of certain chemicals—oxytocin, dopamine—and return it with a chemical agent that causes memory loss."

The chill turned to nausea.

"That's awful," he said.

"I agree."

"Let's talk about another species. You said there were Grays on Earth. You called them Scorpiians?"

This time, she was the one who shivered. She put her arm back across his chest, hugging him close.

"Now I'm really freaking out. They're worse than the Tau Ceti?"

"So much worse," she said.

"You said they're shapeshifters. All they need is some DNA to take on another form. Does it have to be a being with similar biomass?"

"Nobody knows the extent of their abilities for certain. They're very secretive."

He wondered if he had her distracted enough to bring up Craig and Barbara. His palms were starting to sweat. With her head resting on his chest, she could probably hear his heart rate increasing.

"Let's see," he said. "What other systems are nearby that we've found possibly habitable planets for? There's Cygnus."

"Cygnus-1 is populated. There's a black hole nearby, which causes gravity fluctuations that actually protect the planet from too much Coalition interference. Plus, they've evolved to have incredible strength and speed. Their skin is incredibly hard as well—almost like stone."

"They sound like gargoyles."

"I haven't come across that word yet."

"They're decorative stone statues that we have legends about coming to life and moving around. You should look them up." This was the perfect segue into asking about the Lyrians. "Speaking of legends… I'm starting to wonder how many of our legendary creatures are actually alien visitors. Take Bigfoot, for example."

Vay snickered. "Who?"

"Bigfoot. The Sasquatch. It's a really tall, hairy creature that roams through the woods. They leave big footprints, hence the name."

"I was wondering."

"Most legends say they're brown, but some people think that the Yeti might also be a form of Sasquatch, and those are white…" He let his voice trail off, hoping she would fill in the rest.

"Sounds like a Lyrian."

Yes!

"Oh? What are those like?" He hoped he was doing a good enough job keeping his voice calm.

Her grip loosened on his chest. At least she didn't seem to be afraid of them.

"They're tall and have spines that I've heard are really soft. They even look like fur. The spines are colorless, but appear white due to how they refract light. Lyrians can actually bend light around themselves at will, giving them a natural cloaking mechanism. It helps them with their criminal activities."

"Come on, they can't all be criminals."

"Of course not. But the ones we encounter are almost all involved in something that goes against Coalition law."

"The Coalition has sounded pretty crappy, from everything you've told me."

"Well, yeah, but I'm talking about thievery and smuggling."

His hopes of Vay getting along with Craig and Barbara started to tailspin. "It sounds like you don't think highly of them."

"There's a saying on Sadr-4. Lyrians have four arms to help them steal."

"Okay, I get it. Let's…move on."

It wasn't just that she was confirming his fears about her people's opinion of Lyrians. Henry couldn't stand to hear her badmouthing people he respected and trusted, even after talking to them for such a little while.

If only she could get to know them as he had. All they wanted was to help other sentients. He was sure they would help her, once they understood the situation.

"Henry…"

When she didn't continue, he said, "Yes?"

"Where did you get that scarf?"

Crap.

He didn't want to tell her—on many levels. He didn't want to think about it himself, even though the scarf really was the warmest and softest thing he'd ever worn. And it was sort of a sweet gesture.

Lots of humans wore clothing made from animal fur. The donors just usually…weren't sentient. Or so insistent about it. And they didn't pluck out their fur and weave it into a scarf right in front of you.

"Henry, you haven't been talking to a Lyrian, have you?"

"No."

Technically, he hadn't. "I've been talking to two."

Chapter Thirteen

Vay pushed herself up on Henry's chest so that she could look him in the eye. She had to be sure that he was serious about what he was saying. But how would he even know to make a joke about such a thing?

"They're really nice," he said.

"That's insane. Do you know how dangerous Lyrians are?"

"I do."

"Obviously you don't, or you wouldn't have associated with them."

He sat up and shifted away from her. The motion chilled her in a way that went beyond the physical absence of his body heat.

"I'm going to give you a pass on that one, since I'm assuming that your uber-controlling government has given you false information about them."

"Henry..."

"Have you ever talked to a Lyrian? Just sat down and had a conversation? Maybe played some cards. Sang some songs."

"Sadirians don't do those sorts of things."

"I know. But Lyrians do. Did the Coalition include that aspect of their culture in your training on their civilization, or did they focus on the whole 'if they get mad, they tear your arms off' thing? Because yes, they do that—which is really disturbing. But their physiology is so different than ours it means something totally different among their kind. And they don't do that to other species. Usually."

Her heart was thundering. The Lyrians would only have given Henry a scarf made from their fur—one of the most sought after and precious commodities their planet offered, and one they very seldom willingly shared—if they considered him kin. Which meant their protective instincts would be fully engaged.

Anyone they perceived as a threat to him would definitely fall outside of that "usually" addendum about them not pulling off other species' arms. She didn't want Henry to learn about their violent tendencies by watching them tear her apart.

And she really didn't want to be torn apart.

"Henry, this is—"

"They can help you."

She let out a laugh before she could stop herself. "A Lyrian is not about to help a Sadirian. They hate us."

"From what you've said, the feeling is pretty mutual."

All the warmth had left his tone. His lips were pulled in a tight line—lips that she had so recently felt caressing her skin. She wanted his laughter back.

Most of all, she wanted him safe.

"There are some beautiful aspects of their culture," she said. "But there are also records of attacks. Plus, they're notorious smugglers."

"I believe it."

She was so stunned by the revelation that she just stared at him. She couldn't think of what to say.

"I absolutely believe Lyrians have attacked Sadirians," he said. "And that Sadirians have also attacked them. But without having full information on what happened in those circumstances, I'm withholding judgment—on both parties. Maybe you should give that a try."

Her eyes filled with tears. He had obviously become attached to the Lyrians, too. And he'd assimilated their hatred for Sadirians—for her.

"This was a mistake," she said. "I shouldn't have come here."

When she turned from him and tried to stand, he grabbed her arm, holding her in place.

"This wasn't a mistake. Please don't think that. Never think that." He pulled her close against his chest, smoothing her hair with one hand as he held her tight. "I'm sorry. I guess I'm just...protective of them."

She let out a small laugh, wiping at her eyes as she leaned back to look at him again while they spoke. "I don't know what to think about this."

"Just open your mind to the possibility that what you

believe about them might be wrong. Or at least skewed in favor of the Coalition."

That wasn't hard to do, actually. Everything the High Council did was skewed in favor of the Coalition.

Moons, she'd reacted just the way she'd been trained— had jumped to the conclusions they planted in her brain in her initial programming sessions. After everything she'd learned about the Coalition, everything she'd seen with her own eyes, she knew better.

And there was also so much beauty to the Lyrian culture. Their intense love of family, their incredible sense of community.

"You're right," she said. "The Coalition is terrible to sentients who can't—or won't—conform to Sadirian standards."

"From what you've told me, they're not even good to their own people."

She nodded, her mind trying to wrap itself around this new—and stunning—information.

"The best lies are the ones that have a bit of truth in them," he said. "Lyrians do get mad and tear off each others' arms—or even their own sometimes."

"Why would they do that?"

"If one of their arms is damaged beyond their ability to heal it, they'll pull it off. And if that throws off their balance, sometimes they do the same to the one opposite it, knowing that both will grow back."

"That's deeply disturbing."

"For you and I, it's alien."

She arched an eyebrow at him.

"Let me rephrase that," he said. "It's outside of our experience."

The smile she loved so much pulled at the corners of his mouth. Warmth spread through her chest at the sight.

"What about the smuggling? The thievery?"

"Another misinterpretation," he said. "At least, in the case of my friends. Earth's biomes are incredibly diverse. We have ecosystems that match dozens of inhabited planets—planets that have singular environments."

"Earth's diversity is part of why it has preservation status. It's an alluring target for sentients who want to exploit your resources."

"They aren't here to exploit us. They're gathering seeds."

The misgiving that she was fighting against came back full force. "Henry, that is a serious crime in the Coalition. How is that not stealing from your planet?"

"They aren't stealing. I'm giving them what they need," Henry said. "After talking to them and learning about their mission, I'll help them any way I can."

"You don't have the authority."

"Who are they going to ask for permission? Your government? Mine? I can go to any garden shop and buy what they need with my own resources."

"But that's what this is all about. Resources. Earth isn't capable of supplying resources to every planet with sentient inhabitants who feel slighted by the Coalition."

"Slighted? We're talking about worlds that have been completely stripped of what they need to sustain life. People that are now dependent on the Coalition for survival."

"People who traded their resources—"

"Who made a mistake. A huge, terrible mistake. Some of them hundreds or even thousands of years ago. And they're still suffering."

"You can't damage your own planet to save theirs."

"I don't have to. All Craig and Barbara need are a few samples of each specimen, and they can replicate them to distribute to planets in need. They just need the genetic templates to use as a baseline for the worlds they're helping."

"Craig and Barbara?"

Henry shrugged. "Those are their chosen Earth names."

Their efforts almost sounded like what Brendan's sister, Paige, was proposing. She had left with Khel to try to convince the High Council to let her use her knowledge of environmental science to repair the damage to worlds in the same type of situation Henry was describing.

"They're just trying to help other sentients to lead better lives," he said.

That didn't sound right. Lyrians had always been

described as mercenary. They were the Earth equivalent of pirates. But now that she was thinking about it, she didn't remember hearing stories about Lyrians selling anything for profit. Her training mostly said that they were focused on "leading planets away from the Coalition's care".

She let out a breath that seemed to empty her as she actually felt her paradigm shift.

"Are you okay?" Henry said.

"Yeah. I'm just...processing all of this."

"I don't mean to heap more on you, but there's a time factor here."

"Are they on a deadline or something?"

"No, but you are."

Now she was really confused. Although, looking out the window, the sun was getting ready to set. She had maybe thirty minutes of daylight left.

"Vay, I have to ask you something that's very important."

"Okay."

"Do you want to go back to the Coalition?"

Her blood seemed to still in her veins. She couldn't breathe, couldn't dare to hope. But if he was thinking of offering her an escape, was it because he felt sympathy for her, or something else? Something deeper?

"I don't," she said, at last. "But I will. To help your planet. To help you. If I don't go back, they'll search for me."

He shook his head. "The Lyrians can help you. Like you said, they *are* smugglers. Just good-guy smugglers."

She almost managed a laugh, but it came out as more of a pained sigh. "There's more going on with Earth than you know."

"Like the Tau Ceti? Centaurans?"

Vay scoffed. "Your friends really do know a lot. But do they know about the Scorpiian?"

"They didn't mention any Grays. I'm assuming they know about the bugs."

She laughed, which was kind of amazing, given what they were talking about. Henry had that power over her. It was its own kind of magic. But this was too serious a matter for Vay to let herself get distracted.

"I'm talking about the bounty hunter that tried to infiltrate both the Department of Homeworld Security and the *Arbiter* itself before it left orbit," she said.

"They might have thought it was too scary for me." He shrugged. "I tried to explain that I'm an adult, but when they found out that my parents had died, they insisted on adopting me as their nestling."

"Your parents?"

He looked away. "Just before Christmas."

Her breath rushed out of her. That was what he'd been dealing with when they'd met. When he talked about letting go of his family's traditions, she'd had no idea what he must have been going through.

"Henry—"

"Yeah, Craig and Barbara were pretty upset about it, too." He smiled at her, but his eyes glittered and she could see thin lines around his mouth, as if he was in pain. "They think I need them. And I guess I kind of do. They're the only family I have now. Except for you."

Chapter Fourteen

From the way Vay's eyes widened, Henry was pretty sure she understood what he meant by that. Just in case he wasn't being clear, he figured he should tell her in his own Earthling way.

"I love you, Vay. I have since we met on Christmas Eve. I dream about you at night and think of you all the time. But not in a stalker-y way." He shook his head. "I'm not saying this well."

"I love you, too." She squeezed his hand, giving him the brightest smile he'd ever seen.

His heart was thundering in his chest. "Does that mean the same thing—"

She leaned in and kissed him. Her lips were like velvet. She ran her tongue across his mouth and he opened himself to her, met her in a dance that they'd been practicing all day, but seemed to have reached a new level with this. They were in love.

When she ended the kiss, she said, "It means I dream about you, too. I think about you. I wonder what you're doing, what you're thinking. I sleep with the fruitcake you gave me under my pillow every night."

He arched an eyebrow and smiled. "Okay, that does sound a little stalker-y. And messy."

"It's in a stasis pod, so it's not messy."

"I guess that's a good thing."

She let out a short laugh. "And I don't know what 'stalker-y' means."

"It's not a real word. And I shouldn't have mentioned it. It's someone who has an unhealthy attachment to another person. They follow them around, which we call stalking, because they want something from them. Recognition, control, to make them afraid—"

Vay's eyes widened suddenly. She dropped his hands and leapt to her feet. "Where's my uniform?"

"Behind the couch." Henry rose as well. Something in the intensity of her movements made his stomach sink. He grabbed his own clothes and started dressing as quickly as he could. "What's going on?"

She was already slipping the silver material on, not bothering with her undergarments. "I have to go."

"Is it because the sun is setting? If we go to Craig and Barbara—"

"That's where I'm going."

"Then I definitely need to go with you."

"No, you have to stay." She stopped and looked around, her eyebrows furrowing as she let out what sounded disturbingly like a groan of despair. "But it isn't safe for you here, either."

He'd finished putting on his clothes and ran to the door. His boots were still wet, but he started putting them on anyway.

"Vay, you're freaking me out. What's happening?"

"Scorpiians are sometimes smugglers, too. They're known to trade in forbidden items of high value."

"Like a space black market?"

"I'm unfamiliar with that term."

"Forget it."

She pulled on her gloves and checked the ring of metal around her neck that housed her helmet. Then she powered up the wristband attached to her uniform.

Henry's fear intensified. He pulled on his coat and grabbed the scarf that Craig had made him—from his own fur—then hesitated for a moment. All the hair on Henry's arms suddenly stood on end and his stomach seemed to turn to a chunk of ice in his middle.

"Craig told me that his pelt can be used as an ultimate cloaking device, even if he's not in it," Henry said.

Vay froze. Slowly, she looked over at him.

"You tracked the Scorpiian here. To this area. It isn't…" He could barely force out the words. "It isn't after them, is it? Craig and Barbara?"

"Henry…"

That was all he needed to hear. He threw open the door, wrapping the scarf around his neck as he ran toward their ship. He could hear Vay's footsteps behind him.

"You can't know for sure," he said, between gasps.

Vay wasn't winded at all. "I tracked the Scorpiian to your cabin. I didn't understand why it was interested in you, but if it's trying to get close to the Lyrians, using your appearance would be a perfect way to do it."

It must have been watching them—watching their ship. How had it even known where to look?

Craig had said he'd been watching Henry. Maybe Craig wasn't always using his ability to conceal himself while doing so. Henry said a silent prayer that it wasn't his fault that the Scorpiian had found them—that it wasn't his stupid hunt for Bigfoot.

By the time they reached the area where the ship was hidden, Henry had a stitch in his side that made it hard to breathe. He stumbled to a stop, bent double and wheezing. The sun had almost set, and the forest was dim.

"Henry." Vay's voice was tight and high.

He'd forgotten for a moment that Craig and Barbara hated Sadirians. They might attack Vay on sight.

She must be terrified. But she had come with him anyway, to help his new, very weird surrogate family. Even though she'd been trained to mistrust Lyrians, she was there for him.

And she had good reason to be afraid.

As she put her hand on his back, Barbara's booming voice came from above them.

"Get your hand off my nestling, Sadirian." Barbara

crashed to the ground in front of them, all four fists pounding into the earth, scattering the snow around her. "If you want to keep it attached to your arm."

Standing, she puffed out her chest. Henry hadn't noticed in the ship, but she was a good foot taller than Craig. And broader. All the spines on her body were standing straight out, quivering, which made her look even bigger—and a hell of a lot more menacing.

Henry managed to straighten himself and get between them. "This...is...Vay," he gasped. "She's...a friend."

"Sadirians don't have friends," Barbara said.

"They have...bondmates." His breath was finally slowing, though his heart still raced. "She's mine."

Barbara's eyebrow ridge rose, her mouth falling open— her mouth with its rows and rows of sharp teeth. It was a strangely human expression, especially considering her barely-humanoid countenance.

Gradually, the menace seeped back into her features. She closed her mouth, leaning forward and sniffing the air. Long, deep breaths. Then she pulled back and laughed.

"I should have smelled it on you," she said. She waved one of her arms at Vay dismissively. "Those uniforms make it difficult to perceive. Stars, Henry, how did you bond with a Sadirian? And why didn't you tell us before? We wouldn't have spoken so freely about them in front of you."

"I didn't know what she was," Henry said. "I just knew

that I loved her."

Barbara snorted at Vay, scowling.

"I love him, too," Vay said.

The corner of Barbara's mouth twitched. Not quite a smile, but it had taken an hour before she'd looked at Henry that way after they'd met.

"This is all happening really fast," Henry said. "Ridiculously fast. But we don't have time to…take our time."

"Nestling, you're not making sense."

"There's a Scorpiian in the area," he said. "It's been in my cabin. It can take my form."

He looked around, hoping that Craig would appear. Maybe jump down from a tree or just de-cloak himself and yell, "Surprise!" But Henry knew from the sick feeling in his stomach that neither of those would happen.

He closed his eyes briefly, taking a deep breath and letting it out.

"Barbara, where's Craig?"

Chapter Fifteen

Despite Vay's utter terror of the Lyrian a moment ago, now she felt nothing but sympathy. She couldn't imagine how she would feel if she faced a similar circumstance.

"He went for a walk shortly after you left." Barbara looked off in the direction of Henry's cabin.

Vay shook her head. "We didn't pass him on our way here. Is there a way you can track him?"

"He's my mate. Of course I can." She sniffed the air again, turning in a slow circle, then pointed. "This way."

Then she was off, and Vay's focus was on keeping up with her—and making sure Henry could as well. As the Lyrian—Barbara—pulled ahead, Vay realized they could just follow the giant trail Barbara was leaving behind in the snow.

"Don't we need...a plan or something?" Henry said, wheezing between the words. "Damn. I need...to work out more."

"I have a plan." Barbara looked back at Vay briefly over one of many shoulders. "You protect your mate. I'll protect mine."

Vay nodded, hope mingling with dread within her.

Barbara was accepting her. They would probably help Vay escape the Coalition—if they all survived this encounter. She was determined to make that happen.

"Go ahead," Henry said. "Vay, help her. I'll...catch up."

"It isn't much farther, nestling. The scent is getting stronger."

With that, Barbara vanished from sight. The trail she was making remained clear for a while longer, but then it stopped. A nearby tree shook, snow dropping to the ground beneath it.

Vay slowed down, then held out her arm to stop Henry. He bent over again, his breath fogging the air. He lifted the Lyrian scarf to his face to breathe through.

"We're close," she said.

"Whatever training they put you through, I need some of it."

She smiled, leaning in to kiss his cheek. "After we're through this and I'm free of the Coalition, I'd be happy to help you get in shape."

His eyes widened and he dropped the scarf away from his mouth. "You're going to ask them? You'll stay?"

"I don't know if I'll be able to stay on Earth, but I want to be with you."

He nodded. "We'll make it work. As soon as we save Craig."

She took his hand and pulled him along, following the signs of Barbara's passage through the trees. It didn't take long before they found another trail—the large tracks of a Lyrian walking with a smaller, human-sized being.

"It took my form," Henry said. "Craig's guard is down. He doesn't know it isn't me."

They quickened their pace again. Vay's wristband let out a warning buzz that she felt more than heard.

"Henry, my proximity sensor is going off."

"Proximity to what?" He kept moving forward, following the trail.

Vay grabbed his arm, but it was too late. She felt the tug of the gravity net just as Henry flew off his feet, pulling her with him. They hit the center of the energy web, hanging ten feet off the ground, unable to move.

"I don't see anything," Henry yelled. "What's holding us up?"

"A gravity net. The Scorpiian must have set traps."

There was a snowdrift below them. If she could deactivate the field, they shouldn't be hurt from the fall. But she had no way of reaching her wristband. And even if she could, she didn't know what to aim it at to destroy the field.

Lights flooded the trees around them, casting odd shadows on the ground as the sun finally set. One of the shadows moved toward them, long and spindly. She expected to see a Scorpiian—gray skin and huge black eyes. Instead, Henry stepped out from behind one of the trees.

Except not Henry.

"They'll throw anything in a uniform and call it a soldier these days," it said.

The hairs on the back of her neck stood on end. To hear an insult in the same soft voice that had whispered in her ear, had told her she was loved… She wanted to get away from it, but she was held fast.

"You're not even wearing your helmet." It shook its head. "Honestly, I'm tempted to just throw you back into the wild. 'Catch and release', as the Tau Ceti say. But you caught me at a bad time and I still need the human for bait."

It pulled a control disk from its pocket and tapped a few commands. Many of the trees around them vanished.

"Vay, what just happened?" the real Henry said.

"Holograms. Scorpiians deal in illusions and misperceptions."

"Right."

Instead of being deep in the forest, they were in a large clearing. A small shuttle was parked in the center of it, all jarring angles and odd isometric forms. For a species that could assume almost any form they wanted, the Scorpiians placed little value on appearances.

"Vay…"

She looked over at Henry. He was staring across the clearing, eyes glittering with unshed tears. She followed his gaze—and wished she hadn't.

A Lyrian was suspended between two massive trees. All of his arms and legs were pulled straight away from his body. His head listed against his shoulder, though, and his eyes were closed.

"Craig," Henry said.

The Scorpiian paced in front of them. "Where is the female?"

"Go to hell."

"Henry, don't." Antagonizing it would only get them both killed sooner. She didn't believe for a moment it would really let them go.

The Scorpiian shook its head, then lifted the disk again. It pressed another control, and this time a burst of silver energy shot out from it. One of the trees behind them exploded in a shower of heat and light.

"Sooner or later—and I'm betting on sooner—she'll show up and get caught in one of my traps. Nothing can run, leap, slither, or fly into this clearing. Trust me, I've thought of all the angles."

It was overconfident. Vay didn't even see a weapon on it—just the control disk in its hand.

She needed to distract the Scorpiian—to keep him talking while they figured out what to do. Barbara had to be close, and Vay had seen for herself that Lyrians weren't the berserk beasts the Coalition had always described. If Barbara was watching and coming up with a plan, Vay had to get her more time and information.

"I don't doubt it," Vay said. "With all the forms you've probably taken."

It shrugged. Its face matched Henry's, but the expression was completely wrong. Cold efficiency. Henry radiated warmth.

"You have the nets to catch things that just walk or run," Vay said. "And I'm guessing nothing's getting in from above either.

"You're stalling."

"I'm a cultural programmer. I'm interested in learning more about your ways, especially since you have a unique understanding of what different beings are like."

"Where is the female?" the Scorpiian said.

Vay ignored it. "What about burrowers? Lyrians have a lot of arms. They're big, but I bet they can dig pretty well."

He punched a few more commands into his control disk, then glanced at his ship.

His ship...

She looked around the clearing and didn't see anything big enough to create the kinds of energy fields he was describing. She doubted he would bother with setting up a portable cloaking generator. Scorpiians didn't usually stay in one place for long. Which meant everything was probably being controlled by his ship.

"So you didn't have that covered?" she said.

"Vay, maybe don't help the guy out?" Henry whispered.

"I don't really think *Barbara* could burrow into here." Vay said the Lyrian's name louder than the other words, hoping to draw her attention.

"Now I have a name," the Scorpiian said.

"You're welcome." Vay nodded toward the ship. "And you should also thank me for letting you know to add the seismic sensor to all the other traps *being generated by your ship*."

A furrow appeared between the Scorpiian's eyebrows. She hoped he wouldn't pick up on her weird emphasis.

"Make this easier on everybody and tell me where she is." The Scorpiian started edging away from them, moving closer to Craig. It knew something was up. "Maybe I'll let you go with mind-wipes."

Vay heard a loud creaking noise, like the wind pushing against the trees. But the air was still.

She smiled, and said, "I think you'll be letting us go regardless."

One of the largest trees Vay had ever seen came crashing down through the clearing, landing right in the center of it. Barbara rode it down, holding on to the massive trunk with all four arms. It landed right on the Scorpiian's ship.

The gravity net failed. Vay and Henry fell to the ground, landing in the soft snow.

The Scorpiian was on the other side of the tree, its eyes wide as it held its hands up toward Barbara. If it tried to run, Barbara would pounce, and he was well inside her range of attack.

"I'm sure we can work out a deal," it said.

It looked at the sparking wreckage of its ship as Barbara rolled the giant tree trunk back and forth, crushing the vehicle further. Vay doubted the Scorpiian had a backup vessel. From the look on Barbara's face, she doubted he would need one soon.

"Take off my nestling's face before I do it for you," Barbara growled.

The Scorpiian immediately started to glow. Its features shifted, for a brief moment appearing as its natural form—all long limbs and gray skin, with huge black eyes. Then it thickened and changed, the glow fading until Vay was looking at...

"Eric?"

The Scorpiian ignored her. This was definitely the same one that Eric and Sorca had dealt with, though.

"I have resources." Its voice had deepened to match Eric's, as well. "This doesn't have to end in violence."

"No, it doesn't," Barbara said. She gestured toward Vay and Henry with one of her arms. "Find Craig."

Then she turned back to the Scorpiian, baring her teeth. "This doesn't *have* to end in violence. But it will."

The Scorpiian started to glow as it lifted its arms to fend off her attack just as Barbara pounced.

Vay might not have been a model soldier, but she knew

how to follow orders. She also knew that she did not want to see what was about to happen to that Scorpiian. She almost felt sorry for it.

"Come on." She grabbed Henry's hand and pulled him up. "We have to get to Craig and make sure he's all right."

Henry nodded, running behind her as they made their way around the clearing's edge. Craig had fallen as well when the gravity nets failed. He lay still in a pile of snow that was almost the same color as his fur.

"No, no, no…" Henry ran to Craig's side, tugging on one arm to try to roll him over. Craig was so heavy, he didn't budge.

Suddenly, the Lyrian shot up from the snow. "I'm awake."

Henry lost his balance, tumbling onto the ground. Which left the Lyrian blinking at Vay, looking disoriented.

"I'm his mate," she yelled.

Henry said, "She's with me," at the same time.

Craig shook his head, then ran his hand over his face. His skin turned purplish.

"I'm aware," he said. "Moons, don't remind me."

"Wait, how do you know?" Henry said.

Vay helped him to his feet. She was wondering the same thing.

"I followed you back to your cabin to make sure you were okay and saw you two through the window." Craig snorted and looked away. "I suppose you *are* an adult of your species, as you keep saying. A little young to be bonding, though. Nestlings grow up too fast."

He sniffed a little. Henry let out a laugh and then grabbed Craig in a huge—for an Earthling—hug. Craig laughed as well, wrapping all of his arms around Henry at once.

A horrific screech pierced the air.

"What the hell is that?" Henry said.

Craig stood, setting Henry down next to Vay. "That is the sound of a Lyrian female protecting her nestling."

An arc of silver liquid flew through the air above the twisted limbs of the oak tree in front of them. Something bounced along after it.

"Oh dear," Craig said. He reached out with one set of hands and covered Henry's eyes, and then, to Vay's utter shock, he used his other set to cover her eyes. "Barbara, if you could shut off the lights… There are children present."

There was another screech, then a lot of banging, and the lights went dead.

"Thank you," Craig sang out. "I think she's going to be a while. Let's head to our ship while she finishes up."

"Yeah," Henry said. "Let's…do that."

Chapter Sixteen

Back at the ship, sipping a warm cup of something Henry couldn't identify, he tried to make sense of the last day. Bigfoot was real—and an alien. With an incredibly violent and protective mate. He'd been adopted by them, which was apparently part of their cultural norms. And he was kinda-sorta married to Vay.

Mated, bonded, whatever they wanted to call it.

It was amazing. His life was amazing, and he had a feeling it was only going to become more so.

"And then he said, 'It means I'm hungry'." Craig let out a huge laugh, regaling Vay with the one and only embarrassing story he had to tell about Henry.

Some things about parenting were universal, it seemed.

She laughed along with Craig, casting a warm smile Henry's way. The only thing missing was Barbara. Craig had said she would be fine, but Henry still worried.

As if on cue, the door to the ship whooshed open and she stomped in. Silver liquid was dripping from her fur.

"Darling, if you're going to shake, do it in the other room," Craig said. "I don't want you getting quicksilver on the kids."

She growled, then stomped past them.

"Where's the Scorpiian?" Henry couldn't help himself. That was a lot of...Scorpiian blood? He knew from the sounds of what was happening back at the clearing that it was very probably dead, but he had to be sure.

Barbara paused, then turned to face him. She grinned, again showing Henry all of those sharp, sharp teeth.

In a rumbling voice that was almost a purr, she said, "Which part?"

Craig stepped up behind her, nudging her through the door to the other room. "Let's leave it at that."

"Yeah, that sounds like a good idea," Henry said.

When Barbara was gone, Craig turned to Vay, picking up a lock of her hair between his fingers and cocking his head to the side as he examined it. Henry was glad to see that she didn't flinch away.

"So, my new Sadirian kin, what will happen next?" Craig let go of her hair, then crossed the small room and sat on a stack of crates marked "C. Addison". Henry wondered if that was the name of one of Craig and Barbara's "open-minded human contacts".

Vay glanced at Henry and he nodded in what he hoped was a reassuring manner.

"Well, Henry and I had talked about me leaving the Coalition, but I'm not sure that's for the best."

He felt like the floor had suddenly fallen out from under him. Did she not want to be with him after all?

"I didn't realize you'd changed your mind," he said.

"I didn't." She reached over and grasped his hand. "I want to be with you. And I want both of us to be able to stay on your homeworld. But with Scorpiians and Tau Ceti and Centaurans on Earth—"

"And about half a dozen more sentient species that we know of," Craig said.

Vay cast a quick glare at him. "Earth is in a very dangerous position. It might actually become part of the Coalition before long."

"Stars guide us away from that path," Craig said.

Barbara entered the room, her fur white and clean again. She sat next to Craig and hooked her leg with his, planting one set of hands on her thighs and crossing her other arms across her chest.

"What are you suggesting, Sadirian?" she said.

"Vay." Henry squeezed Vay's hand. "Her name is Vay."

Barbara snorted. He knew by now that was a good sign.

Vay turned toward Henry. "You said you wanted to join the Department of Homeworld Security. Did you mean it?"

At the time, it had been a joke. Mostly. But there was a grain of truth in it. He was definitely interested.

"Yes."

"And do you still want to, even after everything you've learned and seen?" she said.

"More than ever."

She leaned forward and kissed him, and for that moment, he forgot everything else—Scorpiians and Lyrians and evil space empires and aliens—and it was just him and Vay and the warmth and love between them.

Until Craig cleared his throat. "Children."

Vay pulled back, still smiling broadly, and turned toward the Lyrians.

"You've adopted Henry," Vay said. She turned to Henry and gave him one of those amazing smiles. "And Henry has bonded with me."

"That's fairly clear," Barbara said.

"The law is also clear in this matter," she said. "The formalities will take me forever, but if we follow proper protocols, which are really common sense—don't let other Earthlings know aliens are real or especially that we're on Earth, don't let any of our technology fall into the wrong hands—I can have us classified as a family with an Earth connection. We'll all be allowed to stay or go as we wish. It'll take time—and a lot of authorizations, but I really think I can make it happen."

Barbara kept glaring. Her mouth started to twitch. The twitch spread until her lips were pulled in a huge smile. Then she threw her head back and laughed.

Craig had his eyes covered and was shaking his head, but his body trembled with laughter. "Stars, Sadirians are hilarious. They make all of these rules and laws to control the universe."

Barbara finally stopped laughing, but her grin remained huge. "If we can use those laws to our advantage, we're all for it."

"And more importantly, it will let us keep our family together." Craig nudged her with a shoulder.

"Of course, sweetheart." She leaned closer, until their ears touched and started…caressing each other.

"I'm beginning to understand those kids who aren't comfortable with their parents being overly affectionate," Henry said.

Both Lyrians turned to him and grinned, but this time, the look was downright diabolical.

"We have many arms," Barbara said.

"And we are fond of hugs," Craig added.

The room wasn't that big, so when they reached across and grabbed Henry and Vay, there was nowhere to run, even if he'd wanted to. But as they pulled them both into the biggest, furriest hug he'd ever felt, he *didn't* want to run. He finally felt like he was home.

Epilogue

Every trudging step was agony. The snow around Zemanni's feet sizzled and melted, little puffs of steam rising from his footprints.

Almost there.

Henry's cabin had melted into the rest of the forest in Zemanni's blurred vision. Only the little lights that the human had strung over the structure helped Zemanni pick it out from the brown and white background of the wintry trees.

Sweat ran into his eyes. Human sweat.

What's happening to me?

He fell against the door, the cold wood heating against his fevered skin. Even if he survived the intensely high body temperatures cycling through his system, he would eventually succumb to the cold if he didn't get covered.

The group who had nearly killed him had headed in the direction of the Lyrians' spacecraft while Zemanni began the agonizing process of pulling his body back together from the pieces Barbara had torn him into. He'd lost so much of his quicksilver. Almost all of it. And now he was trapped.

But not for long.

He fumbled with the handle of the door, knowing Henry kept it unlocked. Stumbling into the cabin as the door opened, Zemanni veered toward Henry's closet.

Clothes. He needed to find clothes that would fit him. And then he needed to find a base of operations where he could regain his strength and figure out the logistics of his next move—obtain more quicksilver and purge his system of this alien DNA that was infecting him.

He paused by a small mirror that hung on the wall, staring at the reflection that wasn't really his.

"Eric Peterson," Zemanni growled, as if the DNA matrix could hear him. The *human* DNA that was changing him in ways he didn't understand. But he did understand one thing with a certainty that he felt in his bizarrely stiff human bones.

This was not the end for him.

—

I'll let you all in on a secret. I originally planned to kill off the Scorpiian assassin in *Tied up in Customs*, but he was too fascinating for me to let go of that easily. Of course, I realized the best way to get to know him better was to give him his own book. And thus, the sixth book in *The Department of Homeworld Security* was born! Read on to see what happens to the Scorpiian assassin in

Duration of Stay.

USA TODAY BESTSELLING AUTHOR

CASSANDRA CHANDLER

DURATION
OF STAY

THE DEPARTMENT OF HOMEWORLD SECURITY

Duration of Stay

The Department of Homeworld
Security
Book Six

Cassandra Chandler

Dedication

For Joey N.—my writing bestie.

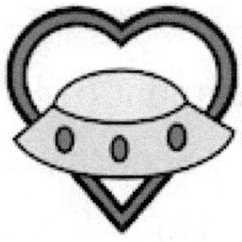

Don't miss out on any of the alien action.
Subscribe to Cassandra Chandler's newsletter at
cassandra-chandler.com!

Chapter One

The windows of Brooke's car were covered in fog. If she'd been sitting inside—maybe drinking one of the gazillion hot drinks she'd made for customers that day—it would make sense. But she was just getting off her shift, and her car had been parked in the nearly empty lot for hours.

"Elliot, you asshole," Brooke said. "Get out of my car and give me back my spare key."

Not that he'd need it to get in later. He knew that the back driver's side door didn't lock right anymore. She lined up her keys between her fingers, making sure the sharp edges pointed out like claws. He'd only been incredibly annoying since the breakup, but she wanted to be ready in case he'd finally gone off the deep end.

She jerked open the door and let out a disgusted grunt. He was lying sort of curled up in the footwell, his dark hair masking his face.

"Seriously, this is reaching entirely new levels of pathetic. It's been three months. Get over it."

A sudden feeling of misgiving shivered through her. Had he cut his hair? And had he always been that tall? And buff?

Her car was a piece of crap, but it was spacious. And he was suddenly taking up every inch of the available space.

His legs were bent and he was hunched over with his arms wrapped around his torso. Her skin felt electrified as she realized that whoever this guy sleeping in the back seat of her car was, he wasn't Elliot.

She raised her key-studded hand. "What are you doing in my car?"

The man lifted his head and turned to look at her. Her heart thudded in her chest.

His dark hair was a little longer at the front, dusting across his forehead. It was short in the back—nothing getting in the way of her view of his shoulders, which were massive. He had a long, straight nose, perfectly curved lips, honey-brown eyes, and an angular jaw covered in a thick coat of stubble. He was absolutely gorgeous.

The sweat coating his skin glistened faintly in the dim light. Why was he sweating when all he had on was a pair of jeans and a flannel shirt? He wasn't even wearing shoes.

She lowered her arm and stepped forward, poking her head into the back seat of her car. "Are you okay?"

He was shaking violently, his whole body trembling. He held up a hand to her and his sleeve fell back enough for her to see his corded forearm—and the line of silver light circling it. His skin was *glowing*.

"I won't hurt you," he said.

His voice sent a frisson through her. It was deep and strong, even with the obvious strain in it. Who the heck was this guy? *What* was he?

"You need help," she said.

"No doctors."

"Duh."

She slammed the door and quickly climbed into the driver's seat. It took several tries, but her decrepit car finally started. She had almost walked that morning, but it was too cold even for the couple of blocks between her home and work. Before putting the car in gear, she looked over the bench seat into the back.

"Do you promise you won't try to eat my face off?" she said.

"I won't try to eat your face off." He looked vaguely insulted at the idea. The furrows between his eyebrows deepened.

Crap, even his forehead was sexy. How was that possible?

"Or anything else?" she asked.

"I'm not going to eat you." This time, there was definite frustration in his tone.

"Okay."

She turned back around and took a deep breath, then exhaled. This was like something out of a movie.

Hopefully not a horror flick.

As she pulled out of the parking lot, she said, "So what are you? A ghost? Fallen angel?"

"Scorpiian."

"What, like a bug?"

"I'm from Scorpii-2."

"Is that a company or something? Are you an android?" The silver glow could be some kind of LEDs in his body.

He let out a frustrated grunt. "It's a planet in the Scorpii system."

"Oh my God. You're an alien."

"Yeah."

An alien. In the back seat of her car.

"Are you having some kind of allergic reaction to our planet?"

"What? Why would I…"

"No offense, but you don't look so good."

She turned into the parking lot for her apartment complex. Luckily, there was a spot right next to the stairs up to her apartment. At midday in the middle of the week, no one was around.

"I mean, you look hot," she said. "But you also look… hot."

"Thanks for clarifying."

She ignored the crack, though she was glad to know he understood sarcasm. That would make it easier to communicate.

"Are you supposed to glow like that?" she said.

"No." He let out a groan and she heard him shift around more.

"Crap, you're not dying, are you?"

She set the parking brake, but didn't turn off the engine. She understood his desire to avoid any organization that might stuff him in a lab and experiment on him, but if it was a choice between that or death, he might have to reconsider the whole "no doctors" thing.

"I'm not dying. I'm acclimating."

"So it *is* some kind of reaction."

He let out another frustrated sigh. It was easier to handle than the little pain noise he'd made.

She stepped out into the frigid air, keeping her apartment key ready and wondering how she was going to get him up the stairs.

"Mom always said I was a rescuer," Brooke murmured. "If she could see me now."

The alien had managed to get himself out of the footwell and onto the back seat. He was dragging himself across the bench toward her. She opened his door and reached in to help him. His skin was burning hot.

"You have a fever," she said.

"I'm acclimating."

"Right. Whatever." She draped his arm over her shoulder and shut both car doors. "Let's go."

He started to pull away from her, veering toward the

mound of snow piled at the edge of the lot. "I need to lower my body temperature."

"If someone sees you lying in a pile of snow, they'll call the cops."

Especially since he was still glowing. She could see more lines now that he was up—soft silver light gleaming around his neck, shoulders, and arms. There were even dim circles around his thighs that she could see faintly through his jeans.

He let her take the lead, though he stumbled a few times. It seemed like he was mostly able to support his own weight, which was helpful. All that muscle would make him way too heavy for her to drag up the stairs. They made it up to her apartment without drawing any attention, and she unlocked the door and helped him inside.

She slid the deadbolts and chain into place, just in case Elliot decided to show up unannounced—again. He needed to give her back her damned spare keys. If he walked in on Brooke while another guy was there... She didn't have the energy to handle the tantrum he'd throw.

She led the alien hottie further into her place. "The bathroom's over here."

"My body doesn't eliminate waste the way human bodies do," he said.

"Ew, really? Do you eat?"

He didn't answer her, probably because his body had

started trembling violently again. If lowering his body temperature was necessary, they needed to get on that right away.

There were a lot of ways she'd like to get on his body, alien or not.

She dragged her attention back to the task at hand, pushing the other thoughts away. She was supposed to be helping the poor guy, not drooling over him. She kicked open the door to the bathroom.

"We need to get you in the tub. I can get snow from outside to help you cool down." She leaned him against a wall, then plugged the drain and started the cold water running.

When she turned back to him, he'd already unbuttoned his shirt. He was even more built than she'd thought. His chest was broad, without an ounce of extra fat. His abdomen rippled with muscle, and dark hair cascaded down his chest and belly, disappearing into his jeans.

"I'm trapped in this human form," he said.

"I can think of worse fates than being trapped in *this* one."

His shirt tangled around his arms as he tried to pull it off. He leaned heavily against the wall, as if just unbuttoning it had exhausted him. Lines of silver traced down the chiseled muscles of his abdomen, but they weren't smooth, as she'd thought earlier. They were jagged, almost like scars. But if they were scars, it looked like he'd been torn limb from limb and reassembled.

"Vapor pits," he said.

She shook her head. "I don't understand. Do you need some vapor pits or something?" Not that she had any idea what that was.

"It's a…" He let out an aggravated grunt. "I'm angry."

"Oh, it's a swear." When he stared at her blankly, she said, "Next time, try, 'fuck' or 'dammit'."

He glared at her, then tugged at his shirt.

"Let me help you." She peeled the shirt down the knotted muscle of his arms and then tossed it aside. As he braced himself against the wall, she reached around and unfastened his jeans.

"Normally, I can just form whatever clothing I need," he said. "This external material is impossible to manage."

"So, you're some kind of shapeshifting alien?"

He grunted. It wasn't a denial.

"You picked a good look."

She tugged his jeans past an ass that could be put on display in a museum, then dragged them over legs that surpassed her wildest fantasies. He had just the right amount of hair covering his perfectly sculpted thighs and toned calves.

He stepped into the water as soon as he was free of his clothes, then slid down the wall. He let out a sigh as he sank into the water's chilly embrace, not bothering to try to cover himself.

The dark hair on his chest continued in a trail that led to the thicker triangle around his dick. The water was freezing. Wasn't that all supposed to *shrink* in the cold?

Wow...

Not lusting after him was going to be a hell of a lot harder than she thought.

Chapter Two

"What's your name?" the Earthling said.

She was hovering over him, staring at him with eyes as blue as Neptune. They weren't as small as most humans'. Her face was oval—a bit like his own kind. It was strangely pleasant to look at, even surrounded by all that yellow-gold hair. Still, he wanted her to leave so he could deal with his humiliation privately.

"Zemanni."

"Cool." She cleared her throat. "I mean, are you cool enough? Should I get some ice?"

"More cold water."

"I guess they don't have manners on your planet," she mumbled, turning up the water to make the level rise. She took off her coat and tossed it into the hallway.

The water was heating quickly from the energy he was putting off. The parts of his body that were submerged felt better. He slid beneath the surface and let out a sigh. Through the water, he could hear the Earthling make a bothersome noise.

He remembered the form of a being with gills, and tried to modify his body so that he could siphon enough oxygen from the water to tell her to shut up. It was more out of habit than anything else, but his idiotic human body interpreted the thought as him wanting to breathe, even though he was submerged. Water rushed into his lungs.

How could it burn? It was *water.*

His body reacted with instincts encoded in the DNA he'd stolen from Eric Peterson—the man whose form Zemanni was trapped in. Between that, and the Earthling's frantic attempts to pull him out of the water, he managed to sit up.

Water sprayed from his mouth and nose. He felt more burning deep in his chest. His body expelled it with coughs that wracked his body, further tiring him.

The Earthling pounded on his back, and kept repeating, "Are you okay?"

He glared at her as he sucked in breath after breath into his nearly functionless human lungs. He wondered how the species survived with only *two* when they were so inefficient.

Though he'd been assigned to Earth for months, he'd never stayed human this long. And without enough of the quicksilver that usually coursed through his natural form —allowing him to alter his shape at will—he couldn't change even the simplest thing about himself.

He could feel his cells stabilizing based on the only DNA pattern they had available to them—*human* DNA.

"Are. You. Okay." The woman was gripping his

shoulders tightly, shaking him.

"Stop that," he shouted.

"I'm not going to let you drown yourself in my tub."

"I didn't know I was going to drown."

"How could you…" Her voice trailed off and she shook her head. "Earthlings need to breathe air." She said the words loudly and with crisp enunciation, as if she thought he needed help to understand her.

"I know that."

"So you *were* trying to drown yourself?"

"No, I… I just forgot for a moment."

Forgot his two pathetic lungs. The single pounding organ that pumped the thin, runny blood through his human veins. His barely functional eyes and all of the hair, hair, *hair* everywhere, all over his body.

He grabbed a fistful of the stuff on top of his head and tugged on it, wishing he could pull off this weirdly sensitive skin. But then he couldn't grow back another. He'd used almost every drop of quicksilver he had left in his system to piece himself back together after that Lyrian female had torn him to pieces.

"Stop." The Earthling leaned forward, wrapping her arms around him.

At least *this* female only had two arms. And she didn't seem like she was trying to kill him.

"Calm down," she said. "I'm going to help you, if I can."

Her embrace felt good. Comforting in a way that disgusted him. He shouldn't need to be comforted. At the same time, the fact that she was offering... It made his chest feel tight, his internal pump—heart—suffused with strange energy.

There was a rich and powerful scent on her that flooded his awareness with her proximity.

"You smell delicious." He wasn't sure why he spoke the words out loud, unless it was from the sudden *want* surrounding the smell that flooded his senses.

His brain was different, too. His mouth, his speech centers. This stabilizing form was pushing all that he was familiar with about himself away and replacing it with feelings that were alien. *Alien*.

What a ridiculous species.

She jerked back from him, stumbling away until she hit the counter behind her. "You said you wouldn't try to eat me."

"What? No." He shook his head, leaning heavily on his thighs. Hairy thighs. "Something on your clothing smells appealing."

She sniffed her shirt experimentally. "All I smell is coffee."

He'd smelled coffee before. But only when he was borrowing an Earthling's form. Being trapped in this form was altering his perceptions to a troubling degree.

Vapor pits, he was becoming a human. He might be

stuck this way forever.

His ship was destroyed, his supplies gone. He could try to negotiate with one of the groups of sentients on Earth that he'd been sent to hunt, offering an exchange of resources for the use of their communication systems. But if he managed to send a signal requesting help, his reputation would be ruined.

The greatest assassin in the galaxy, taken down by a pair of Lyrians who'd adopted an Earthling, of all things.

He'd known he was off his game. He had been ever since he'd taken on the DNA of Eric Peterson. Something in the Earthling's genetic makeup had troubled Zemanni since the moment he'd sampled it. Strange impulses and distracting thoughts he couldn't explain.

He'd never questioned what he did before. Never wanted more than to be the best at taking out targets and gathering power.

Now, he wanted… Zemanni didn't understand what.

"Do you want some coffee?"

"What?"

"Coffee." She arched an eyebrow at him when he just stared at her. "Hello? What we were just talking about? It's an Earth beverage that many of us enjoy."

"I know what coffee is."

"Oh my God. Did you use your shapeshifting abilities to become a giant asshole, or is that part of your natural form?"

He glared at her. She met his gaze and held it. It wasn't something he was used to.

More strange stimulation coursed through his body—this time, primarily affecting his skin. It tingled, especially in his hands. His groin was also starting to feel...tight.

"Do you want some or not?" she said.

He needed to get more fluid into this form. With all the quicksilver he'd lost, he felt desiccated.

"Yes."

She turned toward the door, but stopped suddenly. "If I leave, are you going to try to drown again?"

"I wasn't trying to drown in the first place."

"Right."

She reached for one of the silver handles above the bathtub and turned it. Cold water started spraying from a nozzle high above, like rain. The droplets stung where they struck his flesh, but the cold was soothing. She reached into the tub and pulled out a stopper that was keeping the now-warm water in place.

She smirked at him and said, "Just in case."

As soon as she'd left the room, he muttered, "Infuriating Earthling."

He didn't even know her name yet.

Why should he care? He'd be gone as soon as he could manage it. Though being able to call her by name might be helpful while he was in her care.

He shivered. Help and care. Help and care. Words that

came to his consciousness with increasing frequency.

"Eric Peterson." He spat out the words. "Of all the DNA templates to be stuck with, why yours?" Zemanni struck the water in front of him, sending it splashing up along the tile.

He heard the woman's voice from another room. "Everything okay in there?"

"I'm not drowning," he shouted back. His lungs still burned, but yelling released some of the energy coiling inside of him. The emotional energy, anyway.

The other—the quicksilver—was starting to fade as well, what little he had in reserve going dormant.

"What's your name?" he called out.

"Brooke. And if we keep shouting like this, someone's going to call the cops. Not all of my neighbors are at work."

He let himself fall silent. Knowing her name soothed him for some reason. But the very fact that it did agitated him once more.

How the hell was he going to get out of this one?

Cygnus X, he was even starting to *think* like an Earthling. His people had no notion of hell—or heaven. There was only each commission—gaining rank, and watching his back as he tried to get in position behind other people's to strike when they least expected it.

A shiver passed over him. If a rival Scorpiian found him like this, unbelievably vulnerable, he was fairly sure what they would do. His kind had no pity, but they did have what Earthlings might call a mean streak accompanying their avarice.

Zemanni had resources that many would envy. Resources that could only be accessed by a shapeshifting Scorpiian. Of course, if they didn't use the right codes, they'd be in for a most unpleasant surprise.

He was thinking in circles. He needed to focus. Heal. Replenish himself. Then come up with a plan.

His tissues were settling into his new form, the high temperature of his body subsiding thanks to the Earthling's help. It didn't take concentration to make his form stay together anymore. The glow from the quicksilver seams had dimmed, leaving behind small lines of white scar tissue.

He had delved deeper into his shapeshifting abilities than any other Scorpiian he'd ever heard of. He would test the limits of how much of himself he could change internally. As long as he had quicksilver in his system—even dormant—he'd always been able to change back.

But most of his quicksilver had poured from his body during the Lyrian's attack. His emergency supply had been on his ship, which was now utterly destroyed.

Being human would be challenging, but he knew he would be able to adapt to the needs of this new form as they arose. Food. Sleep. Air. Eliminations.

A disgusted grunt escaped him—a low booming sound

from this ridiculously huge chest cavity. Even his thoughts sounded like the specific human whose form he had taken. That wasn't supposed to happen.

He thought through his options. There were several alien factions operating on Earth. Approaching them would be too dangerous. But there were also humans who had made contact and were smart enough to be discreet about it.

One in particular might be of use to him. Dr. Carol Addison. His exhaustive research on the planet revealed that she had traded goods for enough technology to set up an advanced genetics lab. But how would he even get to her?

It was another problem for another time. First, he needed to secure his base of operations with this human. And adapt to his new form.

Zemanni took a deep breath to check and see how well his lungs were functioning now. The smell—the *amazing* smell—was stronger.

He sniffed the air like an animal—and barely managed to care. What he'd smelled on the woman was a pale shadow of this.

He stood and stepped out of the tub. The floor was cool and slippery against his feet. He carefully made his way out of the room. There was carpet in the hall, and the absorbent material made keeping his footing much easier.

The smell grew stronger as he turned a corner and saw

the Earthling standing with her back to him, humming a song. The woman who was helping him.

Brooke.

Another strange pang filled his chest. He rubbed at the muscles, trying to make the feeling go away. The motion made the hairs on his skin pull, annoying him.

The aroma of the dark liquid she was brewing somehow promised healing and contentment. His mind felt more alert already.

Humans talked about the stimulating effects of coffee. It was supposed to make their brains function better. And it smelled delicious.

If he was going to be trapped in this appallingly sensitive form, he might was well enjoy it. He reached for the glass container of the liquid.

Brooke turned, her eyes widening as she saw him. Her gaze slid down his body, then snapped back to his face. He wondered if she was as disgusted as he was by all of his borrowed form's hair and bulk. Assessing her body for reactions, he noted that her pupils were dilated and her nipples had stiffened beneath her shirt, which was still damp from helping him in the bathtub.

"What are you doing?" she said.

"I need to drink."

She looked back at the coffee, then stepped forward to intercept him. She went so far as to put a hand on his chest.

His breath caught and his heart rate increased. A wave of extremely pleasant sensation sizzled over all of his skin. While the stimulus was strong around where she touched him, it was actually most intense in the bizarre reproductive organ at the bottom of his torso.

Strange.

He looked at her hand on his chest, then back to her face. Did she actually think she could stop him? She would not think so for long.

Chapter Three

She was touching an alien. A *naked* alien.

Sure, she'd already pretty much draped his body over hers while helping him in from the car. And she'd had her arms around him while pulling him out of the tub. But this was different.

His skin was still hot, but didn't feel feverish like it had earlier. He was dripping wet from the bath, his dark hair plastered in jagged little hooks around his forehead. The glowing silver lines had faded into what looked like totally badass scars all over his body.

So much muscle. So much strength. He radiated masculine energy. Her fingers twitched as she fought the urge to slide her hand through his chest hair.

Zemanni grabbed her wrist and pulled her hand away. Had she offended him somehow? Maybe he wasn't okay with her touching him.

She was about to apologize, but he grabbed her other wrist and pushed her back against the fridge, drawing her arms up over her head. He pinned her against the cold surface with his body so that she couldn't move.

Oh, damn. Was she in *that* kind of movie? Because with

this guy, she was down with that.

He shifted his grip so that he could hold her wrists with one huge, strong hand. Now that the other was free, he could use it to unbutton her jeans. Maybe slide it up under her shirt.

He reached for the coffee pot.

"Seriously?" she said. "You can't drink that yet. It's too hot."

He let out a grunt, stretching to try to reach it as she squirmed in his grasp.

This was the bathtub all over again. She strained against his grip, but couldn't budge him. It wasn't nearly as sexy with him about to hurt himself. Again.

"Listen to me, Zemanni. You just nearly drowned yourself. You obviously have no idea how human bodies work."

"Yes, I do." His voice was a low rumble.

"No, you don't." She managed to get one of her hands free and immediately used it to latch on to his arm and pull it away from the counter. "That coffee will burn you. Like damaging burns. If you can just wait a minute."

"I need liquid."

"Then I'll get you some water."

"My body has cooled."

"That's not what… Oh my God, you're impossible."

"No, *you* are the one who's impossible. You Earthlings with all of your differentiated nerve endings and tactile sensitivities."

"What does that even mean?"

He shoved himself back against her, pressing his entire body to hers as he recaptured her wrist and pinned it next to the other above her head. Her breath caught in her throat. Part of her knew that she should be afraid. But she wasn't.

She could tell he wasn't trying to force himself on her. Hell, if she thought he was interested, she'd be all over him in an instant. And she truly didn't think he wanted to hurt her.

Himself she wasn't so sure about yet.

He pushed harder, bringing more of their bodies into contact. "How do you even breathe with these solid air bladders? And almost all of your organs have discreet functions, with no backups."

"We get by," she said.

"You have no idea how precarious your existence is. How limited."

Now he was just pissing her off.

"Actually, I'm the one who understands my 'human limits'," she said. "You're the one who tried to breathe water and wants to drink scalding hot coffee straight from the pot. Human bodies can't do those things, and I'm okay with it. There's plenty that's awesome about being human."

"Like what?"

His face was inches from hers, his breath warm on her face. He was staring at her intently, like he was daring her to prove to him that being a human was a worthwhile experience. She decided to go for it.

She kissed him.

All of his muscles locked up. She could feel it. She could also feel the softness and warmth of his lips. He didn't pull away.

She moved her mouth against his, urging him to kiss her back. His grip on her wrists loosened. It was a good start.

With her hands free, she wrapped one arm around his shoulders to hold herself tight against him and used the other to bury her fingers in his hair. She gently raked her nails along his scalp before grabbing a fistful of the dark strands to guide his head to tilt slightly to the side.

She kept working his mouth, trying to get him to open to her, to kiss her back, to do *anything* but just stand there pinning her to her fridge. His hands dropped to her hips.

Better.

Running her tongue along the seam of his lips, she ran her nails over his scalp again. He groaned, giving her the opening she needed. She slipped her tongue deeper, until it met his, caressing it with long strokes.

She really hoped he wouldn't accidentally bite her. Or on-purpose bite her. He might have sensed her doubts, because he shifted his hands to her ass, pulling her hips firmly against his.

A shower *and* a grower. Damn. She was going to make this happen.

She released his mouth, pulling his hair firmly to the side to give her better access to his neck and ear. His hands clenched her tight as she nipped and kissed his neck.

Pulling herself up higher on his shoulders, she sucked his earlobe into her mouth, tonguing it, running her teeth over it. He moaned, rocking his hips against her and tugging at her jeans—which weren't the best wardrobe choice now that she thought about what they were doing. The fabric had to be chafing him.

She managed to tear herself away from the lust clouding her mind, and said, "You're going to hurt yourself."

"I don't give a rank about the coffee anymore."

Give a rank? She'd ask about it later.

"That's not what I mean. You're going to hurt your dick on my jeans."

"My what?" He was still grinding against her.

Why hadn't she worn a skirt to work? Oh right, because it was freezing outside. The heat they were generating made it feel like summer in her kitchen.

"I want your mouth on me again," he said.

It wasn't a sweet nothing whispered in her ear or even a polite request. His tone was commanding in a way she'd never experienced. Sure, she'd dated guys who tried to act macho in the bedroom, but Zemanni... There was an intensity about him that made his confidence completely irresistible.

She'd dated a string of broken men before. This took it to a whole new level.

Rescuer and now this. Brooke wasn't even sure how to classify it. She had better things to think about anyway.

"Now," he said, thrusting against her again and wincing, even as he pulled her hips tighter against his.

She smirked at him. "You asked for it."

Chapter Four

What was she planning? Zemanni had lived far too long to not know when someone was plotting against him. But she was also pressing herself against him, and stars help him, he couldn't get enough of it.

He'd never had cause to kiss someone during an assignment. And if he had, he doubted it would have felt like this while he was only disguised as a human. Beneath his skin, he'd always been a Scorpiian.

The solid flesh that had felt like a prison was beginning to feel like...an opportunity. His heart beat, sending his thin human blood coursing through veins that seemed to swell in anticipation.

His "dick", as she'd called it, had actually grown, the sensation oddly reminiscent of shifting in his natural form. It was no longer soft, but incredibly hard. The skin had been pulled tight, bringing all of the nerve endings within the organ to full alert. He couldn't believe how much he could sense through it.

There was warmth at the apex of her legs. Warmth and wetness. He felt drawn to that heat, driving his dick against her, *seeking*.

Her clothing was a mix of soft fabric and hard seams. Not what he wanted.

He wanted softness and…something he couldn't name.

"Step back," she said.

"No."

She let out a frustrated sound, but then arched an eyebrow and smirked at him. Leaning forward again, she bit his neck in the tantalizing way she'd been doing earlier. His dick throbbed, *need* coursing through him along with his human blood.

Pulling his earlobe into her mouth, she sucked it, ran her tongue around it, and again caught it between her teeth with just enough pressure to resonate through his body. She released it, then blew on the wet surface, making his skin respond in yet another way.

More stimulation. More pleasure. That was what he wanted.

"I promise I'll make it worthwhile for you," she whispered.

Such a promise. For a moment, it was as though she was speaking his language. Offering an exchange—usually services for resources. But she couldn't know how those words would affect a Scorpiian.

What was she offering? More of this? More *than* this?

And what could he offer in return?

She pushed on his chest, and he let her move him back a pace. If her offering wasn't sufficient, he wanted to be able to press her against the surface behind her again and resume their earlier activity. The pleasure it gave him was worth the moments of pain.

She raked her nails through the hair covering his chest. A thrum of pleasure jolted along his nerves. The hairs caught against her fingers, heightening the sensation. Perhaps it had a use after all.

Brooke seemed to enjoy looking at it, at least. And touching it. Her fingertips trailed down the line of dark hair, along the ripples of muscles covering his abdomen.

"You want my mouth on you again?" she said.

"Yes." Hadn't she understood him earlier?

"What about my hands?"

Those, too, but he was more interested in—

His thoughts cut out abruptly at the overload of pleasure that hit his brain as she wrapped her hand around his dick. He half-fell, half-leaned forward, catching himself with his hands on the cold metal of the fridge behind her.

Her face was just next to his ear again, and she brushed it with her cheek. She tightened her grip, pulling the flesh of his dick in a long, slow stroke.

"Stars," he grunted out, thrusting against her hand.

What is *this?*

While she kept up her stroking, she went after his ear and neck again, stimulating them with her mouth. So many parts of his body were giving him input that he wanted to pay attention to all at once.

So much sensation. So much pleasure.

It was impossible to track it all. He was tempted to just give himself over to the experience, but that would require allowing himself to be distracted to a degree that he had never allowed before.

And yet…he thought it might be worth it.

She took mercy on the pleasure centers of his brain, ending the kisses and bites along his neck and ear. He missed it.

"More," he said. "I want more."

The look in her eyes disturbed him. He'd never seen that particular form of confidence. She knew what she was doing to him—and was enjoying it. As a Scorpiian, he would have found it an affront. But as a human…

He enjoyed that she was enjoying herself as well—that they were *sharing* this. He wondered if her body was sending her signals at all similar to what he felt, and if not, what he would need to do to provoke them.

"You said you wanted my mouth on you," she said.

She'd just *had* her mouth on him. What was she talking about now?

With that same smirk on her face, she slipped down between his arms, landing softly on her knees. He was about to ask what she was doing, but decided against it. She still had one hand on his dick, lightly brushing the backs of her fingers along its length. Each stroke sent another thrum of pleasure through him.

She was also trailing her fingertips along his thigh. The hairs on his skin again enhanced the sensation—especially when she used her nails. Her lips were so close to where her hands were working, and she had alluded to putting her mouth on him again.

He wondered what it would be like to feel the soft flesh of her lips on his dick, the warm wetness of her mouth. Did humans even do such a thing?

The Coalition had sent him to track down and assassinate rogue aliens operating on Earth without the High Council's approval—and thus without them receiving any benefits. He'd only studied Earthlings enough to fit in while hunting his targets.

He wished that he knew more about their mating protocols. This was part of it—he at least knew that much. But there were so many questions he didn't even know how to formulate.

Instead of trying to ask, he said, "I don't see your mouth on me yet."

"I hope you're not always this impatient."

He gripped the sides of the fridge's door, waiting to see what she would do next, how his body would react. What she was doing with her hand was more relaxing than anything else. Yet at the same time, he could feel it building a tightly coiled energy within him. A gentle stimulus that—

She turned her face toward his dick, holding it still as she darted her tongue along its length. He let out another grunt, his eyes rolling shut as his hands tightened on the metal door.

That was apparently only the beginning. He felt her lips on the tip of his dick, wrapping around it, taking him into her mouth. Her tongue pressed against the underside of his length, flicking it, swirling around. She sucked on him, as she'd done his ear and his tongue, but feeling it here was profoundly...*more.*

He was making himself vulnerable to her. She could bite him, and a wound there would be extremely painful. But she'd only been helpful—so incredibly helpful—so far.

She wouldn't hurt him. That realization alone made his chest feel almost painfully tight yet again. He was a fool. He *trusted* her.

It was hard not to, under the circumstances. He forced his eyes open so that he could watch her work her magic on him.

In and out, she moved his dick around her mouth, her lips, her face. She gripped the rest of his length with both hands, guiding it where she wanted. She ran her tongue up in a long stroke along the bottom, all the way to the tip, before taking him deep in her mouth again.

Stars, the pleasure.

It coursed through him, consumed him, set every cell

on fire in a way that was infinitely more enjoyable than his acclimation had been. It almost—*almost*—made the pain worth it. This experience of physical sensation was unlike anything he'd ever known.

His hips started to thrust against her without his conscious intent, a deep instinct rising up through the human DNA that had taken over his existence. The lines of scarring where he had reassembled himself began to glow, matching the sensation in his solid flesh.

She increased the strength of her grip, tightened her lips around him, quickened her tongue. Her mouth pumped along his length, sucking and licking. His dick throbbed with increasing urgency that echoed through his form. A pressure was building inside of him that felt as though it could break him apart, yet he couldn't bring himself to care.

All he cared about was this moment, this ecstasy, feeling her mouth on him, the tightness of her hands and lips, the constant movement of her tongue and—

"Stars!"

A brief flash of silver light blinded him for a moment, leaving an afterimage burned against his retinas. His body felt electrified, like the apex of a change, but so much stronger. The throbbing in his dick turned into a pounding pulse, each beat sending arcs of pleasure ripping through his body with an intensity that made his knees start to buckle.

As the feeling began to fade, she released him and sat back on her heels. Zemanni staggered back till he hit the wall, then slid to the ground.

His breathing was fast, his heartbeat faster. His body was filled with a feeling of *life* that made all of his other experiences pale in comparison. And his dick just kept tingling, even as it subsided to its original form.

He gasped for breath, finally managing to ask, "What was that?"

Brooke shrugged, then smiled at him.

"Perks of being human."

Chapter Five

Brooke knew she was good. She hadn't realized she was *that* good. But she could tell when she'd rocked someone's world. Zemanni's had definitely been tilted on its axis. He looked kind of shaken, actually.

"Are you okay?" she said.

He shook his head, swallowing hard enough that she could watch his throat work. "No."

Dread knotted her stomach at the thought. He seemed human, and had talked about being trapped in this form. He'd even complained about his human anatomy. Was there something different about him that would make sex harmful?

"I didn't hurt you, did I?"

"No," he said. "I want more."

Oh. Not so different at all, then.

She let out a shaky laugh as she stood. "Yeah, yeah. That's what they all say."

The coffee was still too hot for him to drink, so she grabbed some ice cubes from the freezer and plunked them into the mug she'd set out for him. She watched the ice melt as she poured the dark drink over them. Just to be safe, she took out a spoon and stirred everything, making sure there were no ice chunks he might choke on.

When it was ready, she turned to him with the mug in hand. He was still sitting with his back against the wall, watching her every move with that intense stare of his.

"Here." She handed him the drink.

No "thank you", no smile. He didn't even acknowledge it with a nod. He just threw his head back, chugging the entire contents of the mug.

"Maybe slow down a little?" she said.

He shivered. It was no wonder, with him sitting on the cold floor still soaking wet. But then his scars started to glow lightly—pulsing, almost like they were keeping time with his heartbeat. If he had a heart.

He leaned his head back against the wall, dropping his hand and the mug onto his lap. His eyes were closed, and he let out a sigh as some of the lines of tension faded from around his eyes.

Behold the miracle of coffee...

"So, you really are trapped in this form?" she said.

The look of ease vanished as his eyes opened and he fixed her with that predatory stare. "Why do you ask?"

"I'm just trying to get my bearings here. Figure out what's going on."

"It's best if you don't."

"Really?" She plucked the mug from his grasp, then turned back to the coffee pot and began making him an exact duplicate of the first drink. Once she had finished it, she turned and handed the mug back to him, then said, "I think I need to know at least a few things."

"Such as?"

Dozens of questions started lining up in her mind. Was Earth being invaded? Were there more like him out there? What had ripped him apart and why?

She doubted she'd get straight answers to any of those questions. Instead, she stuck with the more immediate concern.

"You said your body is human."

"Yeah."

"How do I put this delicately?" She realized she probably didn't *need* to, since he was an alien and all. "Why didn't anything come out of your dick when I blew you?"

The furrows between his eyebrows deepened and his lip curled up. "Something's supposed to come out of it?"

She busted out laughing, but stopped just as suddenly. "Oh God. Please tell me I'm not going to have to teach you how to go to the bathroom."

"Why would you have to do that?" He lifted his finger and pointed to the archway that led to the kitchen. "It's around the corner."

"Oh no. Okay, you know what? That's what the Internet is for." As long as she was very, very careful in her search.

She shook her head, hoping they wouldn't have to deal

with that particular aspect of humanity until later. As he took a slower sip of his coffee, his scars glowed again. Maybe it wouldn't be an issue after all.

"The way your skin glows, you can't be completely human," she said.

"I'm not."

"You're a Scorpiian."

He drained his mug, then handed it to her. "More."

"Are you sure you should be drinking this much caffeine?" She started working on his third cup. "I mean, who knows what it'll really do to your system."

"This liquid is highly compatible with my biology. And I need to replenish my fluids."

Maybe that was why there hadn't been "the usual contribution" when she'd blown him. It had thrown her off her game a little, to sense all the other signals of an orgasm without that very important one. It also opened up a whole slew of possibilities, if he lacked that complication that most human bodies came with.

Came. She snickered to herself.

"Something is amusing you?" he said.

"It…isn't something I want to explain." She handed him the third cup, then squatted across from him, leaning against the cabinets near the floor. "A real human would probably be getting jittery right now. Caffeine is a stimulant."

"I can feel that. It's boosting my remaining

quicksilver."

"Quicksilver?"

"A vital fluid among my kind."

"Let me guess. It enables you to change your form."

He paused with the mug halfway to his lips. Very nice lips. That would be giving her very nice thoughts if it wasn't for the serious pair of murder eyes he was leveling at her.

She held up her hands and shook her head. "Lucky guess, that's all. I watch a lot of movies and read a lot of books. You keep talking about being trapped in a human form. That kind of implies you can turn into other ones. There has to be something about your anatomy that helps with that."

Slowly, he lifted the mug again and drank. He kept his gaze trained on her, though. When he'd emptied it, he handed it back to her.

"You're welcome," she said.

She rose, turning toward the counter. Another amusing thought occurred to her—one she *could* share.

"I just realized, you're literally replacing your blood with coffee," she said.

"No, I'm not. I have human blood in my veins now."

She let out a little snort. "It loses something if I say, 'You're replacing your alien blood with coffee'."

"The coffee is only boosting the functionality of my quicksilver."

"Barrel of laughs, this one," she murmured.

Zemanni just stared at her. Damn, that was a cool name.

She pointed to the empty coffee pot. "You want more?"

"No."

"Suit yourself." She shrugged, then crossed the room to the sink.

As she rinsed out the cup, she felt the hairs on the back of her neck stand on end. She turned off the water, but kept the mug in her hand. Her skin felt like there was an electrical current next to her. She'd felt something similar once, when she'd been standing too close to a frayed wire.

What if she was wrong about him? What if he wasn't a friendly alien visitor in need of help? He could just be using her.

Right, using me for coffee and a blowjob. And a cold bath that nearly drowned him.

Out of the corner of her eye, she saw that he wasn't sitting on the floor anymore, and she hadn't heard him move. She wasn't sure where he was. Her heart began to thud as her brain went into overdrive, inventing nightmare scenarios one after another.

He touched her shoulder and she wheeled around with the mug raised defensively. He caught her wrist again, stopping her arm. Then he grabbed her by the back of her neck. The back, not the front. That was reassuring at least.

His gaze was still predatory, but the coldness had left it. The look he cast on her was all fire.

"What do you want?" she whispered.

"More."

"More coffee?"

He lowered her arm so that the mug rested on the counter, then said, "No."

Chapter Six

There was more to explore in this human form. Much more. Zemanni had had a taste, when Brooke had used her mouth on him. His changing instincts told him that was only the beginning.

He would have this woman. As soon as he figured out how.

"Let me guess," she said. "You want my mouth on you again?"

Her voice held a note of tension that he hadn't detected before. It was almost as if she was afraid of him.

Not long ago, he wouldn't have cared. But in this form, the thought sent a wave of prickling heat through him— almost a form of pain. He didn't want her to fear him.

She licked her lips, and the energy of the unfamiliar emotion shifted. He wanted to pleasure her, *needed* to.

He pulled her against his chest, pressing his lips against hers as she'd done to him earlier. She had used his hair to guide him, so he released her neck and ran his fingers through the unbelievably soft sun-gold waves. His fingers clenched around a lock of it, holding enough to not hurt her as he urged her head to tilt.

His nails were too short to stimulate her skin as she had done to him, but she still let out a moan, giving him his first opportunity to strike. As her lips parted, he drove his tongue into her mouth. She wrapped her arms around his neck, pulling herself up along his body. With their heads at a more even level, he could begin his conquest in earnest.

His tongue tangled with hers, demanding reciprocation. He only relented when he noticed her breath starting to catch, small gasps interrupting their sparring.

The next target was to the side. He had been nearly overcome the first time she'd run her teeth along his earlobe. The attentions she had given to his body displayed a level of expertise he strove to match.

He had seen her look of confidence—of *victory*—in knowing how her actions were affecting him. He wanted to experience that thrill as well.

Releasing her mouth, he kissed the skin along her jaw. He didn't want to allow her a moment's reprieve from the pleasure he was giving her. At the same time, he didn't rush his movements. Her brain would need time to process the signals her nerve endings were sending.

He reached her neck, raking his teeth over her skin— being careful not to apply too much pressure. She let out a low moan that resounded through his body. His dick twitched—a movement he hadn't known it was capable of.

With her clinging to him, he had more freedom of movement while they stayed in contact. He released her hair, bringing both hands to her buttocks and pressing her hips against his hard member as he sucked on the side of her neck.

She groaned again, grinding her hips against him. The fabric of her jeans was still uncomfortable. It needed to be removed. All of her clothing did.

Moons, he would have to stop kissing her to deal with that. Preferably for the least amount of time possible.

He reached between them and unfastened her jeans. She had already removed her boots and socks—probably when she went to the kitchen. That would facilitate his work.

Releasing her neck took a surprising amount of willpower. Allowing any space between them did. He felt almost magnetized to her. He wanted their bodies to interlock again, as they had when she took him into her mouth. No—in a different way. He hadn't quite figured it out yet. But it was only a matter of time.

He dropped to his knees, pulling her jeans and panties with him and helping her step out of them. As he did, she practically tore her shirt from her body, tossing it across the room. She reached behind her back to release the elastic material of her undergarment and threw it from her as well.

From where he was squatting, he had a close view of her external reproductive structure. Burnished gold hair in a triangle at the apex of her legs. And the air close to her skin was filled with the most incredible smell—heady and sweet.

He had no idea how humans went about this, but he didn't care to stop to ask. The instincts in this body were strong. Zemanni would follow them. He grabbed her hips, and pressed his mouth to her with the same fervor as he'd shown her neck.

Remembering how she had used her tongue on his dick, he slid his tongue between the folds of her flesh. She gasped, grabbing fistfuls of his hair as his tongue passed over a nub of slightly firmer tissue that seemed sensitive, judging from her response to the contact. Perhaps it was some sort of sensory nexus or nerve cluster?

He returned to the spot, circling it and flicking it. As her grip on his hair increased, so did his attentions. The muscles of her thighs tightened as her breath rate increased. The reaction seemed reflexive, but made access more difficult.

With a grunt, he wrapped his arms around her hips, then lifted her from her feet and set her back down on the counter. Their gazes locked for a brief moment. Her eyes were wide and her parted lips swollen as she dragged breath into her body.

His actions were producing the desired result. He still wanted more.

He pushed her legs wide, assessing her anatomy, calculating how they would best fit together, processing everything that he'd experienced with her so far and what he knew from all the human DNA he'd assimilated. With renewed determination, he put his lips to the nexus of stimulation, sucking it as she had done to him.

She reached out to hold on to the side of her fridge and the edge of a cabinet that stuck out past the counter, her eyes closed. There was so much wetness and heat issuing from inside her. Her slit was slick with wanting. He was understanding more and more.

He pressed his fingers to her.

"Zemanni..." She draped her legs over his shoulders, shifting her hips to give him better access.

He pinched her sensory nexus between his lips as he slid his fingers deep. Her central core flexed around them, squeezing them tight. The musculature of this part of her reproductive anatomy was fascinating.

Remembering how his own body had thrust against her without him even consciously telling it to do so, he started sliding his fingers in and out, swirling her nexus with his tongue.

"Oh, God," she gasped. "How do you know how to do this?"

Instinct.

The same instinct that told him to stand and drive his dick into her, to thrust himself in her core over and over again until that same explosion of energy flooded both of their bodies. But she'd already done that for him once.

He didn't like unbalanced scales.

Her grip tightened on his hair and he increased his pace, the intensity of his mouth on her. He sucked and pulled, alternating the stimuli to try to bring her the greatest pleasure.

He felt her body tense, then her feet dug into his back as her spine arched, lifting most of her body completely off the counter for a moment. The muscles around his fingers pulsed harder and faster.

When his own body had peaked in its pleasure threshold, she had increased her pace. He did the same for her, moving his hand more quickly, his tongue more firmly. She cried out, thrashing on the counter as she bucked her hips against him.

His body responded. His dick throbbed and his entire pelvic region felt tight and heavy. He wanted to feel the full effect of this aspect of human physicality.

And now, the score was even.

Chapter Seven

Stars were flickering in Brooke's eyes as Zemanni pulled his fingers from her. She opened her mouth to speak, but he stood so quickly, she didn't have a chance to say anything.

He grabbed the back of her neck again, pulling her face to his for another soul-searing kiss. His tongue invaded her mouth, conquered it. And that wasn't enough.

She felt his dick at the entrance of her core for a brief second before he drove himself into her. Again, he didn't give her time to catch her breath. He immediately started thrusting into her, fast and hard. His dick was so big, she couldn't believe she was managing him.

On the heels of the incredible climax he'd already given her, her body lit up with a heat that consumed all thought. He stretched her, filled her, compelled her body to give itself to the pleasure that he was pouring into her.

She wrapped her legs around his waist, using them to draw him deeper. He grunted his approval, pulling her closer by wrapping his free arm around her back.

Finally releasing her mouth, he dropped his head, staring at where they were connected, watching as he pounded into her. She couldn't stop looking at him—the gorgeous alien setting her nerves on fire.

He brought his gaze back to hers, and the wonder that she saw there made her breath catch in her throat. A thrill of something more than physical pleasure poured along her nerve endings along with the resonating thrums of his near-frantic strokes.

Maybe he noticed her reaction, because his expression shuttered. He dropped both hands to her ass, lifting her from the counter and turning them around, then staggering a few paces to the wall and pinning her against it.

Without the counter supporting her weight, she slid farther down his shaft. She tightened her legs around his waist, using her arms on his shoulders to rock against him, meeting his thrusts and grinding her clit against him each time he landed.

Damn, she could let him fuck her like this forever.

Her body wasn't as patient. Sparks were already starting to sizzle along nerves that had been stimulated past anything she'd thought she could take. The first orgasm had primed her system—like a warm up before the main event, and her senses were going all out for this one.

He held her with his intense stare, until his eyes widened suddenly, then clenched shut. His fingers dug into her hips, dancing at the edge between pain and pleasure. His dick, already stretching her core as far as it could go, started to pulse, each throb booming through her body like a drum.

The pounding beat pushed her over the edge. Her climax tore through her, hitting her bone-deep. She clawed at his back, hips thrashing against his, lost in sensations that struck at her awareness from everywhere in her body. Her thoroughly kissed lips, her love-bite covered neck, and most intensely, where his dick was still jack-hammering into her.

"Stars." His voice rose as he said again, "Stars."

He pinned her to the wall, his dick buried to the hilt, each pulse of his shaft amplifying the booming aftershocks of her own orgasm. All she could do was try to breathe— to feel his heat soaking into her, the sweat coating their bodies mingling.

His grip on her ass loosened for a moment, but then he tightened his fingers again, kneading her flesh. He angled his hips away from her slowly, but then pushed his softening dick back in deeper.

She'd never had a lover who seemed so reluctant for sex to be over. But Zemanni was keeping their hips pinned together, like he didn't want to slip out of her.

The presence of him inside of her still was the weirdest comfort. Relaxing instead of stimulating.

"Again," he said.

She started to laugh. He sucked in a quick breath, closing his eyes, then blew it out slowly.

"The vibrations you're making..." he said. "I like

them."

"I liked the vibrations you made, too. But we're going to have to wait a while before we can do anything like that again."

The furrow between his eyebrows deepened. "How long?"

"I don't know. Every guy is different. But we're going to have to, you know...disengage."

He looked like he was going to argue, but then he stepped away from the wall, letting her unwrap her legs and put her feet back on the ground. Her knees felt more than a little unsteady.

"Maybe we should go sit on the couch," she said. "Do you want any more coffee?"

"Later."

The predatory stare was back, but this time, it sent a shiver of pure delight through her. She could guess exactly what he had in mind. And she had plenty of ideas of her own.

She took his hand and led him to the living room. She didn't have it in her to dress, and with the heat radiating from both of them, she didn't feel the need to wrap up in the blanket that was covering her couch. Instead, they just sat.

She flopped, resting her head on the cushions.

"You had to have done that before," she said. And yet, the raw abandon that he'd shown, the primal urges that he hadn't held back a single bit, made her wonder.

"No."

"Scorpiians don't have sex?"

He paused for a moment, then said, "Not like that."

"How do you do it, then?"

"You don't want to know."

She shrugged. "I'll take your word for it."

The stare was getting a little awkward. They needed something to do to fill the time.

Elliot's game console—actually, *her* console, since she'd bought it, after all—was sitting on the coffee table. Brooke turned it on, along with the TV, then handed Zemanni a controller.

"What's this?" he said.

"A video game."

As the screen came to life, she had a brief moment of misgiving. She turned to Zemanni and poked a finger into his coarse chest hair.

"Don't you dare enjoy this more than sex," she said.

One of his eyebrows arched up, and then... His face transformed. Not in a scary shapeshifting alien kind of way. In a beautiful, eyes crinkling at the corners, lips turning up in a smile, bright teeth flashing, absolutely sincere smile kind of way.

Her heart started to pound. That smile could do a lot of damage. It could put her feet on the slippery slope of starting to fall for him. He let out a deep, booming laugh, and that was even worse. Her toes curled on the thick carpet.

"Don't worry about that," he said. "I can't imagine anything competing with what we did in the kitchen." His expression darkened, but his lips still pulled into a smile. "Except for variations."

Variations?

She swallowed hard, several different "variations" running through her head. The game beeped, giving her an excuse to look away from him.

The sex was incredible. But she needed to do something else with him—something a little more normal than reenacting a porno with a complete stranger. Who was an alien.

"Maybe it *is* that kind of movie," she murmured to herself.

"What kind of movie?"

"Forget it." She shook her head, activating the load screen. "Do you even know what a movie is?"

"Of course. They're very popular on your planet."

She snorted. "*On my planet.* This is so weird."

The game was familiar. It would help take her mind off of the hot alien sitting next to her, and give her a chance to process everything that had happened. Except maybe not. She'd forgotten that the disk in the console was a scifi game.

"Balls," she said.

"What does that mean?"

"It's like a swear. Something we say when we're frustrated. Literally, it means 'testicles'."

He looked down at his crotch for a moment, then back to the screen. "I guess that makes sense. What do you call the cluster of nerves that you most enjoyed me stimulating?"

"You're going to have to narrow that down. You stimulated tons of my 'nerve clusters'."

"The nub in the slit between your legs."

Damn, he was to the point. Then again, he didn't know when not to be. And she kind of liked how direct he was.

"It's called the clitoris," she said.

"Clitoris."

The game finally loaded, saving her from giving him more lessons on Earth names for sexy anatomy. She talked him through the controls briefly as the opening cinematic played.

"It might take you a while to get the hang of it, but try not to stress," she said. "If you die, you respawn."

"Sounds familiar," he murmured.

Was that what had happened to him? Had someone killed him and he... What? Used his shapeshifting abilities to respawn, but now he was stuck in this form?

Zemanni snorted as a spaceship appeared on the backdrop of stars. "That looks almost like a Centaurian vessel. What's it supposed to be?"

"I don't know. This is my ex's game—I never paid attention when he talked about it. I just like shooting things."

Zemanni's smile quirked up on one side. She swore his gaze seemed to soften.

"What?" she said.

"Nothing." He turned to the game as the level started up.

Chapter Eight

One of the opponents Brooke had described appeared on the screen. While Zemanni experimented with the controls, she managed to skillfully dispatch the combatants —some sort of armored humanoids that disintegrated when struck correctly with the right simulated weapon.

Some of the maneuvers she completed were impressive. At least, they would have been in reality.

He watched her fingers on the control, processing how she used the interface to command the figure representing herself in the game. Thoughts of her fingers working on his dick kept intruding on his focus, and it took him longer than he would have expected to grasp the logistics.

As soon as he returned his attention to the screen, he joined her efforts in achieving their objective. Their opponents were dispatched almost as quickly as they appeared. The experience was strangely gratifying.

Sex, coffee, and video games. Perhaps being trapped in a human form wasn't so bad after all.

"Damn, you're a natural at this, too." Brooke smirked at him, casting a quick glance his way before hitting controls in a sequence that disintegrated several opponents.

Sitting with her and playing this game, working toward a shared objective, made that strange warmth return to his chest.

He didn't like it.

Seeking to distract himself from the sensation, he said, "What's an 'ex'?"

"Ugh." Brooke rolled her eyes. "It's someone I used to date. Until he got all weird and super-controlling. You know what dating is, right?"

"Not really."

He had researched Earthlings and their culture more than other Scorpiians might, but only as much as he thought would serve him in navigating their culture while hunting his bounties. The more time he spent with Brooke, the more gaps he found in his knowledge.

She hit another sequence, flanking a group of opponents that he had drawn out into an excellent ambush area on the screen and helping him dispatch them in a pincer movement. He hadn't even had to tell her his plan. It was even more gratifying to work with someone who seemed to think and react like he did.

"When people seem to click—to get along well—we date," she said. "We go out and have fun. Eat, drink, and generally be merry."

"And play video games."

"Sometimes."

"What about sex?"

"Sometimes that, too."

"Your ex—he enjoyed this video game more than sex?"

She snorted. "Yup."

"What an idiot."

She started to laugh, and kept on going long enough that he had to cover her to ensure their opponents didn't disintegrate her representation in the game. The sound of her laughter made that warm tightness surge through his chest again, but this time, it didn't bother him as much.

He was starting to like it.

"Damn, Z," she said. "I could get used to having you around."

That was a good thing, because he had nowhere else to go. The thought chilled the sensation in his chest. He needed to form backup plans immediately.

Returning to his people like this was not an option. Aside from the ridicule he would face, they would see him as weakened and target him. He doubted he would survive long. If another Scorpiian discovered him on Earth trapped in this form, he would face the same fate.

Before determining his options, he had to make peace with his circumstances. He had no supply of quicksilver and no means to access more. His ship had been destroyed.

Even if he could reach a human scientist like Dr. Addison, there was no guaranteeing they would be able to assist him. He needed to integrate his new reality into his fundamental paradigm.

He was stuck like this for the rest of his life.

The only comfort was knowing that he'd already lived longer than most Scorpiians. Spending the next fifty or so decades in a human body was something he could do. Especially if he could spend them like this.

He glanced over at Brooke, watching the intensity she displayed while taking out her opponents in the game. Coffee was intensely enjoyable, both in flavor and the effect on his body. He was sure there were many other experiences that would rival it while he explored the foods he would need to sustain this body.

But nothing could compare to the incredible feeling of his dick buried in her. Everything she'd done to him—and even what he had done to her—had given him pleasure unlike anything he'd ever known.

His dick began to harden at the memories, tingling sensations spreading through him though they weren't even touching. Human bodies were amazing.

He wasn't sure if Brooke would let him stay with her forever, though.

Most Earthlings pair-bonded, much like Sadirians. If he could get her to bond with him, that would facilitate securing this location as a base of operations—and the perks that came along with it.

"You don't have a bondmate, right?" he said.

"No. And I'm up on my shots and don't have any STDs

and I'm on the pill. I'm guessing since you don't 'make a contribution' when we're having sex, that I don't need to worry about getting anything from you, either."

"My form is mostly human, but I'm still fundamentally Scorpiian," he said.

His DNA hadn't *quite* forgotten that, even though the tiny amount of quicksilver remaining in his system had gone dormant. It would be enough to destroy any pathogens that attempted to invade his body, preventing him from passing them on to her.

"Thanks for the reassurance. Excellent job."

He could detect the insincerity of her tone. He shouldn't feel compelled to reassure her, but he did.

"I won't transmit anything to you," he said.

"Cool."

"You don't enjoy video games more than sex, do you?" he asked.

"Of course not. Well, I should say I don't enjoy them as much as sex with *you*. There have been a couple of—"

Before she could finish her statement, he knocked the controller out of her hand, dropping his on the table in front of them. He shoved the table away, giving him more room to maneuver.

"Hey, what are you—"

He swallowed the rest of her question with a kiss, covering her body with his. Her skin was chilled. She must have been growing cold while sitting next to him on the couch naked.

He'd been considering exploring other things they could do with their bodies, but he had to feel himself buried in her again. He wanted to warm her—to *share* his warmth. The emotional desire was as alien to him as the physical ones. He shied away from thinking about how he had been altered at such a profound level and what it meant for his future.

Right now, he wanted to focus on this. Brooke beneath him. Her tongue tangling with his, her passion rising up to crash against his own.

He grabbed her thigh and pulled her legs apart, settling between them. She was still slick, or had become so again. He didn't care which. He just wanted inside of her. Immediately.

Plunging deep, he felt her core wrap around him, muscles tightening. She arced against him, arms sliding around his back and holding him tight. For a moment, he held himself still, taking in the shock and desire on her features.

He ground his pelvis against her clitoris and she gasped. This was different from what they'd done against the wall in the kitchen. He liked this. Their bodies were touching over more of their skin. His heat passed into her, her legs wrapped around his waist.

There wasn't much room on the couch, and the soft cushions were further hampering his movements. He pulled himself from her, and she let out a soft disapproving grunt.

"That was fast," she said.

Did she think he'd already climaxed? He smirked and shook his head, then pulled her from the couch, dragging them both to the floor. The carpet would provide a comfortable location for them. He placed his hand over the apex of her legs, cupping the entire area as he let his fingers press into her slit.

"What is this area called?" Knowing a common vernacular would aid him in pleasuring her.

"Pussy," she gasped, as his thumb circled her clitoris.

He nodded thrusting his fingers into her, deep. She arced off the floor, her hips writhing against his hand. Her breasts shifted in a mesmerizing wavelike pattern. He reached for one, wanting to know if it was as soft as it looked.

As he squeezed it, she gasped again, her eyes rolling shut. Her nipples had stiffened to hard peaks. He ran his thumb over one and she let out a moan. Another sensitive area?

He kept his hand working in her as he bent his head to explore this new opportunity. Pulling her nipple into his mouth, he sucked on it as he had her neck earlier.

"Yes. Z, yes!" She grabbed his hair again, nails dragging across his scalp and sending pinpricks of pleasure along his skin.

No one had called him anything but his name. Hearing her call him 'Z' was yet another special way that they could connect—one that stimulated his chest instead of his groin.

He increased the pressure of his hand on her breast, kneading the soft tissue, circling her nipple with his tongue. When she seemed to start to calm, he shifted to the other side and was met with renewed responses.

There was so much to learn.

His dick was starting to ache again, a dull throb building in his balls. He gave a final pull on her nipple with his mouth, sucking it hard, thrusting with his hand and flicking her clitoris every time it was in range of his thumb. Then he released her and let his body fall on top of hers, only supporting himself enough to give her room to breathe.

He wanted them connected. As much as possible.

Wrapping his arms around her back, he grasped her shoulders to make sure his thrusts wouldn't push her away from him. He knew he'd be landing hard, and wanted her to take it—to take every inch of him. He pressed the tip of his dick to the incredible softness and heat of her core, and slowly pushed himself inside.

Her flesh resisted. He felt his dick stretching her, filling her. Her muscles clenched around him, already so close to the pulsing glory of a climax. He wanted to draw out the experience, and at the same time, he could barely contain his desire to push her over that edge and join her in the ecstatic release these forms could provide.

His pelvis hit hers, his dick bottoming out inside of her. He thought he was as deep as he could go, but she wrapped her legs around his waist again, tilting her hips up to meet his and letting him sink even deeper.

He let out a moan, holding himself still as he willed his body to calm. Nuzzling the side of her neck, he said, "Stars. I could do this forever."

Chapter Nine

"You and me both." Brooke wished she could stay in the haze of lust and pleasure he was keeping around her. But she knew eventually she'd have to return to reality.

She had a job and people who counted on her. She couldn't spend all of her time indulging herself with her alien sex toy, no matter how eager he seemed to keep—

He started to move, and the friction sent sparks through her nervous system that shorted out whatever thoughts she'd been about to have. Something about responsibilities?

Two slow thrusts, and he started to build up speed, that huge dick of his demanding her full attention. She'd never walk straight again after him. And she couldn't care less.

"Dammit, Z. You feel too good."

He chuckled against her neck. "I could say the same about you. And I love it when you call me that."

"What, 'Z'?"

She actually felt a tremor flood through his system. She nipped his ear, and made sure her voice was extra breathy against it as she said, "I can think of some other things to call you."

"Like what?"

"Do you know what a jackhammer is?"

He laughed again. Her stomach did a little flip-flop at the sound.

Zemanni lightening up. Zemanni murmuring against her ear, covering her with his body.

She loved how much he took charge during sex. If he wanted her to move, he moved her. If he wanted to touch her, he touched her. And if he wanted to drive his dick deep into her core, making it feel tight and full and so very, very good, she was down with that, too.

He gripped her shoulders more tightly, his hips shifting back and forth faster and faster. He landed harder each time, pulling away and then pounding in.

Yeah, he definitely knew what a jackhammer was.

The way he was holding on to her, keeping them as close as possible, was threatening to bring her feelings into play, though. She was fully ready to lust after this guy. But to care... She wasn't sure about that yet.

Everything he did was so genuine. Sure, he seemed like he could be an asshole, but who couldn't? He'd treated her well enough so far. But then, she hadn't really pushed him.

"Stop." She spoke so suddenly, she even surprised himself.

Z went still immediately, his dick buried inside her. His eyes were wide and his mouth slightly open as he panted for breath. He licked his lips, and her gaze followed the movement of his tongue. Pushing himself up onto his elbows so less of his weight was on her, he glanced down at her body, then back to her eyes.

"Are you okay?" he said.

Her heart felt like it had fallen through her stomach.

Dammit. I just had to test him, didn't I?

She shook her head. She wasn't okay. With a guy like this, she was in dangerous territory—and she wasn't even thinking about him being an alien.

He was gorgeous, strong, confident. He knew what he wanted and wasn't afraid to go for it, unlike most of the guys she'd dated. They'd been broken on the inside, in need of someone to take care of them, and that had lured her like honey.

Z had been broken on the *outside*, but he was solid steel within. She'd known he would challenge her. He'd been doing so almost nonstop. But she hadn't known if he would be decent to her. Until this moment.

"Am I hurting you?" The furrow between his eyebrows deepened and he started to pull away.

She tightened her legs around his waist, holding him deep. A ripple of pleasure shuddered through him, but he kept himself still, staring at her intently. She had a weird feeling that he could be *hers*, if she wanted him to be.

And she did.

"You're not hurting me," she said. "I just…"

He brushed her hair back from her face in a remarkably

gentle movement. Tenderness and passion. Damn, she was in trouble.

"I need you to guide me through this," he said. "I don't know what's going on."

"Neither do I. That's the problem." She let out a sigh. "How long are you going to be here?"

His expression shuttered and he looked away.

"I mean, if this is a pit stop for you, and I'm just a diversion, I need to know not to get attached," she said.

He looked back at her, his eyes widening. The look on his face was the closest thing to sincerity she'd seen from him—aside from his beautiful laugh.

"You aren't a diversion," he said. "Not at all."

"Okay. Well, that's good." She forced herself to maintain eye contact while asking the one question she wasn't sure she wanted answered. "When are you going back?"

His lips pulled into a smirk. "I'm not."

Her heart started to pound. Was he staying? Did he mean Earth in general, or with her? And why the hell was she already thinking in long-term…terms with him?

With utmost care, he slowly pulled his hips away, then slid his dick back into her. Her eyes started to roll shut as tendrils of pleasure wound through her body.

Okay, yeah, that was part of it. But not all.

The sense of potential that surrounded him— surrounded *them*—was stronger than anything she'd experienced before. She wanted a chance to explore it. To explore *him*. And not just his magnificent body.

"You've shown me that Earth has much to offer." His eyes seemed to glitter as his smirk deepened.

Smug bastard. Maybe she *was* the only one interested in things beyond the physical.

"Yeah. We Earth girls can be a lot of fun."

She turned away, no longer wanting to see the look in his eyes. With her neck bared to him, he ran his tongue along its length, catching her earlobe between his teeth gently, as she'd done to him.

Damn, he was good at that. At all of this.

She shivered in response, her body remaining open to him even as she tried to shutter her heart. For someone new to being human, he sure was catching on fast.

"I've met many 'Earth girls'," he said.

Now she was confused. "What?"

He chuckled again, nipping at her neck and suckling her flesh. "Did you think I'd just crashed here or something?"

"Well... Yeah. Or something."

"I've been on Earth for several years. If I'd wanted to explore sex or coffee or video games, I could easily have done so."

"Why didn't you?"

He bit her neck harder, raking his teeth along her skin in a way that set goosebumps flying along her arms and legs. Her core clenched around him involuntarily.

"It never occurred to me to try," he said. "Until you."

Her heart pounded harder. That was the nicest, sexiest thing anyone had ever said to her.

Rather than let herself get swept up in the sentiment, she tried to keep herself grounded. Which wasn't easy, with him teasing the skin of her neck and the feel of his thick length buried within her.

"What did you do with your time?" she said.

"I was hunting down rogue aliens who aren't supposed to be here."

"Oh my God. There are more of you?"

"No."

He pushed himself up so he could hold her gaze as she turned to face him. The intense, predatory cast was back in his eyes.

"There is only one of me," he said. "And be very glad for that."

A shiver ran through her. She didn't want to look too closely at the implications of that statement—of what kind of alien he was, or had been.

"But there are other aliens on Earth?" she said.

"Yes."

"And you're some kind of…space cop, hunting them down?"

He snorted. "There are some who would see it that way."

"But not you."

His smirk deepened. He did another of those long strokes with his dick, shifting his hips back, then slamming into her. Again and again.

Damn, what had they been talking about? The pleasure was rocking against her brain, just like his body rocked against hers. Eroding her defenses.

He quickened his pace, grinding his pelvis against her clit every time he landed. There was purpose in his gaze. He pushed himself up on his hands, angling himself to land deeper. He was taking them to the edge and ready to leap right off of it with her.

Two could play at this game. She clenched her core around his dick, gripping him as hard as she could. Just for kicks, she added a little shimmy-twist to her hips as she rocked against him.

The extra friction turned the tendrils of pleasure coursing through her body into torrents. He let out a groan, slamming into her faster. He didn't hold anything back. She couldn't believe she could take it—could meet his passion and match it.

The lightning finally struck, arcing along her nerve endings and setting everything on fire. Her skin, her muscles, her bones. Her heartbeat was thunder, increasing the pleasure, the ecstasy of the moment. And he was right there with her.

Glowing silver light flashed along his scars, growing

brighter as he kept thrusting into her. It was almost too much to look at. The lights pulsed faster until a flash nearly blinded her as he yelled her name.

Her name. Not some weird alien expletive.

The aftershocks of her orgasm relit into a pounding beat that matched the throbbing of his dick within her. He kept pumping, as if he was trying to experience every ounce of pleasure their bodies could possibly give. His arms were trembling when he finally stopped, his dick pushed firmly into her.

"Brooke," he moaned.

Sweat beaded across his forehead. He lowered his lips to hers, another moan sounding low in his throat as he tasted her, sank into her again, his tongue languidly stroking hers. He finally released her mouth, his hips shifting against hers in a move that made her body echo the pleasure he'd just given her. It was like the afterimage of the lines of silver along his body that was still fading from her retinas.

He rolled off of her, but didn't let her go. She tucked herself into his side, trailing her fingertip through his chest hair. While she did, he grabbed the blanket from the couch and pulled it down over her.

"You were chilled earlier," he said.

Damn. He was a keeper. And she *could* keep him. He was going to stay.

It seemed a little weird that a cop would be so willing

to give up protecting people, though. Most of the ones she'd met were more dedicated to the job. Maybe he was trying to get away from a bad situation. If he'd been ripped apart, she could see him wanting a different line of work.

She let out a laugh, and said, "My mom will be so happy that I'm dating a cop. Just leave out the 'space' part."

"I didn't say I was part of law enforcement. I said there were some who would see it that way."

The happy bubble her thoughts had been building around her brain popped. A feeling of misgiving took its place.

"Then what are you?" she said.

"Were."

"What?"

"I'm not what I was when I came to this planet."

"Fine," she said. "What *were* you?"

He was quiet for a moment. Then he said, "A bounty hunter. And assassin."

"Assassin?"

"That's the closest word for it in your language."

A contract killer. She was fucking an alien contract killer. And she *had feelings* for him.

Her seeming superpower of finding the most messed up guy possible and then falling for him had landed her in bad situations before. Elliot the ever-annoying was a prime example. But this?

This took it to a whole new level.

Chapter Ten

"Something is wrong."

Zemanni had been holding Brooke in his arms, feeling more at peace with the universe than he ever had. That contentment had been shattered when she practically leapt away from him, hurrying to the kitchen. He'd followed her, and was standing in the open archway, watching as she gathered her clothes and dressed.

"Nothing's wrong." The strain in her voice made plain that she was lying.

"I told you that I *used* to be those things. I'm not anymore."

"Right. Because you're trapped in human form."

Did she think that if he could go back to his natural form that he'd pursue the same objectives?

Wouldn't he?

He wasn't sure anymore. That thought alone was extremely unsettling.

"I'm not just trapped in human form," he said. "I'm *this* human. Eric Peterson."

"Who the hell is he?"

Zemanni wasn't sure how to describe the human whose

DNA had already started overwriting his personality before he became stuck in this form. He settled on, "A very strong-willed man."

"Okay." She pulled her shirt into place, then glared at him. "Wait a minute. You didn't kill him to take his place, did you?"

"No." He left out the part where he'd *tried* to kill Eric —and failed. It didn't seem like it would go over well. And it was embarrassing.

"I've heard others say that protecting people is hardwired into Eric's DNA," Zemanni said. "I didn't think such a thing was possible, but his form had started affecting me even before I became trapped in it."

"Again, not doing so great on the reassuring."

"What do you want me to say? That I've changed? That I'm no longer a killer? Because the first is true, but the second…" He let his voice trail off. His chest felt tight and his skin prickled unpleasantly. "I've never lied to you, Brooke. I don't intend to start now."

"Wow. So you admit that you would kill people."

"To protect you, I would. And even from the limited experience I have with you, I'm pretty sure you would kill to protect others, too."

"That's not the same thing."

"I can't go back and change the past. This is my present. And I'm trying to focus on my future."

"I have to go."

"Where?"

The prickling along his skin blossomed into warning klaxons. If she was planning on going to the authorities, it might be best for him to leave. But he didn't *want* to leave. He wanted to spend more time with her, to get to know her. Everything they'd experienced together so far had utterly fascinated him. Even in such a short time, he felt connected to her. And he was actually glad for that.

"I have some neighbors who are homebound." At his quizzical expression, she said, "They can't leave their apartment. They have nurses who check on them, but they like my cooking and I bring them meals most evenings."

She stalked to the fridge and threw open the door, grabbing a large dish covered in foil. "It's just another aspect of my stupid rescuer nature manifesting itself."

"What?"

"Forget it. My mom is a shrink. She likes to psychoanalyze why I'm such a total failure."

Rage tore through him at Brooke's words. He felt his lips pull back from his teeth in a snarl. Brooke looked surprised, but she didn't flinch away from him.

"She should not say such things of you," he said.

The corner of Brooke's mouth twitched up for a fraction of a second, but then she scowled. "I'd tell you to take it up with her, but I don't want you to fucking *kill* her."

So that was the sticking point. She didn't like that he'd

killed people. It wasn't too surprising, knowing what he did of Earth's culture.

"I only killed my assigned targets."

Unless he happened across a lucrative bounty in the process. Like the Lyrians—as much good as pursuing them had done for him.

Then again, if it weren't for his encounter with the pair and their bizarre ad hoc family, he wouldn't have met Brooke and enjoyed the physical pursuits that she'd shared with him that day. Having to reassemble himself had only sped the changes that Eric's DNA had begun.

Sentients used to pass through Zemanni's awareness like static against the background of his environment. The only ones that he ever felt he could truly focus on were threats, targets, and opportunities. No one else felt...real.

But after trying to obtain the Cygnian hybrid known as Sorca and taking Eric Peterson's DNA into his body to do so, his *personality* had started to change. Zemanni found himself taking on Eric's form when others would do just as well, because he actually liked noticing other people.

It had been unnerving at first. He'd tried to play it off as research so that he could assimilate more thoroughly. Deep down, he knew better.

"Were they bad people?" Brooke's voice was thin and weak, but still enough to bring all of his focus back to her. He'd never heard her sound so...timid.

"I don't know."

He'd known Brooke wouldn't like his answer. He hadn't known how his heart would seem to lose its rhythm when he noticed tears form in her eyes.

"I didn't care before." Dammit, why couldn't he lie to her?

She glared at him, which was oddly encouraging.

"'Before'," she said. "What about now?"

"Now... I don't know."

"Great. Let me know when you figure that out."

She hit him with her shoulder as she stalked from the room. He could have stopped her. He was still considering it.

Part of him felt profoundly unsettled at the thought of her leaving when she was so angry. His lungs strained to draw in air and his abdomen felt like it was housing a nest of skeelbats.

He wasn't overly concerned about her sending authorities after him, knowing what he did of Eric's status on Earth. But Zemanni couldn't keep himself from wondering if Brooke would come back. His stomach cramped painfully at the thought of her walking out the door and never returning.

She paused at the door. "Put the chain in place behind me. My stupid ex has a key and likes to let himself in when I'm not home. And don't open the door for anyone but me."

She would be back. And she was taking precautions to

keep Zemanni safe. With what she had learned, it surprised him that she still cared.

She *cared*.

Instead of thinking about how he could use that to his advantage, his focus was on how the fluttery feeling in his gut grew in inverse proportion to the tightness in his chest decreasing. He could breathe again and he felt lighter somehow. How did anyone function with such attention-demanding forms?

Brooke didn't look back as she slammed the door shut behind her. He could hear her quick steps on the stairs that led from her apartment.

He locked the door and secured it with the chain, as she'd instructed. Then he smiled.

He could make this work. He would *enjoy* making this work. They would be mated. And he would see to it that she enjoyed their bonding every bit as much as he did.

He headed for the bathroom and gathered the clothes that he had stolen after escaping the forest confrontation with the Lyrians. He would need more. As he dressed, he considered his options for obtaining Earth resources.

Managing his identity could be a problem. Zemanni considered it highly probable that Eric had joined Sorca in returning to Sadr-4 to attempt to convince the High Council of the Coalition to recognize Earth's First Contact committee.

Zemanni doubted they would succeed, which meant

that Eric would very likely receive a mind-wipe and completely forget his new bondmate when he was sent back to Earth. Or he might remain on Sadr-4, working to further his homeworld's best interests.

Assuming Eric's identity on Earth would be problematic. Without being able to assume different identities, it would be a near impossible challenge for Zemanni to gather enough information to fool Eric's colleagues in this country's government. And the attempt would separate Zemanni from Brooke.

No, he'd find another way to contribute to supporting them both. He could always approach Earth's First Contact committee…

The front door rattled as someone inserted a key in the lock. His heart picked up. Brooke was back already.

Except she had told him to put the chain in place. Why would she be trying to unlock the door when she thought Zemanni had secured it from the other side?

He walked out of the bathroom, watching as the door opened as far as the chain would let it.

"What the hell?" The male voice grated on Zemanni's ears. Even worse was the sound of the chain rubbing against the door as the man tried to force it open.

"Brooke?" he said. "Open the door. How did you even get back in here without me seeing you?"

Zemanni felt like his body had flooded with fire. This human had been watching Brooke. Stalking her, like prey.

Zemanni recognized the signs of a hunter—of a *threat*. He approached the door, waiting for the man to have his fingers wrapped around the wood as he tried for a better grip.

Idiot.

Zemanni kicked the door shut with enough force to severely bruise the man's fingers. Not break—or sever— them. Brooke would be okay with this level of damage to her 'ex'. Hopefully.

The screaming was the most grating sound of all. It might also attract unwanted attention.

Zemanni slid the chain free, then opened the door and reached out to the human. Grabbing *his* prey by the front of his coat, Zemanni pulled him into the apartment and shut the door behind them.

"Stop making that sound," Zemanni said.

The human stared up at him with wide eyes. His dark hair was thick with grease and hung past his shoulders. His bangs were long enough to obscure his vision.

"Idiot" seemed too kind a term.

At least the man stopped screaming. He cradled his hand to his chest.

"You will leave Brooke alone." Zemanni kept his grip on the man's coat, lifting him partway off the ground.

"Who the fuck are you?"

"I'm her mate."

"Mate?" The guy managed to laugh, but it was

somehow an angry sound. "That cheating bitch. But she's *my* cheating bitch."

Zemanni knew what that word meant in this context. He didn't know it would make his vision go white with rage.

Oblivious to his danger, the man went on. "She's meant to be with me. And I'm going to make her realize it."

Zemanni shook the man, hard. "If you wish to keep your hands, you will never raise them in harm toward her. If you wish to keep your skin, you will never even *think* of touching her. And if you wish to keep your tongue, you will never use it to speak ill of her again."

The human paled, but still sneered at Zemanni. "You can't threaten me like that."

"It isn't a threat. I'm informing you of the consequences of your choices." Zemanni leaned in closer, and said, "Choose well."

Chapter Eleven

When Brooke returned to the apartment, Zemanni was playing the same video game she'd shown him earlier. It was a little too reminiscent of Elliot. She could almost imagine his body-funk smell lingering near the stairs.

But the guy sitting on her couch wasn't one of the string of losers she'd dated. He was a dangerous alien assassin. And she had a freaking crush on him.

"My neighbor sent home a pair of shoes for you." She dropped everything she was carrying on the table near the door and locked the deadbolt behind her, then latched the chain into place.

Part of her had wondered if Z would still be here when she returned. She had to admit that she was relieved he hadn't left.

"I see you put on some clothes," she said, joining him on the couch.

He grunted in response. Damn, was he turning into another boyfriend that would ignore her in favor of video games? Elliot had been terrible about that.

"You don't have to worry about your ex anymore," Z said. He kept his attention on the screen, zapping alien mechas.

Her stomach lurched. "What did you do?"

"Nothing permanent. He won't be playing video games for a while, though."

She grabbed Z's controller, then tossed it on the coffee table. "What did you do, Z?"

Instead of being mad at her interruption, Zemanni smiled at her.

"Do you have any idea how much I enjoy it when you call me that?" he said.

This time, the fluttering in her stomach was pleasant. It clashed with her worry, though, leaving her feeling confused and vaguely guilty.

"Stop being charming and answer my question."

"Charming, huh?" He leaned forward and turned off the TV, then pushed the table away from the couch with his foot.

"Oh, no. We are not doing that again until I know what happened with you and Elliot."

"He came by looking for trouble."

"Please don't say he found it."

Z shrugged, then his expression darkened. She knew she should be scared—any sane person would be scared. Instead, she felt a shiver down her spine and her arms broke out in gooseflesh.

"Mom is right," she said. "I am so messed up."

"Brooke, I know a predator when I see one. From

intimate experience."

Right. Because he was one. Or used to be—she hoped.

"Elliot was harmless."

"He was not." The force in Z's voice killed the argument she'd been about to make. "The things he said and what he was doing—keeping your keys, watching your place—"

"He was watching my place?"

That was creepy. And she'd had no idea.

"He won't be back," Z said.

"I guess I should thank you."

Z grinned, leaning toward her. She put a hand on his chest to stop him. Well, to hold him off for a few minutes. There were a few things she still wanted to understand.

Someone pounded on the door and she jumped. Z was on his feet in an instant.

"Police," a muffled voice called from the other side of the door. "We need to talk to you."

"Shit," Brooke said. "What did you do?"

"I already told you. Nothing."

"You said 'nothing permanent'. What is 'nothing permanent'?" She jumped again at more pounding on the door. "Go to the bedroom and stay there. I'll handle this."

She ran to the door as Z started toward the hallway. She gave him enough time to be out of sight before looking through the peephole. There were two cops on the other side. She left the chain in place as she opened the door.

"Hi, officer," she said. "How can I help you?"

"We had a report of an assault in this apartment just a little bit ago. Are you alone, ma'am?"

"Actually—"

Before she could finish her sentence, Z appeared behind her. Her cheeks prickled with anger. He was supposed to stay out of sight.

"Actually, I'm staying with her," Z said.

"And you are?" The officer raised an eyebrow, his back stiffening. The one behind him dropped his arms to his sides—nearer to his weapon.

"He's a friend." Brooke tried to step between Z and the officers, but he pushed her out of the way.

"Do you have a fingerprint scanner?" Z said.

The officer seemed a little confused. He glanced over his shoulder at his partner, who nodded.

"Yeah." The closer officer took out his phone and held it up.

Z held up both hands to show they were empty, then slowly reached forward and pressed his thumb to the screen. What the hell was he playing at?

The officer looked at his screen, his eyes practically bugging out of his head at whatever he was reading. He turned and showed the screen to the other officer, whose mouth dropped open.

"We're so sorry, Agent Peterson," the first officer said. "We get reports, we have to run them down."

"Of course." Zemanni's voice was weirdly...affable. "But could we maybe keep our voices down. I'd rather not have anyone know I'm here. It seems like the only way I can get an actual vacation is if I keep a very low profile."

"What's a vacation?" The second officer laughed at his own joke.

The first joined him and, to Brooke's shock, so did Z. His eyes crinkled at the corners as he smiled at the pair as if they were all drinking buddies. He was like a totally different person—which unnerved her.

"Again, our apologies," the first officer said.

"Nothing to apologize for, officers." Z gave them a half-wave, half-salute. "We're all on the same side here."

"Yes, sir." The officers turned and headed down the stairs, still beaming.

Z closed the door and locked it, then turned to Brooke. He studied her face for a moment, then said, "What?"

"Okay, the list of things I need you to explain is now about a mile longer."

"Eric Peterson is a special agent with your country's government."

Brooke stared at him. Her brain seemed to be stuck in neutral.

"I think I need to sit down," she said.

Z gestured to the couch. He followed after her and sat at her side. She stared at him for a long time before speaking.

"So, *did* you assault Elliot?"

"I kicked the door shut. If he hadn't been trying to break in, his fingers wouldn't have been injured."

"Ouch. Are you sure he's okay?"

"He was fine when he left."

Brooke stared at him. She was getting sick of his half-truths and evasions.

Z let out a sigh. "I'm sure I didn't harm him grievously. I can't say what state he's in now. The guy is an idiot."

She couldn't argue that point.

"This is all so weird."

"*You* think it's weird? At least you're in your natural form. This body has so many bladders, I can hardly keep track of them all."

She laughed. She couldn't believe it, but she did. Sitting on the couch with an alien assassin.

"You told me that you didn't used to care who you killed. And you said you *were* an assassin. Past tense. What about now?"

"Now… It's a lot more complicated. But in some ways, more simple."

"How?"

He leaned forward and kissed her.

Chapter Twelve

Zemanni could get used to being human. Pursuing contingency plans for escaping this form no longer seemed important. He rolled over on Brooke's bed, reaching out for her. The sheets were warm, but empty.

He sat up and glanced around. Morning light streamed into the room. They must have finally fallen asleep at some point in the night. She hadn't mentioned needing to go to work the next day, but maybe she had gone and didn't want to wake him.

He heard soft voices in the other room. Maybe not.

He swung his legs over the bed, grabbing his jeans and sliding them on. As he fastened them, he headed for the open bedroom door. Peering around its edge, he saw Brooke talking to Elliot just inside the apartment.

Zemanni grabbed his shirt and swung it on, buttoning it as quickly—and quietly—as he could. He went back to his position, listening.

"I just wanted to apologize in person," Elliot said. "I was an ass. You deserved a lot better than that."

What the hell? Was he trying to get back in her good graces?

"Thank you, Elliot. It means a lot to me to hear you say that."

Crap, was it working?

The now-familiar feeling of possessiveness stirred in his chest again. Zemanni strode out of the bedroom. Brooke turned to him and smiled. He barely registered it, too busy glaring at Elliot—who smirked at him.

Zemanni was going to knock that smirk off Elliot's face and give him a bruise to match the ones on his fingers. Except...

Zemanni slowed his approach. Something was different about Elliot today. Something was wrong. His hair was washed, for one. He was wearing the same outfit as yesterday, but it was clean, too.

"Z, Elliot just came here to apologize," Brooke said. "You can stop looking at him like you're going to pick him up and use him to club something."

"Yeah. Okay."

She seemed taken aback at how easily Zemanni had calmed down. He was too busy processing whatever this new feeling was that his human body was feeding him.

His pulse was pounding, senses hyper-alert. He experienced something similar in his natural form—a preparation for battle—when facing a threat. But Elliot wasn't dangerous at all.

Elliot brushed his long bangs behind one ear—with the same fingers that Zemanni had smashed in the doorway the day before. Fingers that had miraculously healed.

"Brooke," Zemanni said. "Step away from him."

"I told you, he's just here to apologize."

"Brooke, please."

"Please?" Elliot let out a disgusted snort. "I never thought I would witness the great Blorvo Zemanni begging another sentient for anything."

"Blorvo?" Brooke said.

"It's an ancestral name." Zemanni inched closer, hoping to keep this newcomer distracted for long enough to get close and— And what? Protect Brooke?

Trapped in this form, there was nothing he could do. Not against another Scorpiian.

"Wait a minute. How does *he* know your full name and I don't?"

Don't think about it. Don't figure it out.

Her eyes widened and she turned toward "Elliot" and smiled.

"You're another Scorpiian," she said. "Like Zemanni."

Vapor pits.

She wasn't done digging her hole. "Why do you look like Elliot, though? I mean, that form will get you nowhere."

The Scorpiian looked to Zemanni. "She knows about us? You *told* her about us?"

"I can explain," Zemanni said.

"Please do. Right after I dispatch this Earthling."

Brooke finally realized the danger she was in. She quickly backed away from the Scorpiian, but it pulled out a stasis disc and activated it, freezing her in place.

"Are you done with her?" it said.

Zemanni had to think quickly. He couldn't let the newcomer know how far gone he was, or he would lose any kind of influence over the situation.

How had another Scorpiian arrived so quickly to take over Zemanni's contracts on Earth? His ship had only been destroyed a few days ago. It didn't send a distress signal. He wasn't checking in with anyone. This Scorpiian must have already been in the area. It must have been waiting for Zemanni to...

His stomach clenched painfully as missing pieces fell into place. Zemanni had been distracted after assimilating Eric's DNA. He'd been off his game. And he'd blamed that for the Sadirians being able to find him. For the Lyrians destroying his ship.

But maybe he hadn't been as far off as he thought. Maybe someone had been sabotaging him. It was just the kind of thing another Scorpiian would do to try to make their name—and steal his bounties on Earth.

A young Scorpiian. Ruled by greed. Zemanni could work with this. He only hoped Brooke would forgive him if they made it out alive.

"Now that you're here, I don't need her anymore," Zemanni said. "But you can't kill her."

Brooke's eyes filled with tears. He could see the tendons along her neck pulling in strain as she tried to free herself from the stasis field. Ever a fighter.

"Do you want to do it yourself?" it said. "There's no bounty on her, so it doesn't matter."

"Killing her is inefficient." Zemanni forced his voice to be cold and even. "If she goes missing, the authorities will look for her. I assume they'll already soon be looking for Elliot?"

The Scorpiian shrugged. "From what I gathered in my limited time with him, I doubt anyone will be upset enough by his absence to even report it."

Brooke would be. Even knowing that Elliot had been a danger to her.

Zemanni had someone's death in mind—but not another Earthling's.

"Identify yourself," Zemanni said.

"Kagnan."

"Your presence on Earth violates my rights as sole operator on this planet. Explain."

Kagnan shrugged. "I picked up a faint energy reading from your ship, as if its cloaking generator was slightly out of phase. It inspired my curiosity."

Zemanni just bet it did. He also would bet that Kagnan was behind the misalignment in his system in the first place. There was an external vent that could grant access to the peripheral systems of the cloak given the right circumstances.

"I discovered a few remains of your ship," Kagnan said. "Don't worry, I took care of them for you."

"I take it they're now sitting in your own vessel's hold?"

Kagnan smiled. "I did need something to provide proof that Earth is open for assignment."

"Not quite yet," Zemanni said.

"You can't fault me for believing you were dead. I also found a significant amount of quicksilver in the area."

"It takes more than that to kill me."

"Most impressive."

Trying to use false flattery on *him*? Kagnan was such an amateur.

Zemanni kept his tone cold. "I had secured a base of operations with this Earthling and was working toward making contact with one of the groups of sentients on the planet who have a means of communicating with Scorpii-2."

It was what most Scorpiians would do in a similar situation. Zemanni had already dismissed the idea. He *preferred* to stay on Earth. He was enjoying this form too much—and Brooke's company. If only there was a way he could communicate his plan to her, to let her know that he wasn't actually planning to betray her. He was trying to keep her safe.

"It's a good thing I'm here, then," Kagnan said. "I can

send a signal for you."

For a price, Zemanni was sure. He couldn't let Kagnan get the upper hand in their negotiations.

"I will send my own signal," Zemanni said. "Using your equipment—for a fee. And I will also need to use your programming pod."

"Do you need to upgrade your knowledge of Earth's customs?"

"Of course not," Zemanni said. "The Earthling needs a mind-wipe."

Kagnan nodded. "The use of that equipment will be expensive."

"It will be free." Before Kagnan could complain, Zemanni said, "And I will not report that you are on Earth when I am still the designated operator."

He wanted to muddy Kagnan's feelings—to throw Kagnan off *its* game. The fine for encroaching on another's hunting grounds could ruin a Scorpiian who was just starting out. And while Kagnan's thoughts were on its resources, Zemanni could begin to bait his trap.

"There is another matter," Zemanni said.

Kagnan glared at him. "Which is?"

"You have a backup store of quicksilver, correct?"

"Of course."

"I wish to purchase it."

As expected, Kagnan's face lit up. Quicksilver was the most precious resource among their kind. Zemanni could replace his ship for the same cost as replacing his quicksilver. And Kagnan knew it.

"These circumstances are highly unusual," Kagnan said.

Again, his behavior aligned completely with Zemanni's expectations. If this persisted, Zemanni would have no difficulty keeping Brooke safe.

"I understand that," Zemanni said. "Which is why I will pay you half again as much as its worth."

Kagnan's smile deepened. It thought it had Zemanni at a disadvantage. But then, no one knew how many resources Zemanni had been able to secure over his long lifespan. And no other Scorpiian could conceive of him being so willing to part with them.

"We can negotiate on our way to your ship," Zemanni said. "Right now, we need to address the issue of the Earthling."

"I thought you didn't want to kill her."

"I don't."

"Then what could we possibly do about her now?"

"We'll need transportation to your ship. Rendering her unconscious and carrying her to her car will appear suspicious to anyone who might see us. She needs to come with us of her own will."

Kagnan snorted. "Good luck with that. From what I've seen so far, these sentients are highly unreasonable."

Zemanni would have gone with "passionate". He didn't

argue the case. Instead, he turned to Brooke, hiding any sign of sympathy or regret from his features—even though they weighed heavily on his heart.

If he shifted his body so that Kagnan couldn't see his face, Zemanni wouldn't be able to keep track of Kagnan's movements. And Kagnan was still very much a threat to them. When this was all over—when they were safe—Zemanni would explain. He only hoped Brooke would understand.

"Brooke."

Her eyes were the only thing she could move in the stasis field. The skin around them crinkled as she tried to glare at him, no doubt. The tears he had seen before were gone.

"You've heard all that has passed between us," Zemanni said. "Do as I say, and you will have a chance to return to your life as it was. You won't remember me or any of this. But understand that Kagnan will not hesitate to kill you with very little provocation. Do not scream. Do not run."

Zemanni nodded to Kagnan, who turned off the stasis field. Immediately, Brooke lashed out, her fist flying toward Zemanni.

He considered letting it connect. It would no doubt help her feel better. But it would weaken him in Kagnan's perception, and Zemanni couldn't have that. He caught her wrist, twisting it around and pulling her up against his chest.

She writhed against him, and he had to clamp down on his body's reaction to her. Her scent, her heat. If Kagnan had any idea of how much Zemanni cared for her, they would both be in much greater danger.

"Brooke," he said. "Stop struggling."

After a few more thrashes, she went still. She looked up at him, her eyes filled with fire, and spat in his face.

"You bastard." Her voice was low and raw.

"I've never said otherwise." Zemanni kept his hold on her, waiting to see how Kagnan would react.

"These things are disgusting," it said. "I can't wait to wipe her and be rid of her."

"The sooner you both are out of my life and brain, the better." She shoved away from Zemanni, and he let her go.

He kept his face impassive as his heart seemed to crumple in on itself within his chest.

Chapter Thirteen

"Quicksilver first."

If Brooke heard Zemanni harp about the fucking quicksilver much more, she'd throw *herself* in the "programming pod" that Kagnan was so eager to get her into. She'd been listening to the two of them argue for the last half-hour as she drove them out of town to the sparsely forested field where Kagnan had hidden his ship.

She should be excited. Curious. Frightened, for God's sake. She was sitting in an alien vessel, arms and legs crossed as she glared at the two men in front of her.

Kagnan wanted to erase Brooke's brain first, then send a signal to the other Scorpiians, then give Zemanni some quicksilver. Zemanni wanted to do it in reverse order. And, of course, Kagnan wanted to be paid before anything else happened.

"Not until you have transferred the resources we agreed upon," Kagnan said. Again. "We should get rid of the Earthling first."

"Oh my God," Brooke said. "Just transfer half of what you agreed on, then get your quicksilver, then transfer the rest and send your stupid signal."

Both men turned and stared at her.

"What?" she said.

Z's lips quirked up a bit. "That's actually a good idea."

"Strange." Kagnan cocked his head to the side as he looked at Brooke. "Surprising that it came from her."

Brooke covered her face with her hands. "I can't wait to forget this conversation."

Except, she could. As much as she'd said the opposite earlier, she wasn't eager to forget Zemanni. What the hell was wrong with her?

There was even a tiny part of her brain that kept telling her that this was all a trick he was playing on Kagnan. That Z was trying to get them both out of this alive and with their memories intact.

He'd saved her life already, right? He could have just let Kagnan kill her. Like Kagnan had killed Elliot.

She was glad her face was covered. Of everything she'd experienced since Z came into her life, that was the part she had the most trouble believing was real.

Sure, Elliot was an asshole with delusions of stalkerhood. But Brooke could have handled him. Maybe even—

She stopped her utterly useless train of thought. Elliot was past her ability to help him now.

Always a rescuer.

"Without quicksilver, I can't make the transfer," Z said.

"You can if you give me your code."

Brooke dropped her hands to her lap. "Ugh, this is the most boring alien abduction ever. How about a simultaneous exchange? You know, like you both meet partway across a bridge?"

When they both stared at her again, she let out another grunt of frustration. "Get out the quicksilver and let him have it the moment he gives you the code you need. Haven't you done anything like this before?"

"This sort of situation doesn't really come up," Z said.

She glared at him for having the nerve to address her directly. She was also weirdly relieved that he was still talking to her, especially since Kagnan only talked *about* her.

Wasn't there something about surviving by making the kidnappers see you as a person? Except they weren't the same kind of people, and she wasn't entirely sure she *wanted* them to see her as a fellow Scorpiian.

Kagnan turned to the wall of his ship and pressed his hand on its surface. His skin rippled, then glowed with a bright silver light. His flesh seemed to melt, flowing into the control.

No wonder Z was so eager to get his quicksilver back. It looked like the Scorpiians' technology revolved around their shapeshifting abilities.

A panel opened in the wall, revealing a clear cylindrical container filled with liquid that looked like mercury.

"Huh," Brooke said.

Z glanced over at her. "What?"

She shrugged. "It's just like in the movies."

Kagnan ignored her. He set the container on the floor, then held out his hand to Z.

"The code?" Kagnan said.

Z reached down for the container. As he did, he held his hand above Kagnan's. A single drop of shining silver liquid dropped from Z's hand onto Kagnan's.

"Gross," Brooke said. "Was that like your DNA or something?" She remembered reading about genetic codes back in high school.

Z glared at her as he backed away from Kagnan. She wasn't sure who she should focus on.

Z opened the cylinder and shoved his hand inside. The silver fluid crawled up his arm, wrapping around it as it flowed into his skin. He shivered, and not in a good way. She knew when something felt good to him, and this didn't. Somehow, the thought was encouraging.

When the container was empty, he let it fall to the floor of the ship. The lines of silver that she had traced repeatedly the night before started to glow so bright, she could see them clearly through his clothing.

Meanwhile, Kagnan was still standing with his arm embedded in his ship. His eyes widened suddenly.

"There's so much here," he said.

"Yeah, I've been busy." Z walked to the other side of the room and placed a hand over one of the weird access ports. His fingers, wrist, and part of his arm glowed silver, becoming near liquid as they flowed into the ship's control.

The tiny bit of hope she'd been feeling vanished. She had sort of wanted it to not work. She'd wanted Z to stay...Z. Now he was an alien, and—

Kagnan suddenly stood straighter. His body twitched as if a current was running through it. His skin blackened, like paper being consumed by a flame. He made a tiny grunting noise, and then fell to the ground, his arm still stuck in the wall. Wisps of smoke came out of the top of his head.

"What the hell?" Brooke was on her feet, hands up, ready to defend herself. Against what, she wasn't sure.

"Calm down," Z said.

"I will not calm down. Did you just kill that guy?"

He glared at her. "Yes."

"What? How?"

"I distracted him by offering him what he wanted. He was so focused on my resources, that he didn't notice the failsafe he had activated by using an incomplete genetic sample."

"But you said you gave him the code he needed."

"It was incomplete. Most Scorpiians aren't capable of giving a partial genetic sample, and so it's used as our primary means of identification. He wouldn't have guessed that what I gave him would activate security countermeasures."

Brooke looked at the charred body hanging from the wall.

"Scorpiians take their resources very seriously." Z retracted his arm from the wall. It coalesced into a human-looking hand. "Kagnan also didn't realize how quickly I could reassimilate quicksilver. This amateur had no idea who it was dealing with. Its ship is now mine."

Z approached her—cautiously, as if he thought she might run. If she thought she could escape the ship, she might. Except… She wasn't done here. Not with this. Not with him.

"You lied to him," she said. "You told me you never lie."

He was right in front of her, wall of solid-seeming chest. It was an illusion, she knew.

"I told you that I had never lied to *you*."

"Well, gosh. Doesn't that just make me special."

She was starting to build up hope, and that was making her feel stupid. This guy was a killer. There was a body of a person he'd just killed in the room with them.

And he was an alien. Absolutely alien, now that he'd gotten some quicksilver back into his system. He was a shapeshifter, and she had no idea what that really meant or what the limits to his abilities might be.

"You are special, Brooke. To me." He lifted her face to his, one hand under her chin.

As he leaned down to her, she said, "I'm not kissing you in the same room as a dead body."

"Right." He stood straight again. "I suppose that's fair."

"I'm so confused right now. I don't know what's going on or what will happen next."

"What's going on is that there was a threat to you. I have neutralized it."

"That's one way of putting it."

"As to what's next, that depends on you." He stepped to the side, blocking her view of Kagnan's blackened form. "Aside from this ruse that saved both of our lives, I truly haven't lied to you. I told you back at your apartment that you would have a choice. You can go back to your life, either with or without your memories of me intact."

"What if I don't like those choices?"

He smiled, then brushed a lock of hair behind her ear. "Haven't you learned yet? I always leave something out."

"Another choice?"

He nodded. "It won't be easy and I'll need your help to pull it off."

"Again. I totally saved your bacon with Kag-man there."

He laughed, and her heart seemed to skip at the sound.

"It would mean that we could stay together," he said.

She shrugged one shoulder, shifting a little closer to his chest.

"I'm listening."

Chapter Fourteen

With the main bay doors open, the hangar was chilly, even with the small ship's heating system trying to fight back the cold air. Brooke sat on a crate that Zemanni had carefully inspected for hazards before letting her use.

"You can still change your mind," he said.

"Shut up."

He smiled, walking toward the open doors with his hands held up. His feet crunched on the snow

"I surrender," he shouted.

The air rippled as a ship decloaked in front of him. It was shaped like a thin crescent moon, with a hull of gleaming black. A standard Sadirian skimmer.

A voice shouted out from a loudspeaker set in its hull. "Do not move."

"I wasn't planning on it."

He heard movement behind him—footsteps on the ramp. Brooke joined him, but she couldn't lift her hands.

She was holding the container of quicksilver.

"I told you to stay inside." Zemanni stepped forward, putting himself between her and the skimmer.

"Yeah, and since when do I do as you say?"

"We said don't move," the voice from the skimmer boomed.

Zemanni let out a sigh. "She's an Earthling. And I am not a threat to you. We need to talk."

The skimmer landed in front of them. Its hatch opened and a ramp descended. Within seconds, two male figures approached. They both wore the silver uniforms of Sadirian soldiers.

One filled his out impressively, his chest bigger than some of the young trees around them. The other was thin and wiry, and walked with a hesitance that no Sadirian soldier would show.

Curious.

The large one held his arm up toward them, pointing his bracer—along with all its weapons—at them. The other didn't.

"Brendan," the big one said. "Your wristband."

"Oh, right." The thinner one held up the wrong arm, then quickly shifted. "Don't try anything," he said.

"Where are you guys getting your soldiers nowadays?" Zemanni said.

"I ask the questions." The big one took a few more cautious steps forward. "You both read as humans, but it wouldn't be hard for Scorpiians to fool our sensors."

"I'm aware," Zemanni said. "But your sensors are correct in this case."

He stepped aside, revealing Brooke—and the canister

of quicksilver. When he nodded to her, she set it down on the ground, then they both backed away.

"What is that?" the thin one asked.

The large one tapped on his bracer a few times. He paused, then tapped again, more urgently.

"Quicksilver," he said. "And a lot of it."

He tapped the side of his helmet. The opaque metal broke into inch-wide segments that folded in on themselves before collapsing into the housing around his uniform's neck.

His skin was dark gold, his scalp and face either hairless or shaved. He glared from Zemanni to Brooke and back again.

"Awesome." The thin one hit the control to remove his helmet as well. As soon as it was in its housing, he took a few deep breaths. His bright orange hair made a striking contrast to the snowy background around him. "Those things make me claustrophobic."

"An Earthling?" Zemanni shook his head. It was the only explanation that made sense.

He knew that the Sadirians were working with humans on their First Contact committee. He didn't know they were letting them run around in Sadirian uniforms.

"I'm Brendan." The thin man waved. "And that's Ari."

Ari glanced over his shoulder, casting a glare at Brendan.

"What?" Brendan said.

"I'm Brooke." She stepped forward and waved back. "And this is Blorvo."

"*Zemanni.*"

"It's a family name." She smirked at Zemanni, even when he glared back. "He doesn't like it."

"So, she's definitely human," Brendan said. "Only Earthlings can make aliens glare quite like that."

Brooke laughed.

"Which makes him what?" Ari kept his wristband trained on both of them. "Standing in front of a Scorpiian vessel, holding a container of quicksilver, wearing a friend's face."

"I was kind of wondering about that, myself," Brendan said.

"Change it," Ari said.

"I can't." Zemanni gestured toward the quicksilver. "All of my quicksilver is in there. Well, almost all of it. I had to keep a little bit to hold myself together."

He slowly pulled down the collar of his shirt, letting Ari see the scars around his neck. "I hear you've let the Lyrians join your group. How's that working out for you?"

"Actually—" Brendan said.

Ari interrupted him. "I said *I* ask the questions. I'm just…kind of stumped about where to start."

"Let me help you," Zemanni said.

"Scorpiians don't help anyone." Ari said. "Not for free."

"True. But I'm not a typical example of my kind." Zemanni gestured toward the huge Sadirian, and said, "I'm guessing you know something about what that's like?"

Ari's glare intensified. Zemanni knew it was a gamble to try to connect with Ari on such a sensitive subject, but it was the only thing he could think of that they had in common. They were both what their people would consider "glitches".

Zemanni tried a different approach. "You're looking for sentients who aren't supposed to be on Earth. So was I."

"We're trying to help them," Brendan said. "Not skin them."

"Oh my God, did you try to skin somebody?" Brooke said.

"I'll explain later." Right after he came up with a plan for how he was going to get the Lyrians to not tear him apart again as soon as they saw him.

"You can't believe anything he tells you," Ari said. "Scorpiians are masters of deceit."

Brooke crossed her arms. "I know. But Zemanni doesn't lie to me."

"Unless he's lying about not lying," Brendan said.

"I'm not lying to any of you. I know I have choices and actions to atone for, but I *am* interested in helping you."

"Why? What's in it for you?" Ari said.

"Protection for myself and my mate." He gestured toward Brooke.

"Mate?" She dropped her arms and smiled at him. "I'm your mate?"

"Again, now is not the time," Zemanni said.

"What is it about these Earthlings?" Ari muttered, shaking his head.

It seemed a good sign that he hadn't disintegrated either of them. Zemanni tried to push the matter further.

"I have changed. Give me a chance to prove it to you."

"How?" Ari had lowered his arm a bit, but brought his wristband back into firing position as Zemanni slowly reached for the front pocket of his shirt.

"I have removed all of the quicksilver from my system that I don't need to survive," he said. "I'm trapped in this human form unless I receive an infusion."

"Which is sitting right in front of you," Ari said.

"I could have escaped with Brooke and this ship. But I stayed. I intend to give this quicksilver to the Department of Homeworld Security. I will only be able to resume my shapeshifting abilities when and where you deem appropriate. I'm putting myself at your disposal, in exchange for you keeping Brooke and I safe."

"And also providing meals to a really sweet elderly couple that lives in my apartment building," Brooke said.

Zemanni glanced at her.

She met his gaze without flinching. "What? They depend on me. You said Brendan has money and could hire them a private chef or something if we had to leave."

"Sure, I can—" Brendan stopped and cleared his throat when Ari glared at him again. "But first, finish your demonstration."

Zemanni pulled out the small pocketknife he'd borrowed from Brooke. He cautiously opened it, not making any sudden moves with Ari's weapons trained on him. Zemanni rolled up his left sleeve, then cut a shallow line along his forearm.

Thin, red blood flowed from the wound. He held it out for Ari to see.

"Okay, that seems legit," Brendan said.

Brooke nodded. "That *is* how they do it in scifi movies."

"We need more than…" Ari's voice trailed off, his gaze fixed on the red seeping from Zemanni's wound. He ran a hand over his face, lowering his other arm to his side. "Actually, that's pretty convincing. Scorpiians don't bleed."

"Well, unless an angry Lyrian rips them into pieces." Brendan shrugged when Ari glared at him. "What? Henry and I are BFFs and he told me all about it."

Brooke took off her scarf and started wrapping it around Zemanni's forearm. He folded the knife and put it back in his pocket.

"Does that mean you'll help us?" Brooke said. "And let us help you?"

"A Scorpiian working with the Department of

Homeworld Security," Ari said.

Brendan inched toward them, his attention on the cylinder. "It was his mission to hunt down the sentients that were on Earth without permission. And let's face it, we could use all the help we can get finding them and sorting out the good guys from the bad."

Ari shook his head, glaring at Zemanni. "You won't be loyal to us. Don't think you have me fooled on that point."

"You know the man whose form I'm wearing," Zemanni said. "When I try to revert to my natural form, this is now the shape I take. His DNA has altered me as much as Brooke has."

"I don't know how I feel about that," Brooke said.

Zemanni pressed on, sensing that they were close to the beginnings of a...bond with this group. "I'm loyal to Brooke and—"

"And I'm loyal to Earth." She shrugged. "Plus I love helping people. From what Zemanni has told me about you guys, that's what you all do."

Brendan smiled broadly. He patted Ari on the shoulder, then reached down and picked up the container of quicksilver. "I'm going to go call Kira."

Ari sighed. "If our planetary liaison says you can join us, I can't go against her orders. But I *will* be watching you, Scorpiian."

"I have no doubt about that."

"So, that's it?" Brooke said. "Because if we're going to

be waiting around for a while, I'm going to do it inside where it's warm."

"I'll join you." Zemanni started after her, but paused and turned back to Ari. "My loyalty isn't just to Brooke. It's also to Earth. It feels like... It feels like my homeworld now."

Ari shook his head. "It has that effect on many sentients, it seems. But I can't help but wonder how long it will last."

Zemanni smiled. "As long as she'll have me. And as long as there's work to be done."

Epilogue

"What is it about this planet?" Ari shook his head, gazing out at the mountainside through the windows of the mansion where the Department of Homeworld Security was headquartered.

The senior officers of the *Arbiter* had fallen for Earthlings. More people were pair-bonding with Earthlings every day. Sorca had been defeated in challenge, which Ari still could hardly believe. But the most unbelievable of all...

"A Scorpiian bounty hunter." He had to say the words out loud. It just seemed too insane when he repeated them in his head.

Ari would have thought it physiologically impossible for a Scorpiian to form an emotional bond with anyone— or to feel anything but cold, calculating assessment toward another lifeform, for that matter.

But then Ari had seen Zemanni and Brooke together. There was definitely something going on there, and it was anything but cold.

Vay and Henry were together, too, and that... That was the one thing that made sense to him. Vay had been his best friend since they'd been assigned to the *Arbiter* together. He was glad to see her so happy. He just didn't know how long it would last.

One or two pair-bonds with Earthlings might be recognized. This many? It was unlikely.

It was much more probable that the High Council would order everyone's memories wiped and then change Earth's status from a preservation site to a banned planet, seeing it as a source of cultural contamination. And if Earth lost preservation status, the smugglers and invading species would arrive in earnest.

He felt a pang for the Earthlings if that came to pass. What his fellow soldiers and the Department of Homeworld Security were doing was dangerous. In bonding as they tried to protect Earth, they could be opening it up to even more dangers.

At the same time, Ari couldn't stop wondering what it must be like for them. How deep must their connections be that they were willing to sacrifice so much to be together? And what was it about this planet that was making people he'd known and served with for decades suddenly make such huge changes?

He had a feeling these were just the initial ripples of a huge change that was coming to the Coalition whether it was ready for it or not. When all was done, he didn't know if his friends would find more happiness or if they would lose everything they'd found. He didn't know how to help

—them or himself.

"Ari."

He turned at the strong female voice behind him. Kira. She was standing in the doorway, arms loose at her sides.

"I have a mission for you," she said. "There's a reading coming in from Florida and I need you to check it out."

"Of course." His heart pounded strongly, his throat suddenly dry.

Missions are what had started most of these relationships for the others. What if he met someone, too? What if the strange effect of Earth crept over him and—

"Ari?"

He shook himself. "Yes?"

"Were you listening?"

"I'm sorry, sir. I was lost in thought for a moment. You have my full attention now."

A crease appeared between her dark brows. "Good, because you're going to need your full attention for this mission. The readings are unlike anything we've seen before. Could be a lead on the Centauri base, could be something new."

"I'll run it down, sir."

"We leave in two hours."

He followed her as she turned and strode down the hall. The Tau Ceti had obtained technology that was beyond anything they had encountered. General Serath—Adam— had taken what survived their encounters onto the *Arbiter* for analysis and to help him make his case with the High Council.

If there was more technology of that level on Earth, Ari would certainly need his wits about him. And yet...

He couldn't stop thinking about his fellow soldiers. At the way they looked at their mates, the way they always seemed to gravitate toward each other, even without realizing it.

Before the huge change hit them, he wondered if perhaps he might get a taste of that happiness for himself after all.

—

Thank you for joining me in the first *Department of Homeworld Security* Omnibus Adventure! Read on for bonus content set in *The Department of Homeworld Security* universe!

The Department of Homeworld Security

Short Stories and Bonus Content

Cassandra Chandler

Close Encounter—Evelyn

It was over. It was all over.

Evelyn stared at the poster covering the door to the hotel, wishing there was one more day to enjoy the company of her kind. But the convention was over, and everyone was heading home. Tomorrow, she'd return to the ranks of graduate students spending their summers working on research projects at her college, resigned to studying the stars instead of dreaming about being among them.

The poster was more entertaining than her thoughts. It showed a green-scaled alien with a—presumably—human woman slung over his shoulder. And, of course, she was wearing a bikini and endowed with the ultra-curvy figure that had been popular in the 50's.

Evelyn had the hips, but lacked the rest. Well, that and the whole, "damsel in distress" thing. Not her scene.

The silver disc-shaped spaceship was more her style, and matched the one on her T-shirt. For the last day of the convention, she'd been too tired to do more than throw on her favorite understated costume—the spaceship T-shirt with the words, "I want to believe", plus a sign hanging around her neck that read, "Help! I'm an alien stranded on this primitive planet."

Not everyone thought it was funny, but that just helped determine who to talk to and who to avoid. People's reactions to the sign were always a good indicator of how she would get along with them.

She reached out and gently touched the spaceship in the picture, realizing she was being ridiculous and letting herself enjoy it. "Next year..."

Just as she touched the picture, someone placed a hand on her shoulder with a firm grip. She wheeled around, coming face to...chest...with the most perfect set of pectoral muscles she had ever seen.

They were covered with a snug, pale green T-shirt that hugged every curve so beautifully that she actually had to exert willpower not to touch him. Because that would be even worse than staring at his chest.

"Oh, wow. Sorry," she said. "Your eyes are up... *Meep!*"

Words were vaporized by the chiseled lines of his jaw, cheekbones, and nose. He was almost crystalline in his perfection, right down to the unnaturally vibrant shades of his eyes. *Shades.*

One was a bright cerulean blue and the other as green as a peacock's tail. He had to be wearing colored contacts.

His hair was jet black, shortish and tousled like he

hadn't done more than run his fingers through it in a while. Her hands ached to give that a try herself. It wouldn't be hard to do, with him standing well inside her personal bubble. She'd just have to stand on tiptoe and stretch her arms way up. If she lost her balance, his chest was only a couple of inches away, waiting to catch her.

Wow, he was tall.

"I wish to initiate conversation." His voice was commanding, and his word choice odd enough that she laughed reflexively. Which made him scowl.

"Seems like you just did, there," she said.

When his scowl deepened, she laughed again.

"Forgive me," she said. "Perhaps you will be more comfortable if I address you in a similar manner. Conversation has been initiated. I am Evelyn Chambers." She lifted her hand into the narrow space between them, just to see what he'd do.

Instead of getting ticked off and walking away at her teasing, he actually seemed to relax. He grabbed her hand in a crushing grip, pumping it up and down. She had to weave her head back and forth to keep from getting bonked in the chin by his exuberant greeting.

"I am Adam Smith."

"Definitely a cosplayer," she murmured. Now she just had to figure out what character he was trying to be. Or at least what story he was playing at.

"I am not familiar with the Cosplayers. What is their

origin?"

"Nerd-dom, as with us all." She covered his hand with hers and managed to get him to stop shaking her arm loose from her shoulder socket. Squeezing tight in the hopes of bringing his attention to her reddening fingers, she said, "That's quite a grip you have there."

"My apologies."

He relaxed his grip, but didn't let go. Then again, she was pretty much hanging on to his hand. She wasn't sure she could bring herself to release him back to the wild.

"Now that conversation has been established, what did you want to discuss?" she said.

His gaze dropped to her chest. For about half a second, she wondered if he was checking her out. Then she remembered that there really wasn't much there to see. Except her sign.

Adam leaned in closer—so close, she had a momentary daydream that he might be about to kiss her. Instead, he lowered his voice, and said, "Do you require assistance?"

"What? Oh, the sign." She laughed, until she realized he was still staring at her intently. "Wait, you know I'm not an actual alien, right? Just a run-of-the-mill Earthling."

"Of course." He let out a weird, forced laugh—possibly the fakest sound she had ever heard.

This was weird. She wasn't sure he actually was a cosplayer. She'd just been thinking that she wanted the convention to continue. He could be a kindred spirit in that regard, and trying to stay in his role a little bit longer.

But something about him was off. There was a sincerity to his demeanor that made her think he wasn't pretending.

Weirdo, then. Amazingly hot weirdo. Who was still holding her hand.

"You're not from around here, are you?" she said.

"No, I am not." His mouth twitched up at the corner. *That* at least seemed real.

"Forgive me, I am unfamiliar with…" He looked past her at the poster.

"Scifi conventions?"

"Sigh-Figh…"

"Science Fiction? As in the greatest form of entertainment to have ever been developed in the universe?"

"That is a bold claim." He cocked his head at her, his expression thoughtful. "Fiction is an exercise in creating falsehoods."

"Falsehoods?" So many arguments tried to come out of her throat at once that she nearly choked.

Where the heck was he from? And did they even have *books* there? She suppressed a shiver at a thought of a place—any place—without books.

"You mean *stories*," she said. "Stories that can help people uncover truths about themselves at a deeper level than they could ever have imagined on their own."

"I do not wish to offend you. I am merely trying to

understand. The combination of science and fiction does not seem…appropriate."

"I can't believe you just said that. Science and fiction are a magnificent pairing. It's looking at what could be through the veil of what we know—or *think* we know. It's building on what we conceive of as possible for our future, while holding true to everything we are as a species. It's like…chocolate and peanut butter." At his blank look, she said, "Chocolate and peanut butter? You have had chocolate and peanut butter, right?"

"I am aware of them."

"Aware. But you've never tasted them? *Either* of them?"

"No."

"Oh. My. God. You need help, my friend." She turned around, tightening her grip on his hand and pulling him after her. She was half-surprised he didn't balk. "This is going to take a while."

"Where are you taking me?"

"To the nearest coffee shop." She shook her head, determined to introduce him to her experience of the world. "Adam Smith, welcome to Earth."

—

Close Encounter—Adam

Adam surveyed the humanoid female again, looking for any clue as to her species or origin. She was wearing a sign that proclaimed herself an alien stranded on Sol-3. *Earth.*

She was being much too open about that fact. He was under orders to impose punishment on anyone who dared to let a native population learn of the existence of aliens. Not until the High Council was ready to allow their planet to join the Coalition.

He needed to understand the situation better to know how to proceed. All he had at the moment were questions.

How had she become stranded on Earth? Where was she from? How did the Coalition not know that she was here? Was she alone?

A surge of emotion coiled in his stomach and his chest tightened at the thought. He couldn't imagine being stranded on a primitive world. And yet, if the planet happened to be as lovely as Earth, he could think of worse fates.

He was even more confused by the image she was staring at. He had been studying it from a discrete distance when she stepped in front of the display and blocked his view. With her slight build and small stature, he could easily see it again over her shoulder once he had approached.

The image depicted a green-scaled humanoid, much like the Tau Ceti had looked a few hundred years ago, carrying what was probably a human woman. A Sadirian woman would not have hips so wide or breasts so large.

Now that he thought more on the matter, the woman in front of him had full hips as well. Her limbs and face were also softer than a Sadirian's, though her build was compact enough to perhaps pass as a failed specimen—a glitch, like himself.

She would be useful for repair work aboard a ship or on one of the space stations built for standard-sized civilians. Adam was too large to fit in most of the maintenance tunnels.

The woman was wearing a shirt with a ship that matched the one in the image. Both of them looked remarkably like an interceptor, with their simple disc shapes.

She reached out and gently touched the spaceship in the picture. "Next year…"

Her rescue would come much more quickly if she was truly stranded on Earth. It was against protocol to make contact, but he had to figure out what was going on. He reached out and gripped her shoulder to let her know he was behind her.

She spun around, her gaze seeming to get stuck on his chest. Adam was accustomed to such scrutiny from other Sadirians—individuals whose genetic engineering had been more successful. Even as a General, he was forced to endure curious stares and open questioning about his abnormally large physique and mismatched eyes. Her expression behind the large vision correcting lenses she wore was less voyeuristic and more…awed.

"Oh, wow," she said. "Sorry. Your eyes are up…"

She made a strange, half-strangled "meep" sound, like the offspring of a Lyrian ixtu. A strange warmth spread through his chest as he imagined the small furred creatures and gazed into her warm brown eyes.

Near her scalp, her hair was a similar color to her eyes, but otherwise a pale gold. It was pulled back with some form of tie. Her features were soft in a rounded face. Everything about her was soft. He resisted the urge to touch her by clenching his hands into fists.

"I wish to initiate conversation," he said.

She laughed. The sound was not mocking, but still unsettled him. What had amused her?

"Seems like you just did, there," she said.

He must not be following the customs of her world properly. One of the reasons he was ordered to avoid making contact with Earthlings—if she *was* an Earthling —was due to the limitations of the cultural indoctrination programming available for Earth. It was designated as a preservation plant. He was lucky he'd been allowed to set foot on its verdant surface.

She straightened, and said, "Forgive me. Perhaps you will be more comfortable if I address you in a similar manner. Conversation has been initiated. I am Evelyn Chambers."

When she held up her hand, Adam breathed a sigh of relief. This Earth-custom he knew. A "handshake". Her communication style also put him at ease. Perhaps she was Sadirian after all.

He took her hand in his and shook it, trying to read her expression to tell him when to stop. "I am Adam Smith."

"Definitely a cosplayer," she said.

Did she not recognize him as one of her kind? He had never heard of the Cosplayers. Perhaps they had altered their appearance through genetic engineering, like the Tau Ceti.

"I am not familiar with the Cosplayers," he said. "What is their origin?"

"Nerd-dom, as with us all."

She placed her hand upon his. An odd sensation traveled along his nerves, seemingly in response to her touch. His skin felt electrified, the small hairs on his arms standing on end.

"That's quite a grip you have there," she said.

Only then did he realize he was squeezing her hand

much more tightly than she held his.

"My apologies."

He reduced the pressure of his grip, but didn't let go. He wasn't sure why. She didn't seem eager to release him either. Perhaps it was an extension of the customary greeting.

"Now that conversation has been established, what did you want to discuss?" she said.

He looked to the sign on her chest. Speaking to her at all was against protocol. Asking her openly if she was stranded on Earth was out of the question. He must attempt to gather information in an indirect manner.

Leaning in close, he lowered his voice and said, "Do you require assistance?"

"What? Oh, the sign."

She laughed again. The sound flowed so naturally from her that it made his breath catch in his chest. He had never heard someone laugh so easily.

She stopped at last, her gaze returning to his. "Wait, you know I'm not an actual alien, right? Just a run-of-the-mill Earthling."

He had miscalculated. The error was grievous. He must extricate himself from the situation immediately.

But first, he would have to bring himself to let go of her hand.

"Of course." He laughed, trying to approximate the sound she had just made. Judging by her expression, he failed in that regard as well.

Her smiled softened. For some reason, his heartbeat increased, seemingly in response.

"You're not from around here, are you?" she said.

If only she knew how very accurate her assessment was. He stifled a laugh that perhaps would have been more convincing than his earlier clumsy attempt, but might rouse her suspicions.

"No, I am not."

He still needed to gather information. The ship on the image she had ben staring at was highly suspicious. That must be why he was still holding her hand, struggling to think of something to say to continue their conversation without giving himself away. No other reason.

"Forgive me," he said. "I am unfamiliar with…"

"Scifi conventions?"

"Sigh-Figh…" His programming had not covered this. Perhaps she was speaking in one of the many languages of Earth.

"Science Fiction? As in the greatest form of entertainment to have ever been developed in the universe?"

"That is a bold claim."

Entertainment was not something he prioritized in his life, but the Coalition had several options for civilians— beyond supplying all citizens with doses of *Balance* to maintain their emotional equilibrium, and *Coupling* for their sexual needs. He doubted anything on Earth could match technology that was developed to directly stimulate the pleasure centers of the brain.

She seemed fierce in her belief, though. How did Earth combine science and fiction in a way that would generate such an attitude? More information was necessary.

"Fiction is an exercise in creating falsehoods," he said.

"Falsehoods?" She made a choking sound, her eyes widening. "You mean *stories*. Stories that can help people uncover truths about themselves at a deeper level than they could ever have imagined on their own."

"I do not wish to offend you. I am merely trying to understand. The combination of science and fiction does not seem...appropriate."

"I can't believe you just said that. Science and fiction are a magnificent pairing. It's looking at what 'could be' through the veil of what we know—or *think* we know. It's building on what we conceive of as possible for our future, while holding true to everything we are as a species. It's like...chocolate and peanut butter."

Her impassioned speech intensified the electric feeling along his skin. His breath again stuttered in his chest and his heart pounded.

The ideas she was expressing... He had never heard anything like them.

Of course, there were stories in the Coalition. Well, there were accounts of past events. Citizens learned of them in their initial indoctrinations, after being released from their development chambers. Thoughts of the future were handled by the High Council.

The future of everyone in the Coalition was the same as their present and the same as the past for several generations. Nothing had changed, and nothing would change. The High Council would see to that, using soldiers like him as their tools.

"Chocolate and peanut butter?" She said the words again, as if she had expected some sort of reaction from him. "You have had chocolate and peanut butter, right?"

"I am aware of them." If he was not mistaken, they were among the seemingly infinite variety of foods available on Earth. One was a common allergen. Adam had been following Coalition protocol and only ingesting the nutrient bricks in his ship's supply.

"Aware," she said. "But you've never tasted them? *Either* of them?"

"No."

"Oh. My. God. You need help, my friend." She tightened her grip on his hand as she turned, pulling him along after her.

He could resist. He *should* resist. But something about this Earthling—the way her touch stimulated his senses, her words stimulated his mind—made him want to know more, want to experience more. With her.

"This is going to take a while," she said.

"Where are you taking me?"

"To the nearest coffee shop." Her voice was commanding and filled with confidence. "Adam Smith, welcome to Earth."

—

Listen—Brendan

"Greetings, travelers. This is Brendan Sloan, speaking to you from the third rock from Sol." He paused instead of rolling on with his stream-of-consciousness transmission.

Normally, he imagined the dark depths of space, littered with brightly glowing stars, and the infinite possibilities between them. Today, all he felt was the void. The silence in his headphones was deafening.

He let out a sigh. "Is anyone out there listening? Please respond."

Even he could hear the wistfulness in his tone.

There had to be someone else—multiple 'someones else'—out there. Space was too vast to be empty. And Earth was too full of self-serving, misleading... He shook his head, leaning against his desk.

His handler, Eric, had checked in that morning. The conversation hadn't gone well. The group that hired Brendan refused to back down after designating his work as a military project. It was supposed to help *civilians*—supposed to help everyone on the planet.

But Brendan had messed up. His communications system worked too well. The signals were undetectable, which made his relay far too useful.

At least he had realized his mistake before handing the system over. He had locked it up, feigning technical issues, and gone on a leave of absence from the project to "loosen up his mental block". He had chosen to stay at one of his smallest mountainside cabins, trying to figure out what to do next.

Mostly he went for walks around the lake and used the back door he had built into his system to broadcast messages into space trying to contact…aliens. A species intelligent enough to detect and respond to his transmissions had to have evolved a peaceful society.

It was probably a naïve belief, but he refused to let go of it. Maybe they would also be compassionate enough to lend Earth a helping hand. The whole scenario was beyond 'unlikely' and well into the realm of 'absolutely dreaming'.

"I am a fool," he said. "And this is my last broadcast."

He rubbed his eyes, leaning back in his chair. No more delays. No more hoping his liaisons would suddenly see the light and start working toward the benefit of the planet. No more hoping for aliens to come to his rescue.

He had resources. He had intelligence. He had…no idea how to proceed.

He was still only one man.

"Brendan Sloan."

He froze, the strong female voice sounding clearly

through his headphones. Deep, sultry. He would remember if he had heard this person speak before.

"Continue your transmissions," she said.

"Who is this?"

The silence went on for long minutes before she responded. "No one."

Brendan snorted. "Obviously you're someone. Unless I'm talking to myself."

Which was a possibility he wasn't quite ready to entertain. More likely, someone back at the government facility that housed his work was messing around with something they shouldn't.

Another long pause made him start to wonder if he actually *had* imagined the voice.

"Hello?" he said.

"I'm here." She said the words haltingly, almost like she was unsure of herself.

Too many scifi stories wound their way through his head. What if she was an AI just gaining self-awareness? Or she could be one of the alien species he was trying to reach, learning how to communicate with Earthlings.

Or he could have spent way too much time alone in his cabin reading books.

She had to be from the facility. Probably someone assigned to convince him to come back to work. But how had she managed to break into his system? He had locked everything down until he decided whether to return to the project—which was really pissing off Eric's bosses.

Brendan started typing as quietly as he could, running scans to determine how and where she was accessing the relay. But he kept coming up with nothing.

"You know that no one is supposed to be accessing this communications relay, right?" he said.

"Then I guess me accessing it isn't a problem."

It took him a moment to get her joke. When he did, he shook his head and chuckled.

"Because you're 'no one'."

In the silence that followed, he imagined her smiling—wherever she was.

"I take it you're a fan of *The Odyssey?*"

"I am not familiar with that vessel."

He snorted almost loud enough to cover the slight hitch in her breath. He thought he heard her typing, then she said, "I mean story. I am not familiar with that *story.*"

Wow. When did they stop teaching *The Odyssey* in school? Wait, was she actually trying to pretend to be an alien?

"Did Eric put you up to this?"

Brendan had tricked Eric into joining a few live action role-playing scenarios before. This could be… Payback? A peace offering?

Or, a way to trick him into coming back on the project. They all knew Brendan had more work to do on the system.

"I have contacted you of my own volition," she said.

"But you do know who Eric is."

Silence again.

He leaned on the edge of his desk, his cheeks aching at the strange sensation of smiling after so long. Talking to her was fun, if nothing else.

"Not a denial," he said.

"Nor an admission."

"I do love a woman who has a way with words."

That time, he heard her brief puff of breath. He imagined her smiling, wearing a similar headset to his own, the microphone near her lips...

He shook his head, breaking himself away from the direction that particular daydream was heading. Yeah, he'd been alone way too long.

"You also have a way with words," she said. "Your transmissions have...comforted me. For that I thank you."

"You're welcome. I'm glad someone got some use out of them." If she wasn't lying to him to try to gain his trust.

She didn't sound dishonest, though. If anything, she sounded lonely. He sure as hell could empathize with that. And that was dangerous.

He steered the conversation back toward the most important topic. "How did you break into my signal?"

"I didn't break into anything. You were broadcasting."

"On a channel no one on Earth should be able to access."

"No one on Earth," she said.

He let out a sharp laugh and shook his head. "Using my hobbies and dreams against me is crossing the line. I'm calling Eric."

"To do so will bring you difficulty."

"Is that a threat?"

"A warning. I am aware of Eric. That he is your government liaison, assigned to protect and guide you. Hearing of our communication will cause him distress and most likely lead to him escalating the matter to your superiors."

"*His* superiors." Brendan had made sure his contracts were clear on that matter. He was working with them independently.

She had said, "*your* superiors", though. Effortlessly—as if she really wasn't among Eric's peers.

Brendan decided to test that assumption. "And I'm sure it won't cause you any trouble for them to know you failed in your mission."

"My mission is not—" Her voice was tight, but then she let out a sigh. "Eric's superiors have no control over me directly. However, it would also be in my best interest that you don't inform them that we have communicated."

"Right."

"Brendan… I didn't mean to create conflict for you by responding." There was another long pause. "You asked for a response. I gave it."

"I suppose that's true."

"The universe is vast and silent. Earth is small and... noisy."

He laughed despite himself. Her words were an uncanny echo of his thoughts. Eric's bosses might be able to break into Brendan's transmissions, but surely they couldn't read his mind.

"I heard your voice amid the noise. Through all that static, it called to me. Every day, it is the one thing I look forward to."

His heart gave a little tug in his chest. Dammit, she was getting to him. And he still wasn't sure if it was part of a scheme or something else. Something he didn't understand.

"You said you didn't think anyone was listening. Now that you know I am, will you continue your broadcast?"

He wasn't sure—of so many things. But this mystery, this nascent connection... He was sure he had to explore it.

"What's your name?"

She didn't hesitate before saying, "Kira."

Of course just 'Kira'. No last name. He was lucky she hadn't given him a serial number, playing in to the whole alien thing.

But it was enough.

"Tomorrow," he said.

After a short pause, he heard her steady exhale. And he

swore he heard a smile in her voice.

"Tomorrow."

—

Listen—Kira

Kira was late. She'd spent the afternoon daydreaming about Brendan's transmission, and now she might miss it.

Of course, she could play back the recording later, but it wasn't the same. Hearing his voice as he spoke made her feel connected to him in a way that was unlike anything she'd ever experienced.

She ran to her favorite viewport, calling out a command to the listening station. "T5-Alpha, initiate audio for Earth transmission B-447, secured channel."

"Detecting."

The station's cool voice was feminine and detached, designed by Coalition scientists to have the most calming effect on soldiers operating in small-unit assignments. Or, in Kira's case, an assignment of one.

Kira sat in the sill of the viewport, staring down at Earth. After listening to Brendan for dozens of cycles, she could pick out his location on the planet's surface without T5-Alpha's assistance. She had the coordinates memorized.

Her worry grew as the station's audio remained silent. She hadn't missed a single broadcast since she had discovered Brendan's transmissions.

Finally, T5-Alpha said, "Initiating."

Kira closed her eyes and rested her head against the viewport briefly, releasing her breath. She hadn't missed him after all.

"Greetings, travelers. This is Brendan Sloan, speaking to you from the third rock from Sol."

The peculiar warmth that accompanied the sound of his voice travelled down her spine and out along her limbs. She didn't know why, but somehow the particular way he was communicating resonated with her nanNet. She wasn't the only one who listened intently to his transmissions. The nanites installed in her brain buzzed with excitement.

That is, they did when he *spoke*. Brendan was uncharacteristically silent, until letting out a sigh that seemed to carry a great weight.

"Is anyone out there listening?" he said. "Please respond."

Kira's heartbeat increased. His voice was filled with even more pleading than his words. She had to bite her lip to keep herself from ordering T5-Alpha to answer him.

He was broadcasting on a unique channel—one decades ahead of all the other technology on Earth. It was almost like a primitive version of the Coalition's own communication technology.

But it *was* primitive. If she responded, the Coalition

would know. There would be a record.

Unless…

Unless she used her nanites to access the main communication relay instead of T5-Alpha.

The genetic engineers who had created Kira had installed the nanNet because she barely met the baseline requirements for her to be placed in the military—the standard assignment for glitches like herself. But she'd soon realized that the nanNet wasn't functioning as they expected.

Yes, her nanites enhanced her memory and ability to interface with Coalition technology. But she was also able to communicate with them *directly*. She could ask them to do things, and they would send her messages in their own way—like the warmth that spread through her body when Brendan spoke.

They were an independent network living within her. They were her friends.

Talking to Brendan with their help was so tempting. But every time she used her nanites in unorthodox ways, it was another opportunity to make a mistake and leave evidence that the Coalition might find. If they learned that she wasn't just a glitch—that she was an aberration—they would dissect her.

Then again, she didn't think anyone actually knew she was on board the listening station. The *Arbiter* had come and gone, dropping off General Serath on the planet's surface. Somehow, he'd convinced the High Council to let him take shore leave on a planet with preservation status. Her station still received and uploaded data for the Coalition military.

No contact had been made when the *Arbiter* was in orbit. It was like everyone else in the universe had forgotten she existed. For all she knew, she'd spend the rest of her life alone orbiting a planet where the only friendly voice she heard was Brendan's.

"I am a fool," he said. "And this is my last broadcast."

A wave of panic made it hard for her to breathe. Not talking to him was one thing. Never hearing his voice again... She couldn't go back to that loneliness, that silence.

It was worth it. The risk of talking to him.

Her brain was already tingling, her nanites responding to her subconscious desire before she even gave them the command. She felt the click as the station's communication relay linked up with his channel, bypassing T5-Alpha and her record-keeping.

"Brendan Sloan," she said. "Continue your transmissions."

Hopefully that would be enough.

"Who is this?"

She should have known better.

He was waiting for her to respond. She knew it.

She had already gone this far...

"No one."

Brendan snorted. "Obviously you're someone. Unless I'm talking to myself."

She laughed inwardly at the thought. She talked to herself all the time—well, to her nanites. Without them, she might have gone crazy after so much time alone on the station.

"Hello?" he said.

More time must have passed than she realized. That was another side effect of being on the station by herself.

"I'm here."

"You know that no one is supposed to be accessing this communications relay, right?"

She had identified herself as "no one". His wording again struck her as amusing. She hid her laughter, but couldn't resist calling attention to the play on words.

"Then I guess me accessing it isn't a problem," she said.

After a moment, he let out a quiet laugh. "Because you're 'no one'."

She smiled, glad he'd also been amused.

They were talking. She couldn't believe it.

"I take it you're a fan of *The Odyssey?*" he said.

"I am not familiar with that vessel."

Wait, was that a vessel? She quickly tapped on the control band on the forearm of her uniform, performing a search on the name. Movies, books, television programs—

various forms of entertainment all surrounded it. They all traced back to one original story, which seemed the safest term to use.

"I mean story," she said. "I am not familiar with that *story*."

Brendan was quiet or a moment, then said, "Did Eric put you up to this?"

She wasn't sure what he meant by that. "I have contacted you of my own volition."

"But you do know who Eric is."

Eric was the human liaison between Brendan and his government, like the planetary liaison between Kira and the Coalition. She had researched Brendan thoroughly when she first started listening to his broadcasts. Of course, if Kira admitted to knowing about Eric, it would no doubt lead to more questions.

After a few moments of silence, he said, "Not a denial."

"Nor an admission."

"I do love a woman who has a way with words."

She let out a quick laugh. To think that her speech could impress him when she was so out of practice with talking.

"You also have a way with words," she said. "Your transmissions have…comforted me. For that I thank you."

"You're welcome. I'm glad someone got some use out of them." His voice was even more soothing in conversation. "How did you break into my signal?"

"I didn't break into anything. You were broadcasting."

"On a channel no one on Earth should be able to access."

"No one on Earth," she said.

He laughed again, but there was a harsh edge to it. "Using my hobbies and dreams against me is crossing the line. I'm calling Eric."

Dread flooded her system. If Brendan told Eric about their conversation, Eric would definitely look into it. It would discredit Brendan when they found no evidence of the communication. Or worse, it could make them question whether other governments on Earth had access to Brendan's communications relay. It could create schisms in their relations. She had to try to prevent that.

"To do so will bring you difficulty," she said.

"Is that a threat?"

"A warning. I am aware of Eric. That he is your government liaison, assigned to protect and guide you. Hearing of our communication will cause him distress and most likely lead to him escalating the matter to your superiors."

"*His* superiors." The edge to his tone sharpened as he went on. "And I'm sure it won't cause you any trouble for them to know you failed in your mission."

"My mission is not—" She stopped herself from revealing even more than she already had. She still didn't want to lie to him. "Eric's superiors have no control over me directly. However, it would also be in my best interest that you don't inform them that we have communicated."

"Right."

"Brendan... I didn't mean to create conflict for you by responding." She was silent, struggling to find the right words to convey what she was experiencing. "You asked for a response. I gave it."

"I suppose that's true."

This was not the way she had dreamed their first conversation would go. She had imagined them connecting —had felt *something* so strong when listening to him. She had thought speaking to him would increase the sensation.

He had shared so much of himself with her, not knowing his broadcasts had an audience. Perhaps if she opened herself up to him, at least a little.

"The universe is vast and silent," she said. "Earth is small and...noisy."

He laughed, and she was gratified to find that the harsh edge to it had softened.

"I heard your voice amid the noise," she said. "Through all that static, it called to me. Every day, it is the one thing I look forward to."

She was speaking her truth, at last, to someone who seemed to want to listen. That...had never happened before. In her entire life, the only thing anyone had wanted to hear from her were reports and observations, usually in written form.

And it was *Brendan* who wanted to hear her thoughts.

Who had shared his own for so long now, helping her to not feel alone in the universe.

"You said you didn't think anyone was listening," she said. "Now that you know I am, will you continue your broadcast?"

There was another pause before he said, "What's your name?"

"Kira." She had told him this much. Her name seemed a small matter.

She held her breath, waiting for his response. Her heart was pounding in her chest.

Finally, he said, "Tomorrow."

Her eyes clouded over with excess moisture as she let out her breath at last. She was smiling so broad that her cheeks hurt—and she didn't care. All she cared about was that tomorrow she would hear his voice again. Tomorrow, they would *speak*.

"Tomorrow," she said.

—

Hope

Paige's homeworld filled the viewport, oceans darker than the void outside the ship. Starless.

Lights covered the landmass below, diametrically opposite the water. Cities bled into the countryside in veins of bright gold. It was beautiful and terrifying.

Humans had altered the planet so much already. From her vantage point *in geosynchronous orbit aboard a spaceship* it was impossible not to see. She was still having trouble believing this was real. Focusing on her planet helped her feel grounded, even though she was very far from the ground.

She preferred the view while the sun was up. The oceans gleamed sapphire-blue. The land ranged from pale brown to dark green, washed out through the bubble of atmosphere surrounding it. Thick white clouds encroached on the coastline.

A storm was brewing.

She had known Earth would be beautiful from space. She hadn't realized it would look so fragile. So alone.

The *Arbiter* was hovering directly above Louisiana, proving they were not, in fact, alone. More evidence was on the way in the form of another vessel—filled with aliens whose motives she wasn't sure about yet, but whose destructive powers she had seen all too clearly.

She was surrounded by technology capable of simulating gravity, providing her with the air, water, and food she would need to survive—and vaporizing her instantly. Her 'hosts' had insisted that she don one of the silver catsuits they all wore as uniforms as soon as she was aboard. She'd received a rudimentary guide on how to use them, and was further amazed at how much the thin material could protect her from. Heat, radiation, even the vacuum of space for a time.

They hadn't bothered with any sort of decontamination procedures that she could see. Her clothes had just been placed in a small storage compartment.

The Coalition was so arrogant. From what she had learned, that arrogance was about to cost them. She had to find out if Earth would be paying the price as well.

She kept staring at the dark shape beneath her. So alone.

But not really.

Khel walked up behind her. She heard his footfalls and knew it was him even before he wrapped his arms around her waist and pulled her against his chest. Finally, she closed her eyes for a moment, letting herself sink into his warmth.

He pressed a kiss against her temple and said, "The

meeting will begin shortly. Are you ready?"

"Ready to represent the interests of not just the billions of people on my planet but every life form that calls it home?" She let out a laugh. "Not really."

He turned her to face him. She waited for him to say something, but instead, he leaned down and kissed her. Gently, his hands running along her arms to take her hands in his. He left their foreheads touching as he spoke.

"You won't be the only one on the First Contact committee for Earth."

"Right. I'll be with my brother and some woman I just met, both of whom are starry-eyed at the whole 'being in space with aliens' thing. Some committee."

"You're all brilliant scientists representing a variety of fields. You'll do fine."

She laughed again. "It sounds like the start of a joke. *An engineer, an astronomer, and an environmental scientist walk into a spaceship...* We need more voices. More perspectives."

"Sorca has already been dispatched to bring back Brendan's government contact, Eric. More voices will join. But they must be carefully selected."

She took a deep breath and blew it out. "It's a big responsibility."

"You can handle it."

She wished she had as much faith in herself as he did. He interlaced their fingers and pulled her toward the hall that led to the conference room where they would be meeting. She looked back over her shoulder once more. She wouldn't let her planet down.

—

There's plenty more to explore in this universe, including a second omnibus, starting with Ari's story in *Duel Citizenship!* Everyone around Ari is falling for Earthlings. His fellow Coalition soldiers, even the ruthless Scorpiian assassin. He doesn't know what to make of all this pair-bonding...until he meets Sarah. Read on for a sneak peek at *Duel Citizenship.*

Duel Citizenship

The Department of Homeworld Security
Book Seven

Chapter One

"This planet's diversity is remarkable." Ari checked the readouts on his screen again. The geological scans were returning data he wasn't sure he was interpreting correctly. "Are we really hovering over a sandbar? That people *live* on?"

Kira smiled. "Earthlings are innovative, especially considering the level of their technology. Perhaps because of it. They're unable to build space stations that can support large numbers of people and don't have the technology to make dome worlds. They have to make do with what they have, and the planet is heavily populated."

"Yet they still leave vast areas untouched." He wished he could see more through the viewports, but the sky was still dark.

"That's a good thing. They're already starting to understand the importance of managing their resources." Her smile faded. "And we need to help them stay on the right path—especially once they find out about us."

"Understood." Ari turned his attention back to his scans with more focus.

Someone was using advanced technology nearby. Technology that rivaled—if not surpassed—that of their own scout ship. Kira kept the vessel steady, hovering high above one of the smaller cities in the region while Ari tried to pinpoint the source.

"I can't get the source of the reading narrowed down to more than a few miles radius," he said. "I think we need to move in closer."

"We only have twenty minutes till the sun rises. I need to be back at headquarters by then."

"I'm detecting a stretch of road near the area of interest that isn't heavily traveled. If you drop me off there, I can investigate further."

"You'll need to set up a base of operations. You'll be here for days and will have to interact with Earthlings."

"Yes, sir."

She didn't respond at first, except to scowl as her brow furrowed. "Are you sure you're up for this? Earth can be...bewildering."

"I've been acclimating for months. All of us have."

And yet it was still strange to see his commanding officer wearing Earth clothing—jeans and a light sweater. Her dark brown hair was in a loose ponytail instead of the regulation bun that was required when she was in uniform. If their scout ship malfunctioned, they needed to be able to blend in with the Earthlings of the area. Their shining silver uniforms would not help with that.

Ari's outfit was designed to match the culture of this region of the continent. They had anticipated the possibility that he would need to scout out the area.

Brendan, Kira's Earthling bondmate, had insisted that Ari wear ridiculous shoes called "loafers". They barely felt like shoes at all, especially compared with the boots he was used to. Apparently, wearing heavier shoes in the warm climate of Florida would make him stand out, even during their early spring season.

As if the shoes weren't bad enough, he was also wearing a brightly colored button-down shirt that was decorated with what was called a "tropical pattern" and pale tan shorts that barely reached his knees.

At least the shorts had plenty of pockets.

He was supposed to look like a tourist so that anyone who noticed he was out of place wouldn't think too hard about him. Brendan had packed a duffle bag with everything Ari should need for his mission. Money, clothing, identification cards.

The watch Ari wore integrated Coalition technology with Earth's in an inconspicuous form—another innovation from Brendan, though with the help of Coalition engineers. In addition to being a communication device, it could act as a small scanner, letting Ari covertly search for the alien technology he was looking for.

He had to admit, the Planetary Liaison had chosen well in pair-bonding with Brendan, even if she had done it for something as irrational as love.

"This isn't going to be like interactions at the mansion," Kira said. "You've been spending time with specific Earthlings in the controlled setting of our headquarters— which is in a radically different ecosystem from this one."

That was true enough. It was hard to believe that they had flown from mountains covered in snow to the sub-tropical setting around them on the same planet. He'd been on worlds with variations in their ecosystems, of course, but planets with diversity as extreme as Earth's were rare.

Once more, he wished they could fly during daylight so that he could see the change in vegetation with his own eyes instead of scanner readouts. Coalition protocol dictated that all in-atmosphere flights had to take place at night, even when their ship was cloaked.

Kira watched him silently, lips pulled in a concerned

frown.

"I can handle it, sir," Ari said.

She nodded curtly, maneuvering the ship toward the road he had pointed out, then setting it down in a gentle landing. He released the clamp that kept his chair still and swiveled around to face the back of the small ship.

"The ground will shift beneath your feet," she said.

He paused in unfastening his safety harness. "Excuse me?"

"I read your file. You've spent most of your time aboard ships and stations."

"That's right."

"You're about to step onto a sandbar. When you walk on sand, it moves."

He smiled, trying to reassure her—and himself. "I'll do my best not to fall."

"See that you don't." She was grimacing again, dark eyes narrowed. "This mission—what we're doing here—it's important. We have no idea how many alien species have invaded Earth. If we can't get this under control, the High Council may revoke the preservation status for the planet and bring it into the Coalition."

He nodded. "And Earth isn't ready for that. I understand."

"I'm not sure that you do. But you will, after you spend some time here." She smiled faintly. "Enjoy it while you can."

"Yes, sir."

"Check in every three hours outside of your rest cycle. Dismissed."

He half-crawled out of the chair, keeping his body hunched over as he grabbed his bag. Kira opened the hatch and a ramp slid out from within the ship's hull, which had decloaked to help Ari make his way outside.

He had to turn sideways to exit the ship, bypassing the short ramp and stepping out with one foot on the road while ducking to maneuver the rest of his body through the opening. Most Sadirians were genetically engineered to be small and wiry. Living on dome worlds and space stations, creating citizens who were bigger was considered a waste of resources. Of course, accidents happened—like Ari.

His size had bothered him until he'd been assigned to the *Arbiter*. The first time he'd watched General Serath— the highest ranking military officer in the Coalition's fleet —do the same twisting maneuver to exit a tiny scout ship was the first time Ari had actually felt proud to be a glitch.

He was in good company, at least, especially aboard the *Arbiter*. Most of the crew were glitches. Serath's first officer, Khel, was even bigger than Ari, though not by much.

The *Arbiter* had been the first place that had felt like home.

Being among the team assigned to find and contain the aliens who were trespassing on Earth was a huge show of

Serath's trust. Ari still sometimes wished that he had remained with the crew when the ship went back to Sadr-4 to try to convince the High Council to recognize Earth's First Contact committee, though.

Earth had a strange effect on his fellow Sadirians. General Serath had been the first to pair-bond with an Earthling, going so far as to change his name to "Adam Smith", not that Ari had been able to start thinking of him that way yet. *Adam* wore his hair differently, carried himself differently, and seemed to have been fundamentally changed by his experiences on Earth.

As if that wasn't enough, Kira had bonded with Brendan. Sorca with Eric. Moons, even Khel had bonded with Brendan's sister, Paige. And then Vay had fallen for an Earthling named Henry.

The others in their small team were already talking about possibly bonding with an Earthling. Most were excited, after seeing how happy their fellow soldiers were with their chosen partners. And it wasn't just the Sadirians who were bonding.

The Scorpiian that they'd been hunting for months had fallen in love with an Earthling and pair-bonded with her. Ari still couldn't believe the cold-blooded assassin now smiled and laughed—and even went on missions alongside the team. At least, when he wasn't busy playing video games or "spending quality time" with his bondmate.

Zemanni had actually been able to convince the pair of

Lyrians living at headquarters that he'd changed. That was a good thing, since the female—Barbara—had been eager to tear him apart *again* when he first showed up.

It was a lot to wrap his head around.

Ari trotted away from the scout vessel as the hatch closed and the ramp retracted. Kira swung the ship around, nodding to him through the main viewport. A rippling wave passed over the ship's hull as it vanished.

He felt a slight turbulence in the air as it took off, heading back for headquarters. She'd be back with her own Earthling bondmate before Ari made it to the town. Especially if he didn't get moving.

Kira's warning about the shifting sands had unnerved him a bit. The road was solid, at least. He crossed to the edge, using the pre-dawn light to note where the dark material ended and the white-tan sand began. Stabilizing himself on one leg, he poked his free foot over the edge.

The sand barely gave any resistance at first. He had his shoe buried up to the toe before he had to apply pressure to dig deeper.

A blaring, discordant noise behind him made him jump forward, trying to spin on the soft surface. He flailed his arms to keep his balance, ending in a fighting crouch. The car that had made the awful noise kept speeding down the roadway.

Ari needed to be more careful. He would get plenty of practice walking on sand as he made his way toward the town. He checked his watch once more before setting out.

—

You can get *Duel Citizenship* now as a novella or as part of *The Department of Homeworld Security Omnibus 2!* I'd love to keep in touch. Join my newsletter at my website, cassandra-chandler.com, to hear about all the adventures happening in Cassland. And if you enjoyed this book, please consider leaving a review at your favorite book review site. I'd really appreciate it—reviews help readers and authors alike!

Thank you for reading *The Department of Homeworld Security Omnibus 1!*

Cassandra Chandler

About the Author

USA Today Bestselling author Cassandra Chandler uses her vivid imagination to make the world more interesting, spawning the ideas she turns into her whimsical Science Fiction romcoms and darkly evocative Paranormal and Urban Fantasy Romances. Fast-paced and funny, lighthearted or dark, her stories will introduce you to characters you want to be friends with and worlds where you'd like to build a vacation home.

www.ingramcontent.com/pod-product-compliance
Lightning Source LLC
Chambersburg PA
CBHW070339030726
47504CB00001B/5